The daughter of a Norwegian Viking and a Finnish goddess, Karina Halle grew up in Vancouver, Canada with trolls and eternal darkness on the brain. This soon turned into a love of all things that go bump in the night and a rather sadistic appreciation for freaking people out. Like many of the flawed characters she writes about, Karina never knew where to find herself and has dabbled in acting, make-up artistry, film production, screenwriting, photography, travel writing and music journalism. She eventually found herself in the pages of the very novels she wrote (if only she had looked there to begin with).

Karina holds a screenwriting degree from Vancouver Film School and a Bachelor of Journalism from TRU. Her travel writing, music reviews/interviews and photography has appeared in publications such as *Consequence of Sound*, *Mxdwn* and *GoNomad Travel* Guides. She currently lives on an island off the coast of British Colombia with her husband and her rescue pup, preparing for the zombie apocalypse.

To discover more about Karina visit www.authorkarinahalle.com, find her on Facebook, and follow her on Twitter @MetalBlonde.

Why you should lose yourself in a Karina Halle novel:

'Karina Halle has done it again with this violently beautiful tale of love, pain, revenge, and loss, that will rip you apart, piece by piece, and put you back together again' S. L. Jennings

'A story that just about jumps from the pages directly onto the big screen. Fans of suspense and twisted romance will be overjoyed with Halle's talent' *Romantic Times*

'I'm officially addicted to Karina Halle's writing, but I don't plan on seeking a cure for this obsession anyt   ' Chelsea M. Cameron, *New York Times* bestselling author

'I knew from the moment I began   kindred spirits' CJ Roberts, *USA Tod*

By Karina Halle and published by Headline Eternal

KARINA HALLE

Shooting Scars

headline
ETERNAL

First published as an ebook in Great Britain in 2013
by HEADLINE ETERNAL
An imprint of HEADLINE PUBLISHING GROUP

First published in paperback in Great Britain in 2014
by HEADLINE ETERNAL
An imprint of HEADLINE PUBLISHING GROUP

1

Cataloguing in Publication Data is available from the British Library

ISBN 978 1 4722 1168 2

Offset in Times Lt Std by Avon DataSet Ltd, Bidford-on-Avon, Warwickshire

Printed and bound by CPI Group (UK) Ltd, Croydon, CR0 4YY

Papers used by Headline are from well-managed forests
and other responsible sources.

HEADLINE PUBLISHING GROUP
An Hachette UK Company
338 Euston Road
London NW1 3BH

www.headlineeternal.com
www.headline.co.uk
www.hachette.co.uk

For Bruce Willis MacKenzie

Shooting Scars

CHAPTER ONE

Ellie

"You wanted me to catch you, didn't you?" Javier's voice cut into my thoughts like a drill. I blinked at the dry, rough desert of Arizona as it flew past my window, trying to remember what was happening. This wasn't a dream, this wasn't a scenario; this was real. I was in the back of an SUV driven by a thuggish man and the ex-boyfriend of my nightmares was right beside me. I had given Camden a second chance at life, at love, at everything by taking a step backward with mine. I was Javier's prisoner now, his six years of chasing after me having finally come to a close.

I was trapped with a man who would either love me or kill me. There was no middle ground with Javier Bernal.

"Didn't you?" he repeated. Out of the corner of my eye I caught him wave his hand dismissively, his watch catching the sun that streamed in through the tinted windows. "Oh, it doesn't matter. I know."

I didn't want to take the bait. I wanted to keep looking out the window, pretending this didn't exist. I wanted to ignore the anger that started to prick at my toes, rising up my limbs, and the disgust and defeat that was about to sink in my chest.

He had found me.

"You tracked my cell phone," I said, my tongue sticking to the roof of my dry mouth.

He chuckled. The hair on my arms stood up.

"Seriously? Your cell phone. Angel, you aren't Jason Bourne."

I wanted to laugh derisively at the way he pronounced Jason and sneer at the use of my old pet name, angel. I had been angel six years ago. That angel had died on broken wings and with a broken heart.

He continued, "I can't track your phone unless I have physical access to it."

"Then you were tracking the car," I said, still to the window.

Another chilling laugh. "Tracking that car all this time? I had people looking out for it—you took quite a big chance driving around in a flashing find-me sign. But no, there was no tracking device in the car. Why would I plant one in my own car?"

"Someone might steal it."

"Only you, my dear."

His voice lowered over that last phrase, twisting in a curiously compassionate way. I brought my eyes over to look at him and immediately regretted it. I realized that up until that moment, I'd been trying to see through him, as if he were a hologram.

Javier's hair was longer now, but just as thick and dark. His face had thinned out a bit over the years and his build was somehow wider, stronger. He looked like a citron-eyed lion in a white linen suit, a creature larger than the sum of his parts. The more I stared at him, the more the space around me became smaller.

He smiled at me, his eyes glinting. It wasn't a kind smile, and I quickly cast my eyes downward, feeling that the less eye contact we made, the better it was for me. I caught a glimpse of his *Wish* tattoo on his wrist, partially covered up by his watch.

"Ellie Watt," he said smoothly. "It didn't take me long to figure out your real name. In fact, it was almost like your name came floating in my window one day. So, you must realize that when you're on the run and using your real name, well, any fucking idiot can track you down."

I blinked hard and turned my head to the window again. I'd been so careful with Camden's name, going through all the steps to make sure he could never be found as Connor Malloy. I didn't do the same for myself. The minute we knew that Javier and his men were after me in Palm Valley, the minute we headed for Nevada, I should have been more cautious. I should have concentrated more on myself than on Camden. Javier had tracked me to the resort in Laughlin, and after that I thought I was playing it smart by taking on an old persona.

I hadn't been smart enough.

"I had people waiting in Las Vegas, you know," he said, and I could sense him examining his fingernails. "It wasn't hard to figure out that's where you'd be going next, that you needed to keep laundering your money.

You were cocky enough to stay on the Strip. One of my men saw your car—*my* car—driving through. Followed you to your hotel, where you went through a halfhearted attempt to hide it."

I swallowed hard. Disgust was beating out defeat at the moment.

"I realize now, angel, that I didn't know you very well at all. I don't know who I knew. But I do know you're not an idiot. You wanted me to find you. Perhaps you've been asking for it since you ran away."

"Where are we going?" I said, trying to keep my breath from shaking.

He sighed. "I told you. To the past."

"I have many pasts. Pick one."

He leaned back in his seat, his legs splayed, the tip of his knee touching my leg for a brief second. Just a tap. His way of reminding me where I was. I eyed the rocky landscape flying past and wondered when jumping out of a moving vehicle could be considered too reckless.

"Child safety locks," he whispered, and I wished he'd get the fuck out of my head. "And *our* past. Do you remember it?"

"No." It wasn't that much of a lie. I'd had so many pasts that it was easy to bury them all with each other. After I'd left Javier all those years ago, I remembered the pain he brought me, the humiliation and deceit, only for as long as I needed to. For as long as I needed to become someone else, to never make the same mistakes again. Then I let it go.

"Now you're just trying to hurt me." He couldn't have sounded less sincere.

I cleared my throat. "I'm thirsty. Do you have any water?"

"Later. First we have something to discuss."

I turned my head and shot him a deadly look. "We have nothing to discuss."

The corner of his wide mouth twitched up into a smile. I wondered how I ever found this man charming. I must have been out of my mind.

My phone rang, jarring me. I reached for my jeans pocket but Javier was quicker. His fingers wrapped around my wrist, twisting it painfully away from me while he deftly got the phone out with his other hand. He held my arms down, pinning me against my door, and checked the screen. His eyes blazed for an instant before he punched the button for the window to go down and then chucked my cell out of it.

In a second, the window was back up and he was sitting in his seat like he never moved and my wrist was left aching in my lap. He smoothed his hair back behind his ears and grinned to himself. "Don't worry. We'll get you a new phone."

I looked down at my wrist, the red marks from his fingers quickly fading. He'd never used force on me before, at least not in a nonsexual way, and to tell you the truth, it was sobering. For the first time since I'd gotten in the car, I was actually afraid.

What had I gotten myself into?

"So, tell me about this Camden McQueen."

My heart rattled in my chest. "I'm sure you know more about him than I do."

"I found out a lot, yes. But you . . . you seemed to be *intimate*."

Acid burned along his words, seeping through his smooth facade. I really didn't want to discuss my relationship with Camden, although I felt like doing so out of spite. It bothered him, somehow, after all this time, that I had been with another man. And I guess somewhere, somehow, I still held a grudge.

"I fucked him, if that's what you mean," I said bluntly. *I told Camden I loved him too,* I thought to myself, playing with the sentence like a hand grenade but deciding it was safer keeping it inside.

Javier stiffened beside me for an instant. "So crude."

"Yeah, well," I said. "It is what it is."

"Nothing more?"

Against my better judgment I glared at him. "What is it that you want, Javier? I'm sure it can't be whether I got nailed by Camden or not, because you have your answer."

"I want," he said slowly, drawing it out. He licked his lips. "I want you and me to work together."

I nearly laughed. In fact, a small snort escaped from my lips.

He raised one perfect brow and tilted his head toward me. "You find this funny?"

My fingers were splayed against my collarbone. "I find this horrifying."

"Eden," he said, then squeezed his eyes shut and shook his head. "Ellie. You don't think you're here just for the sake of being here, do you?"

"You tell me. You fucking kidnapped a mother and

child in order to get me. You paid I don't know how much money. You have me now. For whatever you want. And you're telling me, after all these years, you found me because you want us to *work* together?"

His eyes were on me, growing more golden in the light. Steady. Not blinking. Unnerving if I wasn't so sure this was a test. He who looks away first loses. I wasn't losing yet, not when I was unaware of the prize.

I stared right back.

"Yes," he said after a few beats. He licked his lips again, and it made me realize how thirsty I was. "I could have found you long ago, if I really wanted to. I would have let you go. The car, the money, the lack of answers—"

"The lack of answers?" I repeated.

"You just left. No note, no phone call. No answers." He slowly broke into a grin and then turned his attention to the window where a truck was thundering down the highway, dirty exhaust in its wake. "You know I love my answers, angel. You left me as high and dry as my mother's bedsheets."

My mouth gaped, tongue fumbling for something concrete. "What the fuck are you talking about? I left you high and dry ..."

He shrugged. "No matter, it's the past."

It *was* the past. The past he was totally wrong about.

"You cheated on me!" I spat out, instantly ashamed at how much passion there was in my voice.

"Right," he said. He raised his hand in the air as if to shut me up. "I did. I forget that sometimes, that what I did was wrong on some accounts. But that's nothing."

It wasn't nothing. What he did, me finding him in bed with some ginger-haired bitch, it shaped who I was. It ruined my heart, my ability to love, to trust, to... live. He scarred me just as much as Travis had done. It wasn't nothing. Maybe, maybe it should have been.

I took in a deep breath, knowing he probably loved the fact that I was getting so riled up. "Okay, so it was nothing. You could have found me years ago, so you say. Why now? You're lonely, is that it? Having a lot of money not getting your dick up enough?"

His eyes fastened into slits. "I'm not the person I was six years ago, my dear. And, I can see, neither are you."

He was right about that. Javier had obviously changed for the worse. Had I?

Stupid question.

"I can understand why you think I'd pursue you for, uh, delicate reasons," he continued. "But that's not the case. We both want the same thing. And for once, I think you have the upper hand in getting it."

My forehead scrunched. "Don't tell me you need lessons in being a con artist."

I saw the first genuine smile yet stretched briefly across his face. "You're a lot better at other things, Ellie. You have something that I don't. You have access, contacts, and in some cases... womanly charms. Jesus knows how I fell for them once."

His eyes glided up my body from my jeans-clad legs to my bare arms. To where the tattoo, his tattoo, wrapped around my bicep like an anaconda, squeezing the life out of me.

"And what if I won't help you?" I said, rubbing at

my parched throat. I was thirsty, and the more I thought about what Javier might do if I ever refused him dried me out even more.

"I don't think you'll refuse," he said with total confidence. He leaned forward and tapped on the tinted glass that separated the driver from us. "*Agua, dos,*" he said, and the bald driver leaned down and brought out two water bottles. Javier handed one to me and the window went back up.

I quickly unscrewed the cap and took a large swig. It was cool and strangely sweet and took a lot to quench my thirst.

"And if I refuse?" I repeated, wiping my mouth.

He slowly sipped his water, his eyes on me, far too intimate, far too observant. "I have ways of making you see the bigger picture. Now, drink up."

At that, I immediately brought the bottle away from my lips.

"So suspicious, Ellie," he crooned. I felt the bottle slipping out of my hands as I tried to grasp it. He plucked it from me and pressed down on my shoulder so I was back against the seat. His fingers were rougher than I remembered but hot, as if fueled by a radiator. Everything was starting to go loose and numb. The interior of the car swirled.

"Naturally," he went on, leaning forward and peering into my eyes, "you have a right to be so. Eden White was far too trusting."

My head had lolled back onto the seat. I could see the lightning jags of gold and green meeting his pupils, the tiny lines that formed at the corner of his eyes, the one strand of salt-colored hair that dared to show its face at his widow's peak. Javier had aged. There was nothing scarier.

"Sleep well, my angel." His voice came to me on a wave of vibration. There were swirls of light and then everything went black.

CHAPTER TWO

Camden

She'd lied. She fucking lied.

I should have seen it coming, should have known this wasn't going to end easily. I should have known the minute Javier called that there was no way he'd let her go once he had her. He wasn't weak like me, I'll give him that. He wasn't the one left in the rock garden, two assfuck thugs' meaty hands wrapped around him, holding him in place as he watched her leave. No, that was me, Camden McQueen.

I had to watch her leave again, but this wasn't high school and this wasn't a hallway.

She left me in a cloud of dust, a swirl of crushed cherry blossoms that choked my heart.

I must have been screaming in the aftermath, outside of my body with my old friend *rage*. I hated this part of being me—when I lost it, lost myself—the blackness that settled into my bones, that took over and

booted my brain out of my skin. I was seeing everything from another angle, and it looked just as fucked
from up here.

And there was crying. My beautiful son, Ben, just
three years old, was crying in his mother's arms and I
knew I needed to get control back. Screaming, fighting,
it wasn't going to solve anything. I had to think about
him and my ex-wife, Sophia. I had to think about getting us out of there or getting Javier's men out of my
tattoo parlor, Sins & Needles. I needed control.

I shut my mouth, nearly clamping down on my
tongue, as my heart ached and crumbled and slowed
in my throat. The tunnel vision ended and suddenly the
desert sky was as bright as it had ever been.

The SUV—Ellie—was now long gone.

"Get your fucking hands off me," I snarled, jerking out of the men's grasp. Their stupid, thick fingers
finally let go. I turned around and finally got a good
look at them. They were both built like linebackers,
large heads with nothing inside, programmed to do
Javier's bidding. Pussies to the core.

"Are you going to leave or do you want me to call
the cops on you?" I asked, knowing I wasn't about to
get my father involved. As the sheriff of Palm Valley,
he was someone who could easily out-asshole them
while grinding me down in the process.

The men exchanged a look but were silent.

"That won't be necessary," Raul said from behind
me, the stairs creaking as he came down. I'd forgotten
he had been there, hovering behind Sophia and Ben
during the whole transaction like a yellow jacket in a

fancy suit. "That is, unless they're already on their way because of the scene you just caused."

I swallowed down the volcano in my chest and exhaled sharply through my nose as his skinny, catcher's-mitt face came closer. "If you think that was me making a scene, you haven't seen anything yet."

His smile was wry; it belonged to a prick with empty power. If I hadn't been certain that the thugs were carrying guns, I would have kicked his teeth in.

"We're leaving," he said, folding his arms across his chest. My eyes focused on the scar at his jaw and for a painful second I saw the ones on Ellie's leg, felt them under my tattoo gun, under my hands, under my tongue.

"Are *you*?" he continued, snapping me out of it before I could drown further.

I glared. "None of your fucking business."

He shrugged like Javier Jr. "If you were a smart man, you'd leave this place. Take your wife and your kid and your dirty money and get out of here."

Ex-wife, I wanted to say, but the dirty money comment stung even more.

"Or what?" I challenged stupidly. I should have shut my mouth again, just kept it all in and gone, but I felt like being an annoyance, if anything.

He raised his brow. "Or nothing. We"—he nodded at the thugs and their blank, bloated faces—"are done with you." He jerked his head to the street, where people were driving past like lives weren't being threatened and ruined and changed before their eyes. The men nodded and the three of them walked past me, out of my trampled rock garden where plants would continue to thrive even when I left the shop to cobwebs and dust. Because I had to leave, though not on account of Raul. I had to leave because I'd made my decision weeks ago.

Raul stopped on the sidewalk, the heat rising off of it. He took a pair of shades out of his jacket pocket and handled them for a moment, his eyes two dark dots in the harsh sun.

"But," he said louder, his voice thick, "just because we are done with you doesn't mean Javier is. Don't go looking for her, whatever you do. Or it's your funeral. And hers."

He slipped the sunglasses on his face and he and the thugs disappeared down the street toward whatever getaway they had planned.

Although I believed him when he said he was done with us, it didn't make me feel any safer. I slowly turned around and looked at Sophia and Ben. She was holding on to his hand, my boy leaning up against her leg. In her other hand was the briefcase full of money. She held on to that just as tightly.

Our eyes met, perhaps really, truly, for the first time today. Man, even with her in the shade of the porch, I could see her eyes blazing, full of fire, and not the type I wanted to go up in. Fuck it, there was no avoiding it. I'd avoided this for way too long.

After everything—everything—I'd gone through, it was ridiculous that I'd feel the slightest bit scared of my ex-wife. But I was. I could admit it. I'd admit to anything at this point. I was afraid of what she was going to make me feel, of what she couldn't *wait* to make me feel.

Meanwhile, Ellie was in a car with Javier. Was she afraid too? Was she afraid of what Javier could possibly make her feel? Or was that fear exclusively mine?

I brushed it out of my thoughts like a loose strand of hair and walked up the stairs to them, my fingers flicking past one another, trying to disperse the nervous energy that was building up.

I stopped in front of Sophia, on the last step so I was at her level. She was petite, not so much in shape but in height. She was always a foot smaller than me though her hips and thighs had weight to them, something that lured me in all those years ago.

"I'm sorry," I said thickly, my eyes on hers, and meaning it.

I never thought she'd let go of the briefcase. And when she did, it landed on the porch with a bang that echoed in the overhang. The next thing that happened was her open palm meeting my face. She hit me fast, a quick draw, one side of my cheekbone, then the other with the back of her hand, catching the corner of my lip. It stung like hell and I sucked in my breath. Getting angry would do me no good—getting angry was the reason she was my ex-wife.

"I deserved that," I said quietly, avoiding her eyes.

"Shut up!" she cried out, spittle falling out of her mouth. Ben, bless his innocent heart, whimpered and hugged his mother tighter, refusing to cry. "You shut up. You asshole! You..."

She trailed off and just when I thought all of this was too much for her, she hit me again. Then she burst into tears, her head hanging down, briefcase at her feet.

I couldn't help but look at Ben, my son, who was looking up at me like I was not only a bad man, the bad man that made his mother cry, but a total stranger. I was a stranger to both of them, and it didn't matter how many letters I wrote. We were all lost to each other.

"Hey," I said softly, and wrapped my arms around her. She stiffened but let me hold her. I stretched one hand down and placed it on Ben's head and we stood there for a good few minutes, a family by blood, not heart, while she continued to cry.

"I don't even know where to begin," she said, her voice muffled into my tear-soaked chest.

"I did a stupid thing," I told her, figuring it was better to attempt it than not.

"I know," she said, the edge returning to her voice. She raised her head, her face inches from mine. I remembered how hard it used to be for me to not kiss her and how easy it was now. The bruises around her eye and cheek where someone—Javier?—had hit her were blooming. It made me feel sick all over again.

"I'm sorry," I whispered, and she pulled out of my grasp. "I had the best intentions for Ben in mind throughout all of it. I wanted to escape this life, the life your…brothers…put me in."

She wiped hard at her tears like they burned. "You put yourself in that life. You—"

"I hit you," I said. Even she looked a bit shocked at the way I admitted it after all this time. I placed my hands on her shoulders and held her firmly, lowering my head, eyeing her closely. "I hit you. There's no excuse. I'm done excusing myself. I hit you and I hate myself for it and I hate that it ruined what we had. A family. I can never take it back and I have to live with it. I'm sorry, Sophia. Really, truly sorry for what I did to you."

She sniffed, seeming to take it in. I didn't expect her to forgive me and I didn't even care if she did. As I said to Ellie once, I didn't regret the consequences of my actions but I did regret the action. And I had been making excuses for it all this time, blaming Sophia for something that was entirely my fault. My temper, my anger, my old friend rage—I wanted to finally kick it to the curb. I wanted to own it, destroy it. Wasn't that what second chances were about?

I crouched down and pulled up the briefcase. I put it in her hand. "I didn't earn this money. I didn't ask for it. I hate what it stands for. If it can give us a second chance, then maybe it's not all for nothing."

"Who said I wanted a second chance with you?" she said. She was right. I never assumed she would.

"Because it feels like the right thing to do, to try. Listen, Sophia. I can't let you go back to the way things were. Your brothers...they turned you over to a fucking madman. That life, that wasn't a life, that's not a family. I can be your family."

"Even though you're in love with another woman," she pointed out. "Who was she? Who was this woman who was worth all of this?"

"An old friend," I said simply, ignoring the nails in my heart. I didn't even want to say her name, not now while we stood there in Palm Valley, where I could almost feel her getting farther and farther away. I had to focus on what I had right in front of me: Ben and Sophia. Money for a new life. I had to make sure they were safe first before I could even indulge in thoughts about Ellie.

I hated that I had to choose.

"Please, let's just get out of here. Somewhere safe. We can lay it all out, discuss our next move."

She turned and looked behind her at the shop, my beautiful shop, built on lies and ink. "This isn't safe? It's your home."

"This will never be safe. And it's done being my home."

She nodded, seeming to understand. "So what, you're going to leave right now, like this? Your father..."

"I've already left, Sophia. I shouldn't even be here." I shouldn't have been so careless to think a man like Javier wouldn't go after me and take the things I loved. He had given some of them back to me, and I had to make it work.

I looked at the GTO, the car that Ellie named Jose, sitting in the driveway. It had seen so much already. It was time for it to see more.

I grabbed Sophia's hand and tried to grab Ben's but he pulled away from me. Would he recognize himself inked on the back of my leg? Would he one day realize how much he meant to me? I wanted to feel like a father again. I wanted him to feel like he had a dad.

We had just reached the car when I heard someone call out from the street.

"Camden!"

"Shit," I swore under my breath, and turned to look.

It was Audrey Price, one of my clients. Her pale skin glowed under the hot sun like skin cancer waiting to happen. On her arm was the sleeve of cherry blossoms I had partly filled in a few weeks back. The day I met Ellie. The same cherry blossoms I would later add to Ellie's leg.

"Who is that?" I heard Sophia whisper.

"A client," I said, and put on my most charming smile as Audrey approached us. "What's up, Audrey? How's the tat?"

She stopped in front of us and quickly glanced at Sophia over her retro shades. She took her in first, then Ben, who was still as quiet as a mouse. Finally she looked to me.

"I came to see you the other day. You were closed," she said uneasily, and slid her shades back on.

I shrugged as casually as I could muster. "Going on a vacation with my family."

She frowned, then her head swung to Sophia and Ben again for a better look. Her mouth dropped open. In the stark light, it wasn't obvious off the bat that Sophia had been knocked around. "Family? I...I had no idea you were...I'm sorry."

"Don't be sorry," I told her, knowing that Audrey was running over a few scenarios in her head. She'd always had a female hard-on for me, that much was obvious. It didn't help that I tattooed her ass late one night and in turn she sucked my dick. Now, all of that, combined with what seemed like a hidden wife and child and obvious case of spousal abuse, probably made things seem that much more wrong.

She never really knew Camden McQueen, did she?

She smiled tightly at me and I went on, trying to put her at ease. "I'm just going off for a bit, need some quality time, that's all. I'll reopen when I return. Did you want another session? Let me take a look."

I reached for her arm as I would normally do, to inspect my work, just to see how it was holding up and if it had somehow gotten more beautiful as it melded with the skin, something I'd noticed time and time again. They say tattoos are permanent, but in my eyes they adapt, ever changing.

She jerked her arm away as if my fingers were needles themselves and shot me another one of those awkward smiles. "I should be going."

I swallowed my fear, the kind that would paralyze me and keep me here to make sure I wasn't given a bad name, so no one would think ill of me. "All right. Well, drop by in a week or so." I could see now I was no longer the hot tattoo artist but something more sinister. In a week, she wouldn't return. And I wouldn't be here anyway.

Audrey gave me a vague nod, turned, and quickly walked away, her sex heels echoing on the sidewalk.

"Are all your clients that awkward?" Sophia asked as she moved over to the passenger's side door of the car.

"I guess none of this looks very good," I said with a forced shrug.

"It's beyond looking good," she said, throwing the briefcase inside and squinting at me gravely. "Because this is all very, very bad, Camden. I don't think you realize how bad this all is."

Oh, the thing was, I did.

I took one last look at Sins & Needles and got in the car, not even feeling the heat that only an old car can hold.

*   *   *

I'd been driving for only twenty minutes before the depraved finality of everything settled in. Beneath my hands was the wheel of a car that wasn't mine and wasn't his and wasn't hers, but it was all I had left. I had lived too fast and too hard, and now I was just supposed to accept it, accept that it was a parting gift, like the briefcase in Sophia's hands, my reward for giving up my love.

I wasn't giving up, was I? Every bone in my body ached to turn the GTO around, to go back for Ellie, to take her from something she didn't need to do, from a life she didn't need to return to. From a love that never was, that could never be what she needed.

"We're about to run out of gas." Sophia spoke up, her voice hoarse and emotionless. My eyes drifted sideways to Ben sleeping in her lap and my lungs burned as if I had swallowed a pint of sand. I couldn't give up on Ellie. But I couldn't give up on Ben either. I had made my choice when I drove away from Palm Valley. I just didn't know if I'd get my second chance one more time.

I pulled the car over to the next gas station and filled up as quickly as possible. I needed to keep it together, I needed to keep control. I needed, needed, needed.

The passenger door opened and Sophia got out, Ben still in her arms, still asleep. "I'm going to get some food," she said, nodding at the convenience mart with the garish lights that wouldn't hide a thing.

I put the pump back in the receiver. "Why don't you leave Ben with me? You don't need to take him with you."

She shook her head. "I don't want to wake him. He'll sleep as long as I'm holding him."

Things I should know about my own kid. Things that I didn't.

"Don't you trust me with him?" I asked, coming around the car.

She raised her brows. "No, Camden. I don't. You might be his father by birth, but that's the only father you've been."

"I wrote letters . . ." I trailed off.

"No, you didn't," she snapped.

It fucking figured. My heart began to pump loudly in my ears, my fingers twitched. "I did, Sophia. I wrote him. I sent you money too, but I'm guessing you never saw any of that."

Her eyes darted to the store and back. She licked her lips and looked back at me. "No. I haven't gotten a dime from you."

"Fuck," I muttered, trying hard to keep myself from pounding my fist on the back of the car.

"If it makes you feel better, I believe you."

I raised a brow and unclenched my fist. "Just like that?"

"Just like that." Still, she walked off toward the store, Ben's head on her shoulder.

I sat back in the car and rested my head on the steering wheel. I needed to think and think fast.

I had two problems: Sophia and Ellie. Both seemed impossible to fix, to make right, but it didn't matter. I had Sophia in my hands, and that was the one I'd have to fix first.

Sophia was turned over to Javier by her brothers in exchange for the money I stole from them. It didn't really surprise me, not really. They'd always been the types to throw each other under a bus if it meant coming out on top. Her whole family was fucked up that way, rotten to the core. Ellie had theories that they were tied to the mafia but they weren't Sicilian, just Italian. They were tied to something big and bad, that's all I knew.

Now, obviously Sophia couldn't go back to them. She wasn't living with her brothers. Last I knew they were in LA, near her in Silverlake. They were too close for comfort, and I was pretty sure if they ever saw my head popping up in their neighborhood, they'd shoot it clean off. I had to convince Sophia to leave LA with Ben. I had to get them somewhere far away and safe. At the depth of mud I was sunk in, I couldn't take things to the police, not without going to jail myself. Fuck, if I really thought about it, there was a grocery list of felonies I'd committed in the last week alone.

Once I got Sophia away, maybe even in another state—Oregon, who knows where—I'd contact Gus, the guy Ellie vouched for. We could get Sophia a new name. We had money. We could start again.

It sounded all too familiar.

What about Ellie?

What about Ellie?

What about Ellie?

What happened to her? Every day I was apart from her was a day she was farther and farther away. Three lives were at stake here, and I couldn't save all of them at the same time.

I exhaled loudly feeling nothing but hopeless, and my eyes fell to the passenger's side. The briefcase was gone. I sat up and craned my neck to look at the store. I couldn't see Sophia inside. No...

Panic rose inside me. She wouldn't take the money and leave me here? She didn't hate me that much. She couldn't...

I didn't know *her* at all, did I?

I quickly got out of the car, my footsteps sounding hard on the asphalt in a rare moment of quiet from the highway. The store looked empty for all I could see, and we were the only car on the lot.

I opened the door, the bell jangling too loud for my liking. A double-chinned man with fuzzy gray hair was looking at a crossword puzzle. The store was empty.

"Excuse me," I said, trying to hide the anxiety in my voice. The clerk didn't even look up. I walked over and leaned over the counter, getting between him and the puzzle. Finally his tired red eyes met mine. I knew those eyes, they were desert eyes, dried out from too much sun and too little joy.

"Can I help you?" the man asked. I could sense he was about to reach under the counter for the alarm so I backed off.

"Did you see a woman and a young boy come in here?" I asked.

He frowned then relaxed a bit. "I saw a woman. Can't say I saw a boy."

"Was she petite, you know, short, dark hair, Italian looking?"

He rubbed his lips together in thought. I didn't have time for him to ponder this shit. I needed to find out if Sophia left me, and fast.

"Think!" I barked, losing control for a moment. "Was she here?"

The man froze, taken aback. At the same time, I heard a door slam behind me. I turned to see Sophia coming out of the restroom with Ben at her side. Her eyes were drawn thin, eyeing me suspiciously.

"There you are," I said, turning and giving Ben the most genuine smile I could muster. Relief never felt as soothing as it did just then.

"Where did you think I went?" she asked. I nodded at the briefcase. She shook her head and quickly pushed the door open. "Come on, sweetie," she crooned to Ben.

I followed her out to the car, trying to burn away the guilty feeling. My first thought was that Sophia had taken the money and run. I wondered when I'd ever trust anyone again.

"Sorry," I muttered to her after I got in the car and pulled it back on the highway. The sun was sliding low in the sky, casting a warm golden light that made you feel warm and safe, like your mind was flipping through photographs of summers long ago. It was nostalgic and good and terribly misleading. I hated this time of day.

She was silent, mulling over my distrust.

"Sorry," I said again, passing the roadside dinosaurs of Cabazon. "I thought you'd left."

"You *would* think that," she said.

"Mama, I'm tired." Ben finally spoke, tugging on her sleeve as she held him. His voice brought tears to my eyes. I'd never heard him speak before. My mouth was torn between a gape and a smile. In another life, this would have been ordinary, and I would have turned the car around and shown Ben the dinosaurs. In another life, he would see me as his father. In another life, I wouldn't be trying to find a new one for us all.

"Watch the road," Sophia said, tapping her hand on the dashboard. I looked up in time to see I was crossing over the dividing line. I corrected myself, my heart racing loud, and rubbed my forehead until I could feel. I needed to hold it all together, if only for a little while longer.

I swallowed hard and let out a long, calm breath. "Sophia, we need to think about the next steps. You can't go home again." As eloquently and noninvasive as I could, I explained what we needed to do. To my amazement, she didn't put up a fight, even when I said she'd have to change her name and cut off all contact with her old life. Perhaps she knew that Ben's well-being was worth every sacrifice.

"I understand," she said as she smoothed back Ben's thick, beautiful hair. My God, he was going to be a lady-killer one day. "But I can't just up and leave like that." She snapped her fingers. "We have to go back to the apartment so I can get my stuff."

"Your brothers—"

"Aren't even in town anymore. They're in Fresno."

"How do you know?"

She shot me a dirty look. "They might have sold me out, but I'm their sister. I knew their plans for the week before any of this happened."

I flipped down the visor, squinting at the sun spearing the I-10 with golden flames. "Sophia..."

"What?"

I shook my head. "Aren't you...surprised? Upset? You *are* their sister, and they sold you out."

She sat back in her seat, silence blanketing us. "Yes. I am surprised and I am upset. I don't know what to tell you, Camden. One minute I was at home feeding Ben, the next..."

She sniffed and her whole body started shaking.

"It's okay," I soothed her. "We don't have to talk about it. We'll get you home tonight, but in the morning, we're gone. For good. You understand what's happening?"

Sophia nodded. "I hope to see LA again."

I hoped, for all our sakes, that she was right.

CHAPTER THREE

Ellie

I woke up in hell.

At first, I couldn't see anything but flashing lights and moving shapes. That alone did not make it hell. Neither did the increasing urge to vomit and the pounding blood in my head that made me wince painfully with each breath.

What made it hell was when my eyes opened enough to focus on the flashing lights. It was the soft, baby-new glow of morning being scattered by an azure blue curtain that waved back and forth by an open window. Despite the bars that created zebra shadows on the carpeted floor, the window was familiar.

The curtain was too. I'd picked out that curtain from Bed Bath & Beyond, thinking the blue matched the surf outside. I'd hung that curtain myself.

Six years ago.

I sat up, limbs and head heavy with a tincture of

chemicals, panic, and total disgust. I was back in our old bedroom, the one I used to share with Javier. I was *back*.

And the slippery son of a bitch had drugged me.

I got out of bed and nearly fell flat on my face, my legs tangled in the sheets. The room had stayed the same. Save for the security bars on the window, everything looked exactly as it had before. For six years, it had stayed the same while the man who slept there grew something terrible in his heart. I could see it in his eyes, the coldness, the games. Or maybe I could see now what I couldn't see then.

There was no use dwelling on it. He wanted me to swim in this past, that's why I was here. He wanted the past to drown me. I wouldn't let it. I wouldn't let him win. I was Ellie Watt, not Eden White, and I was stronger than this.

I had no past. There was only now.

I took the next step—as unsteady as I was—and tried the door. It wasn't locked.

I peered out into the hallway and fought the memory that wanted to intrude, that time I discovered Javier slitting the throat of one of his friends. I shot down the memory, threw fresh dirt over it. I moved on and moved down the hall, my feet bare and sticking to the hardwood floor.

Sunlight dazzled the kitchen, streaming in through the large windows that overlooked the dune grass, sand, and ocean. Javier was sitting at the table, drinking orange juice and flipping through the *Los Angeles Times*, eyes darting from page to page.

It could have been a Norman Rockwell painting. I was about to throw red paint on it.

"The fuck is going on?" I asked, one hand leaning against the wall.

He finished flipping to the end of the paper—agonizing seconds of paper flipping through his deft fingers—before he laid it down and looked up at me.

"Good morning," he said, looking amused without smiling. "Did you sleep well?"

It took all of my self-control to keep from tackling him across the table and clawing his eyes out. I knew we weren't alone though. I knew there were people, somewhere, watching us, making sure I was following the straight and narrow. I knew I had to keep everything inside as much as I could.

"Why the hell am I here?" I asked, my jaw clenched.

"Because I live here," he said simply.

"Still?"

He smiled, just a twitch at the corner of his snake-like mouth. "Painful memories?"

"Fuck you," I said. I instantly regretted it when his grin broadened.

"I see. So they are."

I brushed my hair back behind my ears, as if that would help me think. "Why am I here? Why am I here *where you live*?" I mimicked his accent.

He folded his hands in front of me and the damn watch started glinting like a gold spark in the sun stream. "I brought you here because this is our first task."

"First task?" I asked dumbly.

"Sit down," he said, gesturing to the seat across from him. Where I always used to sit. Same damn seat. "Please."

"No." I crossed my arms across my chest. His eyes briefly lasered in on my cleavage. "I want you to tell me what the task is. I want to know why I'm here."

He leaned back in his chair and clasped his hands behind his head. "So impatient, my angel."

I shot to the opposite side of the table and shoved my finger in his face. My razor blade necklace swung like a pendulum. "Talk. You owe me that much, you piece of shit."

He eyed my finger and had the courtesy to wipe the smile from his face. "Okay."

I backed off, my nerves firing in all directions. I waited, shoving my itching hands in my back pockets.

He breathed in delicately through his nose and folded up the newspaper as he spoke. "The task, why I brought you here, why I sought you, finally, is this: I know what you've been doing for the last however many years."

"Six. You know it's been six."

He raised his brow. "Time flies."

"Keep talking."

He sighed. "All right. You've been a thief."

"Just like my parents," I filled in, knowing what else he'd throw in there.

His smile wavered for a second. "Yes. Just like them. Anyway, I'm not judging."

Wouldn't that be rich.

"So," he continued. "You've been doing that. Being

generally immoral, such a far cry from the Eden White I loved."

The way he said *loved* creeped me out. It was like watching the devil himself say it. The word didn't belong on his tongue.

"And while you've been Ellie Watt, I've been... making adjustments. Making money. Going places. Moving up."

"If that's moving up, then I'm moving out," I muttered under my breath, making sure he could hear me.

"No more Dire Straits?" he asked. "Billy Joel now?"

"Get to the point."

"The point is, I know about you. I know why you were with me, at least for some of it. I know the truth about your scars. I know the truth about Travis."

I swallowed hard, the hairs standing up on my arms and prickling along my neck like tiny ants. Of course he knew. I remembered what Jim had told me about Javier.

Jim.

My uncle Jim. My only real family. The memory of him hit me like a brick. But it wasn't anything nice. It wasn't the good times. It wasn't something fucking normal. It was when he was dead. The bullet in his head, his shocked expression as he hit the floor in that motel room.

And I was staring, just feet away, at the man who killed him.

"Something wrong?" Javier asked.

What would be the point in bringing it up? Jim didn't deserve to be mentioned in his presence. Another memory to bury deep inside.

"So you know the truth," I said with a shrug. "Must have been enlightening for you."

He nodded gravely. "It was. Ellie...if I had known what Travis had done. If I had known then..."

Right. If he had known that I sought him out under false pretences, pretending to be interested in him in order to get closer to Travis, I'm sure things would have been just peachy between us. I could only imagine what Javier would have done if he discovered at the time that our whole relationship was based on a lie.

"I don't care. What do you *want*?"

"It's one and the same, don't you see? I no longer work for Travis. I went my own way a year ago."

"A regular Stevie Nicks," I said, masking the sorrow that picked at me. Uncle Jim. His memory kept floating to the surface.

He went on. "Travis...I grew more powerful than him."

"You must be very proud."

He tilted his head in agreement, not recognizing my sarcasm. "There were too many traitors in his organization. He'd gone mad with power. Things were unraveling. He began consorting with our rivals, Los Zetas. The very people who killed my parents. If I hadn't split, I might have died."

What a shame, I thought.

"I had Raul and Alex. I had a few others. I had the means and the connections. I left here and headed to Florida. I made a good life for myself." He noticed my expression. "Yes, maybe running drugs isn't a noble life. But neither is conning."

"What," I said through grinding teeth. "Is. The. Task?"

"Travis hurt you, Ellie. He was the reason you found me those years ago. You wanted revenge for your scars, for your life, for what he'd done to you. I'm handing you the gun. Together, we can get your revenge. And I can get mine."

Despite everything sounding absolutely ridiculous, I had to ask, "What's your revenge? What did he do to you?"

"It doesn't matter," he said, his eyes drifting to the *LA Times* again. Why he was reading the LA paper when we were in Ocean Springs, Mississippi, was beyond me. Everything was beyond me. "What matters is that I said I would kill any man that hurt you. Now, you have seen that I keep my word. I keep my promises. Travis hurt you, maybe more than anyone else. I want him dead from the barrel of my gun."

I swallowed uneasily. "Maybe you oughta turn the gun on yourself then." *Because you hurt me too* is what I didn't say.

He blinked warmly. "Maybe I will. But first, this is the task. We kill him. Together. Eye for an eye, tooth for a tooth. Promises are promises."

I couldn't believe what I was hearing. It was raining down on me in slick fragments that I just couldn't grasp. One minute Camden and I were heading for a new life together. In the next I was with Javier, who wanted me to kill the drug lord that ruined my life. As much as I believed in revenge, I couldn't muster up the rage that blinded me enough to do such a thing. I couldn't do much of anything except try to get my brain up to speed.

"I'm a con artist," I stated. "Not a killer for hire."

"I know," he said softly. He got up, pushing his chair back and leaning on the table. "Unfortunately, you don't have much of a choice."

My breath hitched. I would not let fear set in. Fear made me weak. Fear had drugged me.

"I *always* have a choice." I grimaced at my warbling voice.

"Not always," he said, walking around the table. His wing-tipped shoes echoed in the kitchen. "The choice you did have—to stay with Camden or turn yourself over to me—you took. Now you have to live with the consequences. It's time for you to own your decision."

His eyes were getting to be too much. I looked to the floor. "Why do you need me to do this? Why can't you kill him yourself?"

"Because we are enemies now, my dear. Because he knows to look out for me. Because I have tried before and, yes, I failed. I am not perfect."

"No one ever said you were," I muttered. My heart was threatening to beat out of my chest, but as long as I kept my eyes on the floor and my head clear, I was going to be okay. No fear. I had to play it cool, play it safe and have no fear. The minute my mind started focusing on the *what if*s was the moment I lost it.

I was very close to losing it.

"You," he said, coming up to me. My body seized with his just inches away. I concentrated on his black shoes, expensive leather with scuffed tips. Tailored suit pants. It didn't go. His shoes should have been shiny and as black as oil. "You. You can get to him. You can get close. You don't even have to pull the trigger." He said *trigger* like it was a new sexual position.

Another thought I didn't need.

He took another slow step forward. I sucked in my stomach.

His voice lowered till it was rough and smooth like ice in a milkshake. "You can get your revenge. The revenge you couldn't get with me."

"Maybe I don't need revenge anymore."

"Maybe you're lying to yourself."

I dared myself to look him in the eye. I raised my chin defiantly, pretending I was suited in armor. "Maybe lying is what I do best."

He gazed at my lips and let out a small laugh. "Aren't you tired of searching for that something to put your demons to rest?"

I ignored him. "Aren't you tired of pretending you know me when you don't know shit? You didn't even know I was Ellie Watt."

"I knew enough," he said vaguely. "And I know you'll help me."

"I'd like to prove you wrong."

"Ellie, he doesn't know who you are. You can get in. You can get close."

I jerked my head in disbelief. "Like hell he doesn't know who I am. Javier. I was your...I was here. I lived with you for a fucking year. Travis knew about me, you told me he did. He saw pictures of us, of me."

"He never met you."

"Doesn't matter."

"You look completely different."

"He'll know." I started shaking my head up and down and back and forth. "Oh, he'll know. How can he not?"

Javier frowned and rubbed at his chin. I could almost see puzzle pieces coming together behind those eyes. "Because he didn't know you when you were a child. And he didn't know you when you were with me. And he doesn't know you now." His head dipped. "Angel, you were nothing to him. Unmemorable. He probably doesn't even remember pouring that acid down your leg. You're nothing special. Not to him."

I felt like I'd been slapped in the face, and I had to dig my fingers into my pockets like desperate claws to keep from slapping him in the face. Lord knows he deserved it, and more. But now wasn't the time. Because as much as it hurt to hear Javier say it, I knew he was right. I had always thought that Travis was watching for me in the way that I watched for him. But who was I to him? Just a ten-year-old girl with stupid, reckless, selfish parents. He got his money back. He probably never gave a second thought to what he did to me. He was the be-all and end-all in the back of my mind, my heart, my spine, my soul. His actions piloted my every moment until now. And they would probably affect the next. I knew he hadn't given me more thought than just that moment, when he scarred me. It was as natural as wiping his ass. He probably woke up the next day and forgot all about what he did to me. I *wasn't* special. I was a mere second to him yet he'd become my Moby Dick. In some way, he'd become my everything. Too many monsters had inserted themselves into my life.

"You see," Javier whispered. Sugar sweet. Poison. "He ruined your life and it didn't mean a thing. He'll do that to you. That's how he got so far. That's why we're going to take him down."

"I'm not doing anything with you," I snarled, finding violence in my veins.

That smirk of his. "You'll change your mind. You did before."

Then he moved away from me in one swift moment. He plucked the orange juice off the table, drank it empty, and slammed it down. "I have some business to attend to. I'll be back, you'll be delighted to know. In the meantime, make yourself...at home."

He gave me a wink and then ran down the stairs to the front door. It opened before he even got there, a burly man on the other side. Then the door closed, sealing me in the prison of my past.

CHAPTER FOUR

Camden

I dreamed about Ellie.

We were walking together between the rows of date palms on her uncle Jim's farm. As usual, my dreams were vivid. I could smell the dates as they squished beneath our feet, the earthiness of sun and soil. Me, in my high school gear: long black trench coat that was never as hot as it looked, vinyl pants that *were* as hot as they looked, black Doc Martens that I'd drawn on with a silver Sharpie. Ellie was wearing the same boots, albeit smaller. I had decorated hers with gold scribbles. She was dressed in jeans and a strappy top, her uniform. Jackasses made fun of her for wearing pants in the California desert, even in the heat of summer, but I loved her in that. The jeans adapted to her body as she developed over the years, from lean and lanky to lean and curvy.

We'd always been the only kids in Palm Valley who wouldn't be caught dead in shorts.

We walked along the rows, the sun dappling through the leaves making me feel happy. It was always a peculiar feeling, but I was used to it when I was around her. Being around Ellie gave me peace and acceptance. Real life settled in only when she left.

In the dream, I reached for her hand and pulled her toward a date palm. A ladder had been left there after harvesting.

"I want to show you something," I told her.

She shook her head, her brow wearing a faint sign of panic. She looked so fucking cute, it was always so damn hard not to kiss her. I remember always wanting to and never working up the nerve. She had let me be so true and free (as free as a teenager can be), but that was the one thing I could never let on—how much I wanted her, needed her. It was puppy love at its dirtiest.

"Come on," I had said to her. "Don't tell me you're afraid of heights."

Her fourteen-year-old face grew hard with stark determination. I knew that would work on her.

"I'm not afraid of anything," she said. She grabbed the ladder and began to speed up it.

"Careful!" I called after her, and followed.

We seemed to climb on and on, forever and forever, the palm tree stretching from twenty feet to thirty feet to fifty feet to a hundred. We finally reached the top, crawling through the thick fronds like kittens in a jungle. I took every opportunity to touch Ellie, my hand on her arm, her back, her thigh.

"Oh my God," Ellie said as she settled in. Her eyes were fastened to the horizon.

In the distance you could see the San Jacinto Mountains looming like lions. They were on fire, the peaks flickering with flames that edged their way down the mountainsides and toward the towns below. The fire spread like a blanket of lava over the valley, faster and thicker until it reached her uncle's farm. Date palms disappeared in front of our eyes, going down like blackened matchsticks, leaving tiny puffs of smoke floating above a sea of red.

Ellie looked at me, young and scared. She reached for my hand as the hiss and pop of the fire gathered at the base of our tree.

"Will you burn with me?" she asked. "Or will you go free?"

I grabbed her face as the heat pressed in. "I'll burn with you."

My lips touched hers for one second. Our screams covered us in the next.

*   *   *

"Camden." A voice came shuddering through the dark. "Camden, wake up."

Soft hands on my arm, shaking me awake.

I opened my eyes. Instead of seeing Ellie's face in a sea of flames I saw Sophia's, peering at me with something a little less than concern. Her hands were still shaking me but she was keeping her distance, clutching her mauve robe to her chest. I blinked and tried to sit up.

I was on her couch in her tiny, toy-strewn living room. There was a fuzzy darkness that came with dawn. Light was taking its time outside her windows.

"What's wrong?" I groaned while pinching the bridge of my nose. I'd fallen asleep with my glasses on, ensuring that the frames felt permanently pressed into my skin. We'd gotten to her apartment as night was falling. After scoping out the joint and peering through the blinds every five minutes, watching for her brothers or anything suspicious, I stayed up for as long as I could. It was a second-story unit with views of the street, easy pickings. Sophia didn't seem as worried as I thought she would be. Perhaps her focus was on Ben. He may have been young, but he was observant and knew something bad was happening. Sophia did what she could to make sure he was calm and happy before putting him to bed.

I had watched from the doorway. It was as close as I could get without intruding. My heart pinched as she sang him a nursery song, the same one she had sung to him as a baby. When I was around. In those days, she'd pick him up during his midnight cries and whisper it, so soft and so sweet. Sometimes I'd take over, just to give her a break. I could never hit her high notes—I wasn't much of a singer. But Ben would stop crying, just like that.

Later, when Sophia started pulling out of the marriage, out of life in general, I sang that song all the time. After a while, it stopped working. He missed his mother. I did too. And no matter how soothing I tried to sound, I couldn't stop Ben's tears. Things crumbled beyond repair.

Ben had been a year old when I last saw him, days before the divorce was final. Though now I had been looking at the face of an older boy all curled up in his bed, in some ways it was as if I had never left. I knew him, deep inside, and everything on the surface was slowly catching up.

He had been almost asleep, round face, my beautiful boy, when he opened his eyes and stared right at me from across the room.

"Mama, who is that?" he had asked, as if seeing me for the first time. It had felt like I turned a tattoo machine on my heart.

She had brushed back his hair. "No one you need to worry about. Sleep well, my Ben."

Any other time, I would have said something. The words, the anger, were fighting their way out of my chest and up my throat. To be brushed aside like that. I was his motherfucking *father*. But that wasn't the time for my own insecurities, for the tragedy of our family. As long as Sophia and Ben were around her traitorous brothers, they were in danger. I needed to save them first.

The technicalities could come after.

And that's how I ended up falling asleep on the couch. Sophia had retired to her room, something I had no interest in being a part of, even if the offer was on the table (which it wasn't). I had lain down on the couch and waited. Waited for people who never came. Waited for the reason to run.

"You were yelling," Sophia said, straightening up. She started tugging at her dark hair, something she did when she was nervous. "I thought you were in pain."

"It was a dream," I reassured her.

"A bad dream. You cried out for that woman. For Ellie."

It was weird to hear her say Ellie's name. She didn't say it with venom, though, just curiosity. I couldn't blame her. Ellie and I had quite the story, and she hadn't heard any of it. There was no point in explaining, not when the wound was still raw.

"Did I wake Ben?" I asked, suddenly worried. My eyes darted to the hallway where his door was open. His room was still dark and quiet.

She shook her head and smiled. It was a sad smile. "He sleeps in. And he sleeps through everything. Just like his father."

I watched her face carefully for telltale signs of insincerity. There weren't any.

I smiled back carefully. "I've gotten better. I get up at nine now."

She smirked. "Oh, nine. Must be nice being a tattoo artist. Your clients are probably all hungover anyway and stumbling in at noon."

That wasn't exactly true but, of course, that was the stereotype of people with tattoos. Despite the popularity of shitty-yet-hot tattoo artist chicks and the locust swarm of hipsters, people still had the wrong idea about tattoos and the artists who gave them. They were untrustworthy, dirty, trashy, and dishonest as a whole. Yet I'd tattooed valedictorians and soccer moms. I'd inked businessmen and actors. Reverends and teenyboppers. Tattoos were self-expression in its rawest and most permanent form. They weren't for one set of people or another.

Despite the facts, I was used to the stereotype.

It wouldn't die but then neither would I as long as I ignored it. Even Sophia, who had met me because she got a fucking tattoo, clung to it as if it were the only way to describe me.

Of course, the fact that I turned into a money launderer didn't really help my case. I'd never much cared for what people thought of me.

"I don't care when they stumble in, as long as they let me use their body as a canvas." Then I would continue to be immortal. My ink, my work, my *self*, would live on. I didn't say that to her though because that would definitely add another bar to the *my ex-husband is a nut job* scale.

Her features drew together. "So what are you going to do now?"

"Now?"

"Will you keep being a tattoo artist? Or will you try something else?"

The way she said "something else" reminded me of the way my dad often talked about my choice of career.

"One step at a time, Sophia," I reminded her, easing myself to my feet. Sleeping on a thin couch never did my back any good, and I had a strange feeling that I would need to be agile today.

"Do you want me to make you coffee?" I asked, my head starting to ache for it.

She studied for a moment before shaking her head. "Where are my manners? You stay. I'll make it."

She swept herself into her tiny kitchen. "My father gave me one of those Keurig coffeemakers for Christmas last year. I love it."

Her father. My eyes did another sweep of the room, and even in the fuzzy dawn I noted things I hadn't the night before. Flat-screen TV, not new though nothing to scoff at. Ikea couch that I'd slept on. Ben didn't have an obscene amount of toys, but from the ones that I saw, they looked new. Despite Sophia telling me that her dickhead brothers never passed on a dime of my child support, she seemed to be doing well enough for herself. This could have been her father—always Mr. Madano to me—or her job (she was an aesthetician) or the government. It should have made me feel good inside, to know she was doing okay without my money going through, yet for some reason it made me madder. It highlighted the money that was wasted. It made me feel like a fucking chump.

The coffee machine whirred and spurted, and in minutes I had a steaming cup of coffee in my hands. The mug had a picture of Ben on it, smiling, wearing reindeer antlers on his head.

"You still take it black?" she asked.

"Some things don't change," I said with a nod, taking a sip. It tasted good. Not as good as I made it, but good enough. The way I did it took patience, as do all the best things in life.

"You're wearing glasses now," she noted.

I smiled and took them off, slipping them into my pocket. "I was just trying something. I'm putting my contacts back in."

I pulled out my cell and glanced at the time: 6:30 AM. No calls or texts. I wasn't really surprised.

I cleared my throat as I sat down on the couch.

Sophia hovered above me like a nervous bird, darting her head down for a quick sip.

"How fast do you think you can get yourself packed up?" I asked, feeling like the neck of the hourglass was starting to widen. "I'll help, of course."

"Oh," she said, and shrugged, her face noncommittal. "Not long."

I squinted at her. "Not long? You're packing up your whole life, Sophia."

I was getting the impression that the severity of what we were taking on wasn't sinking in. I leaned forward, elbows on knees, and tried to rein her in. "I know this isn't easy. I know this doesn't even feel real. But, Sophia, you know what your brothers did to you. What makes you think they wouldn't do it again? What makes you think you'd ever be safe if you keep going on like you are? What about Ben?"

I knew I reached her. A pain expression flashed across her eyes, then it was gone. She smiled politely. "I know what I have to do, Camden, and I will do it. Whether I'm calm about it or freaking out, it doesn't matter, because it must be done. I'd rather do it now and worry about it later. Give me until 11 AM. I'll be ready to go."

It was a specific time, but I liked that about her. After we'd finished our coffees, the sun was up, trying to cut through the fog that covered LA like parchment paper. I helped Sophia gather most of the important stuff—clothes, books, documents—while Ben slept. She was trying to keep his distress to a minimum, she said. I wondered how well a three-and-a-half-year-old can adjust to a new life. If he was anything like his father, I figured pretty well.

After he'd had his breakfast of banana Cheerios and as Sophia was trying to clean him up, I asked her where the briefcase was.

"Why?" she asked, sounding strangely cagey.

"Well, I don't think it's very safe to have fifty thousand dollars just sitting around in a briefcase, do you? I'm going to deposit some of it in the bank."

She shook her head and patted Ben on the butt. "Ben, go to your room and get your Bubby."

Ben nodded and ran off to his bedroom. I looked back at her. She was tugging at her hair.

"Look, you can come with me," I told her. "It's smart if we deposit it."

"You can't. We can't. We'll set an alarm off if we deposit more than ten thousand," she said.

I chewed on my lip for a second, watching her. "I know that. We aren't going to get dinged. The money technically isn't dirty anyway. I can deposit nine thousand in my bank account and nine in yours. That gives us eighteen grand that we know will be safe. We can repeat this tomorrow. And then the next day."

"No..." She kept shaking her head.

"Sophia, what is wrong with you?"

I watched her throat move as she swallowed hard. "You can't do that."

I threw up my hands. "What's the fucking difference? Look, we don't have time to squabble over money here. As much as I hate it, the money is ours. We need it."

"Don't you have the money that you and Ellie stole?"

I cocked my head. "What makes you say that?"

She shrugged, trying to be casual and totally failing. "You and Ellie stole my brothers' money. You have that money in your bank account already, don't you?"

"No," I said slowly. "It's..." The money we laundered. The checks from the casinos. Ellie had them. Either they were still on her or they were in the car somewhere. With the trauma of the last day, I'd forgotten all about it.

"Well, where is it?" she shrieked. "You can't hold out on me, Camden."

I raised my hands. "Whoa, calm down, okay? There's a lot going on. There are the checks that we got from the casinos. I think they're on Ellie."

"You're lying to me," she said, walking toward me. "They're in the car somewhere, aren't they?" She yelled the last bit. "You have them!"

"Maybe. I'll look," I said, trying to placate her.

"I'm coming with you," she said. "And if they're there, we're depositing the money in your account today."

"Oh, so now there's a rush?"

She smiled quickly. "Now it's legit. These kinds of transactions won't make the bank suspicious. It's just casino winnings, right? We can deposit the cash some other day. We'll just be really careful with it."

I frowned, feeling strange about everything. Was she really afraid that I'd hide money from her? Didn't she understand I was doing and risking everything to protect them, to provide for them, to do the best I could?

Or maybe Sophia had a supremely fucked-up idea of what a family was all about.

"All right," I told her. "Grab Ben. We'll search the car and, if we're lucky, I'll go deposit what we find."

She nodded quickly and grabbed her purse from the counter.

"And the briefcase?" I asked, blocking her.

She frowned. "It's in my room. We're not taking it with us."

"I'd rather we did. It's safer on us than here."

I could tell she wanted to argue, but maybe she figured it wouldn't do any good. She gave me an agreeable sigh and then came back with the briefcase in hand. I let her hold on to both it and Ben, things I wasn't allowed to touch.

It only took a few seconds for me to locate three of the checks. They were in a metal box in the trunk, the place where Ellie carried a "spare life." Unfortunately, one check was made out to Ellie, two were made out to Connor Malloy, and one was made out to Camden McQueen. Each was worth about seven thousand dollars, which meant Ellie must have the remaining checks on her. I wanted to think that was a good thing, that she'd have money, wherever she was. But I had a bad, bad feeling that she wouldn't get to use them.

After I calmed Sophia down and told her that I could eventually deposit Connor Malloy's check, once our new life was under way and I got some help from Gus, we headed off to the nearest bank branch that Camden McQueen belonged to. All I had to do was smile at the teller when she commented on my "lucky Vegas winnings" and that was it. The money was in the bank. It was a small amount in the grand scheme of things, but it was a start. And I hoped to God that was enough for Sophia to start showing a little faith in me.

Yet, as we drove back to her apartment, she became quieter and more nervous. She was pretty much ripping her hair out as we pulled up to the tiny complex.

I popped the GTO in park and stared at her earnestly. "Are you afraid that your brothers are back?"

She shook her head. "No. I'm just afraid." Then she started to cry. Ben squirmed in the child seat we had outfitted in the back.

"Hey," I said, putting my hand on her shoulder. "We're going to be okay. This shit sucks and I know I'm the last person you want to be running away with, but maybe things will all work out for the best."

"How can it?" She sobbed through wet, nasty tears. "How can you and I ever work?"

I sucked in my breath before saying "Maybe it can work if there's love. If not for each other, at least for Ben."

This only made Sophia cry louder. I was never very good at being sappy. Good thing my job wasn't writing greeting cards.

I sighed and sat back in the seat, ignoring the fact that it was feeling more and more like my car when it very much wasn't. I rubbed her back, despite her flinching from my touch.

"I know you're upset, but we're almost packed. We're about ready to go."

She sniffed but didn't look at me. "Why don't you

start bringing your stuff down? I don't want to take Ben back in there if we're only going to rip this life away from him."

Fair enough. I nodded and left her in the car and took the car keys—the briefcase was in the trunk, after all. I made my way up the stairs to the unit, the sun beating down on my back like a hot hand, and opened the door.

I was wondering how Sophia would adjust, if she would ever adjust, if maybe we'd part ways in a few months after our new lives got settled and if she'd take Ben away from me again, when I stepped into the apartment.

Something was different. Something was *off.*

For the life of me, I couldn't tell what it was—a smell or the fact that all the shades were drawn—but I suddenly knew I wasn't alone.

I suddenly knew why Sophia stayed in the car.

I suddenly knew there would be no new life for me.

Not if I didn't act on instinct.

Now.

Before there was a shuffle, the sound of a gun's cartridge being handled, and the exhale of breath, I ducked. A gun fired from somewhere behind the couch. My own gun was tucked away in the car's glove compartment. I had to improvise.

I rolled out of the way and sprang to my feet in time to meet one of Sophia's brothers. He was the one I called Sloppy Seconds, or "Not Vincent." I was taller than Not Vincent and a fuckload angrier. Before he could fire again, I brought my elbow down between his eyes until I heard the crunch of cartilage. Then I struck him in the throat, driving his Adam's apple in until he and his gun dropped to the floor. Out of my reach. I had no time to think or act before launching myself over the couch right before another gun went off.

"Camden." It was Vincent, his slimy, manipulative voice. "This can end now."

I kept my mouth shut. I had nothing to say to him, no bargains to make. I heard him take a step closer, coming from maybe Ben's room. In the distance there were a few cries, worried neighbors. This was going to all happen fast, before the cops showed up. Vincent was in a hurry. He planned to kill me now, make it look like a break-in. A domestic dispute. Perhaps Sophia would back his claim and the brothers would look heroic.

"This bullet can go straight through the couch."

He was right. Fuck Ikea for making such flimsy furniture. I listened for the sounds of Not Vincent, trying to gauge if he was still a threat to me. He had fallen so fast—had I killed him? I couldn't hear him sputtering.

Vincent went on, sounding breezy, apparently not caring that his brother was hurt or possibly dead. "I'm giving you a few seconds to tell us where the rest of the checks are. The checks with my money."

"You already have your money," I grunted, trying to breathe in and out, trying to get oxygen into my brain. *Think, Camden, think.*

"What Javier gave me was a bonus," he said, closer now. Maybe just a few feet away. He was right behind me, and he wasn't pulling the trigger until I answered. "I still want what you dared to steal from me."

"Was all the money worth handing over your only sister and nephew to a drug lord?" I spat out.

Vincent chuckled. "It was practically Sophia's idea."

The room froze. It was hard to breathe.

"Aren't you tired of people fucking you over?" he went on.

Apparently, I hadn't been tired enough.

My eyes fought through the disgust that had lodged itself in my chest and drifted to the floor. One of Ben's toys, a robotic dog, was lying a foot away from me, half covered by the couch's slipcover.

"I don't know where the rest of the checks are," I said while my arm slowly reached over. My fingers curled around the toy.

"You're lying," Vincent said. Now he was right on the other side of the couch. I could practically feel his breath. If he took one more little step, he'd be able to see me, hands on the toy, my shoulder pressed against the couch back. He would see me waiting.

Ready.

"You couldn't cash them anyway," I told him. "They're all in Ellie's name."

"Then I'll make her cash them for me."

That would have been a believable threat if I hadn't known that Ellie was with Javier.

"I'm afraid you'd have to go through another psychopath first," I sneered.

"You really are naive, aren't you, tat boy? What

makes you think that wouldn't be a problem? What makes you think this isn't all part of the plan?"

Plan? I shook my head, refusing to let him rile me. He knew all the right buttons to push. "All of this for forty grand."

"Easy money gets you rich," he said. The gun cocked.

It was time to move.

I pressed down on the button on the robotic dog's back and flung it up and over the couch to the right. It barked as it went, loud and jarring, and I hoped it was enough to confuse him. Flying robot dogs probably weren't part of his "plan."

It worked.

The dog exploded into silver smithereens as Vincent shot it.

In the next second I focused all my energy into a squat, my years of surfing at Long Beach finally coming into play, and with a giant groan I sprang up and out, my shoulder driving into the couch back. Ikea made flimsy couches, but they were that much easier to move.

I felt the couch make contact with Vincent, his gun going off again but up in the air, cracking a hole in the ceiling. I kept driving the couch forward until it knocked him down and was out of my way. He cried out and the gun went off again, the bullet this time whizzing over my shoulder and crashing through the window. I burst out the door just in time.

I leaped down the stairs three at a time, my back feeling like a bull's-eye, not knowing when Vincent was going to fire on me. The sunlight was so bright, so terrible and out of place after what I'd gone through.

As I neared the car, I noticed it was empty. There was no time to process where Sophia and Ben were. For once I wasn't worried about them.

I jumped in the driver's seat and, with my hand on the gearshift, stared up through the windshield to the apartment. Sophia and Ben were standing a few doors down, huddled with a neighbor and watching me, watching everything. She was crying and playing the part. It sickened every bone in my bloody body.

Against my better judgment, I stuck my head out the window and yelled at her. "I'm coming back for him!" Call me crazy, call me whatever you will, there was no way in hell I'd let my son live with that devil of a woman. I would come back for what was mine.

She held Ben close to her side and gave me a look of Oscar-worthy revulsion. "Over my dead body!" The neighbor, a round Latino woman, was watching our exchange with horror—no doubt for the poor ex-wife. That poor, poor double-crossing bitch.

"We'll see," I said to myself, though I wondered if it was loud enough to hear, if it would come back to haunt me. I wondered if I meant it.

I popped the car in reverse and peeled out of the parking lot as Vincent came staggering out of the apartment, waving his gun around.

I was already gone before he could steady his hand. The GTO roared down the quiet sunny streets of suburban Los Angeles, and I wondered when the fuck I'd stop being a chump and if I'd ever get to see my son again.

If I'd ever get my life back and take charge.

But I had to.

I *wanted* to.

I was going to find Gus.

And then I was going to find Ellie.

And nothing, absolutely nothing, would get in my way.

CHAPTER FIVE

Ellie

My escape-artist skills had grown rusty. Which wasn't really all that surprising since I'd apparently turned into quite the shit trickster as well. Whether I'd grown too confident and too cocky by driving that damn, damn car around or whether I was doing it, as Javier had suggested, because I wanted to get caught, I was obviously losing my touch. I decided that I'd become too cocky, because wanting the vile Mexican to find me was a whole other can of worms that I wasn't about to dive into.

Besides, I had bigger problems. Like getting caught right after I made a break for it.

You couldn't really blame a girl for trying.

After Javier had left me alone in that rotten house to do whatever business he did (strangling puppies was my guess), I spent the rest of the day devising a plan to escape. The time probably would have been better

spent if I had thought about what Javier had proposi-
tioned me with, but I was so certain I could escape that
I didn't even have to think about the *what if*s.

Another reason why I was losing my touch: A good
con artist always examines all the scenarios, the *what
if*s, the multiple ways the game can play out. But I did
none of that. Instead I observed the burly man on the
other side of the front door and the smaller man in
the black suit who was stationed by the French doors
in the kitchen, guarding the way to the balcony like
some bored bouncer at a club. I decided I'd fake out the
smaller guard, maybe hit him over the head with something (he was smaller, after all, and the kitchen was
full of blunt objects, even if all the knives were conveniently gone), and make a run for it. Once on the beach,
I could book it down to one of the neighbors, providing
he hadn't paid off everyone on the sandy strip. There
was a chance that he did. Javier wouldn't have split
from Travis without being extremely thorough.

I should have mulled on that observation a little bit
longer. At around five in the evening, when the sun was
low in the west and the shore looked fuzzy with light, I
had knocked on the kitchen door. Through the glass, I
could see the short man ignoring me so I rapped again
and stared at him impatiently until he turned to look.

I made the motion for him to open the door, all
while keeping a heavy pestle from a mortar and pestle
set nestled in my hidden hand like a police club. Finally
he opened the door and looked at me expectantly.

"Hi," I said, all smiles. "I don't know if you realize
this, but I've effectively been kidnapped."

His face remained frozen except for one brow that rose.

"And, well, I was wondering if you had it in your heart to let me go," I went on. This was a long shot, playing to a man's sense of decency and morality. As if he'd choose that over going against Javier's orders.

As I expected, he shook his head ever so slightly. At least now his focus was on me. I chose that moment to scratch behind my ear with my free hand and let go of a quarter I'd kept hidden in my fingers. It was like a magic trick gone wrong, but the point was that he wasn't expecting a shiny quarter to fall out from behind my ear and clank down on the floor. His eyes followed it, and before they had a chance to look back up at me, I'd raised the pestle and smashed it down into his temple. The sweet spot.

He cried out, much louder than I was expecting, and grabbed his head. I saw a flash of red but didn't have time to dwell on it. I pushed him down and to the side and then jumped onto the balcony railing. Without hesitating I leaped down, falling a whole story but landing with a *clump* onto the soft sand below. A sharp pang shot up from my left ankle, my weakest one, but I ignored it and started running.

At first it felt as if I were moving through quicksand, like one of those horrible dreams where you're trying to run but can't. Only this was no dream. I made it as far as the property edge, where a row of flax separated Javier's property from the neighbors, flax I'd planted because it looked tropical and pretty, when I was tackled from behind.

I face-planted into the sand as arms went around my legs and brought me down. I kicked out, trying to hit the assailant, but it was too late. The person was straddling me across my waist, preventing me from flipping over or fighting. I bucked, I tried, but the person was too strong.

I turned my head violently, cheek burning against the grains of sand, and peered up. His face was in shadows caused by the setting sun behind him, but I knew it was Javier…and he was smiling. I could always see that flash of white teeth.

"Get the fuck off me," I said, sand coating my lips as I spoke against it.

"I don't think so." He sounded smug.

"What were you doing, waiting for me to run?"

"Yes," he said with a cock of his head. "I wanted to see if you'd learned anything."

I tried to move again, to throw him off with surprise, but his legs were like steel.

"I learned that your chances of escaping diminish quickly after the first twenty-four hours of kidnapping," I told him with a grunt.

"I heard what you said to Felipe. You think this is kidnapping?"

I glared at him with the one eye. "You are so fucking delusional."

"Oh, I believe you are the delusional one, my angel. I never threatened you with force. You didn't have to come with me into the car. You chose me, Ellie. You chose to leave him and his lovely family. This was your choice."

"Then let me go," I spat out. "You don't need me."

"Of course I need you. Please tell me you didn't spend the whole day trying to think of silly little ways of escaping instead of giving me an answer."

I ignored him and his mind-reading ways. "Let me go, Javier. If you're not keeping me here by force, then you'll get the fuck up and let me walk away." My voice shook a little.

He grew silent, and I could hear nothing except the waves and hushed Spanish in the distance. It sounded like his henchmen, somewhere nearby watching the scene, keeping an eye on their boss to see what he was going to do next.

What he did do next surprised me if not them. He cleared his throat and said, "Fine."

Then he got to his feet and stepped away, dusting the front of his pant legs and adjusting his suit jacket. Same scuffed wingtips as earlier. He waved his arm toward the street, as if highlighting the way to go.

"You are free to go, Ellie Watt. I cannot keep you here if you don't want to be here. I thought you were someone else. I suppose I was mistaken. Even I can make mistakes."

I wasn't sure what the hell he was doing, but I wasn't going to waste an opportunity. I snapped up to my feet as quickly as I could and stood across from him, a little unsteady.

He pointed at me, letting his finger trail up and down my body. "You're wearing a lot of sand."

I glance down. I looked like confectioner's sugar had exploded all over my jeans and T-shirt. I didn't care.

"So I can just go," I said warily. This stunk to high heaven.

He nodded gravely. "I brought you here because I thought I was doing you a favor."

"You thought I was going to do *you* a favor," I corrected him.

His eyes relaxed. "This is something we both want. You know you want it, need it, crave it."

No, I wouldn't start bargaining. I wouldn't examine what revenge meant to me now. Being with Camden had taught me that revenge wasn't the be-all and end-all of my existence anymore, that I could go legit, as I had once planned, and that going legit, going moral, meant not throwing it all to shit and killing a man, no matter how evil that man was.

The man who ruined your entire life, your entire family, your soul, something whispered from some deep dark place inside me. It used to be a familiar voice, and that alone made me realize that I'd changed over the last little bit. What once was familiar was now strange and buried.

"What are you thinking?" Javier asked with false politeness. I could see his eyes burning gold and green with curiosity.

"Go to hell," I said, "is what I'm thinking. Now I'm going to walk and pretend I never saw you. You're going to pretend you never saw me. You can go on to kill Travis if it makes you happy. I won't condemn you for it though I can't say the same for everything else."

"That sounds fair," he said, clasping his hands together like he was about to lead a sermon on the beach. "*Adiós*, my dear angel. I'm sorry we couldn't work this out."

I watched him for a few beats, my peripheral vision picking up his henchmen, who were far out of reach, watching, perhaps as confused as I was. Something was up, obviously; I wasn't that much of an idiot. But I figured I should probably run for my life while I could.

I'd turned on my heel and was about to sprint away to the road when he cleared his throat. Here it came. The catch.

"Of course," he said, "there will be consequences for your lack of loyalty."

My jaw came a tiny bit unhinged. I froze in my tracks for a second, then slowly turned to face him. "Loyalty?"

He twisted his lips in agreement. "Yes. I thought you would have stayed loyal, but you're no different from the rest of them. Remember Miguel? When I found out how disloyal he'd been? He was a traitor."

My face was making expressions that I couldn't control. Disbelief and a flood of impatience lay thick on my tongue. "I don't...I don't even know what to say. Are you saying that I'm disloyal to *you*? Javier..." I burst out laughing and leaned forward, hands on my knees. "Javier, you really have lost it, haven't you? You fucking need to be loyal before you can be disloyal."

His expression was stone. "You were loyal."

"I was loyal and then I caught you in bed screwing some fucking chick. How is that for loyal?!" I yelled the last bit, hoping that his henchmen had picked up on it. Not that it mattered to them, but somehow it mattered to me that they knew how fucking delusional this man was.

He frowned and took a step forward. "I'm sorry, angel. I didn't realize that it had such an impact on you, to affect you all these years later."

My eyes narrowed, all my ire reflected in them, and I jabbed my finger into the air. "No. I know what you're doing. You're sick, you know that?" Not only was he trying to make it seem like I was some hung-up ex-girlfriend, he was quasi-threatening me. Slit my throat for not going along with some fucked-up plan? Is that what he was seriously suggesting?

My heart was beginning to beat loudly in my head, throwing me off a bit. Was I panicking? Or just getting a major mind fuck?

Run, my gut screamed at me.

And so I did. I didn't have time to get sucked into whatever trap he had planned. He seemed to think I'd be too caught up with old feelings and sentiment to go anywhere, but he was wrong. Javier's betrayal had been a learning experience. It had taught me to never let my guard down. To never trust men like him.

I ran across the sand, along the flax, and to the path that led between his house and the next. The road was almost at my feet. I had no car but I had memory and I knew if I ran fast enough, long enough, I'd hit up a pay phone by the fried chicken joint and then I'd be calling Gus for one big favor.

Before I could hit the pavement, I hit someone else.

I shrieked and leaped back. I'd run right into Raul, who was raising his hands like he didn't mean me any harm though his eyes said otherwise. Pinched and vulturelike, he made my blood curdle.

"Raul, you're back." Javier's voice came from behind me. Fuck, he was fast, my eyes darting to Raul's side, where freedom lay. I could still run. Raul wouldn't stop me if Javier wouldn't.

"I had to make sure Camden got away in good faith," he answered, his scars stretching as he talked.

The mention of Camden's name filled my limbs with gravity.

My jaw clenched. "How is Camden?" I asked, taking the risk, the bait, the whatever.

Raul looked over my head at Javier, trading a look I couldn't read. "Oh, he's fine."

I was about to ask him to elaborate when Javier spoke. "Fine *for now*." His words were laced with grease.

I turned to face him. That smug son-of-a-bitch look was back on his face.

"What do you mean, fine for now?"

Raul walked over to Javier and stood beside him. There was a difference in him now, something that wasn't there six years ago. Raul had become Javier and Javier had become Travis.

Javier smiled diplomatically. "Well, you do know our score hasn't been settled, Ellie. That's why I gave you the chance to redeem yourself."

My head jerked back. "Score?"

"You stole money of mine. I never saw that money again. In fact, I paid a lot to bring you here. You've put me about a hundred grand in the hole."

My skin was starting to prickle in hot flashes. "I don't have a hundred grand. You know that."

"You have some money, I saw you in Vegas, pretending to gamble. Lucky for you, I don't need your money. It's the principle of the whole thing. You may not feel loyal to me anymore, but you should at least feel like you owe me something. Don't you have some kind of code, or are you just that immoral now?"

"You're a fucking pathetic human being," I jeered, surprised I was even able to form words when my blood was pumping outrage. How dare he insinuate that I was the one with the skewed morals when he was a cold-blooded killer and womanizing, drugging, manhandling bastard.

He tilted his head and eyed me with fake disappointment, as if I were a disobedient child. Or maybe it was real and, if it was, it was much more fucked up. "Such an angry little angel. Your wings are certainly dirty. They're black."

"Like your heart."

"The heart you once wanted. What does that say about you?"

"It says get to the point. You're obviously not letting me go. There's a catch to all of this, and it involves Camden and a score. So tell me what the hell it is so I can decide how screwed I am."

He raised his brows. "Well, I don't know how screwed you are, I only know how you liked to be screwed."

My upper lip wrinkled. "Sick pig."

"This is true," he said unapologetically. He clapped

his hands together, his watch jangling. "Okay, Ellie. You know what I want. I've told you repeatedly. I need your help in getting to Travis. And you don't have to help me, as you now know. But you should understand that I want this bad enough to call in that little score we must settle. You can help me out of good faith. Yet you won't. Because a woman like you doesn't have anything good or anything that resembles faith." He drew out the word "faith" like it was foreign to him.

"You done trying to be an asshole or do you want to throw psychopath in there?"

His features grew hard and I instantly regretted opening my mouth. There was nothing more troubling than Javier when he got serious.

"Since you won't help me on your own good conscience," he said in a clipped voice, "I'm giving you a choice. Just like the one you had before, only more... detailed. You help me with Travis and in return I'll settle your debt."

"I don't owe you anything," I said.

"Right. Did I mention Camden McQueen is part of your debt now?"

My heart came to a sudden stop, crashing into my chest, shards of glass in my veins. "What?"

He smiled, cold as a gravestone in winter. "I gave Camden money for you. That's more money I lost. Because of you. And based on that, I see that Camden's well-being is part of your debt now. Not his ex-wife's, not his son's... I can't be bothered with them. Camden, now, I could destroy him with the snap of my fingers. That is, if you don't help me. So... what shall it be?

Your pride and freedom? Or the chance to save a man you think you love, or at least took pity on, plus the chance to kill the man who put those scars on your leg and in your heart?"

You're the one who left the scars on my heart, I thought to myself. I felt as if I were swallowing a cotton ball. I could barely look at him. "You promised me you wouldn't hurt Camden, that you would let him go. And you don't break your promises."

He exchanged a satisfied look with Raul before smiling at me. "This is true. I think that's why I've become such a threat to Travis. Because I have my own code that never wavers. Integrity is missing from too many men these days." He noted my face grow red with anger and went on quickly, "I gave Camden the money. I gave him his wonderful family back. That was what I promised, and I did just that. This, Ellie, this is a whole new game with a whole new set of promises. Now, what I need to know is, are you ready to play?"

I wasn't ready to play anything, but if I could protect Camden, then I was going to do everything I could.

CHAPTER SIX

Camden

God bless apathetic teenagers. If it wasn't for the bleached blond girl who was busy doing her nails a sick shade of green as I paid for my gas and a mound of energy drinks, I wouldn't have made it to Gus's. I'd probably have been arrested, my ass thrown in jail for who the fuck knows what anymore.

The dry and perpetually unamused girl barely glanced at me and certainly never picked up the *Los Angeles Times* that day. If she had, she would have noticed that yours truly was on the cover. Not a big picture—that was reserved for a report on the country's economics around Christmas time—but I was there, in the corner, right under the headline "Los Angeles Brothers Shot Trying to Stop Domestic Dispute."

I had so called it.

After I left the scene of the ambush—Sophia's set-up—I'd sped up the I-5 until I'd reached the town of

Valencia. I finally checked into a motel under the name Connor Malloy and started planning my next steps.

They all involved Gus.

I brought out the number that Ellie had given me and let it ring a few times before hanging up. What if Gus wanted nothing to do with me without Ellie? What if he wasn't as trustworthy as Ellie had seemed to think? I barely knew a thing about the guy except that he was an ex-LAPD officer, the same police department that was probably combing Sophia's apartment for clues. I was glad that I never brought anything into her house except a case of contacts and solution. Everything else had stayed in the car, including the briefcase.

Gus would have to be worth the risk. I'd have to trust Ellie, even from afar. He was the only way I could find her; somehow I knew this.

I dialed his number again and this time he picked up gruffly, with a slight accent that I couldn't place. Maybe Texas or the Deep South. It wasn't obvious but lately I'd been paying more attention to those types of things.

"Hello?" he'd said.

"Is this Gus? Ellie's Gus?"

There was a pause. Then, "Is this Connor Malloy?"

I couldn't help but smile. "Not quite. I'm getting there."

"I'm going to assume from the tone of your voice and the fact that Ellie's not on the phone that something's happened."

My smile faded. I clutched the receiver hard and sat up straighter on the motel bed. "She's gone."

"On her power?"

"That...that I don't know." I explained, as briefly as I could, what had happened. I left out the part about Sophia and her brothers. That could wait, or so I thought. Besides, I was still too angry and exposed over it. To talk about it, dwell about it, would rub the wound raw.

Gus seemed concerned but fairly calm about the whole thing. I liked that he didn't lose his shit over it, though at the same time I hoped Ellie was as important to him as I hoped she was.

"Where are you?" he asked.

"Ventura," I lied, picking the closest town that could still have the same area code.

He grunted then told me his address: 141 Rosewood Drive, Pismo Beach. It sounded too pretty.

"Meet me tomorrow at noon," he said, then hung up.

It was only luck that got me there at noon. After I saw my face in the paper, the same paper I managed to swipe on my way out without the teenager noticing, I kept my face down and my driving calm as I worked my way up the coast. The ocean was glittering like blue scales, the cliff sides were lush with December rains. It was so beautiful here in contrast to my life in the desert that my heart thumped for Gualala, for me and Ellie on the beach there, living in the freedom that only the surf can bring.

I stopped at one empty lookout spot on my way up and got a better look at the newspaper. There were a few things wrong that might have saved my ass without me knowing it.

In the statement, Sophia had told the cops about us

getting back together in Palm Valley and wanting to start a new life before I turned on her and beat her up. I was in the process of stealing her money, "child support" she was saving, when she called for her brothers to help. One of the brothers was in serious condition in the hospital with a broken larynx (and nose, I was sure, since I busted that fucker up), while the other had escaped unscathed. Sophia told the police that I was driving a green Ford Mustang but she had no idea what the plate number was. In fact, I was driving an olive green Pontiac GTO with racing stripes. Not at all like a Mustang, not to most people anyway. I was more than grateful for her lack of interest in cars.

The next thing that saved me was the fact that the picture of me was one of hers. It was from a few years ago, taken at a friend's picnic. My hair was surfer shaggy and dark brown, no glasses. At that I quickly took my contacts out, flicking them out the GTO's window, and slipped my glasses back on. This wasn't a Clark Kent thing. The fact that the article stated I had black hair now and was covered in tattoos was enough to bust me. Most people would be looking at that picture of me, smiling, dimples, younger, so maybe they wouldn't notice. They'd be looking for him, not a clean-cut nerd, not until they got really close, and hopefully by then I'd be gone and it would be a case of them shaking their heads in my wake saying "Nah, it couldn't be."

Of course, other than those two little glints of luck, I was screwed. My name, Camden McQueen, was out there, in the paper. And perhaps I was even on the news, being pumped into the minds of every citizen of this fair fucking country.

Camden McQueen. Wife-beater. Thief. The worst of the worst.

My mind reeled back to seeing Audrey the other day. She would have put two and two together really fast. I wouldn't be surprised if she was calling the news now to tell them about her escape from Camden McQueen, the bad, bad man who tattooed asses and kidnapped wives and children.

As if on cue, my phone rang. I looked at the display and sucked in my breath. It wasn't Audrey. It was my father.

He knew.

My father knew I was a wanted criminal. That could be the only reason he was calling.

I expected to feel ashamed or guilty or something along those lines. But for some sick and twisted reason, I felt defiant. As if I'd actually committed it and I did it to prove a point. I secretly felt that way during the whole money-laundering operation, as if somehow I was sticking it to the jackass. Now I wasn't just sticking it, I was driving in a stake like the biggest fuck you.

Too bad none of it was true.

Too bad I knew my father would not accept this without a fight. And that was something I couldn't even let myself think about, not at this stage.

So, obviously I didn't answer it. I just listened to the phone ring and ring and ring again. Then I put it on silent and continued cruising up the coast until the shores of Pismo Beach appeared.

Gus's house was a little ways from the beach, down a winding road that barely had room to fit one car. It was a lush and strangely idyllic area, as pretty as I thought it would be and not really fitting for the man I was about to meet.

His house was small, the size of a cottage, but well kept. The garden in the front was overgrown but still tidy, organized chaos. It was like he could bully the plants into behaving even though he probably weeded the place once a year. My rock garden was easy to maintain but it didn't have the same kind of beauty. I think I'd been in the desert for too long.

I rapped on the door and could hear a shuffling on the other side. I knew he was peering through the peep-hole, which was one step better than I thought he'd do. After I'd picked up the newspaper, I'd been so damn certain that he'd pull out of the whole deal. I think he thought I wanted Connor's Social Security number, and that alone was aiding and abetting a known felon.

In fact, the longer I stood there on his steps, a young girl on a pink bike peddling cheerily past his slat-wood fence, the more I thought about what a mistake this was. This was an ex-cop. I was a fugitive. I was a love-sick idiot and a sitting duck.

Before I could change my mind and head back to the car, the door opened a crack and I got a glimpse of a wary eye, gray beard, heavy jowls.

"Camden McQueen?" He sounded even gruffer in person.

What was the use in lying now?

I nodded. "Hello, Gus."

He grunted and then opened the door. "You better get in here before someone sees you."

I swallowed and walked in. The carpeting underfoot was worn but soft. The house smelled like a cabin. It was dark. The TV was playing in the background, a movie from the 1940s. I picked out Peter Lorre's voice though it wasn't *Casablanca*.

He shut the door behind him and set about locking many dead bolts before finally sliding the chain across.

"Tough neighborhood?" I asked. "I saw a girl on a My Little Pony bike outside; she looked kind of nasty."

He didn't laugh. In fact, he looked the opposite of amused. He leaned back against the door and folded his arms across his wide chest, his beer gut sticking out to infinity. His gaze leveled me.

"Something tells me this isn't the time to be making jokes," he said. "Now, I don't know if you realize it or not, but I'm not here to be your friend. I'm not here to give you advice. I'm here to give you what you need because I made a promise to Ellie once and it seems by you being here she's calling in that promise. I'll help you if you understand that I'm not doing it to be nice. I'm not doing it to be good. I've got my own life that I've sliced out for myself here and if I can avoid putting it through the burner, I will."

I was biting my own lip without knowing it. He was waiting for me to say something.

"I appreciate that, Gus" was the best I could come up with. Talking to him was a bit like talking to my dad. Though I'd like to think Gus wouldn't slap me in the face or call me a faggot, there was always the chance that he would. He was unpredictable and completely detached, and that combination was a bit frightening.

"How about you go sit down and tell me what the hell is going on," he said, gesturing to the couch.

I nodded, feeling more stupid by the minute, and took a seat on his gray leather couch while he disappeared into his kitchen. I watched the movie on TV for a few seconds and recognized it as *Arsenic and Old Lace* with Cary Grant until Gus came back in the room with a beer. For himself.

He sat down on the recliner across from me and cracked the top of the can, chugging down half before slamming it on the coffee table in either annoyance or exuberance. Foam dripped down the sides.

"You. Talk."

I took a deep, calming breath and got into it again, rehashing the story, telling him everything I told him before.

"Why didn't you tell me about being wanted by the LAPD?" he interrupted.

And here it came. I eyed the window, expecting to see a squadron pull in right through his garden, squashing the gardenia.

"I thought you wouldn't help me," I admitted. "And I need you to help me. To help Ellie."

"How long did you say you knew Ellie for?" he asked.

"I went to high school with her."

"And?"

"And she came back into my life two weeks ago."

"And?" His eyes were steel as he drank the rest of his beer, slower this time.

"And, well, she was trying to rob me. I was on to her. We struck a deal: I'd ignore her attempt to steal from me if she'd help me escape my old life. She agreed. We took the money and ran."

He rolled his eyes.

"We laundered the money in the casinos," I went on. "We got caught."

"By the police?" he asked, looking confused.

"No, by Javier," I said. "You do know who that is, don't you?"

He raised his hand dismissively. "I'm very aware of who that is. I just don't know why the cops are after you now."

With a pained sigh, I went into my side of things. The after story.

"But," I finished off, "that really has nothing to do with the problem at hand. Javier has Ellie, and I don't know where or what he's doing to her."

I almost saw a smile on his face, but it looked like it was sucked up by his beard.

"It has everything to do with the problem at hand if you're wanted by the police," he said carefully, as if I were a moron. "Trying to track down Ellie just got a little bit harder with your fuckup."

Fuckup, huh. You know, I was having a real hard time figuring out why the hell Ellie would send me to this guy. So far he was a steaming pile of dickshit. Still, I bit my lip purposely, to keep myself from blowing up and saying something I'd regret. I had welcomed my old friend, rage, in the shoot-out yesterday, but not today. Today I needed to suck it up and behave and quit making things worse for myself.

"So will you help me track her?"

He pursed his lips. "And why do you want to find her so bad?"

I gave him an incredulous look. "Because she's in danger. If you know who Javier is, then you know he's a bad man. He shot her uncle in the head."

Gus shook his head. "Poor Jim." And I realized that maybe he knew him too. I was about to apologize when Gus continued, "She *is* in danger of some kind, that's certain. The man she's with is not the man he was, and the man he was ... well, let's just say he went from bad to worse. That still doesn't explain why you care."

"Why I care?"

"You should be hightailing it to Canada. Get your fake numbers and go. You should be creating your new life, your escape, not heading after Ellie. Why is that?"

"Because ..." How did I even explain it?

"Do you love her?" he asked. "Are you in love with her?"

I guess that explained it.

I nodded. No hesitation. All cards on the table. "Yes, to both." I almost said some bullshit like "We're in love," but I couldn't even say if that was true. All I knew is what I felt. And that the woman I loved, had always loved, had sacrificed herself for me. There was no getting past that. She'd embedded herself in my skin, like a tattoo I could never give myself.

"Well, that certainly makes things messy, don't you think?" he asked, leaning back in the chair. Now the hostility on his face had been replaced with pity. I wasn't sure which one I liked better.

"Love is messy," I said. Another greeting card–worthy sentiment.

"So you're a tattoo artist?" he said, getting out of his chair and changing the subject. He went into the kitchen and came out again, this time with two beers. He handed me one, which I thanked with a nod. I fucking needed this.

I took a long swig before I answered. "I am. I used to work at a shop in LA before I opened up Sins & Needles."

"The front," he filled in.

"Yes," I said hesitantly. "But I did actual work there. I had steady clientele. It really was enough to live on."

"Then why bother with money laundering?"

My mouth flapped open and closed. "I didn't have a choice."

"There's always a choice. I get the feeling that you don't know how to say no."

I glared at him. "I'm pretty sure I said no when I stole the money."

"And look where that got you. The best way to say no is before you start. Say no now, not later."

"Wise words," I muttered, gulping more of the beer down. "You having second thoughts?"

"I haven't agreed to anything, now, have I? I'm just hearing you out."

This was getting ridiculous. All this talk and he still wasn't sold.

"Maybe I'm wasting my time then," I said, standing up. I felt better standing. I was a tall guy and I liked to remind people of that. If they couldn't take me and my tattoos seriously, then they at least took my height and muscle seriously.

I started for the door. "I just thought maybe you cared about Ellie since she seemed to care about you...that you cared whether an innocent woman lived or died."

And at that, he laughed. Maybe I was being a little bit dramatic, but it seemed the only way I could get his attention.

"Innocent?" He sputtered. "First of all, we both know that Ellie Watt is the farthest thing from innocent."

The funny thing was, although that was technically true, that Ellie thieved and lied and charmed her way through life, I still saw an innocence in her. When I tattooed her, I saw it all over her leg and swimming in her eyes. For all she'd done, for the heartless, cruel, selfish person she could be, there was an innocence deep inside—there was still a ten-year-old girl who'd lost everything, who never learned to love without repercussions, who never let her real self be free. That was the Ellie I had seen all through high school, the one who hid behind jeans and a tough attitude. She never allowed her real self, its purity, to come out. She had her soul on a very tight leash.

"And second of all?" I prodded him.

"Second of all, you're insinuating that I don't care. Ellie and I haven't seen each other much over the last few years, yet I still look on her like I would a daughter. A very badly behaving daughter who should be permanently grounded, but a daughter nonetheless. Whether I care or not should have nothing to do with whether I'll help you."

I looked at the ceiling in exasperation. "What the fuck does that mean?"

"It means," he said, "that I could take all the information you just gave me and go find her myself."

"Like it's that easy," I scoffed.

"It is when you've got connections, firearms, and an idea of where she's going. Of course, you're still ignoring the big question here, and it's the only reason why I'm hesitant to involve you in any of this."

How the fuck did he just do that? He turned something that was my idea, my plan, and made it into *his*.

And I was biting like a fish on a hook. "What's the big question then?"

He rubbed at his beard. "Does Ellie want to be found?"

I thought maybe I was hearing it wrong because that didn't sound like an actual question. Gus noted the look on my face because he said, "You see. You didn't think of it."

"Of course she wants to be found. She went off with a psychopath, a dangerous uncle killer. She did it to save me and my family. She had to."

He nodded, seemingly to himself. "She probably did have to, you're right. But that psychopath is also her ex-boyfriend. Ex–love of her life. The man, the catalyst, who made her the person she is today. You should have known the twenty-year-old Ellie. She was different."

"I knew the fourteen-year-old Ellie. She was already damaged." I was spitting out the words like shrapnel, appalled by what Gus was suggesting. It created an empty space beneath my ribs that kept threatening to break open. "Ellie hated Javier with a passion. Feared him."

His eyes softened. "She always feared him, from day one, and that never did her any good. And hate, well, we all know love and hate. Hate is the other side of the coin. It takes one good toss to get it facing down. It can happen quicker and easier than you would think."

"Are you talking Stockholm syndrome now?" That I could understand a little better. What he was suggesting was beyond my realm of comprehension.

He shrugged. "In a way. It's just, with someone like Ellie, it'll be really hard for her not to fall back into old habits. Javier was her biggest habit of all."

The hole was opening, my heart threatening to sink in. I dug my fingernails into the palms of my hands and wished they were sharper.

"Camden," he said pointedly. "It would be Stockholm syndrome on steroids."

And suddenly, somehow, in some sick fucking twisted way, that scenario was a million times worse than the one I had envisioned. I thought the worst thing that could have happened would be Javier killing Ellie. Now I knew, I saw, it could get much, much worse.

She could fall back in love with him. He could seduce her and set that soul free.

And, in the end, still leave her dead.

CHAPTER SEVEN

Ellie

Pain saturated my dreams. When I woke up the next morning, lying there stiff in our old bed, I realized I had really bungled up my ankle when I jumped off the balcony. Looking back, it was a stupid move, leaping away like I was in an action movie. Granted, I was trying to escape a drug lord's henchman, so desperate times called for desperate measures.

After Javier blackmailed me into agreeing to help him, I went straight to the room and didn't come out even when he knocked on the door and told me dinner was ready, like we were roommates or some shit. I was this close to opening the door and breaking his perfect teeth, but it seemed the angrier I acted toward him, the more he liked it. He was delusional enough to equate hatred with passion, and I'd seen the way he'd been appraising me, like some cocky player who assumes every woman is in love with him.

The thing was, I *had* been in love with him once. I'd been more than in love with him—it bordered on something between love and obsession, between Romeo and Juliet teenage dramatics and something real. But it never was real. Over the years, I had convinced myself of that. I had to. It was the only way I could make sense of what he had done and what I needed to do to get over it. What Javier and I shared was a deadly cocktail of intense hormones and lies. True love doesn't have a sick desperation to it, an undercurrent of doom. People who burn that brightly still get burned in the end, and I'm sure if it hadn't been for him cheating on me, it would have ended some other way. The whole relationship had been based on deceit, and it had been only a matter of time before it would have caught up with me.

Now, of course, Javier knew the lie. I hoped it ripped his heart out just a little bit when he found out that all that time Eden White wasn't who he thought she was. Probably not, though. He was different now, bolder and more exaggerated, all of his flaws magnified and his good side gone. He wouldn't know the meaning of sentiment, though I had a feeling that it at least ate at his sense of pride, something he had too much of anyway.

I knew I shouldn't have been lying there thinking about him and the past and the ways things had changed. Giving him all that thought was giving him too much credit. It was a hard thing not to do when you were stuck in his house, the house you had shared together. It gave me a sense of comfort and familiarity that was all an illusion. If this was six years ago, I could figure out what to do next and how to get out of it. I could escape once again and go find Camden. I would find a way to keep him safe, even if it meant having to watch him start a new life with his family.

The very thought of him and Sophia brought a heavy knot into my stomach. That was another thing I was trying to keep on the back burner, the fact that he was with his family. It shouldn't have made me feel so... desolate... but it did. And it was partially my fault. I mean, I know I did the right thing, maybe the first right thing I ever did in my life. And yet it didn't feel right or good. It only made me feel a bit resigned that we'd even gotten in that position in the first place. If I could go back in time and change things, I would have split with Camden as soon as we left Vegas. I would have sent him up to Gualala on his own and gotten out of there before I fell in love with him. And, since we're talking about a fictional time machine here, I would have saved Uncle Jim in the process.

The knot in my gut started to twist and bleed, a whole new, less-selfish set of feelings cutting through. Uncle Jim, whose face I still saw in my sleep, the man who'd been so much to me yet was willing to sell me out for a bit of cash. I still didn't know how to deal with his death, feeling so much anger for what he had tried to do to and so much fucking shame that he died on account of me.

And that's what made things that much more confusing and hard to figure out, like puzzle pieces that never belonged together. The Javier of six years ago would have never killed my dear uncle, no matter how badly he hurt me. That Javier wouldn't have kidnapped a mother and her child and smacked her around (or hired thugs to do it). That Javier, for all his smooth intensity and seemingly blind devotion ("seemingly" being the key word), wouldn't bribe me to help him kill someone. That Javier was the one I knew and the only one I could try to figure out. *This* Javier was a stranger, and a dangerous one. I saw no affection in his eyes, no hint of remorse or respect in his movements. As much as I pretended I wasn't, I was afraid of this Javier in a way I couldn't quite put my finger on.

I'd fallen asleep with my clothes on, Javier, Camden, and Uncle Jim on my mind, so when I finally woke up with my buggered ankle, I decided I'd had enough of submitting to my thoughts. I got out of bed carefully and decided a shower would be a good idea after being dusty and dirty for the last three days. Soap and water had a way of clearing my head unlike anything else (except maybe some well-done sex). When I was finished, I searched under the sink for an Ace bandage and found one, then made sure my ankle was wrapped well. It probably wasn't even as bad as a sprain, but I had to make sure walking on it wasn't going to make it worse.

After the shower I contemplated putting back on my jeans and stained T-shirt when a morbid thought crossed my mind. I wrapped the towel around tightly lest Javier suddenly burst inside the bedroom and went to the closet I used to use. When I'd left Javier that one morning, I had scarcely taken anything of mine.

I opened up the door and sucked in my breath. All my clothes were still there. Jeans, palazzo pants, tissue-thin tank tops, maxi dresses, and skirts that reached the floor. A year's worth of wardrobe belonging to a scar-shy twenty-year-old. I couldn't believe they were still there, that he'd saved my clothes all this time. I thought he would have burned them in a beach bonfire the moment he discovered I'd left him without a trace (and stolen his favorite car and a bunch of his money). Maybe he was more sentimental than I gave him credit for.

Or maybe, dangerously obsessed. I couldn't rule out that one either, considering where I was and how I got there.

I took in a deep breath through my nose and shook out my edginess. It didn't matter what the answer was because there was no use in figuring him out. For whatever reason, my old clothes were here and they were clean, and that's exactly what I needed to feel even remotely human.

I quickly pulled out a pair of jeans, super soft from years of wear, and tried to shimmy them on. Well, as clean and comfortable as they were, they barely fit over my thighs. I was a thin girl, but my legs and ass were always on the generous side, and I guess my twenty-year-old body had been a lot more waiflike than I remembered. I was sure it would have bothered any other girl to know she'd gained weight, but since meeting Camden, I'd refused to feel bad about my body anymore. He had loved it, my curves, my scars, the way I was now, and that wasn't something to toss away, especially when his safety wasn't as concrete as I had originally thought.

I mulled that over, wondering how it was that Javier could get to Camden at any moment—was he being bugged, monitored? Did he have a person on the inside? Was it Sophia? I remembered the way she eyed the briefcase like it held every wish she ever had. Then I pushed those thoughts out of the way, deciding I'd get it out of Javier instead, and selected a pair of wide-legged pants, a tight spaghetti-strap top, and a cropped cardigan with three-quarter-length sleeves. Just long enough to hide the tattoo on my arm, the tattoo that Javier had kept staring at as if it still meant something.

I smoothed back my hair, black as ink when it was still wet, and didn't bother with the makeup I had in my purse. I had no one to impress, not now. I opened the door and was immediately met with the rich smells of frying bacon and brewing coffee. My stomach growled, turning over on itself, reminding me that I hadn't eaten a thing so far.

"Good morning," Javier said from the table, looking like a carbon copy of yesterday. Once again he was dressed in a suit, albeit this one was sand-colored, and he wore a plain white T instead of a dress shirt. He was also reading the *Los Angeles Times* again and shaking his head in amusement at whatever was on the page. "Green Mustang? Oh, that hurts my soul."

My eyes flew over to the stove where the bacon was done frying, a few pops and sizzles accompanying the smell.

He waved his hand in that direction, eyes still glued to the paper. "I wasn't sure if you were still on a hunger strike, but I made enough. There's toast as well, one hundred percent whole grain. It's supposed to be good for you." He said this all absently, as if he weren't secretly hoping I'd eat it. Fuck my own spite this time, hunger was winning out.

I picked up a plate he had left out and started scooping up the rest of the bacon and eggs, deciding to commit to it. I pressed two slices of bread into the toaster and attacked the pot of coffee next.

"There's milk and cream in the fridge," he said, and I could feel him watching me now.

I shrugged and filled my cup, turning around and leaning against the counter. "I take it black now."

He eyed my pants. "You found your old clothes."

I nodded and took a sip. It was so strong it was almost poisonous, yet it was exactly what I needed. "I did. Are you going to start an Ellie museum or something?"

I thought that would get a reaction out of him. No such luck. "Glad you're looking a little more...elegant for our expedition today."

My body jerked. "Expedition?" I couldn't be meeting Travis, I wasn't ready. I wasn't ready and there was no plan. The thought of seeing him after all these years, never mind the fact that I was supposed to help kill him—an idea that, despite everything, left my heart feeling numb—nearly brought me to my knees.

Javier raised his brows, still so very expressive. "Don't worry, my angel, we're just scoping things out, as you say. I would not throw you in the pool without a noodle."

I frowned at that phrase, ignoring the tiny twang in my brain that reminded me of how charming I used to find his lapses in the English language, and asked, "So what is the plan then? Where's my ... noodle?"

He smiled, too wide for his damn face. "You made a joke? You must be liking it here then."

"Don't flatter yourself, and get to the point."

He stroked his chin in one smooth sweep. "Ah. We're going to take a look at some things."

"And?"

"That is all."

At that, the toast in the toaster popped with a loud bang and I nearly jumped out of my skin. Unfortunately, Javier noticed this.

"You seem nervous," he commented. To make matters worse, he got out of his chair and took a step toward me. I flatted up against the counter wondering if a coffeepot to the head would be my way out of this. Then he stopped a few feet back, close enough for me to smell his earthy cologne, close enough to grab me if he wanted to, but not close enough to be doing anything wrong. He was good at that, skirting the line between coincidence and intent.

I looked at the toast, sitting just out of reach. To get it I'd have to turn around, and I didn't want my back to him. I could almost imagine his breath at my neck, and that wasn't a good thing.

He smiled gently, following my eyes, then leaned over and plucked the toast out of the toaster, dropping it on my plate. He almost handed the plate to me and then stopped.

"Would you like honey with that?" he said, his eyes blazing into me like the aforementioned sweet.

I managed to shake my head, aware that I wasn't really breathing. *Just go, please,* I thought, a strange kind of desperation running through me, that fear I couldn't place.

Ever observant, he picked up on this.

"You're trembling," he said, voice low and smooth and far too familiar to my liking. "Are you afraid, Ellie?"

I could pretend I wasn't. But Javier liked to make people feel the emotions he thought they should be feeling. In layman's terms, if I lied, he'd *make* me afraid.

"Yes, I'm afraid," I said, averting my eyes. I didn't want to see his reaction, not the real one deep inside where his soul used to be.

"Of me?"

I nodded, keeping my attention focused on the fridge, the clean chrome, the lack of magnets and calendars and take-out menus. The things that used to be there. Life.

"Why are you afraid of me, Ellie?"

If I told him the truth, that I really didn't know, he'd make it into something it wasn't.

"Are you going to kill me?"

His head twitched in surprise. "Is that really what you think?"

I honestly didn't know, not anymore. I knew he'd keep me around for as long as he needed me, but I had no idea what would happen when this was over. He hadn't promised me my life yet.

"Other than the fact that you're an asshole, yes."

He didn't seem to get it. "I'm doing this for you," he said quietly.

"I thought it was for your so-called morals. Your score?" I noticed that the plate in his hand was shaking ever so slightly. Something was happening.

Then it was gone. He swallowed hard. "I guess it's that then. Either way, I'm not hurting you."

No, I thought, *just Camden and me if I don't do what you say.*

"You did in the car," I blurted out.

"I did?"

"You grabbed my wrist..."

He was truly puzzled. I was starting to feel like an idiot for having no control of my mouth. So much for being tough as nails.

"Then I am sorry. I didn't realize you were so delicate. I knew that Eden wouldn't mind that sort of thing. I could bite her hard enough to draw blood and she liked it."

He was standing too close to me to be saying those words. I took the plate out of his hand finally, to do something, to ignore what he was saying and the visual I had of the two of us, younger and in throws of uninhibited passion.

"That was different," I managed to say when I found my voice. "I wasn't the same person back then."

Javier nodded, his eyes fastened to every inch of my face. "Neither was I. One must wonder if we changed for the better, hmmm?"

"I'd say we barely crawled out of a burning wreckage alive."

His brows knit together delicately. "I'd say we evolved. We grew stronger."

I shot him a hard look. "We ruined each other."

"You see it one way, I see it another. It was good for something. Once upon a time I thought it was good for everything."

Me too, I thought, then buried it.

He watched me for a few moments, wheels turning behind those hawk eyes. It used to kill me never knowing what he was thinking. Now I didn't want to know. Our exchange had gotten a little too close for comfort.

I still couldn't rule out the fact that he would never hurt me. Fool me once and all that jazz.

When he was satisfied with his observations, his attention darted over to my plate. "Your bacon is getting cold."

So it was. And then he left, turning sharply away from me and snapping up the newspaper from the table. He rolled it up as if he were going to punish a bad dog and walked swiftly to the staircase. I had to wonder where he was sleeping; perhaps in the spare bedroom downstairs. Perhaps I was alone here at night.

"When is the expedition?" I called out after him.

He paused and looked like he was going to say something smart-assey when his cell phone rang, a sci-fi-type ringtone. He frowned and fished it out.

"Yes?" he said, clearly annoyed already by whoever was calling. He listened and as I moved over to the table with my plate, I watched his face contort in absolute rage, a look that, for all his short-temperedness, I very rarely saw on him. It made me sit down and shut up.

"What do you mean they're gone?" he practically screamed into the phone. "Did they see her?"

Suddenly he was looking at me and switched to Spanish, lowering his voice as if it took all the effort in the world. It probably did.

Now, Eden White never knew Spanish and Ellie Watt was pretty rusty at it but she knew some. I couldn't make out everything he said and I was probably wrong on what I was interpreting anyway, but what I could gather was that it involved me. Or some other woman, but I was going to assume it was about me. It was a problem that I was here or someone knew I was here. Not a he but a group of people, it seemed. Of course, that could be more my paranoia talking than my grasp of Spanish.

Suddenly Javier jabbed at his phone and slipped it in his jacket pocket. His back was to me, which was somehow more frightening because he could be turning into a drug cartel Hulk and I wouldn't know it until he turned around.

He sighed, loudly, gazing up at the ceiling, his fingers clenching and unclenching. Part of me was happy to see him so pissed off, that things weren't going his way; the other part was scared. Because he could take it out on me. Because things might have just gotten worse.

I waited there at the table, afraid to eat, afraid to move, afraid to breathe.

Finally he turned around, his skin dark red at the temples, but otherwise he looked calm. He gave me a smile that read false. "Change of plans."

I raised my brow and remained silent.

"We're going to Mexico."

CHAPTER EIGHT

Camden

She was in my dreams again, Ellie. Only this time, the fire that consumed us came from within. I was in a black, cavernous room with no walls, no windows, and a floor made of ebony satin. She was lying at my feet, naked and curled up, sleeping.

Her eyes opened and she saw me. She smiled. I could barely take my eyes away from her body. She was curved in all the right places, places that felt like home to me, like the area underneath her ass were it melted into her thighs or where her full breasts swooped up into her soft arms. Her nipple ring sparkled, diamonds now, and I felt myself grow instantly hard, wanting nothing more than to tug at it with my teeth. She had groaned with so much pleasure when I had done it before. I'd give anything to hear that sound, even if it wasn't real.

She turned over onto her back, her breasts inviting me for a taste. Beckoning me with her finger, her sly look almost undid me. I was naked as well, my erection impressive. I'd heard that I was a "big boy" from many women. Looming over Ellie like that, seeing the raw hunger in her eyes, the anticipation, I couldn't have been more grateful. I was petty, even in my dreams.

I dropped down to my knees and crawled over her, pinning her body between my limbs. The contrast of the dark hair of my legs to the milky white of hers made the cherry blossoms more delicate and vibrant than ever. I brushed my cock against the fine hair of her pubic bone, pressing it up against her belly, a heavy weight between us. Her breath quickened, mine deepened. I wanted nothing more than to thrust inside of her, feel her warmth, her wetness, her tight grip that felt better than heaven.

I reached under her back and deftly flipped her over and pulled her up so she was on all fours, back arched, ass widening beneath me. She wiggled it, just slightly, and the sight nearly made me come. I was a hair trigger.

I licked my fingers, then trailed them down the slit of her ass, feeling her pucker before dipping them down into the lake of her cleft. She was so fucking wet, so wet for me. I drew the moisture up and swirled my finger into her, one then two. I hadn't known Ellie long enough in an intimate way to know if she was into anything anal. But it was a dream and I didn't care. I'd have my way with her and she'd love it.

My breath hitched and she let out little fluttery moans that made my balls tighten. I slowly edged myself into her, feeling the heat and the impossible tightness, the taboo, the dirtiness. The wonderful, mouth-gaping dirtiness. We both cried out as I thrust in deep, my cock being squeezed until I couldn't handle it anymore.

Then something changed. A wave of cold came out from the darkness and, along with it, the shadowy silhouette of a man. There was only shape to him and thick substance, a figure sculpted out of black tar and clay. The chill he brought made me stop dead, my fingers resting softly on the cheeks of her ass.

The man came closer and still he had no features. Ellie's head was up and watching him, like a playful cat, while I remained lodged inside her. He stopped right in front of her face and she reached for him with one hand, taking his black erect appendage into her mouth and crying out with pleasure.

I shut my eyes tight, willing myself to be the one she was sucking off. My dreams could be somewhat lucid when I wanted them to.

When I opened them, it had worked. My cock was in Ellie's mouth, her tongue running and up and down the underside. But now the black shape was where I had been, pounding her hard from behind. I watched, unable to stop Ellie from sucking me off, not wanting the pleasure to end, while watching the blackness as it spread over her. I came loudly, spurting into her mouth, which she swallowed happily. Then she came, the pounding coming to a climax.

The man of black matter smiled. A flash of white teeth against the abyss.

Then he was gone.

And she was gone.

I woke up on Gus's couch in the middle of the night, my dick in my hands, pumping myself until I was coming all over my stomach with sticky bursts. I bit my lip to keep from crying out, from waking up Gus, and once the sensation faded, I noticed with embarrassment that I'd pulled my shirt up in my sleep, avoiding a mess.

I lay back, breathing hard, staring up at the ceiling. As far as sex dreams went, that one took the cake. I didn't feel a sense of relief and peace as I normally did after climaxing. I felt empty. I felt dirty—and not the good kind of dirty.

I wiped up the mess with a few tissues and threw them in the trash. The door to his room was closed and I could hear him snoring loudly. There was no way I'd be going back to sleep now, even though the microwave clock said it was 4 AM. The dream had thrilled then scared me, and I didn't want to give it thought, to give it power, to think what it had meant. I had to find Ellie; then I'd deal with my subconscious.

Yesterday, after Gus had put it in my head that Ellie could be suffering from Stockholm syndrome on steroids, I could tell he was half expecting me to pull out. To give up, to let him carry out the plan. It was probably what he wanted anyway, better him than some bumbling puppy who was wanted by the police.

But I couldn't. I was invested, as deep as I could be, and as emotionally connected to Ellie as I'd ever been to anyone. In some ways, even to Ben. I didn't quite know why, but that was the thing about love sometimes. It gave you few reasons and the rest was out of your hands.

Last night I had told Gus that I was going to find

her no matter what. If he wanted to help, then great. But if he didn't, it wouldn't stop me. Now that I knew exactly what was at stake—Ellie's life, Ellie's heart—I was all in.

"Even if Ellie doesn't want to leave and Javier dies by my own bloody hands, I'm in it to the end," I had said.

I don't know if was because my veins were bulging out of my forehead or because I felt like a thousand suns were burning through my body and out of my eyes, but Gus finally nodded and agreed. He would help me get Ellie back.

To be honest, I think the idea of killing Javier put a little motivation in him, like a drop of blood in a shark tank. It wasn't something I was banking on, but I was prepared to do it. To know that Gus would be there to back me up helped, and it also made me realize the lengths I was prepared to go to save her, even on my own. It made me realize that in saving her, I might lose myself, lose any morals or convictions I once had had. Camden McQueen might end up a stranger to even me when it was all said and done.

And I was going to have to be okay with that.

In fact, from the tiny visceral thrill that shot through me as I watched Gus go through his collection of firearms and give me the lowdown on each one, I was probably going to be more than okay with that. I was probably going to welcome it with open arms.

*   *   *

I never did fall back asleep, the memory of the dream and the real memory of Ellie clashing violently with each other. I did what I could to hold it all together, the same way I'd been doing it for the last few days, ever since she had left with *him*. When I'd feel rage creeping on up, saturating my limbs from the inside out, I mentally quarantined the feeling. I imagined taking the anger, the panic, the injustice, and funneling it into a compartment in my head. I took it out of my heart and my lungs and the muscles that wanted to curl my hands into fists and have me explode. It was the only way I was able to think clearly, to do what needed to be done.

Every minute I spent with Gus made me realize I needed to become more like him, cool and distant. Somehow it worked for him, and as time went on, it began to work for me. I even applied it to Sophia and Ben and my fucking father who wouldn't stop calling me until Gus destroyed my cell with a quick stomp of his boot. I filed it away, until I felt smooth and snag-free inside, like a machine.

Our plan, according to Gus, was fairly straightforward and simple. We'd head out to Mississippi, where Ellie had lived as a girl and where she had met Javier. We'd poke around, he'd ask a few of his contacts and hopefully find some sort of a trail.

"I'm pretty sure Javier Bernal still lives in the state," Gus had told me as he threw a duffel bag into the GTO. It landed in the trunk with a clatter, and I knew it contained more than his clothes and toiletries. He was a bit wary about taking the car, even with the newspaper reporting it as a green Mustang, but since his only vehicle was a beat-up café racer motorbike, he didn't have much of a choice. I was relieved. As strange as it sounded, I could see why Ellie hung on to the car all those years. There was something very empowering about it, like it made you invincible. Maybe after that stunt on the Vegas highway I even believed it.

I was about to hop in the driver's seat when Gus waved me off with a gruff gesture of his hand. "Nope," he said, slipping on a pair of amber aviators. "Too risky with you driving. You're sitting in the passenger seat, looking straight ahead, never to the side."

"Why don't I just lie down in the back then?" I wasn't questioning his methods, but his tone of voice didn't help.

He gave me the are-you-an-idiot look. "If someone notices, it's only going to draw more suspicion. Look, as of right now, the photo circulating on the news is a far cry from what you look like. They're looking for a pretty boy with a dumbass smile; you look like a piece of shit."

This was going to be a fun ride. "Thanks."

He shrugged. "It's true. Now get in before I change my mind."

I almost wanted him to but I decided to suck it up and file my feelings toward Gus away too.

Once we'd cleared the streets of Pismo Beach and were heading inland toward the I-5, I asked him what he knew about Javier.

Gus pursed his rough lips as if he wasn't sure I was worthy of the information. Then he spoke.

"As I told you before, I hadn't kept in touch with Ellie too much over the years. We'd talk on the phone around Christmas time—she was really good at calling—but other than that it was more that I would help her out when I could. Fake IDs, information on people, yadda yadda. During that time, she never once mentioned Javier. It was like the moment she left him, she erased his memory from her head. And she seemed to be doing fine. What is the point in bringing up the past anyway? So I never spoke a word about him, even though I was keeping tabs—mainly out of curiosity, mainly for her sake. No one just up and leaves a gang member, it doesn't happen. I was so sure he'd come after her right away, but from what I could tell, he never did. He stayed put in Ocean Springs, Mississippi. And then he began to build his empire."

A chill laced my blood. Empire?

Gus went on. "I'd heard it through my grapevine that Travis and Javier were butting heads. He started getting friendlier with their rivals, Los Zetas in particular. That was unheard of, not to mention stupid for someone like him, but Travis Raines cared more about power than loyalties. He believed that their cartel could grow stronger if they became allies instead of enemies and thought going back to Mexico would help. Never mind the explosion of violence in the country, the fighting, the tourists who were getting caught in the middle, the fact that it turned into one big shit show and was getting international attention. Javier did not agree. Javier thought it was too dangerous, too chaotic, and that Travis would slowly lose control. He would rather die than make peace with his rivals. It came down to Javier staying behind and Travis booting him out. Javier siphoned a few key players of his, people who still had loyalty to a cause instead of to Travis. I still don't know who'd win in a fight, but Javier at least has charm to mask his brutality, something Travis doesn't have."

I winced at the word "charm." I remembered meeting Javier for the first time, in that café in Palm Valley. I wouldn't say he had charm, but he definitely had something. Mystery, if I wanted to sound quixotic about it.

"There was an incident, of course," he continued. "Before Travis left, he'd managed to get two of Javier's men killed. And once he made it to Mexico, he went one step further and hunted down one of Javier's sisters. Raped her, killed her, all that stuff. This was about three years ago, mind you, though nothing really came of it. Javier still stayed in the U.S. and began leaching from another cartel, trying to build his own power. That was his revenge, I suppose. Who knows, maybe Javier didn't give two shits about his sister. Nothing would surprise me with that guy."

I cleared my throat, watching the green hills whiz by. "You knew all this stuff all this time and you never told Ellie."

He looked chagrined, or maybe that was wishful thinking. "It didn't concern her. And by the time it did concern her..."

"Well, you obviously knew he was coming after her."

"Actually, I didn't. I'd stopped paying attention about a year ago. I got dragged down into some money and health problems, I just didn't have the time. Javier seemed to be holding steady, and at that point I figured he'd never come looking for her."

"Which begs the question, why now?"

"Good question. That's what we're going to find out. I doubt it was something as simple as hearing a love song on the radio."

"Perhaps it is as simple as that he's still in love with her."

He glanced at me, his eyes hazy behind the aviators. "Men like Javier don't know what love is. I wouldn't worry too much about that."

But Ellie did know. And that's what concerned me.

"I'll tell you one thing that I thought was odd," Gus added. "About a few months before I stopped keeping tabs on him, I'd heard there was a couple that jumped ship—they'd been working for Javier and then went to the other side. To Travis. Javier sent some men after them, but who knows what happened."

"A couple?" It didn't seem like the line of work that a husband and wife would get roped into, like opening a bed-and-breakfast.

He nodded. "Yeah. A couple. An older couple at that. White folks. Amanda and Bob Williams."

There was something loaded in what he was saying, but I wasn't getting it.

"You know, I used to be friends, good friends, with Amelie and Brian Watt."

The light went off in my head. AW. BW. Same initials.

"Ellie's parents?" I asked in disbelief. "That doesn't make any sense."

"No, it doesn't."

"Do you know for sure?"

"I don't. Just a gut feeling. I hadn't talked to them

since they up and left poor Ellie with her uncle. I wouldn't put it past them, but I don't see the point of it all. Why go through all of that with their daughter only to go back to the man that did it?"

"Maybe they got into some trouble." It would have to be some major fucking trouble to go back to Travis or work for Javier. Was it a case of Javier recruiting her parents, hoping he would get close to them, or was it the other way around? No matter the reason, my damaged, beautiful girl was still getting screwed over, even without her knowing it.

The anger must have been showing on my face because Gus tapped the steering wheel.

"Hey, aggro, don't you go losing it on me. You said you were prepared to do whatever you could to get her back. Things are only going to get harder and more complicated from here on out."

I sucked in my breath and sat back in the seat, giving him a quick nod. We fell into silence punctuated by the staticky radio. I fell into my own head, facing my fears.

I wondered what Ellie was doing right then and where she was. I wondered if she had any idea about her parents, if Javier would tell her and taunt her with it. I wondered just what the hell he wanted with her, a question that would drive me crazy until I knew. It couldn't be as simple as a love-struck ex-lover, not when Gus had explained what had gone on over the years. Javier hadn't simply followed Ellie all that time, as she assumed. He went ahead and built up an empire. Was it a matter of the ex-boyfriend trying to make something of himself before attempting to win her back? In a way, I understood that. But I didn't want to understand him. I didn't want to think about how she apparently got under his skin the same way she got under mine. I didn't want to find any similarities between us.

I could never turn into him.

CHAPTER NINE

Ellie

Later that day, we set off. I barely had time to pack, which was ironic since I actually had things to pack when I shouldn't have. Javier brought me a large carryall bag for me to stuff my clothes inside. It was creepy as hell, folding up my old stuff, knowing that we were heading to another country like some couple on vacation.

"I hope I don't need my real passport," I remarked as I hauled the bag out of the room. I had only one passport in my bag. It belonged to Eleanor Willis, and I'd never crossed a border with it before. Gus had made it for me, so I assumed it would hold up, but this wasn't the time to test it out. Getting busted with a drug cartel leader would be very, very bad for me. Almost as bad as *not* being busted.

Javier stood at the end of the hall, white pants, white shirt, looking like the devil in a snowbank. "Angel, this is Mexico. And you're an American. They wouldn't even look at your ID. I, on the other hand...well, I'm pretty sure it won't be so easy."

"So we're crossing the Rio Grande against the flow?"

"That's messy," he said. He took a step forward to take the bag from me, but I held on tightly and yanked it out of his reach. He glared ever so slightly, then turned on his heel and went down the stairs.

"We'll be crossing over in style," he tossed over his shoulder and headed out the front door, held open by the burly man I think was called Carl or Carrell. It was hard to tell with his accent sometimes.

I followed, the bag dragging behind me. Outside the air was bright and airy, as if it wanted to fool me again with that whole vacation feeling. Palm trees and live oaks waved in the breeze, a very picturesque scene that people never thought could happen in Mississippi. Even though my years in the state were full of emotional turmoil, there was a beauty here that most people overlooked. For me, the beauty had turned a shade deadly.

The SUV was roaring in the driveway with Javier climbing in the backseat. Oh joy, I was going to be trapped with him again. That peculiar kind of fear, the one that made me wince with disgust, came trickling down my neck. Or maybe it was sweat. The temperature was unseasonably hot.

Raul took the bag from me and tossed it in the trunk, then held the back door open as if he were the perfect gentleman. I suppose I should have been thankful that it was Javier I had to sit with, not Raul, but a creep is a creep.

I hopped in, buckled my seat belt lest Javier try to do it for me, and leaned against the armrest on the door. Every part of me was crammed up away from him. He wasn't trying to get close, but the scene from the kitchen was still fresh in my mind. I did not want to feel his breath on me ever again. The memories and the reality did not jive.

After we were driving for a few minutes and, notably, not taking the highway, I had to ask, "Isn't Mexico in the other direction?"

"Patience, my angel," Javier said, his eyes glued to the front of the car, a small smile on his face.

I didn't have fucking patience, especially when he kept calling me *that* name, but I had to remind myself that the more I gave, the more he wanted. I bit down on my lip to keep quiet and pulled my cardigan around me, for modesty's sake and to ward off the Arctic air-conditioning.

Ten minutes later we were pulling up to yet another familiar place: the marina where Javier used to keep his sailboat. Another disturbing trip down memory fucking lane.

I suppressed a shudder, knowing Javier was watching me like some science experiment. How much of our past can I torture her with? Am I breaking down her defenses? And other such thoughts.

"You remember this place?" he asked delicately.

I ignored him and spoke to the window as the SUV pulled into a loading zone lined with wheelbarrows. "I don't have amnesia. Why the hell are we here?"

He made a *tsk*ing sound, the type that made me look

at him just to see how disappointed he looked. "Ellie, really."

I looked back at the marina. The panic started somewhere below my gut. He couldn't be serious. He wasn't that delusional, was he?

"We're not going to Mexico on your boat," I said, more of a statement than a question. Even if I was jumping the gun a bit, at least it was out there.

He gave me that sly smile again. "Would that be a problem for you?"

My mouth opened and closed like a fish, no words coming out. I knew that Javier probably had to lie low as we traveled across the country, but this seemed a bit extreme.

"It's not the same boat, don't worry," he said. He opened his door and hopped out just as Raul opened mine.

Javier's old sailboat was a sleek, gorgeous thing that held far too many memories for us. It was big enough to sail anywhere, really, but that wasn't the point. I could barely handle being in the same vehicle as Javier, let alone a boat.

I guess I must have stood there shaking my head or something like that, because Raul's cold fingers clamped around my forearm as he yanked me forward.

"Let's go," he growled.

"Don't touch me," I growled back, yanking my arm away from him.

Javier gave both of us an amused look as he walked off toward the docks. "This trip will be easier if the two of you learn to play nice."

"Fuck you," I yelled after him. A family decked in nautical gear were unloading their car nearby and gave me an odd look. In fact, they gave all of us an odd look, and I couldn't blame them. Big bald driver was hauling our bags out of the back of the black SUV, while the devil in white led the way for one henchmen and the damsel in distress. I wondered if we appeared suspicious enough for them to report us. Technically we weren't doing anything illegal, but if I had seen a similar scene, my radar would be going wild.

What would happen if I mouthed to the father, with his wary eyes and nervous twitch, "Help me." What would he do? Would he help? What would I even say? Could I get away and still ensure that Camden would go unharmed? Or was my freedom always going to be joined to him in that fate?

I didn't say anything. I was used to being the one trying to get away, not the one wanting to be caught. I just walked toward the docks, feeling like oxygen was slowly being leached from me, that the farther we got away from solid ground, the less chance I had. For life, for liberty, for love, maybe for everything. My situation kept changing from day to day, moment to moment, and I wasn't quick enough to keep up.

Just when I thought my legs were turning to jelly, we stopped on the farthest dock in front of what I first thought were a bunch of sailboats tied together. I was wrong.

"This is my new masterpiece," Javier said with a too-wide smile, his arms spread wide, as if he built the boat himself.

He wasn't kidding when he said it wasn't the same boat. I didn't even think you could call it a boat; it was more like a floating apartment complex, a hotel on the sea, a mother ship. This boat, this yacht, this monster had to be almost 200 feet long and one of the largest *things* I had ever seen. It had two masts that seemed to stretch into the hazy heavens, it sparkled in the sunlight, glossy navy and white paint and teak accents, and boasted a crew of four people, all men in their twenties, who stood in a row on the deck like subjects greeting the king. There were less obvious ways of jetting off to Mexico but this wasn't one of them. Javier was nothing if not obvious sometimes.

He'd been waiting for my reaction, for me to say something, but I couldn't do it. He wanted me to be impressed when all I could think about, despite the size of the sea beast, was that I was going to be stuck on that ship for quite some time, with no way off except a watery grave.

"Come on, let's get you introduced to the crew and settled," he said, waving at the driver to bring the bags on board. I peered at the boat's name as everyone shuffled around me. It was called *Beatriz*, which happened to be the name of his eldest sister. I wondered why it was named after her, if something had happened, before I realized I didn't care. I *couldn't* care. Men like Javier used sympathy as a fuel.

"Are you having second thoughts?" Javier asked from up above, holding his hand out for me. "Because you don't have to come with us, you know this."

I didn't know if he was saying it for the benefit of

the crew, who were all facing forward, stony yet eager expressions on their faces, dressed in black shorts and black polo shirts.

I watched them carefully as I said, "If I don't come with you, you'll kill Camden McQueen. It's not a hard choice to make." Out of the corner of my eye I saw Javier sneer, but none of the boys even blinked. They couldn't have been younger than me by more than a few years, but apparently they were already hardened to this life. Javier's empire was a lot larger, and went a lot younger, than I had thought. It made me wonder what lives those men must have led to get dragged into this kind of mess. Super-yacht or not, I could only hope Javier paid them well.

"Then you've made your choice," Javier said calmly, though I could see his temples going red. "So take my hand and come aboard."

I ignored his hand and walked up the stairs to the deck.

The boat, as Javier soon explained, was a 187-foot, 550-ton Royal Huisman mega-ketch. Everything else went over my head as I got the grand tour. All I could gather was that it must have cost tens of millions of dollars, all filthy, bloody drug money. It had a flybridge in the middle of the boat, a raised deck complete with outdoor dining, sofas, and a damn barbeque. A private sitting area at the very back had a spiral staircase that led down to an office and Javier's gigantic bedroom. There were three levels in total, with dining and living rooms, a theater deck for movies, numerous bedrooms and spacious bathrooms. The rear of the boat even folded open with the hiss and whir of hydraulics to provide a sunbathing and diving platform. It was to be my prison for the next six days until we reached the city of Veracruz.

"What do you think?" Javier asked as my bags were placed in the room that was to be mine, conveniently right next door to his.

I looked him squarely in the eye. "I liked your other boat better."

His lips twitched in amusement. "You always had simple tastes, Ellie. Except, perhaps, for me."

He spun around and started to shut the door before he paused and said, "We set sail in an hour. You might want to get one last look at land. You won't be seeing it for a while."

The door closed with a sleek *click*, leaving me alone in my cabin. It was spacious enough, but I could already feel the walls starting to come closer.

*   *   *

It turned out I missed the big farewell. After I'd unpacked a few items, I lay down on the bed to ponder my fate. Exhaustion took over. The next thing I knew, I was very slowly rolling out of the bed and coming face to face with the upholstered cabin wall.

I sat up and blinked at the light streaming through what I thought was a shuttered window but was actually a well-disguised panel of lights meant to mimic daytime. I got up, finding my sea legs, and started fiddling with the lights, turning them from morning brightness to night. But they always sprang back, preprogrammed.

The fact that Javier could control the way his crew perceived the days was chilling.

I made my way out of the cabin and went down a narrow hallway lined with handrails. The boat was no longer heeling over, making walking seem painless. Aside from the gentle sloshing sounds of water along the length of the boat, you couldn't even tell you were on a ship. The yacht was that big; it was like being on an airbus compared to a seaplane.

The hallway led me past three more cabin doors, all closed, before I came to a small set of stairs, flooded with natural light. The area I was in ended about midship, which meant the crew's quarters were at the front of the ship and had a separate entrance. I cautiously climbed the stairs until I recognized I was on the second deck, the main living area. The back was open, not fully enclosed, the sea breeze fluttering through. Past the elaborate dining table setup, teak table and white high-backed chairs that could easily rival any house, I could see Raul and another man lounging on the couch, drinks in their hands, the wind ruffling their hair. They both looked at me sharply, unkindly, before turning back to each other, talking in Spanish. Behind them I could see the lower deck, all smooth wood, Javier's private cockpit and the stern of the ship, the American flag waving in the breeze. The water here was green, and a few islands dotted the horizon, slowly disappearing in our wake.

I went up another flight of stairs, holding on to the rail in case the boat decided to pitch, and came up to the top deck, half covered like a pilothouse. Javier was there, sitting in a leather captain's chair, hands on one of the two steering wheels, eyes focused ahead through the wide, tinted windshield. A large sail had billowed out from the mast, an immense noise that reminded me of happier times but that didn't make any sense to my brain, since the only time I'd ever been on a sailboat would have been with Javier.

"You're up," he said without turning to face me. His hair was waving slightly against the nape of his neck. I found it annoying how his longer hair still suited him. It shouldn't have, it should have made him look more like a cheesy drug lord, but it didn't. My stomach twisted.

I turned my attention to the large cockpit, at the row of the glowing radar screens, GPS, and weather charting systems at his fingertips, at the sofa and chairs in the open area behind me, another fantastic viewpoint. I took it all in yet it didn't seem to stick. Nothing in this situation seemed real.

"I passed right out," I said when I recovered my thoughts. "Did you drug me again?"

He let out a small laugh. "I promise I won't drug you anymore."

I didn't find his words particularly amusing, but I was glad at his promise.

"Here, take a seat," he said, gesturing to the co-pilot's chair. "Can I get you a drink?"

I shook my head but sat down next to him. There was a pleasing amount of space between us, and having a wheel at my fingertips was exciting.

"What happens if I start steering?" I asked, closing my fingers around the suede-encased wheel.

"I'll countersteer," he said. "And I will override you."

I pressed my lips together and watched as the water flew past the boat, delicate white sea spray that matched the fluffy clouds. In the distance were ghostly shapes, oil rigs obscured by the haze.

"I don't think I've ever been this far out before."

"Soon it will be blue water," he said, shaking the glass in his hand, the ice cubes rattling. Gin and tonic. "And then there will be no land in sight." He finally turned to look at me. "Does that scare you?"

Actually, it did. And so did he.

Instead, I gave him a shrug and turned my attention back to the sea, to the dizzying height of the mast. It was only then that I noticed a crow's nest about halfway and one of the crew members up there.

"What's he doing?" I asked. The young man was so high up that he looked like a black blob.

"He's being punished."

I stared dumbly at Javier. "You're kidding me? What for?"

He shook his glass and took a long sip before saying "I didn't like the way he was looking at you."

I couldn't believe my ears.

"Looking at ... how was he looking at me?"

"You don't want to know, angel."

"Javier, you can't punish the guy, he's just a fucking kid!"

"He should know better. You're the lady of the boat and you deserve respect."

This was doing my head in.

"Respect? You wouldn't know respect if it crawled

up your ass and died. You're blackmailing me, how is that for respect?"

"I have a special relationship with you," he said softly, then looked back at the boy on the crow's nest, eyes narrowing.

"You have *nothing* with me," I said, and got out of the chair. Javier reached over and grabbed me by the bicep, and I was thankful for the layer of fabric between our skin.

"I'm not hurting you," he said, pulling me closer. His eyes burned into me, mine burning right back.

"And if I struggle?" I sniped, raising my arm, letting him know I was all for it. Anything to let me hold something above him.

"Then I'll change my tactics," he said, getting up and taking a step closer.

"You stay back," I said, so glad that we were alone in the cockpit. I didn't want anyone else to see how this was playing out, seeing me so damn weak.

"Or what?" he asked nastily. "You'll hit me?"

I thought about it, I really did. It's all I had ever wanted since we left the dust of Palm Valley behind. But not like this. Not when he wanted it. Why did my ex-boyfriend have to be such a sick son of a bitch?

"I'm going to my room," I said, jerking my arm away from him. His grip loosened and his hand slid down to my wrist, where he held on. It felt electric in an extremely disturbing way.

"Dinner is going to be ready soon," he said, voice lower, smoother, as if he were confiding in me. "One of the boys, Marc, is actually a very good cook."

"I'm not hungry."

"Starving yourself isn't proving a point, you know."

I wasn't starving myself, not really. I just knew he'd take pleasure in watching me eat, food that probably was absolutely delicious, and I didn't want to give him anything. I was already doing enough for him, coming on this trip, committing to something I didn't even want to think about.

"I'll see you tomorrow," I told him. Then I snatched my hand out of his grasp and walked off quickly down the stairs and down others, until I was back in the bowels of the ship. I went into my cabin, locked the door, and sat on the bed, my knees tucked under my chin. I had a whole evening to think, and hoped the rock of the boat would jostle my brain into reacting.

I didn't like the way things were going. Well, that was an understatement. For maybe the first time ever, I was in a bad situation and I didn't have a plan to get out of it.

I pulled up the wide right leg of my pants and gazed at the bright pink and red flowers that adorned the scars. Its beauty was breathtaking. Something so ugly had been transformed into something so lovely, all by Camden's very skilled hands and his very skilled heart. A rush of emotions began to flood up from my chest, choking me. It felt like an unending flow, the budding blooms the source, and my small sob caught me by surprise. I hadn't let myself think about Camden, to feel, and now it was catching up with me. He wasn't here. He was somewhere else. And until he was placed in danger again, because of something I would or would not do,

I had to get over him. He wasn't here with me. He was with his ex-wife and his kid. Knowing the good person that Camden was, the messed-up and angry but undeniably good soul that he had, he would be with her. Maybe falling in love with her again, or maybe not, but he was with her and I was alone. I was here. And though I'd lived so much of my life on my own, being with Camden, no matter how briefly, had brought me something I had never had before. He made me feel safe, whether I was in his arms or at his side or just in his presence. For the first time in my life, I had a protector—and I never knew I needed one until then.

Now he was gone and I was on my own. I'd been alone long enough to know I wanted more, someone to believe in me, to love me, to have my back and serve as a shield at the front. It made me realize that I wasn't invincible, immortal, and that I wasn't always going to be able to make it on my own. Of course, now I had no choice. Camden was gone. Though I'd been good about keeping him out of my head, ignoring the little welts on my heart, the pain—the strange emptiness—was surprising.

My defenses were crumbling.

There was a knock at my door and I quickly shoved the pant leg down. Javier hadn't seen the tattoo yet. I felt like if he saw it, he'd be intruding on a private memory. His very eyes would taint it.

"What?" I asked, brushing the hair off my face while checking to see whether my eyes had leaked tears or not. They hadn't. I was good.

The handle was jiggled, followed by another knock.

I sighed and got off the bed, unlocking the door. I took a step back and it opened. Raul stuck his head in. Not that I wanted to see Javier, but I especially didn't want to see *him*.

"Are you all right?" he asked, all beaky nose and widow's peak. "I thought I heard you crying."

I glared at him. He couldn't have looked less concerned; in fact, it looked like he found the whole thing funny.

"I'm fine. Do you mind giving me some privacy?"

His face grew still for a moment before he smiled. "Sure thing. You know, if you ever need to talk to someone who understands, who is just outside of the equation, you know you can talk to me."

As if that didn't sound insincere enough, his eyes traveled down to my chest and back and he ran the tip of his tongue over his teeth.

Before I could tell him to get the fuck out he winked at me and shut the door. I locked it again, hoping he could hear the sound, and went back to the bed. I put my fingers up my pant leg, tracing them over the scars, imagining Camden's hands on top of mine. Then I lay on my side and hoped for sleep to come so I didn't have to suffer a moment longer.

CHAPTER TEN

Camden

We had gone as far as La Cruces, New Mexico, when we met the first of Gus's contacts. After following I-10 for the last few days with minimal stops for gas and sleep, the blistering sun making the interior of the GTO swelter like a fat man's armpits, La Cruces was a sight for sore eyes.

As was Gus's contact. Lydia DuShane was a Louisiana native who gave up running her coffee shop battered by Hurricane Katrina to run a pie shop in New Mexico. Though she was an older lady, late fifties, she had aged better than any of the plastic-coated women in LA. Her skin was relatively smooth and freckled, her hair a mixture of red and gray, and her blue eyes were nicely wrinkled from smiling too much. She made me feel at home immediately, which was a bit surprising considering what Gus had told me about her.

"When she's not baking pies, she's bounty hunting," he'd said as we pulled into town.

"Uh," I said, fidgeting in my seat, "isn't that kind of a problem for me?"

Gus gave me a dry look. "Hey, kid, there's no bounty on your head yet. Besides, you're with me. You're one of the good guys."

I raised my brow. Right.

Soon after Lydia sat us down in her shop, the last few customers dwindled out as the 3 PM closing time approached. We each had a slice of apricot blueberry pie in front of us. That, combined with the steaming cups of coffee and the vintage posters of farm life on the walls, did work as a wonderful front. Who would ever believe that sweet, patient Lydia had a knack for nabbing America's Most Wanted?

Yet, after she flipped the sign on the front door to CLOSED and locked it, she slid into the booth with us, took out a small netbook, and slipped on a pair of glasses, ready to get to the point.

"So you're hunting Javier Bernal, is that right?" she asked. In the reflection in her glasses, I could see her flicking from website to website.

"You know him?" I asked.

She snorted. "I know everyone. If I'm not keeping tabs, I'm not doing my job."

I leaned forward eagerly. "Is he wanted for something?"

She shook her head. "Nah, not yet. The police have ideas but then again half the force is corrupt in Mississippi. You think the New Orleans PD is bad, you ain't seen nothing yet." She took her eyes off the screen and tilted her head at me. "I like to know what the baddies are doing so when they do finally do something to get them in trouble—and believe me, it catches up to all of them—I know their next step. I was watching this one guy for years before he slipped up and was wanted for a DUI. Considering the guy's unofficial rap sheet, I knew the reward would be a big one. I knew where his safe house was and I nabbed him the next day. Cops were already on the way."

"How do you do it? I mean, you're not frail but…"

She smiled slyly in a satisfied way. "I'm a woman. And that's the secret. I've been around the block. You'd be surprised what a retiree can get away with. Ain't that right, Gus?"

Gus scratched at his beard and I could have sworn his cheeks turned a shade of pink. That was something to ask him about later, even though I knew his answer would be a glare and a grunt.

He cleared his throat. "So where is Mr. Bernal now?"

"Ocean Springs, Mississippi," she said, sitting back in her chair. "Are you boys going to eat your pie or what?"

"I'd love to but we really need to get a move on," I said apologetically. I got up but Gus's arm shot out and he planted me back down.

"Relax, Camden, we'll get there," he said. "A town isn't enough. We need a plan."

I shook my head. "We can plan in the car. If he's in Ocean Springs and that's where Ellie lived with him, then I have no doubt that he's living in the same house he was six years ago."

"Who is Ellie?" Lydia asked, eyes wide.

I shot Gus a look to keep quiet but he ignored me. "Ellie Watt. She's Bernal's ex-girlfriend and is, we think, being more or less held hostage."

"Ellie Watt," she said, tapping her pink fingernails on the table. "Ellie Watt. She's no innocent, is she? She wrapped up in the cartel?"

"No," I said quickly, and probably too defensively. I cleared my throat. "No, she was never involved in that."

"But she's not innocent. She's a con artist," Gus supplied.

"*Was* a con artist," I corrected him.

He gave his head a shake. "A tiger doesn't change its stripes, boy."

"Ellie's better than a tiger," I shot back.

"Either way," Lydia said slowly, "Ellie Watt has been wanted for something before. She was on my radar briefly."

Gus and I both looked at her. "For what?" I asked.

She pursed her lips, flamingo pink like her nails, a color I'd used many times in my work, and began scrolling through her files again. After a few tense moments, she shrugged.

"I'm not sure. This was like three years ago. It wasn't anything major, maybe just twenty grand, or I would have gone after her."

"But her name was Ellie Watt..." I reinstated. "Not Eden White or Ellen Williams or anything like that?"

"Nope. Ellie Watt. I remember because my sister's name is Ellie."

Now, that was troubling. Ellie hadn't been Ellie since high school. Whoever had placed a bounty on her was someone from a very long time ago. I glanced over at Gus and his furrowed brow told me he was thinking the exact same thing.

"Well, if you do think of anything else, please let me know. I've got my cell," Gus said. "About Ellie, that is. Everything about Bernal, we'd like to know now."

She nodded. "I can tell you he's got several body-guards around him at all times."

"Raul," I said.

"And that he's very careful, almost to a fault. He never slips up, at least not enough for me to act on. The man has patience and is ruthless, and that's a mighty terrible combination."

"Tell us something we don't know," I said under my breath.

It was loud enough for her to shoot me a sharp look. "Tell me what your plan is when you find her."

I looked at Gus, but he was staring at the wall now, eyes drifting over a pastoral landscape, too-green field, bright red barn.

"I'm not sure," I said slowly when Gus didn't respond. "We haven't really worked out the kinks yet."

She smiled before growing serious. "Well, let me tell you this, there are some things in life that you can do by the seat of your pants and there are others you need to plan. What I said about Bernal being careful, it's no lie. He'll smell you a mile away if you're on his territory. If he has his ex-girlfriend, and they're in the place they used to share, I would bet he wouldn't give her up easily. You're obviously after her for a reason. He was too."

I swallowed hard and tried to bury the seeds of doubt that were popping up in my head, the fact that I was green, new to this, didn't know what the fuck I was doing. I was a tattoo artist, for crying out loud, not a vigilante. Hell, I wasn't even a bounty hunter like this middle-aged lady was. I had absolutely no skills to my credit except that I knew how to fire a gun and could kick the shit out of any unarmed man. And I doubted I'd be able to throw a couch and get away with it a second time.

"Well, thank you for your time, Lydia," Gus suddenly said, getting to his feet. "I'm sorry we couldn't stay for pie, but the kid is right. We need to get going so we can start planning."

I scooped up my pie and wrapped it in a mound of napkins from the dispenser. "For energy," I said, trying to give her an easy smile. I think I failed. Her own smile faltered in return.

As we were leaving the shop, I saw Lydia pull Gus aside and whisper to him, "Are you sure you don't want me to come? For company? Just for old times?"

He grunted. "I'll be all right, Lyd."

"I worry about you. You've been through so much, and this man, Bernal…"

"I'll be seeing you." Gus patted her on the shoulder, and I quickly turned and headed to the car so they wouldn't know I'd been eavesdropping.

She waved good-bye to us, standing on the stoop of her shop, as we got into the car and roared off down the dusty desert streets, sand it seemed I could never escape.

I shot Gus a look. "I guess we need a plan."

"We need a plan *and* a prayer," he said, eyeing me over his glasses. "But you knew that already, didn't you?"

I did. Yet knowing it didn't make it easier.

I started nibbling on the pie—absolutely messy but delicious—and got to thinking. We would descend on Ocean Springs soon.

Tomorrow I might be able to hold Ellie in my arms again.

Tomorrow I might also lose everything.

*   *   *

Ocean Springs definitely wasn't what I pictured when I thought of Mississippi. Granted, we had driven through Gulfport and Biloxi, a mix of new casinos and post-Katrina destruction. But Ocean Springs was fresh and charming. A little too quaint for someone like Javier, but what did I know?

We pulled into the small town in the late afternoon, the humidity swept away by the evening's incoming breeze. We hadn't even spent a night in a hotel; instead Gus had me take over during the middle of the night, somewhere in Texas. He figured it was safe enough to not draw any suspicion, our car anonymous among the others on the dark stretch of highway.

While he snored from the backseat, utterly out in a matter of seconds, I had more time to think and go over the plan.

Gus had known where Ellie had shacked up with Javier, in case of emergencies. We were able to locate it using his cell phone's GPS, as close into the street view as we could go. Looked like a nice place, a fact that kind of picked at my heart a bit. It was ridiculous to be jealous over this, over something that had happened a long time ago, but I couldn't help it. I always was a jealous guy. I guess it came from insecurities and all that nonsense. Well, that's what the shrink had told me all those years ago when my father shuttled me off to him once a week. Even though I knew that Ellie despised Javier, that she was in a terrible place and needed my help—*our* help—I wondered what had attracted her to him in the first place. What caused her to give up on her revenge and live with this man? The beauty of their house and the location disguised the truth.

Gus had decided we'd first need to do to a bit of a stakeout—which totally went against what I wanted to do, which was pretty much to barge in there and take out everyone in our path. That method would probably get me killed, but every second that we spent staking out the joint was a second that I felt we were losing Ellie. Still, Gus was right. Of course. I'd started wanting to second-guess him out of spite, but the fact was, he knew what he was doing.

After the stakeout, when we got an idea of how many people were there and how they were armed (that's assuming they were at the house—this was just our hunch, after all), we'd formulate our plan of attack. One person to act as a diversion, the other to rescue Ellie. Obviously the trick would be the diversion so we didn't get caught. It also depended on how many men were there and if Ellie was heavily protected or not. Gus seemed to think that she wouldn't be. Javier probably had his bodyguard or Raul. Javier, like everyone in the world by now, had to know I was on the run from the police and would want to stay low, so coming for Ellie would be the last thing I'd do.

Javier would have totally underestimated me.

Once we followed the GPS's chirpy voice down a few seaside streets, we eased up several blocks away. Javier's car was still Javier's car, and our cover would be blown in a second if we went any closer.

Gus brought the duffel bag into the backseat and began sorting through the weapons. Yeah, that word pretty much encompassed what he'd packed. An assault rifle, a few handguns of various calibers, plus a sniper rifle. Then there were two knives, a small ax, a small plastic bottle, hornet spray, various gas lighters, and a container of Coffee-mate.

I picked up the Coffee-mate and shook it. "Now, what's *really* in here?"

"Coffee-mate," he said, face serious. "You get a cloud of that in the air, there's nothing more flammable. Not to mention how easy fireballs are to make."

"Okaaay," I said. My nerves were starting to twitch a bit. I wasn't counting on doing anything that involved igniting a puff of nondairy creamer. Also it made me wonder if people knew what they were putting in their coffee every morning.

I nodded at the unmarked bottle, afraid to touch it. "What's that, breast milk?"

His eyes twinkled at that though his mouth remained flat. "A bleach bomb."

"Perhaps we should stick to guns," I said. I didn't want this to turn into Gus's science experiment.

He nodded. "You just use your own, you're more comfortable with it."

I was. I also had a secret weapon. I wasn't planning on using it, but if I ever got the chance—if I happened to come across Javier alone—well, it paid off to plan ahead. Guns didn't always have a way of making people talk.

Gus slipped one gun into his boot, a knife went into a sheath under his pant leg, and he tucked another gun into the waistband of his jeans. He seemed to consider the bleach bomb for a bit before he grabbed the can of hornet spray and stuffed that in the front of his pants.

"So I'm going to assume here that I'm the diversion," I said, grabbing a small backpack I had stowed in the back.

"We'll have to watch them for a bit, but yes, that's the plan."

As childish as it seemed, I wanted to be the one who came breaking into the house in a blaze of glory and rescuing my woman. But things didn't work out the way they did in the movies. Instead I'd have to fake and run and leave the rest up to Gus.

At first I assumed we'd be waiting until nightfall, but Gus assured me that daytime was the safest. This was an affluent neighborhood, and Javier was the leader of a Mexican drug cartel. They couldn't get away with a lot during the day, so the risk of a shoot-out was kept to a minimum. That said, we'd be in a lot of shit if we were spotted. Sadly, that was the risk we were going to have to take. I was a wanted man now, what the hell was the difference? Might as well get nabbed for something I actually did.

We left the car and started walking toward the house, taking the street that dipped along by the ocean. It was stunningly beautiful, the glimpses of crashing waves that you could spot between the properties, the way the sun was setting in golden shimmers. Still, the scenery did nothing to abate the anxiety that was starting to eat at me. I'd never experienced panic attacks, not the way that Ellie had anyway, but this was as close to one as I'd ever felt. My lungs felt like they were shrinking with each and every step we took. The gun tucked into my jeans felt like a bomb about to go off, my backpack felt weighted and heavy.

Luckily, Gus and I didn't look out of place. He was wearing a yellow and pink Hawaiian shirt that I joked made him look like a combination of Jimmy Buffett and Nick Nolte when he got arrested for drunk driving; I had on a baseball cap and a long-sleeved gray Henley shirt that covered up all my tats. We both had sneakers and sunglasses. We could have been a father and son going out for their sunset walk. No one would suspect that Gus was a walking weapon.

Soon we were upon Javier's house, which looked the same as it did on Google Maps. Only this wasn't a concept, an idea, an image on a phone. This was the house, all white with its raised porch overlooking the beach. Idyllic and deadly. And Ellie could have been inside, maybe in one of the windows that had bars on it. The thought caused a jolt of anger to run through me.

As usual, Gus picked up on my mood. "Take it easy," he whispered out of the side of his mouth. We were just walking past, two guys on a walk. No one should suspect anything, not if we kept going on our easygoing way.

Once we were a few yards from the house, Gus stopped and pretended to look at his watch. "What time is sunset, do you know?"

I swallowed hard. Was that code for something? I could barely even think.

I could tell his eyes were on me underneath the glasses. He lowered his voice, pretending to adjust his watch. "Just the one car. Recognize it?"

I nodded, unable to find my vocal cords.

"Come on, let's go see how Dana's garden is doing," he said more loudly, and began walking again. I followed, wondering if we were being watched or followed but knew I couldn't look around to check. The skin at the back of my neck prickled.

We turned down the next street and once we were out of sight of the house, he pulled me to the side into the flowering bushes of someone's yard.

"We might be lucky," he whispered gruffly. "One car means less people. Maybe. Either way, I'm going to go around and up through the beach. Enter from there, probably from the main floor. I didn't like the looks of those windows, but I'm going to assume that's where she's being kept. Unless Javier is that paranoid. Which the bastard probably is. Still. You wait here."

He pulled his cell from his pocket and checked the time. Then he took off his watch and handed it to me. "In five minutes from now, you knock on the door or ring the doorbell and ask if Dana Prescott is home. They'll tell you you have the wrong house and give directions. Maybe. And hopefully you'll be on your way."

"Hopefully," I said with a grimace. "Who is Dana?"

He shrugged. "She lives around the corner. I Googled home businesses in Ocean Springs and her location came up the closest. Home computer services. You'll be more believable if you're asking about someone who lives here. Maybe Javier and his pals are the good neighborly types."

"Like a Neighborhood Watch," I said. The shakiness had come up into my voice. I needed to hold it together if I was going to be any help.

He gave my shoulder a hearty slap. "You'll do fine. You'll know when it's time to go. Then you run, you get back to the car, and you bring it three houses down. Ellie and I will be running along the beach and will come in between that red house I pointed out. You got it?"

I nodded. He watched me for a few moments to make sure, then suddenly he was off and running in the opposite direction, moving a lot quicker than I'd given him credit for. He disappeared down the next street, heading for the beach.

I slid the watch around my wrist, my hands shaking,

the leather slipping. Five minutes. Five minutes. Five minutes.

Oh shit, Camden, I told myself, and suddenly my head was between my legs, nausea sweeping through me like a bat out of hell. I hadn't been this nervous in a long time. Not even when Ellie and I had been going to get Sophia and Ben. The last time I'd felt this nervous was when I'd been planning to catch Ellie in the act of robbing me.

I had to admit that still stung from time to time. How the whole time I knew she was scoping me out, wanting my money, not giving a shit about leaving me high and dry. Not caring about her old friend Camden, the doormat, the lovesick puppy, the goth queen. She looked me in the face and lied time and time again. And then she broke into my house and robbed me.

But that was the old Ellie. When she traded herself for me, sacrificing herself for my freedom, for Sophia and Ben's freedom, I knew that old Ellie was dead. Still, being here in Mississippi, in the very place where she gladly lived a lie for over a year, a part of me had to wonder if the old Ellie would be resurrected. It was something I tried not to think about, because it only added an unnecessary fear. The fear that when Gus and I came to get her, she would not come with us.

I looked down at the watch. It was time.

I breathed in deeply through my nose, adjusted the cap on my head, and came out of the hedges, striding down the road and turning onto Javier's street. There was the house, just as before, and for once I could gaze at it through the cover of sunglasses and take it all in. After all, I was looking for someone now, Dana Prescott, and I'd heard she lived here at 425 East Beach Road. I heard she had a lovely garden and fixed computers.

Fuck, what was I doing?

It was too late. Gus was probably somewhere on the beach, heading to the house like a lost beachcomber. Without a diversion, Ellie's chances of getting out of there would get a lot more difficult. I had to keep going. One foot in front of the other. A gun tucked in my jeans. A new weapon in my backpack.

I walked down the bend of his driveway, past moody, weeping trees, and went straight for the front door. Half of the house at the back was on stilts, leaving a spot big enough to park two cars—the black SUV being the only one there—and to the side a stone walkway led to the front door, trimmed by flowering pots. It was surprisingly well maintained.

I stopped on the low stoop and fought the urge to hesitate. If Javier's men were worth their salt, they'd already have spotted me and been watching my every move. If I looked to the window to the side of the door, I'm sure I'd see the venetian blinds move. But I was there to see Dana and had no reason to cast a suspicious eye upon the house.

Seeing there was a doorbell, I rang it, a loud chime that nearly made me jump out of my shoes. I had to, had to, had to watch myself. I needed to do this for her sake, my sake, Gus's sake.

Be cool.

The door opened and a short Hispanic man appeared,

dressed casually in a white polo shirt and khaki shorts. Did we even have the right house? He didn't look to be much older than me, and his posture was relaxed. The only thing that gave me a hint right away was the fact that he had a bandage across his temple, the area red and raised.

"Can I help you?" he asked. He was polite too, though I detected a hint of suspicion in his tone.

I smiled. "Hi, is Dana home?"

He frowned. "Dana? No."

"She does live here though, right? 425 East Beach?"

The man crossed his arms and I got a glimpse of some pretty badass tribal tattoos on his biceps. I could take him easily, but he'd put up a good fight. He leveled his stare at me. "This is 425 but there is no Dana here. Sorry."

He was about to close the door when I raised my hand to stop him. A ballsy move, but I wanted to make sure Gus had enough time.

The man eyed my hand, then fixed his eyes on me. He didn't look relaxed anymore. He looked annoyed. I was pressing my luck.

I kept grinning like an idiot, like I wasn't picking up on the obvious signals he was giving me. "Do you know if there's a Dana in the neighborhood? She's supposed to offer computer services." I patted my backpack. "Got my laptop right here."

"All I do know is that if you don't get the fuck out of here right now, I'm going to break your balls with my foot."

I let my smile fall because that's what anyone would

have done. I was half tempted to break *his* balls. Instead, I raised both hands as a peace offering and gave a meek "Sorry, man, sorry" while backing away.

The man didn't move. He kept staring at me. I started thinking, maybe, just maybe he already deduced something about me, maybe I'd given something away.

Then I heard a gunshot.

CHAPTER ELEVEN

Ellie

"So, how would you like to kill Travis, Ellie? A bullet to the head or something more subtle?"

I turned and glared at Raul. It was day two at sea, and the massive yacht was already starting to feel too small. I was alone only in my cabin. Everywhere else I went it was Raul, or the other guy, or one of the crew boys following me. Unlike the other two, the crew boys were nice enough and kept their distance lest they incur Javier's wrath, but I could tell they were watching me. Little matching spies all in black.

Oddly enough, Javier hadn't been around a lot. Most of the time he was at the helm of the ship, even though one of the crew boys seemed to be adept at handling a sailboat, even one of this size. Javier always had a thing for control, but I started to get the feeling he was avoiding me. It was somewhat unwelcome, and I couldn't figure out why.

"Who said I'm killing Travis?" I shot back at him and took a large, medicinal gulp of my wine. I had been sitting in the theater lounge area, hiding out from the relentless sun and trying to occupy my frazzled mind with books. The peace didn't last long. Raul had sat down across from me, leaning back in the seat, one leg crossed, drink in hand. His eyes had gotten extra lecherous, even though I was wearing breezy pants and a flowing peasant top. His eyes were so much more intrusive than Javier's.

Raul tipped his chin down and smiled. "I suppose you think Javier will be the one to do it, that you're just the trap. The bait."

"Something like that," I muttered, and looked down at the book I was attempting to read, Stephen King's *Duma Key*. It seemed fitting, the storm and boat on the cover.

"Doesn't that bother you," he continued, "knowing he only sees you as a pawn?"

"I'd rather him see me as a pawn than anything more than that," I said.

"Hmmm," Raul mused. "And I see you mean that too. Do you still have feelings for him?"

I lowered the book again and gave him the most disgusted and incredulous look that I could muster. Considering I was already buzzed from the wine, I'd say it was probably pretty good. The drunker I got, the nastier I became—facial expressions included.

"Sorry to disappoint you, Raul." I drew out the syllables in his name, mocking it. "Whatever feelings I had for Javier died six years ago, when I found him cheating on me."

He raised a brow. "Oh yes. That. Have you ever asked him about it?"

My heart stopped a bit. Raul knew. This was public knowledge. Oh, of course it was. Javier was probably screwing everyone, calling anyone with legs—even scarred ones—his angel and coming all over them. Somewhere deep inside I flushed at that last memory and shook it off.

"No I haven't, because I honestly don't care. I'd like to find that chick and shake her fucking hand. If it wasn't for her, I'd probably be wasting my life, attached to a complete psychopath with an addiction to pussy."

"And being a con artist wasn't a waste?"

"What are you, a shrink?" I asked, and looked away. The book wasn't helping anymore. The wine was. I got up and made a move to the bar (there was one in every single room on this ship, a total booze cruise), but Raul beat me to it. He was quicker than he looked and within seconds my wineglass was being filled with expensive Sauvignon blanc and I was slightly too buzzed to care.

He sat back down across from me and brushed back his hair. My God, why did cartel members have to be so ugly? I'd lucked out when I picked Javier for my plan all those years ago. He was the only one who was pleasing to look at. Even more than pleasing, when you added in the fact that that whole primal animal vibe slithered off him.

Why was I thinking so many pleasant adjectives about a man who was blackmailing me and essentially holding me hostage on a ship that launched Raul in my direction at every turn?

"How are you going to kill him?" he continued after a moment.

"I told you, I'm not. I'm the bait."

"You know, if I had you in my possession, I'd set you free."

I glared at him. "Right. And I'm not in his possession."

"Maybe he's in your possession."

"Seriously, what do you want? If you want to annoy me, you're succeeding. If you want to be creepy, you're succeeding at that too."

"I'm just wondering how it is that you're going along with all of this so well. It's like you belong here."

"It's called making the best of a bad situation."

Raul leaned forward and lowered his voice. "I think you only do your best in bad situations. Because you're a bad, bad little girl, Ellie Watt. And I can teach you to be worse."

"What's going on here?" Javier's voice broke in.

I swallowed the sour feeling in my mouth and looked over at Javier, who was standing by the entrance to the lounge, eyes boring into Raul.

"He's annoying me," I said, not caring if it got me in shit with either of them.

Raul only smiled, his eyes darting to me and back to Javier. "I'm trying to prepare Ellie here for what's to come. You know, Javier, for an assassin, she's awfully blasé about the whole thing. Doesn't that worry you? Perhaps she might flake out, maybe fuck everything up.

On purpose, no less. She really seems to harbor some sort of grudge against you."

Javier didn't look at me. "She'll get it, sooner or later. And I trust her."

I almost snorted wine through my nose. Javier trusted me? I'd dump him over the side of the ship at the first opportunity if I knew that Raul wouldn't kill me right afterward.

"That trust might get you killed, *señor*," Raul said bitingly.

I raised my brow at that comment, but Javier's face was blank.

Finally he cleared his throat and said, "Well, Raul, I think you're done with annoying Ellie for today. Why don't you go join Roberto at the helm, huh?"

Raul narrowed his eyes at him and got up. He left without saying a word, brushing past Javier with utter disdain.

The whole exchange had put a weird vibe in the room. For some reason I felt like things had gotten even more off balance, or perhaps that was the combination of the wine and the ship. Not seeing land for twenty-four hours didn't help.

Javier folded his arms and looked at me. "Are you okay?"

I raised my glass of wine. "Drinking away the blackmailing blues."

"That's funny," he said, though his tone was flat. He walked over, smooth and sleek. That whole primal animal analogy darted into my brain again. Today he was a cat dressed head to toe in olive green. He stopped right behind the chair I was sitting in, so I had to twist around to look up at him. "What was he talking to you about?"

"About how I was going to kill Travis." *And if I had feelings for you anymore.* Of course I didn't want to say that. I didn't even want to go there.

He peered down at me. "That wasn't all. He said he was going to teach you to be a bad girl."

"Well, I don't know what he meant by that..."

"I do. I don't like the way he talks to you."

"Well, I'll tell you what. If you want to go stick Raul all the way up the crow's nest, you have my full support."

Finally his mouth twisted into a smile. He raised his brow and nodded at my glass. "I say the drinking is working. You've got a little spring in your step."

For a split second I was able to fool myself into thinking we were old lovers who were having a lovely cruise together, old sparring partners, shooting the shit. But that couldn't have been further from the truth.

His face grew colder as he studied me. He turned around and left the lounge, calling over his shoulder "Enjoy your book. Dinner is at six."

He didn't remind me to eat like he'd been doing at every meal, even though that's one of the reasons the wine was hitting me so hard. And just for that, I decided I would finally partake of dinner. My stomach punched me in anticipation and I went back to reading.

*   *   *

As much as I hated to admit it, dinner was fabulous. The snapper was so fresh I could have sworn that it had just been caught off the side of the boat. The coconut rice and mango salad was amazing. The cocktails, syrupy hurricanes, were phenomenal. It was almost good enough to make me forget why I'd been avoiding meals in the first place.

I did my best to put a damper on my enjoyment of the food and instead paid attention to what was going on around me. It was just four of us, since the crew had their own mess hall in their quarters. The other man was Peter. He seemed fairly intelligent if not quiet most of the time. I didn't know why he was there with us or what he did, but Javier seemed to treat him with respect. Maybe it just seemed that way because he was getting increasingly short with Raul while Raul was acting more and more like a petulant child. I could feel Javier's authority over him crumbling little by little, and it kind of scared me.

Once dinner was over, cleared away by the boys who seemed to appear out of nowhere, Raul and Peter retreated to their cabins, leaving me and Javier sitting across from each other at the dinner table. When we were alone, I felt the weight of the star-filled sky crushing me. The boat's deck was lit up with tons of mood lights, making Javier's eyes shine as he gazed at me.

It was a steady gaze, not adoring or concerned. But interested. He had always seemed so intrigued by me.

"It's beautiful out," he said, his voice dull. "You can see so many constellations out here. None of those city lights. You can feel how…insignificant we really are. Can you feel it?"

I didn't know if this was a trap or a trick question.

Still, I nodded. "Yes. Like God might flick me away with his finger."

He tilted his head, his mouth drawing into a slight pout. "God would never do that to you. You're Ellie Watt."

"Sometimes I am," I said, hiding my uneasiness with another sip of my hurricane.

"You always are. I see that now. I might have only seen bits and pieces of you before. But now you're... formidable."

Was that a compliment? If it wasn't, I didn't think I could take it as one since it came from Javier.

He smiled. "It is a compliment," he said, back to that whole mind-reading thing. "You're so strong. I'm lucky to have you."

I nearly rolled my eyes then decided it was a little more serious than that action portrayed. "Javier," I said slowly, "you don't have me. Your only luck is how far you've gotten in life without someone chopping your head off. Yes, I am strong. And I'm afraid that Raul is right. You shouldn't trust me."

"Why?"

I frowned, taken aback at the sincerity in his voice. "Why? *Why?* I don't think I've ever hated a person more than I hate you."

He seemed to mull that over, his eyes shining even more. He took a sip of his drink, then sat back in his chair and placed his hands behind his head. "That's funny. You treat me quite well for someone you hate. What do you do to the people you love?"

"You should know." I blurted it out before I realized

my mistake. The alcohol was ruining me. I was saying things I'd once locked inside my head.

His eyes widened momentarily. I saw a look in them that I never wanted to see again. I quickly drank the rest of my drink and slammed the glass down on the teak table. "Well, here I am drunk and talking absolute nonsense."

He appraised me before saying "Apparently. But I find your lack of censorship amusing. Care to entertain someone that you hate by having another drink with me?"

"Are you drugging me again? Because if I have another drink I'll probably pass out anyway, and you'll have to get one of your little crew boys to drag me back to my room."

His face became instantly stern. "No one touches you on this boat."

"Not even you?" I asked wryly, testing him, pushing him.

He shook his head. "No. Not even me. You are not mine to touch."

"Oh, of course not. I'm just yours to use as a pawn."

"Ellie," he said. Then he got up and held out his hand. "Come join me and I'll explain."

"Explain what?" I asked, eyeing his hand as if it were diseased.

"Explain what's going to happen. I don't know what Raul told you, but I want to make some things clear."

I didn't understand what the point of that was. What did it matter what he told me? I probably wasn't going to like it, which didn't matter if it meant keeping Camden alive. I was in a shitty shitty situation, and I was tired of trying to wrap my head around it.

Finally I put my hand in Javier's and he helped me to my feet. His hands were warm and rough. Familiar and strange.

As soon as I was up, though, he dropped my hand like a hot coal. I'd found that to be the strangest thing about this whole thing with him. He really did see me as a pawn, not as his ex-lover or ex-girlfriend. Of course I still saw his eyes on me from time to time and that hopeful expression on his face. But for the most part, whatever feelings, mental, physical, he had for me in the past, they weren't the same anymore. He was detached, unpassionate, and utterly focused on this task at hand, the one my brain kept skirting. Part of me found his distance admirable. I didn't want him to keep playing the part of the creepy, obsessive ex-lover. The one who kept all my clothes yet took six years to come chasing after me.

I just didn't understand *this* Javier. And maybe that's why I let him pour me a stiff drink and why I followed him down the stairs to the main deck and to the back of the ship to his private cockpit. I wanted to understand him, whether it would do me any good or not. Understanding the enemy was to my advantage, wasn't it?

I hadn't spent any time at his cockpit before, a round depression that led down to his office and quarters below, two curved couches on either side, plus a bar that popped up with the touch of a button.

I sat down on one couch, spreading my legs out, hoping that would deter him from sitting near me. It worked though I had a feeling he was going to sit opposite from me anyway.

"I think this is the best part of the ship," I said. I put my head back and looked up at the stars. I still felt the weight of the universe on my shoulders.

"It's my favorite too. It reminds me of the old boat."

My mind jumped back to the first time I had stepped foot on his old boat. The first time we had made love on it. He had wanted to stain me. And he did, just not in the way he had hoped.

I knew I shouldn't have been thinking of it—it was the booze, plus Raul's words that had implanted the seeds there. But I was thinking it and, before I knew it, I was saying it.

"Why did you cheat on me?" I kept my eyes on the stars, feeling the dark bruise-colored sky lift a bit.

Javier was silent. Stunned or formulating an excuse? Maybe preparing to tell the truth. I didn't know what I hoped to gain out of this aside from having a weight lifted. Unanswered questions can stay with you a long time, riding on your shoulders, wearing you down.

I heard him take a sip of his drink and place it on the side table. The sounds were all louder now, the drone of the engine since we weren't under sail, the water as it crashed behind the stern of the boat.

"I cheated on you more than once," he said cautiously, as if he were waiting for me to spring up and kill him. I didn't. It hurt my pride just a tad, but the anger was on the way out.

I cleared my throat, feeling stupid despite the circumstances. "I see. It figures."

"Why?"

"That I would be the one with the wool pulled over my eyes. The whole time I thought I was keeping a secret from you and you were the one keeping a secret from me."

"Ellie, it wasn't exactly like—"

"I don't care. It doesn't matter. Forget I asked."

"I can't forget you asked. What if I asked why you lied to me all that time?"

"It doesn't matter," I repeated.

"It *does* matter," he said, loud enough to make me jerk to attention. He was gripping his glass, eyes blazing. "I was a different man then, just a boy, but I did love you and I never would have done anything intentionally to hurt you."

"Love and respect don't have to go hand in hand," I retorted, recalling what a wise woman had once told me. And they say you never meet anyone worthwhile at roadside bars. I still had that woman's driver's license in my scrapbook: Marda.

"That can be true," he conceded. "I had reasons for being unfaithful. It went beyond sex and love."

"You loved her?" I exclaimed, feeling sick despite myself. I could blame the wine and the boat all I wanted.

"No, I didn't. But I had revenge. You of all people should know how far you are willing to go for it."

"What does revenge have to do with sleeping with someone else?"

"What does revenge have to do with loving me?" he said, his voice collapsing over the last two words so they spun out in a hush.

I slowly sat up, feeling dizzy. "It shouldn't matter, but I did love you."

"You broke me," he replied. His eyes went to steel.

I didn't want to hear any of this anymore. "Why did you cheat on me? And don't give me that revenge shit. If it was this revenge, this *thing*, then tell me exactly how it was."

"Her name was Patricia," he said.

Oh, so she had a name. A dumb one at that.

He continued, looking down into his glass, "She was a nice girl. Nice enough. Pretty. She liked me. That's all I needed. She was the sister of Enrique Morrow."

"Who is Enrique Morrow?"

"Enrique was one of the higher-ups in Los Zetas. Patricia lived in New Orleans, he was in Nuevo Laredo. I got to know her, I suppose in the same way you got to know me. I used her to get to him."

I stared at him. "And did you get to him? Did it work?"

He nodded and shook the ice in his glass. "Yes."

"What happened to them?"

He eyed me briefly. "They are both dead. I killed them. Killed her first, in front of him, to prove a point. Held her down and took her hand. Then slit her throat. And made him watch. Then, when I thought he'd suffered enough, I cut off his head. Seemed fitting, considering that Los Zetas practically think they invented the act."

My mouth dropped open. I needed to shut it. To say I was horrified was an understatement. "You ... you did that to the woman you were cheating on me with?" A memory flashed in my head, the one of when I found them together, that terrible act of intimacy, him calling her pet names as they lay beside each other on the bed—*my* bed—laughing. They looked so...in love. So in touch with each other. That's what had hurt me the most, more than the sex.

"How could you do that to her?" I said softly. "You...you were capable of that when I was with you...I..."

He finished his drink then filled up my own glass with more. I was too stunned to wave him off. "This happened a few months after you left."

"You were just a young kid," I said, unable to accept it. Seeing him kill his best friend in our kitchen was one thing. But knowing that just a few months after I left him he was the kind of man who was capable of murdering a woman he was sleeping with, pretending to be in love with, in such a brutal way, to prove an awful point was...I didn't even know what it was.

"Everything changed after you left," he said, watching me closely. "Everything."

A burst of indignation flared up inside my chest. "Don't you dare blame this on me. Don't you dare!"

"You left without even a note..."

"You fucked another woman, in *our* bed!"

"I told you, it meant nothing."

I nearly crushed the glass with my hand. "I didn't know that at the time! I didn't know how little she meant to you. How obviously little human life means to you! You did what you did and you never had to do it. Your so-called excuse only makes things worse. Fuck,

Javier! All of this for nothing. Just so you could have your fucking revenge and kill people. You're nothing but a beast, a cold-hearted monster, not even fit to have two legs. Not even worth that heart beating in your chest."

He was staring at me like he hadn't heard a word I said, so I added, with as much venom as I could muster, "You *disgust* me."

He blinked a few times, then put his arm around the back of the couch and eyed his watch and the *Wish* tattoo it was covering. "Well, at least disgust is still something."

I shook my head, words and sentences trying to come together inside, but nothing fit. Nothing made any sense. I downed my drink in one go.

"You said we ruined each other," he went on, his voice lower now. "Both of us wouldn't be here now if we hadn't."

I wiped my mouth. "And what makes you think I like where I am?"

He crossed his ankle on his knee, a flash of dark gold skin between his Top-Siders and navy pants. No socks.

"Because I introduced you to your true self. I made you see the world as you were born to see it. You're not good, Ellie."

I scowled at him. "You sound like Raul now."

"No, I am nothing like Raul. I only see the truth. I opened you up to the life you were born to live. You came from...you only knew this growing up. It is in your blood just as it is in my blood. We lead the lives we were meant to, lives that are exciting and dangerous and full of power. We are strong. We are so alike, so very alike, that sometimes I wish you had told me back then who you really were."

"You would have killed me if you found out," I said. I feared it then but I knew it now. My hand would have been tossed into the sea, like that angel doll.

He seemed to consider that, angling his head. "Maybe I would have. I loved you so much, so much."

"Loving someone enough to kill them?"

He smiled caustically. "It's the romantic in me."

Suddenly he reached forward and put his hand on my knee. I flinched, my heart exploding in my chest, my eyes frozen wide.

"I'm glad you are afraid of me, my dear," he said, his fingers tightening on my knee ever so slightly. "I'm glad I disgust you. The more you feel these things so strongly, the more you'll realize how right I am. That you and I are the same. That I can help you get what I have—the power, the pride, the respect. I can make you my queen. And you'll give up on trying to be good, to be better. You *are* better now."

I felt as if something were lodged in my throat. "I sacrificed my life in order to save Camden and his family. I *am* good."

He leaned forward, his lips going to my ear. I held absolutely still, watching the dark waves roll past beyond his shoulder.

"You sacrificed nothing and gained everything. You chose to be with me. Now own it." His breath tickled hot, even when he pulled away.

After placing his drink on the side table, he began to descend the stairs to his quarters, his silhouette stark against the glow of the cabin. His voice called out, "Sleep well, angel," and was carried away by the night wind on the gulf. Even then, I still felt his breath on my neck. The lingering heat. Those damaging words that were oh-so-slowly getting under my skin.

CHAPTER TWELVE

Camden

One moment I was backing away from the guy slowly, hands in the air in a show of peace. In the next a gunshot rang out from somewhere inside the house. I froze in place, forgetting what Gus had told me, which was to run and get the hell out of there. Instead I acted on instinct.

As the man whipped around in surprise to stare back into the house, I grabbed the gun out of my waistband. I was smart to do so because, in the next second, before he even turned back around to see me, to see the pistol, he was going for his own gun.

Unfortunately for him, I beat him to it. I held the gun steady in my hand, pointed right at his head, and said calmly, "Don't you fucking move."

The man raised his hands slowly, a stupid smile plastered on his face. "Hey, man, we don't want no trouble."

"Gus!" I yelled at the house, coming closer until I was a foot away, gun still aimed and ready. "Ellie!"

"Oh," the man said in surprise. "You are here for the bitch."

Without thinking, I whipped the neck of the gun on his temple, right on his injury.

The man cried out and grabbed his head, dropping to the ground, but I pulled him back up by his shirt collar. I flung him against the door, his head rattling against it, and shoved the gun underneath his chin.

"Listen to me, you piece of shit," I said, my voice breaking with rage. "Where is she? You tell me where she is. *Tell me!*"

The man didn't look scared at all. Then blackness settled in, stoking the fire, and made me drive the end of the gun farther into his throat, until I was sure I could feel his pulse riding down the barrel.

"Tell me!" I screamed, not caring if I was attracting attention. If that gunshot was for Ellie . . . so help me God. I'd burn the entire house down with everyone in it.

He clamped his lips shut, as if daring me to shoot him. I knocked him in the temple again, the blood running harder down his face, then dragged him inside the house. It was dark on the first floor but the upstairs led to rooms bathed in the sunset.

"Gus!" I yelled again.

"Up here," he said from the second floor. He sounded fine.

"Where is she? I've got someone but he won't talk."

"Mine won't either."

I went up the stairs, dragging the man up until his shirt began to rip. I dug one hand into his arm and kept the gun firmly pressed against his ribs. He kept stumbling over the steps thanks to the blood in his eyes but I didn't care.

I walked into a small sitting area and a kitchen that faced a porch through two French doors. One of the doors was open, a salty breeze coming through. This is where Ellie would have had her dinners. Had she cooked for him? Did they have morning coffee together?

"I'm here," said Gus, and I followed his voice down a hallway to an open door at the end, ignoring the cramp in my hand from holding the gun so tightly. I peered inside the room and saw Gus standing at the foot of an unmade bed, a bullet hole in the wall. On the floor was a large bald guy, shot in the shoulder, a gun a foot from his open hand. Blood was soaking the carpet beneath him.

I know what I'd just done to the man in my hands, but the sight still took my breath away.

"Is he dead?" I asked.

Gus nodded, eyes still on him, as if he were expecting the guy to jump up from the grave. "Unfortunately I had to shoot first, then ask questions." He looked to me, noticing the guy for the first time. "Who is that?"

"I don't know," I said. "He answered the door. He knows about Ellie."

Gus shook his head. "She's not here."

"How do you know?"

He shrugged and kicked the guy's leg. "I just do. They're gone, Javier and her. Raul. His bodyguards. These guys are sloppy. They're the ones who get left behind to water the plants."

The man in my hands grunted, as if insulted by that remark.

"Well, I guess we should try to get him to talk," Gus said, coming closer. He peered at the man, then shot me a look I would have taken as impressed on any other day. "Reinjuring an injury. Smart boy." He pointed at the bed. "Here, set him down. We've both got guns; he's not going anywhere."

I yanked him forward and then pushed him so he went flying. Blood sprayed on the sheets. It was only then that I realized what I was seeing. Ellie and Javier's bedroom.

I almost joined the man on the bed, if only to smell the pillow. I needed to know that she had slept here, that she was alive, just to remember what she smelled like. But I kept it together. Instead I noticed a pile of clothes leading into the bathroom. I went over, confident that Gus was watching Javier's house sitter, and picked it up. Ellie's jeans. Her tank top. The very ones she was wearing the day she went with him.

I held them to me, like they were some injured creature.

"No blood," Gus said, his gun out and aimed at the man though his eyes were on the clothes. "Just dirty. Weren't ripped off either by the looks of it."

I took a step into the bathroom. The shower was dripping sporadically, the towel damp to the touch. She had been here. She had showered. Shed her dirty clothes. And then what? What did she wear? Was she alone getting changed or . . .

I had to choke back the bile that was flooding my throat. The thought of Javier and Ellie together. Her naked, him touching her. Taking advantage of her.

The blackness spread quickly. I felt myself floating away.

I spun around, throwing her clothes in the sink and marching right up to the man, gun back in his face.

"Did Javier hurt her?" I seethed, spitting in his face.

The man let out a little laugh, and I immediately whipped the gun across his face. It cracked, crashing against bone and teeth.

"Hey, Camden," Gus said sternly but gently. I pretended I didn't hear him.

"I'll do it to the other side to make things even," I threatened. "Now tell me if he hurt her. Tell me what happened to her. Tell me where she is."

The man spat out blood and peered up at me through a running red eye.

"I'm not telling you anything. Except that she deserves whatever is coming to her."

"Camden," Gus warned me. I bit down on my tongue until I tasted copper, my lungs squeezing and squeezing, a hot black hand wrapped around them, egging me on, wanting me to let loose and drive that gun back into the guy's head. I knew he was saying this shit to aggravate me, and it fucking worked. He didn't see how serious I was. He didn't know how far I would go.

Even I didn't know how far.

But part of me was really curious.

"Rope," I grunted through grinding teeth. "Get some rope, Gus."

Gus hesitated but went straight to the closet. He opened and let out a low whistle through his teeth.

"What is it?" I asked, not taking my eyes off the

guy. He was still staring back at me, daring me to do something, to shoot him. I didn't want to shoot him. I wanted answers.

"Ellie's clothes," he said quietly. "They're all here. That nutter saved them all these years."

That wasn't helping. "Rope, Gus."

I heard metal jangling and he came over to me with a belt. "Belts work just fine."

"I need three more. We're tying him to the bed."

He sighed and came back with more. "Do you mind telling me what you're going to do?"

I shook my head. "I want answers. Then we'll leave."

"Well, you better make it fast because unless they have gunfights here every evening, someone's going to report that. You can probably bet on the cops showing up."

"It'll go fast if he talks. If he doesn't talk, we've got nothing."

The man smiled at that. I took the energy I wanted to pummel into his face and put it toward wrapping the belt around one arm and looping it around one of the bedposts. Gus took care of the rest. Because the guy was quite short, we had to improvise around his legs with the addition of Javier's silk ties. It felt somewhat poetic.

It didn't take long before the man was tied spread eagle on the bloody bedspread. He still didn't look scared, didn't look like he was in any pain, didn't look like he was worried.

"Now, talk," I told him.

"You both are so dead," he said, slurring his words

around his fat lip. "What are you going to do, shoot me in the leg? You'll only attract more attention to yourself. Besides, I've had worse."

"Oh, good," I said, coming closer. "It'll be a nice experiment then, to see if I come close." I wasn't really sure who was talking, the words that were coming out of my mouth, the strange sense of calm, almost a high, that was replacing the rage. It scared me more than the anger had, than the blackness. This was something else. Sinister.

"Camden, maybe you should let me handle this," Gus said, taking a step closer.

I waved him off. "You can have the next go. I think he'll tell us where she went."

I shrugged off the backpack and pulled out my secret weapon, my tattoo machine. It still had ink in it too, bright blue.

"What the hell is that?" Gus asked, even though we all knew what it was.

"Tattoo gun," I explained. "Well, we call it a machine. In this case, gun seems more fitting. Doesn't fire bullets but it can fire a lot of pain if you apply it in the right place and press down hard enough." I took the needle and pressed it against the man's stomach just below his chest, feeling his pulse beneath his skin. "I've always wondered if I could tattoo someone's organs. You know someone is going to ask for that someday."

Finally I saw the man's eyes widen ever so slightly. I smiled back. "Really," I went on. "I'm curious. Care to be my experiment... what did you say your name was?"

The man's jaw wiggled back and forth. Debating.

"That's your first question. What's your name?"

"Camden, we don't have time for this."

I ignored Gus. "This is a liner needle, thick enough. Similar to what did the tattoos around your arms. Except that yours were done properly, and I've made some adjustments with the length of the needle. I bet I could at least puncture your stomach if I pressed hard enough. Maybe fill it with ink? Wouldn't that be something? I'd tattoo you from the inside out."

"Jesus," Gus muttered under his breath.

I plugged in the machine and stepped on the foot petal. "Your name," I repeated.

The man hesitated. I didn't. I plunged the tattoo needle into the middle of his abdomen, just below his rib cage, pressing it as far as it would go. It felt so incredibly wrong to do this, going against everything I'd ever been taught. It went beyond art now. It took me to another level. A bad place.

The man cried out from the pain and I kept the needle there as deep as it would go. An inch of a vibrating tattoo needle was a pain that no one should ever feel.

I almost felt sorry for him. Then I remembered who was on the line.

"F-Felipe," he stuttered, "Felipe Alvaraz."

"Good, good," I said, taking the needle out of his chest. A swirl of red blood and bright blue ink came together to form an overflowing pool of purple. "Next question. Is Ellie okay? Is she hurt?"

He shook his head. "She's not hurt. She's f-fine. She's the one who did this to my head."

I smiled to myself. Good girl.

"And where is Javier taking her? What does he want with her?"

Felipe's lips formed a thin line. I raised the machine, reminding him.

"Tell me and I won't do anymore. Where are they going and why?"

"Fuck you."

"Wrong answer. Gus, hold the back his head please."

Gus didn't move. I shot him a steely glance. He was frowning at me, the most concerned I'd ever seen him. "Gus, do it now. We don't have time."

He nodded ever so slowly and then leaned across the bed, pressing his big hands down on the man's forehead. Felipe shook his head back and forth, trying to escape, but Gus put his other hand on his chin, pinning him in place.

"What are you doing, Camden?" he asked.

"Women are going crazy for permanent eyeliner tattoos these days. Thought I'd jump in on a trend. Get some practice on what *not* to do."

The man's eyes flew to me in horror. I felt nothing. I didn't have any nerves left, and my hand was as steady as a rock. If this was what it felt like to be Javier, putting that bullet in Uncle Jim's head, well in some sick fucking way I could understand the pull.

"Hold him steady. I don't want to miss."

I took the machine, turning it on again, relishing the buzzing, and held it just above Felipe's eye. "It'll hurt less if you keep your eyes closed."

Actually it didn't matter. But he didn't have to know that.

I lowered the needle and the man shut his eyes tightly, struggling under Gus's sure grip. I pressed it, just a bit, into the scrunched-up eyelid. The man cried out. Then I pressed it in further, like puncturing a really dense grape.

Screams filled the room.

"Camden, stop," Gus said.

"Tell me where they went and why he has her or I'll remove it with your eyeball still attached." I pressed it a bit farther. Ink filled the hole. If he was lucky, he was getting ink around his cornea, causing permanent color but no major damage. If it was through his retina, he'd be blind for life.

"Fine!" Felipe screamed and then started hyper-ventilating. "T-they, he, Javier, he took her to Mexico."

I exchanged a glance with Gus. "Why? What's in Mexico?"

"Travis." The man sobbed. "Oh, please just take it out of my eye."

My lungs felt filled with sand. "I will," I told him, trying to breathe. "Where in Mexico?"

"I don't know. Veracruz, maybe. The gulf coast. Travis has places all over."

"Why is Javier taking her to see Travis?"

Felipe started shaking, convulsing, succumbing to the pain and panic. "I don't know! It wasn't part of the plan."

"What was the plan?" Gus asked quickly. The urgency was spreading.

"Her parents. He wanted her to kill her parents. He thought they'd come back here."

Those words sank over the room.

I shook my head. "Why would they come back here? Aren't they working for Travis?"

"I don't know. Please, please just let me go."

I looked to Gus for his opinion. He only nodded. It was over. We had the info and now we had to get out of there.

"Hold still, Felipe," I told him. While pressing down around his eyelid, I pulled the needle out. He let out another cry of pain and I stuck the machine in my backpack. "Now open your eye. Don't worry, I'm just checking to see if there's damage."

Felipe shook, afraid.

"Camden, we have to go now." In the distance sirens could be heard, wailing on the breeze.

"Look at me," I said, getting up and leaning over him.

Felipe tried to open his eye but couldn't. I placed my fingers on either side and forced it open. It was total fucking mess. Blue ink bleeding out from the white. But his iris and pupil were uncolored. "You won't be blind. You'll just look like an idiot for the rest of your life."

I turned around, wiping my hands on my jeans. "I guess we should leave him tied up, right?" I said to Gus. "If he's lucky, someone will set him loose."

"Yes," he said in an odd voice. I turned around to look at him. Gus had a gun pointed at Felipe's head.

"Gus, no!" I yelled, but it was too late.

He pulled the trigger. He shot Felipe right in the temple, causing his head to slump to the side. Alive one minute, dead in the next.

I had trouble speaking, the gunshot still ringing through my ears. "He would have been okay," I finally said. "I hadn't really hurt him."

He gave me an odd look. "No, but you could have. You wanted to."

"No. I didn't want him dead." It felt like a lie on my lips.

Gus came over to me and placed his meaty hand on my shoulder, looking me in the eye. "He would have talked. We still have the element of surprise. We can't afford to take any chances, not after tonight."

He walked toward the hall and paused in the doorway. "This is a different world now. You're not Camden McQueen. You're Connor Malloy. In this world, you will have to do things you never thought you'd do, things you'll wish you never did. I think you already got a taste of that today. That flavor will stay on your tongue. Now come on. We have to get out of here."

I followed him out the door, fighting the instinct to turn around and look at the mess we'd made. Felipe's death was as much on my hands as it was on Gus's.

Ink and blood.

CHAPTER THIRTEEN

Ellie

After the incident in the cockpit, Javier went back to ignoring me for a few days. Well, maybe he wasn't ignoring me so much as he was keeping quiet and oddly professional. Whatever intimacy we shared, those secrets dredged up from the past, was gone, as if it had never happened, and we were back to the strained relationship of blackmailer and hostage.

The next few days crawled by, time going slower out on the Gulf of Mexico. We saw very few boats, I suppose because it was still considered hurricane season. And yet the weather was absolutely beautiful, clear skies that mimicked the expanse of water, stretching forever and ever. We were sailing through nothingness. This was the place you'd come when you wanted to feel each and every minute pass through your skin.

I became more comfortable on the ship yet, at the same time, my nerves were frying in my chest like eggs in a pan. I didn't know what was expected of me when we finally got to Mexico, and I was too afraid to talk to Javier about it. Was it as I thought? Was I bait, or was Raul right, and I was the executioner?

Those words of his echoed in my mind, that I was no good at heart, that I was born to be bad. The way he said it was cheesy and laughable, but there was no mistaking his conviction. I knew deep down that I had spared Camden because it was the right thing to do, because I wanted to make up for every bad thing I had ever done to him, for everything in my life. I knew that was the reason I went with Javier. But Javier believed otherwise, and I knew he wasn't going to stop until his point was proven. He held the shackles to my past and was threatening me with them.

On our last evening out at sea, we spotted land. Actually, *I* spotted it. I was at the front of the boat, sitting on a beach towel I'd spread out on the deck. Massive Attack's "Angel" was playing from a set of iPod speakers I'd brought out from one of the lounges, the bass building up to that first glimpse of hazy landmass, just appearing on the smooth curve of the horizon. It was so jarring, so strangely terrifying and different.

"Land-ho!" I yelled, then laughed despite myself. I'd always wanted to say that.

I could hear some commotion on the back of the ship, maybe the crew or Raul taking it in. It was funny how something as normal such as land could be thrilling, but out at sea, in this dream state of deepwater blue and flying fish, it meant something for us all.

I hugged my knees to my chest, unable to take my

eyes away from the land as it came closer and closer. Suddenly there was a shadow over me and the air burned. Javier sat down on the deck beside me, matching my pose. He was all in cream today.

"It's strange, isn't it?" he asked, his eyes fastened on the horizon along with mine.

"Yeah. Hypnotic."

"It doesn't belong."

"You think?"

"We're free out here. Don't you feel that?"

I gave him a quick, curious glance. "You sound like a true sailor."

He nodded subtly. "It's why men everywhere head for the sea, all these years. Here you can be you. And that is it."

"Who are you out here?"

He squinted. "I don't know. But I think I'm happier."

I rubbed my lips together, spreading the last remnants of lip balm. "Then why are we going there? Why don't we sail forever?"

He turned his head to me sharply, brows raised. "You would like that? To be sailing with me?"

That wasn't exactly what I had said. "I'd be happier if we turned the boat around and went back the way we came."

He looked disappointed at the answer and brought his attention to the horizon again. "Is that so?"

Now was as good a time as any to bite the bullet. Even though the boat was turning slightly to run parallel to the coast, the land was still in sight, within reach, just beyond the haze.

"Javier," I began slowly, "do you want me to kill Travis? Do you want me to pull the trigger?"

He sucked in a breath through his teeth and tapped his fingers against his leg a few times. "Ellie, I don't want you to do anything you don't want to do."

"Yes you do. I don't want to do any of this. I want to go home."

"But you don't have a home. You don't have a family. You have nothing. You don't even have Camden."

I tried not to wince. "I don't need any of those things." That was a lie, of course, because I did need Camden. I needed him, to be good. But the farther we sailed, the more I knew I couldn't have him. He'd be enveloped by his own past, just as I was slowly getting sucked into mine.

"You need to let it go." He placed his hand on the deck and leaned on it, his watch gleaming. "Let go of what you thought was going to happen. Things changed. You chose this path and this is the one you are on. We'll be anchoring off a beach north of Los Tuxtlas. Then we'll take a car to a place near Veracruz. You will find Travis and you will...get to know him. This is where your path is going, Ellie, and this is the only way now."

I swallowed hard. "And what then? I get to know him, which I still think is ridiculous since he'll know who I am."

"I told you, he won't."

"He *will*."

"Do you think I'd set you up to fail?" he asked so sharply that I had to look at him. The sun had browned his face even more over the last few days and by contrast his eyes seemed lighter than ever. I wished he was wearing sunglasses.

"I don't know what I think," I finally responded.

"You will get to know him. You will lead him to me. I will kill him."

"And not me?"

"Only if you want to. Only if you think you're strong enough."

"Killing people has nothing to do with being strong."

He dipped his chin, locking me in a gaze that was becoming harder by the second. "It does when it's someone who deserves it. Who needs it. Do you not remember what he's done to us?"

My head jerked. "To *us*?"

His nostrils flared and he quickly got to his feet. He walked down the length of the boat toward the twin anchors, his loose pants billowing in the breeze like a flag.

I don't know why but I got up, placing the speakers on top of the towel so it wouldn't blow away, and followed him. We were motoring today, the jib and mainsail furled tightly, the ship easy to walk on.

He stopped at the front and leaned one arm against the jib mast. I stood a foot back, feeling the weird energy that was rolling off of him. I waited for him to speak; it seemed like hours.

"Once I found out that Travis wanted to cozy up to them, to Los Zetas, I knew in my heart of all hearts that things would end badly. Travis switched sides, even knowing what had happened to my father and my mother. He knew I would never make nice with them, that I would always fight them, that I would always try to bury them. Travis did it anyway, I think, to get away from me. Because I was threatening to him, you see? He knew everyone liked me better, that I was younger, smarter, faster. I was better than him in every way and he wanted me out of the picture. What better way to... *hurt* me...than to join them? Almost brilliant, right?"

I nodded even though he couldn't see me. He sighed and went on. "We split. It got ugly. Then it got uglier. We were alike so he wanted to make the same points that I tended to make. But he is a brutal man. You may think the same of me too, but you don't know him."

"I kind of know what he's capable of," I said quietly.

At that he turned around and his eyes drifted down to my leg before turning around and facing the horizon. "Yes, yes you do. And so Travis, Mr. Raines, he went and took something very dear to me."

It all clicked together. The ship rolling beneath my feet. "Beatriz." I breathed out.

"Yes, my eldest sister. The one who was in charge of the younger ones. My closest friend, really. He found her. He raped her, forcing her husband to watch. Then he killed her. Killed him. Killed their children. Cut off their heads and put them in front of a busy hotel, just outside the lobby. Burned the bodies nearby. Took a lot of pictures."

I gasped. I'd actually seen this on the news.

He acknowledged my expression. "So you know. You've seen it. He made his point and was sure the whole world saw it, made sure I'd see it no matter where I was. My sister and her family were an example of what Mexican drug violence was becoming. No one would ever forget what happened. And, of course, he made sure I knew what was coming next. That no one that I loved would ever be safe."

I wiped my palms on my pants. "Are your other sisters safe?"

"For now," he said, before turning to face me. "That's one of the reasons I am going to Mexico. Even when Travis is dead, I can't count on someone else not coming after them. We are like those zombies you see on TV, you know. We never really die. Someone else pops up in our place that looks like us and talks like us. We're all interchangeable."

"You're not like—" I began, and then cut myself off because I was going to say he was not like Travis when I knew he was. He wasn't as depraved as Travis, but he was still something else. Something bad and deadly and deplorable.

"I am," he said with a small smile. "And because I know I am, I know when we're safe and we aren't safe. Not while he's still alive. We have to kill him. Do you see now?"

I nodded, finding the fact that I was understanding his logic crazy. Once upon a time I'd wanted to throw acid in Travis's face and watch as his skin melted away. I never did it—Javier got in the way. And now he was in my way again, this time to end it once and for all.

I *did* want Travis dead. I knew it now. But whether that made me strong or not wasn't part of the equation. I would do this for myself, for Javier's sister, for her children, for the countless others who died or were tortured at his hands. For everyone that ever suffered because of drugs and money and guns and crime and everything I had once cloaked myself with.

"So," I said, feeling the landmass change in front of my eyes, turning from fear to something I wanted to embrace, "tell me everything I need to know."

A grin slowly spread across his face.

*   *   *

The next morning I awoke to a deep rumbling and excited cries. I got up quickly, feeling the excitement, and slid on a dress that reached the floor. It was one I'd picked up during an outing to Miami with Javier back in the day, a bright green and yellow floral thing that managed to look both fashionable and hide my scars at the same time.

Of course, my scars were beautiful now that Camden transformed them. But old habits still died hard.

I ran up to the first deck and peered off the side. To our left was the huge expanse of a sandy beach flanked by rich green cliffs and lush forest farther inland. The sight literally took my breath away.

"Beautiful, isn't it?" Javier's voice came soaring from the bridge. I shielded my eyes to look up at him. At the front of the ship, the anchors dropped in, the mechanics whirring until they made contact with the soft seafloor.

I looked back at the land. We were here. Mexico.

I stood at the railing for some time as everyone strode purposefully around me, getting prepared. The beach seemed to go on forever and looked deserted at first, with no sign of civilization. But when my eyes adjusted to the glitter of the water and the haze of the morning sun, I could see a couple of bright tents set up on the beach, nestled into some palm trees, and a fishing boat dragged onto shore. It wasn't the white-sand beach I expected to see but something more earthy and wild.

A hand was at my elbow. I knew who it was without looking.

"Are you all packed?" Javier asked.

I nodded. "What beach is this again?"

"Playa Escondida. Hidden Beach." His hand dropped away and I could feel his eyes slicing down my back. "I loved you in this dress."

Then he walked away, barking orders in Spanish at the crew as they prepared the Zodiac to be lowered into the water. I chewed on my lip for a few seconds, my mind quieted, my insides tumbling.

Soon I, Javier, Raul, Peter, and one of the crew boys, Oscar, were taking careful steps down the ladder and into the Zodiac. A wave flowed past and pitched the boat away from me as I climbed in. I lost my footing momentarily, but Javier was there, wrapping both hands around my arms, holding me in place.

"Are you okay?" he asked, holding me too close to him.

I nodded, wanting him to step away. But he held on, leading me over to a seat. Oscar followed and lowered the rest of the bags onto the boat. Then one of the crew boys threw the rope back in the boat and we were puttering backward. It felt like we were all moving as slowly as the waves, rolling up and down, the ship, Javier's beautiful *Beatriz*, growing smaller and smaller as we headed toward the shore.

Javier told us that landing on the beach might be a bit tricky since we'd have to surf the Zodiac in. It wasn't exactly the most graceful or classy way of getting to shore, but a ship like Javier's would have to be as inconspicuous as possible. There was no way we could dock it at the marina without drawing attention to ourselves. Here, at Escondida, we really were hidden. There were no resorts, no restaurants, no roads. Just surf, sand, and jungle.

Luckily, Javier was just as skilled at maneuvering the Zodiac as he was at killing people. We crashed onto the shore, getting only slightly wet, and soon the men had jumped out of the boat and were quickly hauling it farther inland.

Javier came over to help me but I climbed out before he had a chance to touch me again. For someone who said he'd never touch me, he'd been doing a lot more of it lately. Once all of our gear was on the beach, my duffel bag plus a few leather satchels for the rest, Javier nodded at Oscar to return to the vessel.

"I'll be in touch," he told him. "You keep her out there, she'll be good even in the biggest storm. If I call you and tell you to leave, you do it. Take her to the resort near Campeche, to the marina. I have a space reserved there just in case. Wait there until I get in touch with you. That ship, she is your biggest priority."

Oscar nodded eagerly, happy to have this responsibility. I wondered how trustworthy he was, then thought trust would never be an issue with Javier in charge. The consequences of a failure of trust would always be too vile.

The four of us stood on the beach, our ankles soaked from the sea, and watched as Oscar fought the Zodiac back through the waves. There were a few times when it looked like it was going to flip over, but he managed to power through and soon he was tethered to *Beatriz*, the ship gleaming in the distance.

We all looked at each other, and for the first time since landing, I felt the gravity of land beneath my feet. The way it held me there. What it meant to be ashore.

Javier read my face and waved his arm. "Come on, we have to get moving."

He turned and headed off toward a stream that snaked out of the jungle, a tributary that almost made it to the sea. We walked along the sand, my eyes drawn to the campers down the beach. They looked like a Mexican family, lighting a campfire, kids running around. I wondered what they thought of the yacht anchored offshore, of our arrival, or if they thought anything about it at all.

Once we were in the forest, the temperature spiked. We were all sweating in seconds as the overhanging trees and dense vegetation seemed to hold the heat in. We came across a narrow dirt path and took that for a few minutes, all of us silent, thinking and wary.

The smell of horse shit assaulted my nose, as did a beam of sun that suddenly broke through the trees and illuminated the spot in front of us. There was a clearing with a small paddock and a shanty. Six bony horses stood there listlessly swatting flies with their tails.

"Hola?" Javier called out. We waited, hearing a commotion in the shanty, and the door flew open. An old Mexican man with long gray hair half tucked up under a baseball cap came out, a book in his hands. He looked as bony as the horses in his care.

Javier spoke rapid-fire Spanish to him, too fast for me to pick up. From what I gathered, the horses were to be our transportation. I eyed them nervously. I loved horses and had always been comfortable on one, but heading through the Mexican jungle who-the-fuck knows where with members of a cartel was something different.

Finally the man nodded and clapped his hands together enthusiastically before heading back to his shanty.

Javier jerked a thumb in his direction. "That's Burt Reynolds."

"Burt Reynolds?"

He shrugged gracefully. "That's what he calls himself. Doesn't speak English, so don't bother trying. He's taking us to Montepío. Only way in or out of there is by horseback."

"Or boat," I mused, and watched as Burt came back out of the shanty with bridles and packs. He moved spritely for an old, withered-looking man, and in no time the horses were ready. He gestured for us to come over and started yammering in Spanish to me about a small buckskin mare.

"Her name is Churro." Javier leaned in to me. "Try not to eat her."

I grimaced at his bad joke and introduced myself to

the horse by letting her smell my hand. She was entirely disinterested.

There was no saddle, just straps and packs wrapped around the withers and chest, where my duffel bag was now secured.

"If I'd known I'd be getting on a horse today, I would have worn jeans," I said under my breath.

Burt came over to me, giving me the signal for a leg up, complete with a toothy grin. I shook my head, having no interest in giving the man a peep show, no matter how badly he looked like he needed it.

Suddenly Javier's hands were around my waist, his long fingers nearly meeting in the middle. "Here, I'll help you." Before I could protest he was lifting me up, my legs akimbo. I pulled up the hem of my dress just in time, grateful that it was wide and flowing and stretched across the back of the horse.

Burt was on the other side, trying to help me settle in, and he started squawking about something. The word "tattoo." Javier's head looked up sharply, his eyes flaring, mine going straight to the leg on Burt's side. The skirt was hiked up to my knee exposing my cherry blossoms, so bright and daring in the tropical sunlight.

Javier zipped over and looked at my leg. It seemed that Burt was quite pleased with the tattoo, but Javier wasn't.

He ran his finger down one of my scars, following a twisting stem. "What is this?"

"A tattoo, obviously. Even Burt knew what it was." I wish I could say I felt some kind of relief in Javier finally seeing it, but I didn't. I felt nervous and I didn't know why.

"When did you do this? It's still raised!" His voice was hoarse. He kept looking at the tattoo, feeling it.

"When I was in Vegas. Camden did it," I told him. My eyes shot to Burt to see what he was making of all of this. He was watching the both of us, smile locked, until he met my eyes. Then he went off to busy himself with Raul and Peter who were bringing their horses over to the fence post in order to mount them.

Javier didn't seem to be able to take in that information. He looked confused, lost, off guard. This was so rare to see and yet I felt no pride in making him that way. I just wanted to forget about it.

"Why did you do this?" he asked, swallowing hard. "Your leg was fine before."

"It wasn't," I said, feeling irritated now. "And now I'm proud of it."

"This is the first I've seen it. Why don't you ever wear shorts?"

I hated that question—I'd dealt with it my whole life. I gathered the reins in my hands and lightly clucked to Churro, the horse's shoulder pushing Javier out of the way. "I think we have more important things to discuss than a damn tattoo."

Javier reached up and grabbed the reins, yanking the horse's head back.

Burt cried out, admonishing him, but Javier didn't care. He glared at me until I could feel the heat, his knuckles turning white as he gripped the leather.

"You let that boy mark you?" he sneered.

Oh, of course this was a jealousy thing.

"Yeah," I said deliberately, leaning forward on the horse's neck, "I did. I felt like I needed more. One tattoo just wasn't doing it for me."

I hoped that made him angry. Really angry. In a sick way I wanted him to hit me. Just so I could forever throw it in his face and make him feel like less of a man. Another part of me was afraid that it might actually happen. He looked like a snake about to strike, a face that was both ice and fire, someone who wanted blood and vengeance and to prove just how fucking powerful he was.

We were locked in a showdown of pinprick pupils and venomous hearts until Raul got our attention.

"I hate to break up...whatever this is, but we have to make it to Montepío by noon, is that right?"

Finally Javier broke the staring contest, letting go of the reins with a sharp inhale. "Yes, thank you. We do. Let's get a move on."

He mounted his horse with ease, springing up like a gymnast, and Burt led us out of the corral. I straightened up off the horse's neck, feeling dazed, as if I had been caught in some dream. I looked down at my hands, only now noticing that I had balled them up into fists. I opened one and saw blood where my own nails had dug in.

CHAPTER FOURTEEN

Camden

"So, Camden," Gus said, his hands squeezing the wheel like a stress ball. "When did Ellie first break your heart?"

We were right outside of San Antonio and heading toward the border crossing at Nuevo Laredo. Apparently the border there was pretty lax and Gus didn't expect us to get questioned much, if at all. The Mexicans didn't really care who came into the country, even though the border lineup on the other side promised to be a nightmare.

We couldn't take chances, though. I was all poised to cross over as Connor Malloy, a regular Joe and not a wanted fugitive.

"What makes you think she broke my heart?" I asked, looking at the flat, dry scenery skirt past us. Ranches, ranches, ranches.

I saw him shrug out of the corner of my eye. "Only

a hunch. Not many men turn into the tattoo artist version of Laurence Olivier in *Marathon Man*. Just swap torture with a dentist drill for a tattoo needle."

"I've seen the movie," I muttered. I looked down at his watch on my wrist, feeling heavy and foreign. It was four in the afternoon and we'd been driving nonstop since we'd left Ocean Springs. We'd been lucky enough to get out of Javier's house without anyone seeing us, taking the beach around to the car, but we didn't want to push our luck. The Mexican border seemed extremely inviting for both of us, now that Gus had killed two people.

I shook my head, trying to make sense out of what had happened. As before, no sense came. I completely lost every sense of right and wrong and good and bad. I became this black, suffocating thing, everything I feared in others. I became Javier. I became my father.

That wasn't me. I didn't want to see that person again. He was getting locked in my head along with everything else I didn't want to think about.

Or maybe that person was what happened when all the things I hid deep inside finally came out to play.

"Don't want to talk about it," Gus pondered. "I understand."

It was true, I didn't want to talk about it. But Gus talking and asking me shit was the first time in days he'd shown any interest in me at all. He was treating me with a bit more respect now. Maybe he was impressed. Or scared that I'd tattoo his balls in his sleep.

I sighed and sat back in my seat, hands in my lap, fidgeting. "I fell in love with Ellie in high school."

"Sweethearts, huh?"

I smirked. "No. Just friends. And only for a short while. We were the resident freaks of the school. Ellie with her limp and scars. Me and my penchant for wearing makeup and a lot of vinyl."

"Makeup?"

The way Gus said it, I knew what he was thinking.

"Don't worry," I explained. "I'm not gay. At least, that's what everyone jumps to as a conclusion. Even my father. I was a goth, an artist. The art fag, as they called me. Whatever, I had a lot of names. And I was beat on often, as you can imagine. Ellie was my only friend."

"I see. A friend."

"Yup. Isn't that the plight of every geeky teenager out there? Always doomed to be the friend? So anyway, I was in love with her, and every day I'd try to work up the nerve and the guts to tell her how I felt and to kiss her. One day I just did it."

"How was that?"

I chewed on my lip, trying to figure out how best to explain it. "It took something away from me." After I first felt Ellie's lips on mine, the warmth, sweetness, I was never the same. She took a piece of me that I was unable to get back until I was inside her, feeling her heart and her sins in my hands.

I was so afraid I'd never get to experience that again. All those years of longing, of looking for that part of me, and she was the only one who could supply it. She really was the only one I truly, drowning in my passion, *loved*.

Even at her very worst, she made me want to be a better man. To be good enough for the both of us.

"She must have cared about you a lot to walk away with that man."

"He is no man," I spat out. "He's a monster."

I could tell Gus wanted to say something about that but he didn't. He just gave a grunt.

I took the subject around the corner. "Do you think Ellie knows he wants her to kill her parents? I can't figure it out. Why?"

"I don't think there's much reason to any of this."

"I think you're wrong," I argued, jabbing my finger on the dusty dashboard. "You know how calculated he is. He's had six years to come after her. There's a reason behind everything now."

"Knowing there's a reason isn't helping us get an answer."

I studied Gus, his jowly face helped only by his beard, small eyes, gray bushy brows. He looked like your friendly neighbor on a TV show, a real Mr. Friendly. But this was a man who had shot and killed two people and didn't seem to care much about it. I wondered if I'd ever surround myself with normal people again or if this was the life I'd have to lead forever. Was this what it felt like to be Ellie, to never know whom to trust or where you'll next lay your head?

I chewed on my lip again, feeling some of that pain of when I first caught her robbing me come back. If only she'd really decided to go straight and get a job in Palm Valley and settle down. Somehow I would have gotten out of the money-laundering business...at least

I would have tried. I never would have had to catch her. We'd never have to run or worry about getting caught. We could have settled down in my tiny house above the shop and lived a good life.

But I guess Javier would have shown up anyway. Wanting her in exchange for fifty thousand dollars. What on earth was worth fifty thousand dollars? Was it just to kill her parents? To kill Travis? Was Javier seriously going around and killing everyone who had ever hurt her, even without her say?

Or was there something more going on?

A flash of him and her flooded my head, bare legs tangled together, my art on her leg, his hands tracing her scars, the flowers, everything. My throat closed up. It couldn't be that. It couldn't be *that*. Because if it was, it meant one of two things: He would either rape her or take full advantage of her. In either case, I'd take that tattoo machine and draw him a new asshole before I rammed it straight into the motherfucker's skull. And if it wasn't that, Ellie must have wanted to be with him.

"Are you all right, boy?" Gus asked, taking his foot off the gas. "Your lip is bleeding."

I looked down at my hand where a drop had fallen, ruby red and glossy. Like the finest ink. I wiped my hand across my mouth, smearing it. Art.

"Camden!" Gus barked.

I jumped in my seat and looked at him. "What?"

He frowned. "You looked all sorts of wrong there."

I nodded and leaned my head back. "Just thinking of things I shouldn't. So once we get across the border, then what? 'They went to Mexico' is kind of a vague route to take."

"It is. We'll ask around."

"Is asking around about one of the largest and deadliest drug cartels in Mexico, while being two gringos *in* Mexico, really the wisest decision?"

"I have my sources," he said. "If they haven't turned."

"*If* they haven't turned?" I repeated.

He shot me a quick grin. "Everyone has their price these days."

I was getting to know that a little too well.

*   *   *

Despite me fumbling with my passport like a goddamn fool, the border crossing was easy. Gus was right, they didn't really care who was going in. We kept driving until nightfall, when we reached a small settlement just before Monterrey. That's when we were pulled over by a state police officer wearing a ski mask and holding an automatic assault rifle.

"*Buenos noches.* Where are you going?" he asked us, switching to English once he noticed how white we were.

"To see a friend of ours," Gus answered amicably.

The officer peered into the back of the GTO. We might have been able to go through the border with no inspection, but I didn't know if it would be the same case here. I tried not to tense up but, fuck, what kind of a cop wears a ski mask?

Then he rapped on the roof of the car and told us to drive on.

Gus gave him a small wave and we roared off. We were a ways down the highway before he let out a large puff of air.

"What?" I asked him, not used to seeing him anxious. It made me worry.

"The police here are all controlled by Los Zetas."

I watched the buildings grow larger and more affluent as we headed toward the city. "I'm not surprised. But we're good. We don't belong to any cartel."

"He who casts doubt on himself is often as good as dead," he said.

I looked at him askew. "Did you just make that up?"

A beat passed. "Yes. No good?"

I grinned and shook my head, letting out some of my frayed nerves. "No, Gus, it's no good."

We drove around the city of Monterrey, a huge, sprawling mess that grew darker and quieter as we went on. Gus told me the entire city had a sort of unofficial curfew, which made our car with its fake Cali plates stand out. Even though the city was still one of the largest cosmopolises in all of Mexico, it was under a different sort of law. Whether we were looking for Los Zetas or not didn't matter when we were two white dudes in a cool car. Prime kidnapping material.

Soon we were pulling up to a small house in a nearby town that seemed to consist of a gas station and a post office. The building didn't look like much of anything, but it seemed to be an unofficial hotel, and the plump woman who answered the door with two children at her heels, up way past their bedtime, was more than happy to let us stay.

She led us through to the back of the house where we had our own room and a tiny bathroom. American magazines sat on a bedside table.

"I stayed here once, a long time ago," Gus said as he stretched out on one of the tiny twin beds. "She was thin back then, if you can believe it."

"Two jokes in one day," I said. "A record."

He smiled, then covered it up by turning off the light. There was a chance he was finally warming up to me.

I didn't bother getting under the sheets. The oppressive heat filled up our tiny room in minutes, and the rickety fan overhead did nothing disperse it. I closed my eyes and thought of Ellie.

There was a moment back in high school that Ellie never knew about. I never wanted to tell her, what would be the point? We were both sixteen and hadn't talked properly for years. It was after I'd done the photography project on her and frankly I knew she hated my guts. She considered me a freak, thinking I was creepy and obsessive and a bit of a stalker. Sadly, I was all of those things. That was just me, and I couldn't help it.

There had been a school dance, the Spring Fling or something lame like that. Ellie didn't go. I never expected her to. But I did. Just to be a pain in the ass, really. I wanted to show up and have people whisper to each other, "Oh, the queen is here." The attention, no matter how fucked up, was better than staying at home listening to my dad scream at my stepmother. He always would scream at me afterward.

I went, dressed in a tux, like a normal person, except

my tux was pastel blue. Yeah, I was trying to do an homage to *Dumb and Dumber*, and it was lost on most of the school. So, of course, I'd already been shoved around by a few dickheads by the time I'd arrived.

But there was this one dick, Curran Simpson, a real fucking jackass with big fists and a bigger mouth, who came barreling up to me and spilled all of his punch down the front of my tux.

The anger was already threatening to come out. I did what I could to keep it inside, to do what I had always done, which was to take it, take it, take it.

Then he says to me, his voice low, as if he didn't want to be heard, "Where's your retarded girlfriend? The one you're stalking all the time. Have you stolen her fake leg yet? Do you jack off to it?"

None of what he was saying really made any sense. He was a fucking idiot through and through. But it didn't matter. I lost it for the first time, let the blackness out. I was high above my body, pummeling the shit out of the guy. I don't know how I did it. Suddenly he was knocked to the ground and I was on top of him, punching him like a man possessed. I got maybe three good hits before one of his friends pulled me off and held me there while he retaliated. And of course he retaliated worse.

I had a broken nose from the fight, and Curran was suspended for a week. Even though I threw the first punch, even though I actually knocked the big fucker down, no one ever mentioned it. The teachers were so used to me getting beat up that they were more than happy to put him out of school for a while. I wasn't his only victim. As for me, it got twisted into an urban legend, that Camden finally went crazy and we better make sure he doesn't bring homemade bombs to school. The kids definitely stayed away from me, if they hadn't already.

That was probably my first shining moment, that feeling of actually winning for once. The adrenaline coupled with the fear of myself and what I could do, what I *might* do, was addicting. But I never acted out like that again. I wouldn't do it for just anyone.

Only for her. Only for Ellie.

I must have fallen asleep soon after those thoughts because before I knew it, the morning sun was streaming in through the window and I thought I was going to choke on the humidity. I sat up, feeling disgusting. The bed was soaked from my sweat, and when I put my glasses on, they fogged up in seconds.

I got up and pulled off my sticky shirt just as Gus came out from the bathroom, completely dressed and looking ready to go.

"Jesus," he said as he eyed my chest and abs.

I looked down. Sometimes I forgot about my tattoos. Or rather I'd forget that not everyone had them. "Not a fan of tattoos, Gus?"

"Not after seeing you wield a needle," he said, and motioned for me to turn around. I did so, not feeling shy in the slightest. If there was anything I loved to talk about it, it was my tattoos. And, well, I'd been working out pretty much every day for the last seven years. My body was hard and ripped as shit, and it felt good to make Gus take notice, to let him know that I wasn't some pushover, that I could do more than hold my own in a fight.

But I guess I already proved that the other day.

"These are something else. You do them yourself?"

"Only the ones I can reach, but I drew them all. I have a few artists in Palm Springs that I trust to carry them out."

"Are they everywhere?" He was wincing as he said it.

I winked at him. "I think that's between Ellie and me."

He gave me an unimpressed look then went over to the door. "I'll go get us some breakfast for the road. Can you be ready in five? We're meeting someone."

I nodded and ten minutes later we were back in the GTO, munching on a doughy pastry, the smell of hot dirt blowing in through the open windows.

"Who is this someone?" I asked, crumbs scattering in my lap.

He said, "An old friend." Wasn't that always the case? The old friend. That was the case between us right now. Me and Ellie's old friend.

We drove for some time, flipping through an assortment of Spanish radio stations, before the air began to lift a bit and the sharp bite of salt hit us. The Gulf of Mexico sparkled amid refinery plants as we hit Tampico. We went through the city sprawl, the startling amount of Starbucks and Burger Kings and Walmarts, before we entered the real Mexico again and were hurtling down a pale dirt road, dust flying behind us like flour, dodging giant potholes and overhanging branches.

We eventually arrived to a little piece of paradise. A cream sand beach was lapped by azure water while a beach shack stood nestled in a crop of palm trees. Gus pulled the car up beside a mud-splattered Jeep just as a man with an even bigger mustache than his came out of the house, arms wide.

"Gus!" the man cried out. Gus gave me a sheepish look.

"This is Dan," he explained. "He's very…affectionate."

We got out of the car and Dan immediately embraced him. I held back a chuckle as Gus awkwardly hugged the man back. Gus then waved me over.

I shuffled through the sand, absently enjoying the breeze that washed over me while keeping my senses on high alert. As nice—or huggy—as Dan seemed, I wasn't one to trust old friends. Sometimes I wondered if I even trusted Gus.

"Hello, Camden," Dan said, taking my hand in a two-handed shake. He was about a foot shorter than me, in his early fifties, with a huge handlebar mustache and fake Ray-Ban sunglasses. His hair was cropped short and unusually dark, and he had pockmarks on both cheeks leftover from bad acne. His teeth were yellowed. Overall the vibe was genuine and I was glad for the lack of hostility so far, even I knew things could always turn.

If they haven't turned already. Gus's phrase repeated in my head.

"Hello, Dan," I told him, trying to make my smile look easy. "Beautiful little spot you've got here."

"You like?" he said, eyes gleaming. "Oh, you must come inside. I'll get you Americans some beer. Real beer, you know?"

We went inside and sat down on his small screened porch that faced the incoming surf and chugged back three Bohemias. The small talk came first, Gus and Dan catching up on old times while Gus occasionally filled me in as Dan smoked like a chimney, one cigarette after another. They knew each other from when Dan used to live in San Diego, illegally, and Gus's ex-girlfriend and his wife were friends. Dan eventually got deported, even though Gus had tried to pull a few favors for him with the LAPD, and settled here to open his own business renting kayaks to tourists. I didn't know what happened to the business since I didn't see any kayaks and the Tampico area wasn't a big tourist attraction. But fronts were fronts and I knew how to spot one.

Dan's wife was now dead, something he glossed over very quickly, and I knew from the way his eyes burned at the mention of her that it wasn't accidental. The drug cartels had their fingers in absolutely everything in Mexico.

"Now, Gus," Dan said, his face growing serious after he finished off the remainder of his beer. "You know I love to see old friends. When I heard what happened to you…"

A strange hush came over them and both their eyes darted to me and back again. This thing, this mysterious health problem that had afflicted Gus, had come up again and again but I had yet to figure it out. I didn't want to ask. Maybe I was going to have to. I didn't want the man having a stroke on me if that's what it came down to.

"I miss you, you know?" Dan continued. "But please tell me what brought you here all of the sudden."

Gus sucked in his upper lip until the bristles of his mustache stood out. "We need to find Travis Raines. He's somewhere in Mexico, maybe Veracruz."

Dan's eyes nearly bulged out of his head. "You want to find Travis Raines? El Hombre Blanco?"

"What, seriously, that's his nickname?" I blurted out.

Dan ignored me, getting out of his wicker chair and walking over to the kitchen. "My God, my God. We need some coffee. Yes, we do."

Gus and I exchanged a glance as Dan put on the kettle and began carrying things over to the table for us, cups, saucers, a sugar bowl, nondairy creamer. Then he sat back down and lit another cigarette. His hand shaking.

"Tell me why you need to find him."

"It's not so much him that we need to find but a man who is after Travis. He has a woman with him. We think he's planning on using her to assassinate El Hombre Blanco."

Dan blinked a few times, puffing back rapidly. "I see. And this is a bad thing?"

"He will get the woman killed. Getting to Travis Raines isn't easy. If it was, he'd already be dead."

"Yes, Gus, I know this. What do you think I do all day here? Think of fairy tales?"

I looked at Dan imploringly. "The woman, Ellie, is very important to me. The man she's with will hurt her. She's not a gun for hire. She'll have to do it against her will, and it will end very badly, for everyone, if we don't get to her first."

"Who is the man?"

"Javier Bernal," Gus supplied.

Dan's eyes widened and he quickly put out his cigarette. "Javier is here in Mexico?"

"You know him?" I asked.

Dan gave me a petulant look and strode to the kettle, which was just starting to steam. "Yes, I know him. We all know him. We are all part of the same family when you trace us back. Sinaloa."

The *other* extremely dangerous and fanatical cartel.

Dan poured the water into a French press and brought it over to the table.

"This sounds like something Javi would do."

And now he knew Bernal on a first-name basis. This wasn't right. This couldn't be good. I shot Gus a look, but he was focused on the coffee. I wanted to keep staring at him, get him to look up, but Dan was already observing me, eyes narrowed.

I cleared my throat and nodded at the press. "Local coffee?"

Dan watched me for a few painful beats before he said, "Yes, of course. None of that American shit."

Gus smiled. "I'm pretty sure half of the American shit comes from Mexico at any rate."

Dan shrugged lightly. "This is true. But we don't put chemicals in our coffee."

"Not like what you're putting in your lungs," Gus joked.

And suddenly they seemed like old pals ribbing each other again. Maybe I was creating these situations in my head. Maybe my gut was wrong.

But my gut was never wrong.

Dan poured us both a cup of the fragrant, dark liquid and said, "Do you know where Javi is?"

We shook our heads. "No," Gus said. "We figured you could tell us."

"Why would I tell you?"

"To be a friend, I guess." Gus was still smiling, but his posture had changed ever so subtly. He was aware now, more alert. Maybe because Dan was being stubborn. Or maybe because Dan and Javier were friends, something Gus couldn't have seen coming, and friends sometimes go to great lengths to protect each other. If my devotion to Ellie had brought me here, perhaps Dan's loyalty to Javier was just as strong.

The bad feeling in my gut multiplied when Dan put the coffee press down and one of his hands, so easily, so slowly, went to his side and under the table. I didn't look, I didn't acknowledge it. I only sipped my coffee all the while knowing he had a gun under that table, maybe affixed to the underside, and it was pointing at us.

We wouldn't be walking out of there alive. Not unless we could do something about it.

"Well, I don't know where Javi is. But Travis is in Veracruz. Fucking Zetas have taken over the whole city, such a shame."

"Where in Veracruz?" I asked.

Dan smiled wryly and took a sip of his coffee, bringing his hand back on the tabletop. "I do not have his address, if that is what you're asking. It's a large compound in the hills. Where the rich bastards live."

"How do you think Ellie will get close to him?" It

was a long shot, but one I felt I needed to ask. If I was right and there was a gun under the table, he'd be telling us the truth because the dead don't talk. The dead wouldn't spoil this attempt on Travis's life, someone Javier, Dan, and maybe Ellie wanted killed.

"I don't know," he said carefully. He put his coffee cup back down. One hand went under the table again while the other was going for a cigarette.

"Can I have one?" I said quickly, putting my hand out. "I always wanted to try the Mexican kind."

Dan laughed out of the corner of his mouth. "Okay, fine."

He gave me a cigarette, his other hand never straying. I held mine out for the Zippo lighter and he gave me that too.

I really hoped Gus was right about Coffee-mate being extremely flammable and that the theory extended to all nondairy creamers, not just the name brands. If he was wrong, we'd be dead. But if I sat there and did anything else, we'd be dead too. The minute either of us reached for our guns, Dan would know and pull the trigger. He had the upper hand. I had the lower cut.

I started playing with the flame, running my thumb over the wheel again and again. "So you don't know what Javi's plan could be? I thought you were good friends."

Dan stiffened. "We are not good friends. I admire him. He's done a lot for us and he's stayed loyal, unlike Travis." So much animosity seethed off his words. I knew what had happened to Dan's wife now. "Travis knows how hated he is. I think he's even a threat to the

Zetas. No one just switches sides like that for no reason. He has people following him everywhere he goes and, as you would think, he doesn't leave his house all that often. Just to the market on Saturdays where he walks around like he's Marlon Brando."

I made the flame dance back and forth. Dan's one hand stayed under the table. With his other he put a cigarette to his mouth.

I tilted my head to look at Gus. His face was drawn together, looking incredibly sad. It must have hurt, what he was realizing about his friend.

"Hey, Gus, would you mind passing me that non-dairy creamer over there." I nodded at the container.

He swallowed hard and handed it to me.

"Our coffee too strong for you?" Dan asked.

"Yes, quite." I poured some of the powder in my coffee and then screwed the lid off the container. Dan was watching me, puzzled.

Finally he said, "Checking for poison?"

I shook my head. "Want your lighter back?"

He frowned but nodded and put his cigarette between his lips. I reached across to give him back the lighter and said, "Perhaps Gus and I should be going. We seem to be taking up a lot of your time." I wanted to get this show rolling.

Dan's eyes flicked to Gus and back to me. His hands grasped the lighter but I didn't let go. I stared deep at him and gave him a little smile. "You wouldn't happen to have a gun under the table, would you?"

The corner of his mouth hitched up. "You're pretty observant for an American. What gang are you from?"

"I'm a tattoo artist."

"Dan," Gus said in a long breath. "It's me. I didn't come here to cause trouble, you know this. I only want to know where Travis is."

Dan avoided his friend's eyes and kept them on me and the lighter I was refusing to give up. Not now, not yet. "You want to stop something that should happen. I can't let you do that. You are my friend, but my loyalty to my family comes first."

"Revenge over love," I said.

"Yes, though not that poetic."

He adjusted the gun under the table. I chose that moment to let go of the lighter. He leaned back in his chair and brought the lighter under his cigarette.

"I'm sorry," he said, flicking the Zippo.

Here went nothing and everything at the same time. "No, *I'm* sorry."

I flung the contents of the nondairy creamer into his face just as the lighter flamed. The particles hung suspended in air for one moment, a cloud of white that enveloped Dan's face, before the flame interacted with them.

It went up in an orange blaze, the heat and flames making me fall back out of my seat. Dan was screaming, his face, hair, everything, ignited in a horrible fireball that had stretched to the roof before simmering back down into a puff of curdling black smoke.

There was no time to take it all in. I scrambled to my feet and ran out of Dan's house, Gus right behind me.

I got behind the wheel this time and the moment Gus was in the car, I peeled back through the dense sand. Once the GTO hit solid dirt, I spun it around with a hit to the e-brake and bolted forward. We bounced and pitched and crunched down that pale dirt road, the car feeling alive beneath my hands, willing to take us anywhere we wanted, as fast as it wanted.

Gus wasn't driving anymore.

We didn't say a word to one another until we finally whipped out onto the main paved street that would take us back to the highway, overtaking a donkey cart as we did so, chickens squawking in our wake.

"I'm sorry, Gus," I told him, my eyes darting to the rearview mirror to make sure we weren't being followed. I didn't know how badly Dan was burned, if he was still alive with only minor redness, or if he was rolling on the floor suffering as his skin melted away. I didn't want to think about it. I couldn't.

"He would have killed us," he said gruffly, his attention turned to the window. I noticed he was wringing his hands together.

"I know. And I'm sorry for that too."

A moment passed before he said, "Thank you."

That was the most we talked about it. Another incident swept away. Not because there wasn't more to say, because there was. I mean, the goddamn coffee creamer actually worked. I had opened my mouth to say something about that, then closed it, thinking it in poor taste considering what had happened.

It didn't matter because in the next instance I looked at the rearview mirror again and saw flashing lights far behind us. It almost looked like a mirage in the sun-soaked haze of the road.

"Oh, shit," I swore.

Gus twisted in his seat and looked behind him. "Double shit. They'll be with the Zetas." He eyed me nervously. "Do you want me to drive?"

I gripped the wheel tighter and gunned it. "I think I've got this."

The chase was on.

CHAPTER FIFTEEN

Ellie

The trek through the jungle didn't take as long as I imagined it would, but it felt a hell of a lot longer with the tension between Javier and me. Burt led the way, a chatty Cathy to Peter behind him, while I was sandwiched behind Raul in front, Javier in back. I could feel his damn eyes on me the whole time, burning holes at my back, at the tattoo on my leg. As childish as it was for me to enjoy rubbing it in, that Camden had left his mark, it also made me worry for him. Javier was nothing if not jealous and unpredictable. I was doing all of this to protect Camden, but was I putting him in danger all the same?

Aside from being awkward, the ride was unbearably sweaty and uncomfortable, horsehair sticking to my legs, mosquitoes feasting on every bare inch of me. Howler monkeys added to the hostility, hurling animal obscenities from hidden spots in the trees above.

In comparison, the tiny seaside hamlet of Montepío seemed like a godsend.

Javier handed over a wad of U.S. bills to Burt, who took it from him eagerly, stuffing it away in various pockets like a squirrel. Raul helped me off Churro, much to my dismay, especially since his hands seemed to linger a bit around my ass.

I swatted him away under the guise of wiping off horsehair and glared at him. Javier was watching us over Burt's shoulder, cold and calculating, but I didn't care. I just wanted to be in someplace air-conditioned, a cold drink in hand. To be honest, I think I wanted to be back on the boat. Captive or not, it had been the only place I'd been able to get a routine going since I'd left Palm Valley for the first time.

We handed the horses to Burt, who attached them all together in a long line and led them back into the jungle.

"Now what?" I asked Javier, hands on my hips. The four of us were standing on a cobblestoned street corner and getting some pretty curious looks from the barefoot children walking past.

Javier looked to Raul and Peter, completely ignoring me. "There's a car waiting for us around the corner from here. It will take us to Alvarado. We have a house there, disguised as a fish shop. I'm afraid it might smell a bit, but that's as far as we can get to Veracruz without causing trouble. At least, not right away."

I could have sworn that last bit was directed at me.

We followed Javier down the street, past the faded signs of small shops and businesses, past the group of

kids who were hiding behind a phone booth and peering at us with gap-toothed grins, past a produce stand
where an owner and a customer were in a showdown
over the price of bananas. It was such a scene of old
Mexico, but as I followed Javier and his men, all in
their sharp suits, striding confidently, easily, through
this tiny town, I had to wonder how far reaching the
cartels were. Was there nowhere in the country left
untouched? Would the children on the street have to
come home to a murdered father or mother, as Javier
had? The place he described growing up didn't seem
too much different from this place.

Sympathy for the devil, I thought. It crept up on me
more and more.

The car was a Range Rover, at least ten years old,
with a dented fender. I was guessing that it was tough
and fast enough to get us around, but it didn't look like
the vehicle that a drug cartel rode around in. Just your
everyday quasi-Mexican family going out for a drive,
nothing to see here.

Javier checked something on his phone and then
pulled a key out of his breast pocket. He opened the
driver's side door and unlocked the rest of them.

Then he turned and looked at me for the first time in
hours. "You're riding in the front. With me."

My heart clanged in my chest. I forced a smile to
hide my nervousness. "Sure."

I climbed in and was surprised at how high tech it
looked inside. GPS, MP3, the works. "Nice," I commented, feeling like I had to say something.

Javier started the car and knocked on his window.

"Bulletproof glass. I made sure this was totally outfitted. Piece of shit from the outside, a fortress inside."

"Like the Popemobile."

A smug smile spread across his lips and I knew I had appealed to his God complex. "Yes, just like that."

We headed out of the town and crawled our way through narrow, twisting mountainous passages, the sea temporarily disappearing as the Range Rover plunged deep into the heart of the Los Tuxtlas reserve. The green seemed to close around us as lizards ran across the ragged road just in time and the sun poked through the canopies. Waterfalls tumbled out of volcanic remnants, close enough to splash mist on the car. It was nice to see it from an air-conditioned vehicle, especially one that was outfitted in bulletproof glass. I felt safe for the first time in a while, which was so ridiculous considering who I was in the car with.

Suddenly, the switchbacks seemed to be too much and we nearly went off the road when a bus came careening around the corner, the lush mountains leveling out. Soon we were pulling the Range Rover onto the Minatitlán–Veracruz highway, speeding along the plains and rows of fruit crops.

"I bet when you thought of Mexico before," Javier began, relaxing at the wheel, "you thought of Cancún and Puerto Vallarta and all the resort towns."

I swallowed and nodded, watching the immense land, the countless farms and houses flying past. "I did. I never really thought of it having so much space."

"It's a big country, you know. It can be surprising and beautiful too. The people. The little pockets of life."

I looked over at him, feeling that we were the only two people in the car. "Are you happy to be back? Did you miss this?"

He scratched at his sideburn, eyes darkening momentarily. "I miss it sometimes. It seems peaceful and simple in my memories. But I know it's not true. Behind every house you see, there are secrets. And death."

"That's everywhere," I pointed out.

"Yes, it's true." He adjusted his grip at the wheel. "Still, you forget here. You think there are so many people, so many lives, how can there be that many secrets? When I was young, really young, and my mother would drive me and my sisters to Mascota where my aunt lived, I'd watch all the houses go past and I'd play a game with myself. I'd say, 'What would it be like to be that person? To live there? Or there, or there? What life would I have?'" He trailed off and looked in the rearview mirror. It was as if he just remembered where he was. He suddenly shrugged. "I was young and stupid, and I thought the world was good and other lives were better. Well, all of us know that's not true."

He became silent after that, flicking through the radio until he gave up and put a Nick Cave and the Bad Seeds album on. "Do You Love Me?" came out in full bass and creepy organ, and I had to wonder how orchestrated this was. It added an ominous quality to our journey and a flurry inside my gut, something that pulled me in all directions.

I did not think about Javier. I did not listen to the lyrics, those terribly fitting lyrics. I did not fall for his guise of music. This was not *On Every Street*.

The tattoo on my arm itched.

We drove on. By the time the album was over, I felt dirty and squirmy and we were in Alvarado, driving down another narrow street that coasted along the shore. The fish shop that would be our headquarters was two stories, set at the start of a concrete pier that jutted out to sea, a few aging fishing boats moored along it.

Javier and his men exited the vehicle and headed right for the shop. They didn't look around them to see if they were being watched or if anyone was eyeing them suspiciously. They were a bunch of men wanting fish. I sat in the car a few moments longer, enjoying the safety of the glass, before I spotted Javier waving me over.

The bell jangled loudly above my head as I entered the shop. He wasn't kidding about the smell. It was an actual working business, with rows of different-color fish all lying flat on ice. Raul was talking to a small, deeply tanned elderly man behind the counter, the fishmonger.

Javier came over to me and placed his hand at my back, leading me forward. I could feel his warmth through the flimsy fabric of my dress.

"Ellie, this is Pedro," he said, politely introducing me.

Pedro showed me his hands, full of fish guts, and shot me an apologetic look. "Sorry, I no speak much English."

"*Eso no es problema,*" I told him with a smile, and hoped he wouldn't assume I was fluent. "*Hablo un poco de español.*"

"Impressive," Javier whispered into my ear. "What else have you picked up?"

I hid the shiver that rolled down my neck by telling Pedro he had a very lovely shop. That seemed to please him, and it got me out of Javier's grasp as Pedro began to show me the scales on one of the red snappers.

Pedro was one of Javier's father's friends from way back in the day and had no problems with letting us stay there. In fact, it was common. The upstairs of the shop was constantly used as a hotel of sorts for the Sinaloa cartel members who were trying to gain the upper hand in Veracruz. Javier told me Pedro often stayed down the street with his daughter when they took over his shop, working during the day and minding his own business.

Pedro led us upstairs, which was a lot more substantial than it looked on the outside. There was a small living area/dining room and a large balcony overlooking the beach and harbor, complete with another table, chairs, and a grill. The kitchen was tiny but functional. There was one small bathroom and two bedrooms.

"I guess I'll take the couch," I said, eyeing the tiny loveseat adorned with a white fringed shawl.

"Don't be ridiculous," Javier said, gesturing to the bigger bedroom. "You're staying with me."

My eyes widened and a flash of heat went up my legs. "I don't think so."

He gave me a wry look. "Would you rather sleep with Raul or Peter?"

"I'll take Peter," I said automatically. Peter blushed and quickly went into the other room.

Javier grabbed my hand. "I won't touch you unless you want me to."

I glared at him. "There's nothing wrong with the couch. Perhaps you should sleep there."

"Perhaps I'm not that much of a gentleman," he said with a cock of his head.

Understatement of the century, I thought. Then I realized he was still holding my hand. He noticed my eyes and let go.

"We'll have to get your things later tonight. It would look a bit too strange if someone saw us moving our shit in here. When it gets dark, we'll get the bags. Until then"—he gestured to the rest of the house—"get a beer and relax."

"I think I might," I said, wanting to get away from Javier and any talk about a bedroom. I went to the kitchen and got a beer, settling on the balcony. The sea breeze was wonderful, even if it brought up the occasional waft of fish. I sat back and waited for something to happen. Something more than just me sitting on the balcony of a cartel's hideout, sipping a beer and watching the pelicans fly.

I went back inside the house when I was done with my drink and noticed Raul sitting silently on the loveseat, staring into space. I grabbed another beer from the tiny fridge and, when I turned around, he was right behind me.

I let out a small gasp of surprise and nearly dropped the bottle. How the hell did he move so fast?

"Ellie," he said, as if my name felt good to say. "Have you given any more thought to your predicament?"

I frowned. "Where's Javier?"

"Your lover has left."

"He's not my lover," I said nastily. "You should know that." Then a thread of fear ran through me. I swallowed it down. "Where did he go?"

"He went into town with Peter. They had business to conduct."

"Well, okay then," I said, and tried to walk around him. He blocked me. I gripped the bottle tighter, more than prepared to waste a beer on his head.

He leaned in close. "You say he's not your lover. I believe you. He doesn't speak very favorably about you, you know."

I refused to look away, his beady little eyes spearing me. "I don't speak very favorably about him. So it's fair."

"None of this is fair." He sneered. "Think about it, Ellie. He's getting you to do his dirty work. Don't you think there are other people who can better handle this for him?"

"Maybe they aren't as invested."

He took another step closer, his pelvis almost pressed against mine. I raised my drink in the air. "Don't come any closer."

"I'm only trying to help you," he said with false humility. "I don't want you getting hurt. There's far more to this than he will let you know. It's sad how fucking blind you are."

My face fell. I couldn't help it. Raul obviously had an agenda, perhaps to overthrow Javier, I couldn't be sure. At the same time, I felt like I had to agree with him, that I was probably blind and kept in the dark. I also didn't trust him. In fact, if Pedro wasn't downstairs working and it wasn't bright daylight outside, I would have thought I was in big, big trouble. I made a mental note to never be left with Raul alone again.

"Piss off," I said, pushing him out of the way with my shoulder. "And if you ever come that close to me again, I'm telling him everything you said."

"He wouldn't believe you." But Raul looked worried when he said it.

"I'd like to find that out for myself." I went over to the balcony and closed the sliding door behind me. I wished I could have locked the door from the outside, so I could keep him out.

I drank my beer and every so often I turned my attention away from the sea and looked at the sliding glass door. I could see my reflection, looking positively languid in the sun, and beyond that, inside, Raul on the couch. Constantly watching me.

*   *   *

Once darkness fell, Peter brought up everyone's bags and I got settled in our room. Javier had returned just before dinner, with fresh fish from Pedro, but wouldn't tell me where he and Peter had gone, other than it was some stuff he had to work out. It was deliberately vague, but now I couldn't help but think about what Raul had said. How many things was I being kept in the dark about?

After I put a few long dresses, light jackets, and a nice tunic on the spindly hangers and shoved my duffel bag under the bed, I caught Javier walking past the room, heading downstairs to the shop.

"Javier," I called out.

He poked his head back around the door, brows raised. For a very quick moment he looked like the boy I used to know. Or the boy I never really knew.

"Can I have a moment?"

I don't know why I was being so polite.

He came in, nodding, eyes curious and concerned. "Of course you can. What's wrong?"

I guess he was being polite too.

I eyed the door, jerking my chin for him to close it, to give us privacy. He tilted his head, then shook it, his attention going to the wall. Raul and Peter were in their room, and perhaps the walls were far too thin for whatever he thought I was going to talk to him about.

"I was actually going to go up the street to get more beer," he said somewhat loudly. "Someone's drunk most of the supply. Want to come with me?"

I nodded, grabbing a jeans jacket from the closet, and followed him down the stairs and through the triple locks of the shop door. We hopped in the Range Rover and sped off down the road. The *Let Love In* album started playing again. I reached over and turned down the volume.

After we'd passed a couple of convenience stores and supermarkets, I said, "I thought you needed beer."

"We'll get it on the way back. We're going to Veracruz."

I felt jarred. "Right now? It's night." I wasn't ready for this.

"Best time to go. I won't be easily spotted. It's a large city, you know. Half a million people and a lot of them look like me."

"I doubt that," I said despite myself.

He let out a low laugh. "You still think me handsome, Ellie?"

I shouldn't have looked over at him, as if I were actually considering the question, but I did. And then I started considering the question. He was handsome, maybe even more so than he once was. He was almost thirty now and age gave him power. His features were more defined, his confidence was off the charts. It was a dangerous combination and a dangerous question.

"I can see how a lot of women would find you very attractive," I said in as detached a tone as possible.

"Oh, *very* attractive. I like that, I like that." He smiled at me, eyes puppy dog. "You know if you're not careful with me, we could fall back into old tricks."

"Isn't that what you want?"

He pressed his lips together. "I told you before, this is an evolution. For both of us."

I wiped my hand on the length of my dress. "I don't think you know much about evolving."

"You'll see. Now, I'm sure you didn't want to discuss my looks with me, so what is it that you wanted to talk about?" His voice was clipped now, all business.

"Raul told me some things..."

"Of course he did," he said easily, but I could see his knuckles becoming more defined as he gripped the wheel. "What did he tell you?"

"That I was blind and kept in the dark and that I was going to get hurt."

"I see."

"I don't trust him. Do you?"

"I don't trust anyone," he answered. "It's what has kept me alive. I'd say you follow the same creed as me."

"I trusted Camden," I said, bracing for the impact.

It came slowly, the frustration seething off of him like smoke. His teeth clanked together as he bit down, jaw grinding. He waited one long agonizing minute before speaking, more to gather his anger than to keep me in anticipation.

"Camden is your past," he said, trying to keep his voice steady. "I am your future."

"You are my past. Camden is my future."

"Camden," he said, voice rising, "is gone. He is *gone*, Ellie. He has his family, the family I gave back to him. He has moved on. You need to move on too. Weak people hang on to the what-could-have-beens. Strong people build a new future. Whatever...*thing*...you two shared, it's over. He may have his tattoo on you, but so do I."

"How do you know he's moved on?" I asked in a hush. "How do you know he's not out there looking for me?"

"I told you I know where he is and what he's doing," he said. "He isn't coming looking for you. Don't you think he would have found you by now?"

Javier had taken a pick-ax to my heart.

"Maybe he'll take six years," I whispered, feeling the hope drain out of the wound. Javier was right and

I hated it. Camden wasn't coming. He wouldn't get his family back and then leave them for me. He wouldn't give up on them. I wouldn't even want him to do that. I knew then that I had to let him go; it just hurt too much to even consider it.

"I didn't come for you until I was ready." Javier spoke up after a thick pause. "That's evolution." He sighed. "You're right not to trust me and not to trust anyone. But I am not keeping you in the dark. We're just trying to figure out the best way to get you in Travis's path."

That idea made me shudder. "Easiest way possible, please."

I felt Javier's eyes on me. "A dress like that will be a start. Travis doesn't go out all that often, from what our friends say, but he's not a total, how you say, hermit. He goes to the market every Saturday, so three days from now. I would like to see if we could find him before that, though."

"So what, you're going to keep driving me into town and dropping me off and hoping I'll bump into him?"

"Well, no. We'll get you a hotel room in the city. You'll be a female traveler there alone. I have a man who works there. He'll be our day-to-day contact. You won't see me much."

That worried me for some reason.

He went on, "It's better that way. We can't take chances. Once you are in Travis's sights, I'll have to disappear. He probably will have you followed for a bit, so you must keep up the mask of American traveler for some time. If he catches you and me talking, things will be over for you pretty fast."

"Why me? Why not someone else? Why do you think he'll take any interest in me at all?"

He licked his lips and turned his attention back to the dark highway. "You don't know what you are, Ellie. You act strong but everyone can see how vulnerable you are. Men like me, like Travis, we want to protect that. We want to break you, mold you, and keep you as ours. He'll see you and he'll see that in you."

I didn't know how to react to whatever the hell he just said. It was honest and disheartening. I was pretty sure Camden never saw me that way. Pretty sure...

"Besides, you're very beautiful, from head to toe. Any man would be crazy not to have you as his queen."

I kept my mouth shut to that. I was certain that a woman with scars, tattoos, and a nipple ring wasn't the height of beauty.

Javier's original plan that night was to visit the small hotel where I was to be staying. It was just as well that I had decided to come along.

Veracruz was only forty miles from Pedro's place. Before we knew it we were entering the lights of the city, the plazas and malecón aglow for the evening. The hotel was right in the city but backed onto a small preserve that ran along a stream. One two-story building held the office, gift shop, lobby, and rooms, then there was a courtyard and a pool, with two large haciendas at the back with their own private everything. Javier had splurged on the private cabin starting Saturday night, especially liking that it had a hidden entrance at the back that led to a small landscaped patio and the reserve beyond.

The only person on staff that night was Javier's contact, Enrico. Enrico was no older than twenty, with a smooth face and bright eyes. He was sharp as a tack and respected Javier without being all fan-boy about it. At least I'd feel safe with Enrico there acting as Javier's eyes. I had to wonder how many of Javier's men were scattered around town, protecting him from afar.

Before we left, Enrico slipped Javier a piece of paper. I didn't ask about it until we were back in the Range Rover and heading to the fish shop.

"What was that paper he gave you?" I asked.

"The name of someone who can help us." Another person who could help? Javier caught the look on my face and smiled sympathetically. "Ellie, for this, we are going to need all the help we can get."

CHAPTER SIXTEEN

Camden

Swerve, swerve, swerve.

The GTO responded to my touch like I did to lips on my dick. I jetted the car down the road while Gus frantically flipped on the GPS to try to get us a better route away from the cop car that was still on our trail. We didn't know if it was related to what had just happened with Dan or if the cop just happened to see us speeding; either way it was bad news. If the cops caught us, we'd be found out pretty fast with my somewhat "Wanted" face and a trunk full of crazy-ass weapons that the cartels wouldn't want anywhere near them.

"There's a small road up to your left," Gus said, jabbing at the device. "Take it then take the next road to your right; it hooks around to the highway."

"Highway with more cops," I muttered but did as he said and swung the car down a narrow cobblestone road, flying past tiny dwellings and stray dogs that ran out of the way.

"More cops but they'll be easier to lose at this time of day."

"Do they have traffic choppers over here?" I asked, imagining the view from above as broadcast on television.

Gus grinned at me uneasily. "I guess we'll find out, won't we?"

"And so will Javier." At the moment all we had was the moment of surprise. Shit, I hated even to think it, but I really hoped Dan was knocked out. Looking back, we should have tied him up or, well, if it had been anyone else, we should have shot him and put him out of his misery. Now there was a chance he could alert Javier that we were on our way.

Who the fuck are you? I asked myself, feeling the chills spread all over me. Suddenly I was talking about offing someone like it was no big deal.

I shook my head and concentrated on the task at hand. The police car was still behind us, having taken the same corner. I brought the GTO onto the other street Gus told me about. Sadly, it was no bigger than a bike path, lined with low stone walls.

"Shit!" I yelled as we squeezed through, both of the side mirrors of the car smashing off and flying behind us. The car bounced and rocked back and forth, her sides scratched as we sped through the narrow passageway without more than an inch to spare on either side. I couldn't help my wince at the damage the car was taking on, the paint job it was going to need when this was over. Ellie was going to have a hissy fit. Her poor Jose.

That thought alone, that I'd see Ellie again, kept me

focused. I gunned the car harder, even when I heard the cop car coming to a screech far behind me, probably a few inches too wide to come after us.

We almost made it out of the passage when a little girl with her skipping rope suddenly appeared around the corner, coming toward us, her form small between the stone walls.

Gus and I both screamed in unison as I slammed down on the brakes, burning brake pads and rubber filling our ears and noses. The car fought and weaved in what little space it had as it plowed toward the little girl.

I took in her purple summer dress, the braids in pigtails, the pink rope in her hands, her bare feet, her eyes as they stared me down in horror.

The GTO came to a jerky halt, a few feet away from her, the cloud of dust from our wake billowing forward.

My hands were frozen on the wheel, my foot on the brake, my eyes on the girl. My chest heaved, remembering to breathe, while Gus clutched at his chest. For a minute I thought he was going to have a heart attack, that this was his mysterious health condition, when he waved me off and spat out, "I'm fine. Should we check on her?"

I looked back to the girl. She was giving us a pouty look but turned around and skipped back out of the passage, finding another way to wherever she was going.

I slowly eased the car forward once she was out of our path, inching the nose out until the coast was clear. Then I stepped on the gas and took her down another road that led us to the highway.

Once we got there, it was smooth sailing.

For about five minutes. Then we heard more sirens behind us. Someone had called the cavalry.

Gus and I looked at each other as if to say "Time to do this again" and I gunned the car, the engine slightly less responsive now. I swerved it around the commuters on the highway, getting angry glares, horns, and curious glances. I guess with the mirrors off and the side banged up, we were going to attract a lot of attention. Perfect.

Gus was back to reading the GPS. "We're approaching Tihuatlán. The highway is going to start branching off in different directions. We won't be able to stay on this one, even though it's leading us to Veracruz. We'll have to take the side roads and the smaller highways. We can still get there but, sorry, boy, it's going to take longer now. The cops are going to be looking for this car."

I kneaded the steering wheel and swerved around a car just before we almost collided with the back of a semi-truck.

"Well, let's see if we can get out of this one first."

And we almost did, until a cruiser pulled up beside us. The cop wasn't wearing a ski mask which meant he was probably doing radar on the side of the road. He did have a gun pointed at us though.

He pulled the trigger, the bullet puncturing the back door.

I yelped and slammed on the brakes again, trying to get out of his way. The car behind me screeched and swerved off to the side, trying to avoid being rear-ended. Unfortunately, the cop car did the same maneuver as me and the car ended up flying off the road, crashing somewhere behind us. More and more cars crunched and squealed and I knew I'd left a massive pile-up in my wake.

Not that it was exactly my fault. The cop was aiming for me again, and I jerked the GTO into the other lane as he shot again. The bullet missed, striking the rear window of the car next to us. Screams filled the air. The cop didn't give a shit if everyone on the highway ended up dead.

"We have to get the fuck out of here," I said as Gus reached into the glove compartment and pulled out his gun. "Oh please, let's not add to the carnage."

He cocked the gun dramatically. "Our lives are carnage now. Deal with it."

There was truth to his words. We'd gone from two guys watching *Arsenic and Old Lace* in his living room, to torture-tattooing drug lords and igniting ex–best friends. Now we were on the run from the law, in Mexico, nearly taking everyone down with us.

All for a girl. But she wasn't just any girl.

She was mine.

And I was hers.

Until the bitter end.

"Camden, watch it!" Gus yelled.

The cop was right beside us again. I only got a quick glimpse of him as I turned my head to see, cursing the side mirrors that were gone.

I saw the gun pointed at me.

That was it.

Then my window exploded, glass fragments flying everywhere, lacing the air like confetti. Immediately a searing hot pain erupted in my shoulder, like a molten knife had stabbed me there, twisting it through. I didn't have time to worry about it. I had to act fast. I grabbed the wheel and did what the psycho cop wasn't expecting me to do: I rammed the GTO into his car, at enough of an angle so we'd both spin out. Only I was still in control, with one good arm, and was able to get the car straightened out before Gus had to take control of the wheel and I handled the gearshift.

There were a few close calls, another semi changing lanes to get out of the way, a family-filled sedan staring at our car in horror as we nearly rammed them. But we managed to escape from crashing and navigated the moving maze by the skin of our teeth. I felt like I was in a deadly, real-life version of Frogger. My hands started to get cold and clammy, the gearshift slipping under my palm.

Once we were back at optimal speed, I took the wheel back and started booting up the shoulder, overtaking everyone and leaving them in a storm cloud of loose roadwork. Then I chose to look down at my arm. I saw nothing but blood, starting from the shoulder where it met my collarbone and soaking its way down, a red ink blot that took on new shapes before my eyes.

"Oh, fuck," I said, grinding my teeth together as the pain began to manifest itself. "I've been shot."

"Where?" Gus said, alarmed and peering over at me.

"My shoulder," I grunted, then screamed. "This fucking hurts!"

He seemed to consider that for a moment before he said, full-on smart ass, "Yes, being shot hurts."

I glared at him, my glasses fogging up. "If I die on you, you're going to feel really bad about it."

"I'm sure I will," he said. "Just keep driving. I think we've lost them for now. Get us to Ixtapa Road, the next exit's coming up on your right, then take the road until it intersects with 132. Take 132…" And Gus droned on. I was having a hard time hearing him. My vision was beginning to blur and my ears felt like they had cotton balls in them. I guess I subconsciously took it all in because together, with him steering the wheel sometimes, we followed his directions and ended up at an abandoned gas station on the outskirts of a small town. The cops hadn't followed us.

But I'd been shot. And before I could do anything about it, the world around me started getting fuzzy.

Then nothing.

CHAPTER SEVENTEEN

Ellie

As to be expected, sleeping with Javier was awkward. After we returned from our mini-trip to Veracruz, case of beer in hand, we all had a few and then retired to our room. I could sense Raul's eyes on me the whole time, but Javier didn't act any different around him. I was glad for that because I didn't want Raul to think I'd snitched—he wasn't someone I wanted to further antagonize.

Javier shut the door behind me and flicked on the tall standing lamp in the corner, kitschy Mexican décor. "What side of the bed do you want?" he asked.

Then he proceeded to take off his suit. He flung the jacket onto an armchair across the room and began unbuttoning his shirt. I didn't know where to look, my cheeks growing hot like I was a naive teenager. I'd seen him shirtless before. Hell, I'd seen and felt every single part of that man. Still, it didn't make the feeling go away.

"Feeling bashful?" Now his tone was smug.

I looked up and his shirt was off. His body was pretty much the same as I remembered, but wider, in a more athletic and lean kind of way. He'd grown into it and taken great care of his body over the years. His abs and arms looked like he'd done chin-ups in his spare time, yet it was still very elegant and subtle. His skin was a dark bronze, shadowed by the lamp.

"No," I answered.

"Good." And then his pants dropped.

And I'd totally forgotten he liked to go commando.

"Oh my God," I cried out, shielding my eyes and facing the wall. "Please, put some pants on. Or underwear."

"Say 'Oh my God' again. I liked the sound of it," he said, and I could hear him coming closer. "It reminds me of old times."

"Javier, I'm serious."

"When are you not serious, Ellie?"

I kept my eyes clamped shut until he started shuffling through the drawers. "Okay, okay, calm down. There, I have pants on now."

I bent down and snapped up my pajama bottoms and a T-shirt then walked past him to the door, not wanting to risk a look in his direction. When I came out of the bathroom, after a long, hot and much-needed shower, he was already in bed with the lights off. This was exactly what I was counting on. I wanted to go to sleep on my side of the bed and be done with it. No thinking about the situation, no chitchat.

I carefully closed the door and eased my way across

the room, my bare feet padding on the woven rugs, the moonlight outside the open window illuminating my passage. With the sea breeze coming in and the sound of the fishing boats rising and falling in their berths, the whole thing was soothing. Even romantic.

I crawled in, pulling only the sheet over my body, and faced the wall. The moon was bright on my face.

After a few moments, when my heart rate had started to calm and I was beginning to forget where I was, Javier called out softly. "Angel?"

I wanted to pretend to be asleep. I wanted to ignore him. But he'd used a name I hated and I was sick of hearing it.

"Please don't call me that," I whispered back, pulling the sheet closer around my shoulders.

He turned over in the bed and suddenly he was right behind me, causing the hairs on my neck to rise. "Why not?"

I tried to steady my breath. "I'm not your angel."

"You're someone's angel. God's."

"God's? How can you call me an angel when you think I'm no good?"

He was silent for a moment. Waves crashed outside.

"There are fallen angels too. Angels with dirty wings."

"Lucifer was a fallen angel," I pointed out.

"You're right. But Lucifer had no moral code. You and I, angel, I think we fell somewhere in between all of that. We made our place. Our own home."

I closed my eyes at his words, my soul and heart and everything getting sucked back into a vortex of memories, all bright, shiny, and good. Memories of him and me together, memories I thought I'd erased.

His lips were at my ear, his warm hand on my shoulder, holding me in place rather than giving comfort. Instead of stiffening, my whole body relaxed.

"We evolved, Ellie," he whispered, sending shivers down my back. "And we'll keep evolving." Then he moved away, back to his side of the bed, cozying up under the covers.

I didn't fall asleep for hours.

*   *   *

The next day Peter and Raul went off somewhere in Pedro's tiny Toyota, and Javier and I took the Rover into Veracruz to meet this new contact of his, a woman called Amandine.

We had dressed appropriately for the occasion. I was wearing a long peasant skirt and gladiator sandals that wrapped up to my knee, covering my cherry blossoms even if no one could see them. On top, though, I was showing a lot of skin. No bra under a low-cut and tight low-back white lace tank. I spent extra effort on my hair, styling it until it lay straight and smooth, just past my chin, and put on more makeup than usual. Nothing trashy, but I knew I had the ability to stand out when I wanted to.

"That's perfect," Javier had said when he saw me, his eyes savoring my body. "Of course, if you were still mine, there's no way I'd let you out in public like that."

"Good thing I'm not yours," I'd told him.

Just as I looked like an attractive American tourist,

Javier looked the complete opposite of a drug lord. Jeans, a black and orange San Francisco Giants jersey, aviators, and a plain black baseball cap.

Actually it was kind of weird being with him looking like that. Javier had always been a very smooth and elegant dresser, and now here he was looking like any twenty-nine-year-old baseball fan, albeit one with high cheekbones. Even dressed down he still looked extraordinarily...pretty.

We cruised through the busy streets of the city, both of us taking comfort in the bulletproof glass, until we found the address. It was a café across from one of the various small lakes and lagoons sprinkled throughout Veracruz.

We parked across the lagoon and took the long way around, following a small boardwalk. He took my hand and squeezed it before I could take it back.

"You're just an American girl and I'm your Mexican boyfriend," he said with a cheery smile that made him look terribly young. "We're the modern-day Romeo and Juliet."

"*Romeo and Juliet* was a tragedy, not a romance," I answered.

He held on to my hand the whole way, keeping me close to him, occasionally pointing to one of the flamingos on the lagoon. I pretended to take interest, putting on a show for the folks who probably weren't watching us. People were spread about the park, workers on their lunch break, college students having make-out sessions and picnics at the water's edge.

When we approached the café, he whispered "There

she is" with all the skill of a ventriloquist. A woman was sitting at a small table at the very corner of the café, where the patio petered out into the grass. There was no one by her except an old couple reading the newspaper together.

"Amandine?" Javier asked as we stopped at the end of the table.

The woman looked up, surprised. She was pretty hot, right off the bat. About our age, maybe early thirties, long wavy hair done up in honey browns, sun-kissed skin, and blue eyes that matched her top.

"Hi," she exclaimed brightly with incredibly white teeth. "You must be Enrico's friends."

We nodded. Javier gestured to the empty seats across from her. "May we sit down?"

"Yes, yes of course, please do."

Once seated, I offered my hand. "I'm Ellie."

She shook it, nice and firm. "Nice to meet you. And you too, Javier."

He smiled and folded his hands in front of him for a second before I guess he realized it was a bit too formal for his new persona and instead leaned back in his chair, legs splayed.

I almost rolled my eyes at his quasi-gangster pose.

"So," he said, getting down to business. "I'm sure Enrico told you what this was all about. So how can you help us, Amandine?"

Her face grew a little serious. "I'm sure Enrico also told you about my student loan..."

"Money is not going to be a problem," he said with a quick wave of his hand.

"Okay, well," she went on, "I was with Travis for a bit."

Javier and exchanged a look. He straightened up in his seat and looked around at the café.

"Don't worry," Amandine said, taking a sip of her latte. "This place is pretty safe. Mainly tourists come here. No one knows to listen. Do they?"

He shook his head, his jaw tense. "No. They don't. I didn't expect to hear this. What do you mean, you were with him? As his lover?"

She laughed and covered up her mouth. "No, not like that. I took a job cleaning his house. I needed the extra money for tuition. It was only for the summer. Of course, I didn't know who he was, but I figured it out pretty fast. At first I thought he liked to hire really attractive women to be his help, if I can be so modest, and I thought maybe he was a financial banker or something like that. I don't know, I was naive. I'm a good girl and I study hard and I didn't grow up with that. I knew there were drugs all over the city and that the cartels were closing in, but at the time it wasn't all that bad."

"How long ago was this?" he asked.

"Two years ago, two and a bit," she said, thinking it over. "It was nothing like it is now. This is my city, my home. My family's home. Now we have Los Zetas and Los Zetas Killers and who else knows who, all wanting a piece of this pie, and it's rotten through and through. Bodies are left in the streets. People, good people, journalists, teachers, are murdered and no one is doing a thing about it. Not the police. Not the military. Not the government. Organized crime has taken over this city. As soon as I am done with school, I am gone. And when I make money one day, I will take my family with me."

"Well, Amandine," Javier said calmly, "if you are of great help to us, I will make sure you have the money before you even start your next class. And it will be enough to get your family out of here in the meantime."

She looked flabbergasted. I couldn't blame her. How much money was Javier giving this young woman, and why? Just to be nice? That didn't sound like him. Not when he was no better than Los Zetas Killers.

"I couldn't accept that," she said.

"Yes, you can and you will. Because your information will be worth it. The lives of my own sisters depend on it."

Her face fell. "Oh. I see. Travis...Los Zetas. Did they do something to them?"

Javier didn't say anything. I couldn't see his eyes save for the amber reflection of his aviators, and he was probably glad for that. You couldn't read his face at all.

"If you help me, it will stop Travis from hurting them and hurting everyone else in this city."

I ignored what Javier had told me on the boat that day, that the drug lords were all like zombies and another one would pop up to take their place. Did Javier really want the drug cartels, the violence, to stop? Or did he just want to protect his sisters and come out on top?

She swallowed hard and took another sip of her latte. Her hands were shaking now. I placed my own on the table as a show of solidarity.

"It's okay," I told her. "We'll protect you. We just need to know what you can tell us about Travis, that's all. Places he goes, who lives in the house with him, how well protected you think he is—how many body-guards. That sort of thing. It won't take up much of your time, we promise, and then you can have your money."

She slowly lowered her drink and nodded. "Okay."

Javier shot me an impressed look, lips teasing upward.

Amandine told us everything she knew about Travis over the last two years. He liked to go to the Mercado Hidalgo market on Saturdays, where the local police force practically saluted him. Friday nights he'd fre-quent a nightclub or a bar, mainly the Zoo, a touristy joint with high security where he'd drink in his private room. He usually brought women home from these places, and his driver would take them home right after their session in the sack. I wanted to ask Amandine if I was Travis's type, if he'd find me attractive, but I knew how degrading and embarrassing that question was, to admit to what I was going to do.

And, honestly, as she explained his mansion in the hills, all five of his bodyguards, some I could tell Javier recognized, past brothers, I started to worry. I started to freak out a bit, my pulse quickening, waves of nausea sweeping through me. I was sure I couldn't do it, that I'd fail, he'd catch me, kill me, and everything would be for nothing. I didn't want to have my body dumped behind a garbage can or my head on the steps of a hotel. I didn't want to die by that man's hands.

"Ellie?" It was Javier, his hand over mine. "Are you okay?"

I nodded quickly, trying to come back to reality. "Yes. Sorry. What...what were we talking about?"

Amandine was looking at me with a quizzical expression. "I asked if there was anything else you wanted to know."

"No, I'm good. Sorry. I think I've had too much sun," I said, shielding myself with my hand.

"I think you're right," Javier said, getting out of his chair and pulling me up to my feet. "Thank you, Amandine, you have been a great help. I will be in touch with you if I need any more information. Oh." He reached into his back jeans pocket and pulled out a Bank of America checkbook and started scribbling on it with one of Amandine's pens.

"It's in U.S. funds and from an American bank so it might take a while for your bank to clear it, but I can guarantee it will clear." He ripped the check out of the book and handed it to her.

Her eyes bugged. "I can't take this."

"You'll take it, you earned it. Just make sure you share it with your family," he said. "Come on, Ellie."

He pulled me over to him and led me away from Amandine, who was still staring at the check in shock. We were halfway across the park when I asked, "How much did you give her?"

"About thirty thousand dollars, U.S.," he stated matter-of-factly.

"Shit," I said. "You made her life."

"If she has a life for much longer," he said quietly. "After we do what we have to do, I have no doubt it will all get back to her. That's the way things work here.

Those who talk, die. My only hope is that she gets her family out of here first, to at least give them a chance somewhere else."

I bit my lip, wishing that pretty Amandine would somehow get out of this alive. Wishing *I* would get out of this alive. "Is this place really that bad?"

"It's the Wild Wild East, my dear, and the sheriff is nowhere to be seen."

"And who are you? The Lone Ranger?"

"Don Diego de la Vega," he answered. "Zorro."

We got back in the car and drove out of the city and onto the highway that would take us to Alvarado.

We were about halfway there when I started to have a nervous breakdown.

All I could think about was Travis getting a hold of Amandine and cutting her head off, leaving it for her parents to find. What would happen to me if he did the same? Who would mourn me? Camden would probably never know about it. Neither would my parents, wherever the hell they were. The only one I had at that moment was right beside me: Javier.

And that in itself was what set me off.

I hadn't had a panic attack in weeks so it snuck up on me, as if a hand reached around from behind me and began squeezing my lungs until there was no breath left. I started gasping for air, my hand at my throat, taking in nothing. Tears filled my eyes and spilled down my cheeks in dirty rivulets and my body began to shake.

"Jesus Christ," Javier swore, nearly taking the car off the road. "Ellie, Ellie. What's happening?"

I gulped and gasped, unable to stop from crying, panic seizing me all over from my shoulders to my feet. I thrashed back and forth in order to get free.

Next thing I knew, he'd pulled the car down a private dirt road that ran between two orchards and he was undoing my seat belt. He came around to my side and took me in his arms and away from the car. We disappeared into the orchards, the smell of orange blossoms in the air.

He propped me up against a tree and smoothed the hair off my face. His sunglasses and baseball cap were gone, his hair mussed, his worried eyes searching me.

"Hey, Ellie," he said gently, running his hand down the side of my face and feeling the pulse under my jaw. "It's okay, it's all going to be okay."

I shook my head, feeling disgusting and messy and lost. I sobbed. "It's not going to be okay. I can't do this, I can't do this."

He cupped my face in his hands and forced me to look at him. "You can. And you will. You are strong. You are very strong. Right here." He laid his hand in the middle of my chest. "You will do this and you will succeed."

I finally found my breath again, the fresh air flowing through the sun-streaked orchard coming into my lungs. "I will fail."

"You won't."

I sniffed. "I don't even want this," I admitted.

He cocked his head and let go of my face. "Then why are you doing this?"

"Because you're making me!" I cried out. "You're forcing me to!"

His head jerked back. "I am doing no such thing."

"You are! You'll kill my Camden if I don't."

I didn't see the outburst coming. Suddenly Javier was in my face, his skin turning red, his eyes narrowing into viperlike slits, all yellow and full of hate.

"He is *not* your Camden!" he screamed. I closed my eyes.

"He isn't here with you now," he went on, words harsh and short, like bullets. "I am here with you."

"I know!" I screamed back. "And I hate it! I hate it! I hate you!"

Then before I knew what was happening, I had wound up my hand and slapped him hard across his face. The sound ricocheted down the groves.

I waited, surprised at myself, breathing hard. I watched as his face contorted in the same type of shock. And then something odd flashed across his brow. Something like betrayal. I knew betrayal all too well. I knew it had been on my own face when I found out what Uncle Jim was planning to do.

My dead uncle.

I slapped him again, harder this time, my palm stinging like I was being stabbed with a million tiny knives. "That was for my uncle!" I cried. "You killed him."

Now I wound up for a punch and decked Javier right in the side of the head. "You killed him," I repeated, tears streaming down my cheeks again. "You keep taking everyone I love away!"

The whole time Javier just stayed there. Not ducking

my hits, not getting out of the way. He just let me, watching me with that impassive look upon his face.

"Well, come on!" I screamed. "Hit me back. You know you want to!"

I decked him in the head again, my knuckles exploding in pain. "Come on!" I pushed my hands into his shoulders and tried to throw him to the ground. He fell easily, and I threw myself on top of him, throwing punch after punch after punch until he finally reached up and grabbed my wrists with both his hands.

"I'm not going to hit you," he said, gazing deeply at me with wild eyes, his lip bleeding. "You can hit me all you want but if you're doing it so I can hit you back, it won't work. You'll just break every part of me."

"I want to break every part of you!" I exclaimed but gave up and collapsed on him. "I want you to break," I whispered, my head on his chest, my eyes focused absently on an orange tree.

"You have," he said softly, his hand stroking the back of my head. "I told you that you broke me when you left. And you did. I'm not lying to you."

"You always lie."

"No. Not now." His voice dropped a register.

I raised my head to look at him. He brought his hands on both sides of my cheeks and held me there, his eyes searching me for something.

"Angel," he said through a breath.

He pulled my face to his, my lips meeting his, slowly. Just a taste of blood and tears. Lips and tongue. The sensation pulled me under, the heat that spread from him and through me, the memories mixing with the smell of orange blossoms. All the pain disappeared as our kiss deepened, all the worry, all the danger melted like my lips and his did together.

It was wrong. So wrong. And I didn't care. As I had been so many times before, I was willingly bad.

He let out a whimper, his hands disappearing in my hair, his kiss becoming feverish, it in turn spurring me on. Urgency rippled through us. I started ripping off his jersey, pulling it over his head, suddenly eager to feel his smooth, dark skin underneath my hands, the sun warming us. It felt like heaven and hell and danger to the touch.

His hands frantically found my breasts and grabbed a hold of the V-neck, ripping the shirt clear down the middle, the lace tearing easily. Then he sat up, over-powering me and bringing me to the ground. He buried his face in my breasts, letting out a happy grunt when he discovered my nipple ring for the first time, giving it a sharp tug with his teeth and a soothing lick after to calm my cries.

I ran my nails down his back, digging them in when the passion ran over, then took my hands to his jeans and groped hard at his erection. The moan I elicited out of him made me wet as water, and I started grinding myself into him in pure impatience. I fumbled for the fly of his jeans and pulled them down to his knees, wrapping my legs around his bare ass, holding his length against me.

He pulled up my skirt until it was around my waist and tore my cheap thong off with one smooth motion. His lips and teeth went to my neck, biting hard and sucking slow, making my back arch with each touch. His fingers found their way inside me, stroking and rubbing in all the right places until I moaned.

"I need you inside me," I cried out as he swirled his hot finger around my clit, my hips bucking for more.

"Tell me you're mine," he grunted, mouth at my ear, tongue flicking my lobe. "Tell me that you're mine, then I'll take you."

His other hand went to my breast and pulled at the nipple ring again. God damn it, I was going to lose it before it even started.

"I'm yours," I said, my voice shaking. I closed my eyes and threw my head back. "I'm all yours."

"You always were," he said, and he reached down and inserted himself in me with one hard thrust. I felt the small of my back meet with the earth, a sharp pain that melted away to pleasure as he continued thrusting hard, his ass powering through and flexing hotly under my fingers.

He couldn't go hard enough, fast enough, deep enough. I wanted him, all of him, I wanted everything to explode, I wanted stars and heat and waves that would carry me onto another day. I wanted to go back in time before this mess ever started, when it was just him and me and I didn't know any better and we had a home and a place where we could be us.

Javier let out a small cry as I ran my nails down his chest, his eyes blazing into mine, a yellow-gold dream as his face furrowed with the need to release. I needed it too.

He gave it his all, his taut muscles straining, sweat

streaming off of him and pooling on mine, the sun bearing down on him from behind the orange trees, making his back glow. He pounded himself deeper, his fingers coming down, bringing me to the brink again. I closed my eyes and felt myself fill up with the waves, the energy he was creating, the pressure between my legs that built up and up and up until I had to let go.

I cried out, swearing, my nails digging into his ass and lower back as he let out what could only be described as a roar, his body stiffening. He came hard inside of me, his eyes rolling back in his head.

He held that position, one frozen in the pain of pure pleasure, before exhaling and crumbling on top of me, his elbows propping up most of his body weight, his head now on my chest. I caught the smell of his shampoo and closed my eyes, my breath struggling to catch up, our chests rising and falling against each other in unison.

We lay like that for some time, breathing, being. And when the passion, the dreamlike state of our fucking wore off, I was left with thoughts I didn't want to think. Guilt for what I had done. Disgust for the person I had done it with.

And yet a sick part of me didn't regret a thing. It felt destined, bound to happen, something that had never come full circle until now. A sense of closure and peace settled over us, like the tiny white petals that were flying through the air, swept in by the afternoon breeze.

"Ellie," Javier said.

"Yes?"

"You've gotten wilder."

"Have I?"

"Yes. I don't know if I'll be able to handle you anymore."

I smiled to myself but it quickly faded.

I didn't know how I was going to handle myself either.

CHAPTER EIGHTEEN

Camden

I dreamed of Ellie again.

We were back in the large cavernous room, no walls, no ceiling, just a darkness that went on forever. The ground was black satin sheets disappearing into infinity.

Ellie was on the sheets, in cheesy white lingerie she'd never wear in real life, but it made me happy to see her in such a frivolous thing. She looked amazing, curvy and soft, crawling toward me on all fours, her breasts pushed up to her throat. Every part of me itched to touch her, hold her, possess her. I felt that if I didn't, she'd be taken away, becoming someone else's.

"Ellie," a voice called out from the distance. Deep, dark, ominous. "Eden, Eleanor, Ellen, Emily, Elaine."

Ellie turned her head to look, freezing on the spot.

"Ellie," I tried to call to her, to get her to notice me, to keep crawling. But the words were lost in the room, sucked away.

Suddenly a cold wind blasted me, ice crystals forming on my glasses. I cleared them off in time to see Ellie slowly getting to her feet and walking the other way.

"Don't go!" I yelled, though my voice came out in a whisper.

She stopped and turned her head to the side, barely looking at me before averting her eyes down. "He says he'll make me his queen. I have to go."

I made a move for her but only got about a foot before I wasn't able to move anymore. I was frozen in place, crystallizing from the bottom up.

A black shape formed behind her, growing in the moment, something so large and dense and malevolent that it seemed to take up all the space in the room, in the world, the universe. A flash of white teeth, coming for her.

Run, I screamed in my head. Ellie did not. She smiled in awe and stuck her hand out to touch the beast, it disappearing into the blackness.

Then she screamed and yanked her hand out. It was covered in blood.

Run, run, run.

And she did.

She tried.

She turned and tried to run but fell to the sheets.

The black beast descended on her. It grabbed her by the legs, swallowing them whole with that inky darkness.

Ellie screamed for me, fear taking over her eyes, her fingers desperately grasping the satin sheets, trying not to be taken.

The beast dragged her back and devoured her until there was nothing left but the abyss.

And there wasn't a single thing I could do about it.

*   *   *

When I came to, for one split second, I thought I was back in Sins & Needles, lying on the floor of my tattoo parlor. I thought maybe everything had been a dream and I hadn't tortured anyone for information or ignited someone's face or was on the run from the law. I thought maybe none of it happened and I was Camden McQueen again, a good boy. Weak, but good. There was a sense of relief in that.

Then my eyes started to focus on the ceiling and I realized that I wasn't in a tattoo parlor, I was in a veterinary clinic. I could smell the urine and chemicals and fur, hear the twitterings of various animals. Some woman was leaning over me with a stethoscope in her ears.

"He's awake. Hello, Camden, I'm Carlotta Valdez."

I blinked hard and tried to sit up but she pushed me back down with a firm yet delicate hand.

"You'll be all right, just take it easy. You're heavily sedated. Gus didn't know what to do with you, poor man was a little crazy. You're really lucky, that bullet didn't hit any arteries. The wound was pretty clean. You'll heal up nice."

I closed my eyes, feeling the wooziness sweeping over me. "Where is he? Where am I?"

"You're in my clinic. Normally I treat dogs and cats but business is a little slow on Fridays, so I made an exception."

I opened my eyes again and looked at her closely. She was in her mid-thirties, pretty good-looking actually. Large nose though it suited her face, good bones, nice, gentle eyes. Her hair was dark and gathered in a tight bun. She seemed trustworthy, but I guess it didn't really matter if she was or not because I was lying on a cold table used to treat ailing pets and felt like I had enough drugs in me to bring down a horse.

"Hey." I heard Gus's low voice from beside me. I turned my head to the side and gave him a small smile. He looked like he'd aged ten years, the lines around his eyes deeper. "How does it feel knowing you were shot by the Mexican police?"

"Like I'm on drugs."

Gus smiled and looked over me at Carlotta. "So am I his nurse now?"

She grinned and tapped her clipboard with her pen. "Yes, you certainly are. Camden will be a good patient, I'm sure. He's much more agreeable than some of the cats I treat. You'll have to keep him hydrated, and his arm needs to stay in the sling for a few weeks."

"Fuck," I swore. Being disabled wasn't going to help me in the long run. I needed to get to Ellie, and for that every part of me had to work. The blackness that took her still haunted me.

"I'm sorry," she said, not sounding very sorry. "But you've been shot. So that's what happens. Be glad that cop wasn't trying to take your head off, because he could of." She sighed and looked at Gus, her eyes soft. "I really wish you weren't doing this, especially with him banged up. It's too dangerous."

"We'll be careful," Gus said.

Her lips twisted wryly. "I don't think you've been all that careful thus far."

Gus patted my good arm. "Camden is a lot stronger and smarter than he looks."

"I'm sure he is. The glasses help." She reached into her coat pocket and pulled out a business card. "I know you have my number already, but here's my e-mail. Keep me updated. Let me know how he is and if I can do anything to help."

"You've done enough already, Carlotta, thank you." Gus put his hand behind my shoulder and began to push me up. "Slowly now, Camden."

I couldn't move any slower. I felt like I was pushing through quicksand. Once I was up straight, the room spun around until it slowed. Hell, these were some drugs. I was sure my eyes were rolling around in my sockets.

Carlotta appeared by my side with a glass of water and held it to my mouth. "Just a little bit."

The moment the water hit my lips, I wanted more, all of it, but I held back and eyed her over the rim. "I guess you know why we're here."

She nodded. "Yes. Gus was very forthcoming. I'm sorry I can't be much help. I treat animals and worried pet owners. I don't know all that much about Travis Raines and the cartels, just what everyone else knows about him."

"Well, we'll manage. Thank you for fixing me."

With great effort, I got to my feet and outside the vet clinic. We came out the back door to where the car was parked. Night had fallen, and the GTO looked like a ghostly wreck in the parking lot lights.

Gus waved at Carlotta then put me in the backseat, laying me down.

"I thought this was suspicious," I reminded him, slurring my words a bit.

"Have you seen the car?" he pointed out, getting behind the wheel. "We're a moving target for the police now."

"I guess it's time to ditch the old girl," I said sadly.

"Isn't this car called Jose? Funny name for a girl. And I'm not ditching it, there's far too much stuff in here, this was Ellie's life. We'll ditch it when we find her. I'm not stopping until we hit Veracruz."

I was too dazed to argue. Gus revved the engine and peeled us out of the parking lot.

"Where are we anyway? What happened?" I asked.

"We're in Córdoba. A little off course, but Carlotta was the only person that I knew could help us."

And not turn out to be a traitor, I thought to myself.

He continued, "She owed me a big favor anyway. I caught her father without papers in LA. I turned a blind eye and allowed him to stay. Carlotta grew up in California, then moved back home after school."

"Why would anyone move back here?"

"She missed it, I guess. It's not all bad. Hell, they might have the drug wars, but their economy is a lot stronger than ours at the moment. She seems happy. She's married. We had a long chat while you were out."

I nodded, my head rolling to the side. "How far are we from Veracruz?"

"About a hundred miles, give or take. We'll be there in time for the nightlife to get good."

"Nightlife?"

"Carlotta told me that Travis goes to this club every Friday night. It's pretty much public knowledge. It's very cheesy, touristy, frat-boy jackasses, that sort of thing. He has his own room, a lot of guards obviously. I'm guessing he probably owns the club by now. Anyway, security is extremely tight. Metal detectors, passport scanning, the works. But if she's right, he's there tonight. And maybe Ellie is too."

I opened my eyes, trying to fight through the cloud. "How will we get in?"

"Maybe we won't have to. We'll find her and follow her. Either way, we're tourists and we're white. We'll sail under their radar."

"With my arm in a sling?"

"Maybe not. You'll stay in the car. I'll go investigate."

I hated that idea. I wanted to go with him. I wanted to see her with my own eyes. I needed to. It wouldn't be real otherwise.

The monotony of the engine and smooth highway began to lull me to sleep. When I woke up, I'd be in Veracruz.

"Gus?"

"Yes?"

Fragments of my dream were choking me. "Do you think we'll get Ellie back?"

Pause. "We're going to try."

CHAPTER NINETEEN

Ellie

Things got very messy, very fast.

After the incident in the orange grove, we made our way back to Alvarado. Since my shirt was ruined, I had to hike my skirt up to my chest and wear it as a strapless dress. That, of course, exposed Camden's tattoo on my leg, which made Javier sullen and moody and me feel like a piece of shit. Camden. I succumbed to the past and my hormones and years of pent-up feelings. That's all it was. That's all it had to be. I couldn't fall for Javier again. I couldn't.

That's what I kept telling myself. So what if I told him that I was "his"? I didn't mean it.

I didn't.

I wasn't the only one who arrived back at the fish shop looking different. Javier had a shiner forming on his right eye, and his lip and nose were swollen from my punches. The minute we climbed the stairs and Raul and Peter saw what happened, I knew their tongues were wagging.

Javier and I went to our room, closing the door on their questions. I walked over to the window and stared out at the ocean, the low, dark clouds on the horizon that never seemed to come any closer. They just hovered there, ominous and waiting.

I felt his energy at my back, his presence, his gaze. Then he came closer to me and placed his hand on my bare shoulder. I closed my eyes.

"Angel," he said seductively. I didn't have to give in to it again.

"I think that was a mistake," I said softly.

His breath hitched. "It wasn't."

I stared at the horizon. The clouds were still not moving.

"I have to get...I know what I have to do. Now is not the time to start dredging up the past, to get involved in this." I couldn't let him fool me into thinking he's all I'd ever have.

He placed his lips on my neck. I didn't flinch. I pretended it didn't feel good, electric.

"And what is this?" he asked, when he pulled away. I could feel he didn't go far, his mouth was close, tickling my skin.

"Javier, this is a distraction. You know it. I have to get to Travis."

"I admire your sudden dedication," he murmured. "But we both know there is no stopping this. You are my queen, Ellie. And when Travis is gone, you will rule with me."

I didn't want to be his queen. I didn't want to rule over a terrible kingdom, a land of violence and strife. I was good, somewhere, I knew it.

Yet I was going to help murder Travis Raines.

He let go of me and walked over to the closet, rifling through his clothes. "Tomorrow night, I will take you to the Zoo," he said, his voice back to business. "The club Travis will be at. *Should* be at. You'll go to the bar and order a drink and look for him. When you see him, you will not react. You will continue to scan the club. I just want him to see you. Then the next day, at the market, perhaps he'll have something to talk to you about."

I gulped air. Panic fluttered through me, tiny winged insects.

"And what if he wants to talk to me at the club?"

"Then you talk. We'll have you in something like you wore today. If he's anything like me, he'll want to rip your shirt right off you, just to get a taste of your tits."

I spun around in shock. "You want him to do that?"

He shrugged, back to me. "No, I don't particularly want him to. I don't want any man even looking at you. But in the name of revenge, yes, it will have to do."

I glared at him as I went over, stopping at his back. "So I'm a sacrifice?"

"Yes. You're good at making those now, aren't you?" he said sarcastically.

He faced me, a twisted smile on his bruised lips. I felt like making them worse all over again.

"There are things we have to do in order to get what

we want. You shouldn't let your conscience, or your feelings, ever stop you. We are both stronger than that."

The image of him in bed with the redhead. *Patricia.*

"You're a sacrifice," he went on smoothly. "I'm sacrificing you."

"For the greater good," I said snidely.

"Except there is no good here. This is for us. The greater us."

I shook my head. I knew I'd have to get Travis's attention, I just didn't really think it would have to go to that, that Javier would let me, but apparently that wasn't the case here. He probably would care if I slept with Travis—I mean, I *know* he would, judging by the anger in his eyes every time he looked at my cherry blossoms, but he didn't care enough to not have me do it.

"Okay, fine. I go get his attention. Then what?"

"Then we play it by ear. Maybe go on a date with him."

My lip curled. "With that...that man, Javier, I have to go out with *that* man."

He put both his hands on my arms and brought me to him, his eyes staring deeply into mine. "I wouldn't have you do this if I thought you couldn't. I know you can. You will be all the better for it. Can't you see what you'll become?"

I looked down. "I'll become like you."

He brushed my hair off my face. "My dear, you already are like me. You always have been." He placed his lips on my forehead. "Why do you think we work so well together? A soul needs it's other half to truly live. I said that to you once, do you remember? That was a long time ago." His lips trailed down to my ear. "I don't have a soul," he said softly. "You make me feel like I do."

He led me over to the bed and gently pressed me down onto it. He kissed along my collarbone, nibbling as he went. "I have no interest in redemption anymore. If I did, I know I'd find it in you. Deep inside."

He pressed his erection against my leg. Hunger flared up inside me, hunger that made me feel disappointed in myself. For letting him do this. For liking it. For wanting it when I should know better.

He came up off my chest, his fingers already finding me wet for him.

"So drenched," he whispered, taking his fingers up and sliding them across his lips. "This taste. You're ready to be fucked again."

With one swift and powerful motion, he flipped me over on my stomach and pulled my skirt up around my waist. He grabbed the back of my hair and yanked my head back, painful pleasure radiating out from my head. The sex in the orange grove was child's play; I'd forgotten how rough he could be.

He didn't give me much time to prepare for him before he thrust himself inside, my body expanding from his fullness. "You're wet but tight," he growled in my ear. "Perfect." He slipped his hand over my throat and closed it there like he used to do. Instead of applying gentle pressure, just enough to feel taboo, to make me light-headed, he full-on clamped his hand like a vice.

I had no air. I couldn't breathe. I started to squirm,

and he pulled me back harder with his hand, yanking my hair with the other, still thrusting into me in a frenzied rhythm.

"You think I don't know how to handle you?" He groaned into my ear. "Well, I'm handling you now."

I brought my hands up to my throat, trying to pry his fingers off.

"Stop," I managed to squeak out.

"You don't tell me when to stop," he grunted.

I decided elbowing him in the chest was better.

He let go of my neck and I collapsed onto the bed, trying to breathe, my throat tender and sore. He pressed down on me, keeping me flattened. "Angel?"

I coughed, not able to speak yet. What the fuck had just happened?

"Angel, I thought you were tougher than that," he said, his voice a tad apologetic. He put his hand underneath my stomach, rubbing my clit. But the moment was gone and for once my body was responding to my head.

"I couldn't breathe," I said, trying to turn over. He hesitated, as if deciding whether to let me move, then he backed off, pulling out of me. His eyes flashed in a mix of lust and concern, an odd combination for anyone but not for him.

He leaned back, sitting upright, and pulled me on top of him, my legs going around his middle. He cupped my face in his hands. "I'm sorry. I should have been more...considerate."

You scared me, I wanted to say. Instead I nodded, wanting to forget the whole thing.

"Oh, my beautiful Ellie," he whispered once he noted the expression on my face. He kissed me gently. "There I am talking about how you give me a soul and then I go and do a thing like that. I'll need to take it slow with you, won't I? Build up your tolerance, until you are strong enough for me."

I frowned. One minute I was strong, the next minute I wasn't. "I *am* strong enough for you."

He smiled delicately. "We'll see. For now, I'll fuck you gently."

Then he lifted me up by my waist and lowered me onto his shaft. Javier was nothing but precise.

We fucked sitting up, me riding him in waves, long enough for me to forget, for my thoughts to disappear, for the confusion to lift. We were only our bodies, only our lust, and, maybe, just maybe, only two tortured souls.

* * *

The next morning, he and I had breakfast on the balcony. Raul and Peter totally knew what was up after we'd spent most of the evening locked in our bedroom. I was never good about being quiet in bed. Now that it was out in the open, Javier was being very affectionate and physical with me.

Especially around Raul. The moment the slimeball stepped out on the balcony to join us, Javier's arm went right around my shoulder. I was glad for it, looking straight at Raul, daring him to do or say something. I wanted him to. I wanted him gone. And I figured I'd have that happen one day.

I don't know if it was my upbringing or a sick sense of romance, but I had to admit that despite everything, there was something incredibly...thrilling...about having Javier's affections so publicly. Here was a man with an empire, one of the most dangerous drug lords, someone with immense power and sway, and there I was, the apple of his eye. I felt a little like Michelle Pfeiffer in *Scarface*...although that movie didn't really end well for anyone.

So what was going through my head then? Did I really think that we could off Travis and I'd be with Javier? Was that what I even wanted, to be his queen, his consort?

I didn't know what I wanted anymore. I didn't have anything, and the longer I was in Mexico with Javier, the hazier my future became. I'd wanted to be good, to be better than I once was, and even though I was trying, even though I'd been blackmailed into this whole mess, I felt like I was kidding myself. The future I had with Camden was gone, a daydream that was ripped away when I stepped inside Javier's SUV. That me, that Ellie Watt with her new hopes and fresh starts, must have died that day.

Maybe I never really was trying. Maybe I'd been kidding myself this whole time. Maybe a con artist from a family of con artists can't really change.

Maybe I had to accept that I really wasn't good and I deserved someone as bad as me.

I'd start at the nightclub. Javier had gone out in the afternoon to get me clothes, coming back with a lovely, albeit skanky, dress. It reminded me a little bit of Camden dressing me in Vegas, the way his strong hands had put me in that scrap of material that hugged my every curve and made me feel invincible with his fresh ink on my leg.

No, I told myself sharply. I had to stop thinking that way. The past had to be buried. There was no Camden anymore.

Javier suggested I curl my hair into ringlets, producing a curling iron he picked up along the way. Dark smoky green eye shadow. Pale pink lips. He'd gotten everything for me.

By the time I was ready, I had to admit that even I thought I'd get a few looks at the club. The dress was floor length, bright tomato red, slit to my navel. It showed off the tan I'd gotten while on the boat.

"You look amazing," he said as I stood in front of the mirror, hugging me from behind. Our reflection together startled me. I didn't recognize myself staring back. I looked sleek and powerful, as I should maybe have had that crown on my head. Javier's eyes in the mirror were bright like laser beams and he was staring at himself, not me.

It was a bit unnerving.

"I do?" I asked him.

He broke his stare with his reflection and smiled at me, kissing my neck. "Yes. I want nothing more than to come on every single inch of that dress. Let you wear it out to the club like that, so everyone will know you're mine."

"I think that would scare Travis away."

"No. He'd want the challenge." Suddenly he gripped

my hand and spun me around to face him. "Angel, please don't sleep with him tonight. I'd like to keep you as my possession for just a bit longer. I want to be the only one inside you."

I was taken aback. "Believe me, if I can get the job done without doing that, I will. I don't even think I'll survive looking at him." My lungs were caving in at the thought. "Javier, I'm scared. I'm really, really scared."

He studied my face for a moment, a sort of amused glint in his eyes. "I know you are. But take your fear and own it. This is your choice. Make your fear work for you. Make it, how you would say, your bitch."

He kissed me, soft and sweet, then smacked my ass hard enough to sting. "Come on, you're distracting me. I have to get ready."

He grabbed his clothes from the closet and started stripping. His erection was pretty obvious. I raised my brow at it.

"I told you that you looked amazing," he explained with a shrug. He put on his pale jeans and dark, wrinkled T-shirt with a nondescript logo. On his head was another baseball cap, this one blue and white, the Toronto Blue Jays. We couldn't have looked more different, but it's what he had to wear while driving me. He wasn't going to come out of the car since we couldn't take any chances, especially around Travis's club. Javier had a full-on purple and yellow eye now and his lip was still swollen. But no one batted an eye at that anyway, not in this town.

"Are you ready?" he asked me. I shook my head vehemently. No, I was not.

He dipped his chin and then took my hand, leading me out of the bedroom to the living area where Raul and Peter were.

"Very nice," Peter said through his thick accent.

I gave him an appreciative smile, ignoring Raul entirely. I knew he was looking, though, because of the way Javier's hand tightened at my waist.

"Let's get you a stiff drink before we go, okay." He led me to the kitchen and poured a large amount of tequila in a glass.

"Where's my lime and salt?" I asked, eyeing the glass.

"Lime and salt are for children and women."

I raised the glass. "I'm a woman."

"You're Ellie Watt," he said. "Drink up."

I shot it back in several attempts, coughing between each one. I felt a lot better, really fast.

"Normally, I'd suggest you drink the whole bottle," Javier said once we were in the car, pulling his cap farther down on his head, the wisps of his shaggy hair sticking out the sides. "But you're going to need your wits about you tonight."

Yet I was already scared witless.

It was around 10 PM when we pulled into Veracruz. Despite the daily bloodshed, the city seemed vibrant with lots of young people milling about. Maybe living in such a dangerous city made the citizens party harder, enjoy the best of life, while they could.

Javier took the Range Rover down the busy streets while I stared at couples in white dancing gracefully across tiled plazas and brightly colored restaurants with tables and music spilling out onto the sidewalks.

The port and marina shimmered, flanked by tall hotels. The air was heavy with heat but the occasional breeze from the gulf came in and lightened the atmosphere while the thick smell of flowers came in through the window. It was all very romantic, except that I was afraid to lower the window more than in inch, afraid to lose the protection of the bulletproof glass.

By the time Javier found parking on one of the side streets near the Zócalo, a popular square where the nightclub was supposed to be located, my hands were sweating and I was buzzing with nerves again. The tequila had worn off and left me nauseous instead.

"Here you go, darling," he said, slipping a tiny adhesive chip to the fabric that covered my nipple ring.

"What is that?"

"I can listen to you on my iPhone," he said, waving his phone at me. "It acts as a little wireless microphone. There's a chance that the metal could set off the metal detectors in the club, so I figured your nipple ring was a good place to put it. It's going to set them off anyway, and I'm sure they'll have a few good laughs when you explain what it is."

I rolled my eyes. "Oh, shit. Why don't I just take it out?"

He wagged his brows. "What's the fun in that? You'll be fine. Just flash them your tit."

"Ha-ha." I seriously hoped it wouldn't come to that.

"Hey," he said, growing serious and running his thumb over my lips. I held back the urge to nibble on it. "You're a con artist. You built a whole career on lying, on pretending to be different people. This is nothing.

You walk around the corner to the square and you'll see the club, it's a small building. There will be a line already. Get in line. Wait your turn. Show them your passport, they'll scan it, they'll run the detector over you. You'll show your tit. You'll go through and head to the large circular bar in the middle of the room, near the dance floor. Travis's room is up the stairs, but you won't even look there. You'll get your drink, watch the dancers, and, I am assuming, fend off *porteños* looking to take you home. Sit there for at least three drinks. When you're done, if nothing has happened, tell the bartender 'Thanks for the service, have a good night.' I'll hear that and come back for you. I'll pull up to here, the same spot. You get in. I take you home and fuck you senseless. That's how the evening will go."

I nodded. He was right. I *was* a con artist. Travis had made me one. I was born to do this.

I kissed him quickly on the lips as my skin fuzzed and shimmied with all the energy in the car. What we were doing. Who he was. Who I was.

"I'll see you," I told him, stepping out of the car. I stared at Javier for a good long moment, taking in his elegantly dangerous face, wondering how much trust there really was between us. Then I shut the door and walked off toward the nightclub.

I got more than my fair share of catcalls and whistles as I rounded the corner and came across the colorful plaza. It was alive with mariachi bands in the middle, tourists standing around and watching, with open-air restaurants filled to the brim with chatting patrons. I spotted the low mission-style house across the square with its cheesy zebra-striped sign that said the Zoo. Javier was right, there was already a line about twenty people long.

I took in a deep breath and sashayed my way over to it, getting behind a young white couple with New Jersey accents. That calmed me down a bit, knowing that I could blend in with the other tourists. Despite the New Jersey couple in their jeans, everyone else in line was dressed up. I both blended in and stood out, which was exactly what we were hoping.

I did everything I could to stay calm and focused while I stood there, waiting for at least a half hour before I finally got to the door.

"ID," the bouncer said. I handed him my passport and tried to take in his features without looking at him too deeply. I wondered if he worked for the club, for Travis, or both. I wondered if I'd be seeing this man, with his big fat head and coal-black eyes, again, in other circumstances.

He scanned my passport and handed it back to me. He nodded his fat head at the door. "You pay cover there, 250 pesos."

Ouch, that was steep. I didn't say anything, just nodded politely while he looked over my head at the people next in line.

I paid the girl at the door and, when I stepped into the club, I was met with a wall of smoke and a blast from the past. The club was blaring a bumping remix of the Nine Inch Nails song "Wish." The very song tattooed on Javier's wrist. The song I picked out for him, the one, Trent Reznor sings, *without a soul.*

"Miss?" One of the security guards was waving me over to him. I shook myself out of my daydream.

"Sorry," I said. "I guess I need to be screened?"

"It will only take a second," the man said, and started waving the metal detector over my arms and legs while another man went through my purse. As predicted, the detector beeped when he scanned my chest.

The guard looked a bit embarrassed. "Uh, are you wearing a metal bra?"

"Does it look like I'm wearing a bra?" I said, pushing my chest out, making him notice that the dress was cut down to my navel. "It's my nipple ring."

The guards exchanged a look while the other gave me back my purse.

"Do I need to show you?" I asked. Even in the dark blue lights of the club, I could tell his face was darkening. "I mean, if you look close enough, you can see through the fabric." I stretched it across my breast so he could see the shape of the ring poking through. That was enough for him.

He waved me away. "That's okay, you're clear."

I smiled and thanked them, making my way over to the large bar by the dance floor. It was still a bit early so there was a stool available at the end. Besides, it looked like most of the people there were in groups, filling up booths or yelling "Fist fuck!" out on the dance floor. I ordered a rum and Coke from the bartender and watched everyone, the sweaty moves, the flying hair, the lust for each other, for Mexico. I was being speared by small bouts of jealousy, that these people could be having fun and finding love and living life and I was about to offer myself, a lamb to the biggest baddest wolf of all.

I stared down at my drink, lost in my thoughts, in my shame. I was only interrupted to be hit on by a few Mexican guys, the *porteños* that Javier "warned" me about. They were local but harmless, not drug lords, just young guys having fun and looking for American tail.

It was when I finished my second drink and had to break the seal that it happened. I was leaving the bathroom, heading back to my spot at the bar, when I saw him.

Travis.

Oh my God, Travis.

He was walking down the stairs leading from his private area at the top.

He was looking right at me.

I only had a second to recognize him, to take him in. That's all I allowed myself, or I would have frozen there on the spot and given myself away. I would have lost it all.

He was as I remembered him, but seemed taller. I know that was impossible, but that's what it was like. Thin, straight up and down, in a black suit that made him look slightly sideways. He looked about sixty years old, gray hair slicked back with gel that accentuated his widow's peak; a handsome man who carried the same kind of feral elegance that Javier did. I could see people underestimating him, not seeing the danger.

But here, in this city, everyone knew who he was. Everyone knew the danger. He could order anyone in the club to be shot, and there would be absolutely nothing anyone could do about it. It wouldn't even get reported to the police; if it did, the police would turn a blind eye. This man held the power of a small universe in his thin, tanned hands.

And he saw me. Or at least he saw my dress. While his dark, cold eyes were distracted by my breasts, I looked at the bar and kept walking. I didn't dare look at him again or anywhere else. I kept my sweating hands as loose to my sides as possible, trying desperately not to clench them in case he was watching my every move.

When I got back to my seat, the bartender asked if I was all right. I smiled quickly and told him I'd better slow down my drinking. He gave me a bottle of water and a glass of orange juice.

A million feelings worked their way through me as I felt my heart lower itself into my chest, my lungs widening enough for air. I'd seen Travis and survived. But this was only the beginning. There was no telling what I'd have to do.

It was funny, when I heard Javier tell me what had happened to his sister and her family, I felt anger and sorrow for them. When I heard Amandine explain the decline of her beloved city, I felt the need to straighten out the injustice. Yet I did not feel the anger and the horror of my own wounds, my own place in all of this. It was as if what he had done to young Ellie Watt had happened to someone else, some poor eleven-year-old girl whom I felt bad for but had no connection to.

Now, now it was all different. Now I felt the rage pulsing through me. I felt the urge to grab the nearest sharp object and spear it into his jugular. I wanted to cut his balls off and feed them to him. I wanted to make him pay for everything he did to me, that one act of violence to a helpless child, an act that ruined her life, her character, her very soul. I wanted revenge for that, for the pain I still felt in my leg when it was raining, for the scars I had to endure, that showed the world just how ugly I was inside, how ugly he had made me.

I had to get out of there before I did something stupid.

I leaned over to the bartender and slipped him a twenty-dollar bill as a tip.

"Thank you for your service, have a good night."

And then I left. My eyes were cast on the ground, but I still felt Travis looking at me, from somewhere.

The feeling followed me down the street until I turned the corner and got in Javier's car.

CHAPTER TWENTY

Camden

There was something different. The car had stopped. In the distance, I could hear people hooting and hollering.

Gus was getting out of the car.

"Wait," I cried out, my voice groggy. "I'm going with you."

He paused and looked at me. "You look like shit, Camden. You have to stay here."

I shook my head and sat up. My shoulder ached, my head hurt, everything was moving out of the corner of my vision. I didn't care.

"I am going with you. I will not let the chance to see Ellie go by. What if…" *What if it's my last chance to see her again?* I finished in my head.

Gus waited a few beats, chewing on his lip, his bushy mustache moving in and out. Finally he said, "I couldn't stop you even if I tried. I don't think anything will ever stop you."

"I hope you're right," I said. He helped pull me out of the car and I let out a small yelp of pain as my shoulder got caught on the seat belt.

"Easy now," he warned.

"Got any of those painkillers?"

He brought out a packet from his pocket and shook it. "Oxymorphone. You can't drink on it. That's what Carlotta told me. Of course it doesn't say that on the label because not many dogs drink."

"Just give me the drugs," I grunted.

He thrust them in my hands and I chewed two, grimacing through the bitterness.

"Also, you're only supposed to take one," he added.

I glared at him. "Unless you're the guy who got shot, shut up."

He shrugged. "Suit yourself. But if you collapse in the middle of Veracruz because of an opiate high, you're on your own."

I had a feeling he meant it.

It took no time at all for the high to kick in and the pain to go away. We had a long walk ahead of us into the city, though, having parked in a small suburb close by. I felt like I was bouncing on air instead of dirty streets, the garbage blowing in the light breeze looking beautiful. Everything was beautiful, from the perfume of hot asphalt and night-blooming flowers to the ornate streetlamps that lit up the colonial-style buildings as we got closer to the city. Really fucking pretty.

It was about that time that the euphoric effects of the drug started to wear off and the dirt and grit of the city became a reality. The pain was gone but the picture became real. We were here. We were going to a drug lord's nightclub to find my woman and bring her home.

We got a few curious glances from people as we walked through the city but not enough to arouse suspicion. Gus looked like your average grumpy fat man in his ridiculous Hawaiian shirt, a different print from the other, pink and orange. He must have had a closet full of them. I had my black cargo shorts and a long-sleeved plaid shirt that Gus must have pulled from deep inside my bag when they cut off my old shirt to operate. I still had my arm in a sling, but at least it was black. I looked like a hipster who broke his arm at a Vampire Weekend concert or some shit like that.

The Zoo was at the Zócalo, a square on Independencia Street near the harbor. It was pretty, black and white tiles in the middle, lined with busy cafés, palm trees, and beautifully arched buildings that glowed white and yellow in a slew of lights. A stoic cathedral looked over the whole scene. People were dancing, music was playing. It was Friday night in Veracruz, and we were two of the few tourists not looking for a good time.

"How's your arm?" Gus asked.

"I'm no longer high but I'm not in any pain."

We were approaching the Zoo, a small building at one end of the square. The line outside looked ridiculously long. I hadn't been to many clubs in my life, but back in LA I knew a line like that meant at least an hour wait. There was a chance we would miss her.

"What are your thoughts?" I asked, looking around. I didn't see anything out of the ordinary but, then again, I didn't know who else I was looking for aside from

Ellie. I didn't know what Travis looked like, though I sure as hell remembered Javier.

I choked back a rush of anger. A busy square in Mexico wasn't the place to lose it. I needed to keep my head clear and sharp. I could daydream about a million ways to torture Javier Bernal after I saw Ellie.

"Going into the club might not be a good idea," Gus said. "I don't know what their plan is but us strolling in there might put Ellie in jeopardy. It would probably be almost midnight before we got inside anyway."

I nodded at a café nearby. "How about we sit there and have a few beers, just two guys kicking back. Keep our eyes open."

Considering how popular the area was, we had to wait ten minutes before an outdoor table finally cleared, but when it did, it was worth it. The table was right along the edge, giving us a great view of the line to get into the club. We were far enough away that we would blur into the café crowd if anyone was looking at us but close enough that I could spot Ellie or Javier if I had to.

As much as I wanted us to look like two guys kicking back, tourists having a nice night out in Veracruz, I was a nervous, anxious wreck. I couldn't even drink because of the drugs so I had copious cups of strong coffee, which really didn't help. I sat there, my leg bouncing up and down, trying to converse with Gus, unable to tear my eyes away from the building.

I hadn't seen Ellie but every woman who reminded me of her made me jump out of my seat until Gus had to tell me to stop being such a heat score.

I switched the subject on to something else. Gus's health problems.

"So what was wrong with you, Gus?" I asked him, the fingers on my good arm tapping on the table as I scanned the crowds.

He didn't say anything but I knew he heard me.

"First Lydia, then Dan. Both mentioned you had health problems or something for a while. Just curious as to what it was."

When he still didn't say anything, I tore my eyes away from the building and looked at him. He was staring off into the distance, looking utterly lost.

He sighed and looked down at his hands. "It's personal, Camden. No offense."

"I'm not offended," I told him, turning my gaze back to the crowd. "But since we've been through a lot this past week, I figured I'd be privy to some personal things. You know everything about me. What happened with you? Why are you not matching up with the man that Ellie described to me?"

"People change."

"Some people do. They usually have their reasons."

He chugged his entire beer then slammed it down before motioning for the waiter to bring him another. "Ah, hell."

Once the waiter disappeared, he leaned back in his chair and said, "I had mental health problems, Camden. I sort of lost my mind for a while."

He said this so casually that it took me a bit to realize the gravity of it all.

"For real?"

He smiled sadly. "Yes. For real."

"What happened?"

"A girl broke my heart. Isn't that always the way?"

I leaned in closer. "What girl?"

"Does it matter?"

I frowned. "What happened?"

His face twisted as he grappled with something inside. "It . . . it wasn't meant to be. She was married to a good friend of mine. Once upon a time, she should have been married to me. I guess I got stupid, fell back in love with her. It didn't go anywhere. She made it seem like it would, like it wouldn't be just an affair but . . . anyway, I believed her. She made a living out of lying and I should have known the difference. Played me for a fool, like she played everyone else."

I cleared my throat. "Gus, don't tell me this is a cautionary tale meant for me."

His eyes shot sideways to mine. "No, Camden. You asked. I'm telling you the truth of what happened. But if you want to learn anything out of this, it's . . . don't lose your head. Lose your heart but don't fucking lose your head. You don't know if you'll get that back."

"What would you do if you saw her again? The woman?"

"Oh, now it's a cautionary tale."

I shrugged, my eyes back to the line. Still no Ellie and it was getting late. "I'm just curious. I know what it was like for me when Ellie came back into my life. I suppose I kind of lost my head too. Fuck, I *know* I did. How else did I fucking end up here?"

"Touché," Gus said, raising his beer. I clinked my

coffee cup against his bottle. "What a couple of fucking headless chumps we are."

I chuckled at that and drained the last bit of coffee into my mouth.

Then everything around me whirled to a halt.

Slow motion.

Ellie, Ellie, Ellie.

There she was.

She was leaving the club and walking down the center of the plaza. She was alone. She was devastatingly beautiful, so much so that even admiring her beauty in such a moment of complete shock was surreal.

There she *was*.

Her head was down, looking at the ground a few feet in front of her. She was walking fast, in a hurry, in a bright red dress that glowed on a night like tonight. It was cut all the way down to her stomach, showing off a new tan, attracting the blatant stares of every single man she walked past. Her black hair was done up in ringlets, like a film star, her makeup was seductive and smoky. I'd seen her dressed up to the nines in Las Vegas, but it was nothing like this. This was different— she looked different, walked different, was different. My heart clenched painfully as I was assaulted with things I had no time to think about.

"Gus," I managed to say. I couldn't look away.

"I see her," he said. "She doesn't see us."

"She doesn't see anything."

Suddenly Gus was getting up, pushing his chair back with a loud scrape, and Ellie disappeared around a crowd of people. "We need to follow her. Now."

He threw a handful of pesos down on the table and we moved quickly to the plaza. She was far in front of us, a quick red slash in the crowds of people. We tried to walk as fast as we could without looking like we were chasing someone, but after Gus had collided with the third gawking tourist, we knew it wouldn't matter. Everyone was chasing someone in Mexico.

We started trotting as she disappeared around the corner. Where was she going? Why was she dressed like that, and why was she alone?

Then I remembered what Felipe had said back in Ocean Springs. That they took her to see Travis. That they wanted her to kill her parents first. Were the two connected?

Or...

"He's using her as an assassin," I said as we were about to round the corner.

Gus pulled back on my good shoulder when we reached the edge of the plaza. "Wait. We have to be careful."

He poked his head around and then waved me over. I did the same. Ellie was walking down the street but cutting across it to an idling SUV. We walked quickly in the shadows, ducking between cars, trying to get close enough to see who was driving the beat-up look-ing Range Rover. We couldn't see inside.

"Veracruz license plate, YBA something," Gus said from beside me just as Ellie got inside.

I looked down. He had night-vision goggles in his hands.

"Where the hell did you get those?" I asked.

"My pants," he answered.

The car began to drive off with Ellie inside. I leaped out onto the street, contemplating running after the car, waving my arms, doing something.

"We're not going to lose her," Gus said. "Don't worry."

"Oh yeah, you want to run after the car?"

"I'd rather drive," he said. He took out a screwdriver-looking thing from his pocket and jabbed it into the lock of the hatchback next to us. He busted open the lock with ease and motioned for me to get in the other side after he unlocked the door and got started on the wires beneath the steering wheel.

"I'm impressed," I said.

"To know how to catch car thieves, you have to know how to steal a car," he grunted. The car started with a roar as if to punctuate his sentence and we were bounding down the street, trying to catch up with the Range Rover, which was now turning left onto a busy street.

We plowed through the lights as they went amber, under the early Christmas wreaths hung above the intersections. The Rover was now two cars in front of us. Perfect stalking distance.

Gus navigated the stolen car through the Friday night traffic with ease. "We'll return the car tomorrow."

Energy and twisted excitement was flowing through me. "Gus, I don't really care. I'll do anything not to lose her, a car is nothing."

"I can tell."

We followed the Rover as it headed out of the city and onto the highway leading south to Alvarado.

"Did you hear what I said about Ellie . . . I think Javier's using her as an assassin. Or at least some sort of attempt to get Travis, to kill him."

He nodded. "I figured that."

"Why didn't you tell me?" I pulled my eyes away from the Rover long enough to give him a betrayed look.

"Because you'd lose your nut, Camden. I know how much she means to you. Boy, do I ever." He shook his head to himself.

"Javier is putting her in Travis's lap."

"I wouldn't expect anything less from him."

"Then why aren't you upset?"

"Not everyone shows it like you. Just because I'm not setting people's faces on fire doesn't mean I'm not upset."

I couldn't tell if that was a dig at what I did to his best friend or not, so I decided to let it go. We had bigger things to do than argue.

"Why is Ellie doing this? She was there. She was in his club, looking like . . . a goddess."

"Because this is Travis. And Ellie has never forgotten what he did to her."

"Her parents had a part in it too."

Gus's face grew grim. In the flash of headlights from oncoming traffic, his skin was completely white. "They did. And I'm sure that's why Javier thought he could get Ellie to . . . well, whatever that cartel kid back in Mississippi told us."

"I don't understand." I sat back in the seat, shaking my head. "I just don't. Why doesn't Javier kill these people himself? Why get her to do it?"

"Maybe he has his own agenda. Or maybe he thinks

he's doing her a favor. Maybe that's why she was out there tonight. She agrees with him."

"How could she agree to anything that man says?"

"I don't think you really understand the history those two share."

I felt like punching my fist through the window with my bad arm. Just to feel the pain.

"I need another pill," I said, grinding my teeth instead.

"No, you don't," he said sharply. "We need you to be thinking straight right now. We need our Ellie back, you got it?"

Our Ellie. I liked the sound of that.

"I got it."

*   *   *

We ended up following Ellie all the way into Alvarado. The town was quiet and our presence this late at night would be known so we had to take our time, hanging way back and occasionally turning off the headlights.

The Range Rover parked outside of a fish shop on the malecón, right on the edge of the sea. We parked up the street, watching Ellie's and Javier's silhouettes leave the car and go into the building. I didn't need features to recognize the man. Sometimes a featureless black shape was all it took.

We decided to head to the beach and get a better look at the place from there. We edged silently along the malecón wall, the walkway between the sea and the beach, until we came to a concrete pier with a few fishing boats tied up. We jumped into one and crouched down low, hiding behind smelly crab traps.

Gus had out the night-vision goggles and was playing with them when a light went on in the upstairs of the fish market.

"Look," I breathed out. A sliding glass door opened and Ellie stepped out onto the balcony, still in her dress. She closed the door halfway behind her and walked to the railing, leaning against it, staring out at the sea.

I snatched the goggles out of Gus's hands to get a better look. She looked stunning even in the greeny haze of the night vision. She still took my breath away, so much so I didn't have space in my brain to ponder the big picture—where she was and who else she was with.

"She must be being blackmailed somehow," I whispered to Gus. "Otherwise she could jump down onto the sand and leave. She could run away. She's good at that."

"Give me those," Gus said, taking the goggles out of my hands. He peered through them, twisting the knobs, and we both crouched among the crab traps, watching our dear Ellie staring off into the distance. I looked behind me to make sure I wasn't missing something. The moon was obscured by heavy clouds in the distance, settling over the water like giant spaceships. She was staring at nothing or perhaps at everything. I wondered if she thought about me.

"She looks okay, though," he said in a bright tone that came across fake. "I mean, she doesn't look traumatized. Or beaten. Just pensive."

"How do people with Stockholm syndrome look?"

He sucked his lip before saying "They look a lot like her. Not usually as well dressed though."

"Well, I still think there has to be a reason why she's there, why she's doing this. It can't be black and white."

"For as long as I've known Ellie, she's always been gray. No black, no white."

We watched her for a few moments more. She hadn't moved. I started wondering whether we should come back in the morning or just act now, waving underneath the balcony like a tattooed Romeo, when Javier's silhouette appeared at the door.

I sucked in my breath, blackness poking at my insides.

The door slid open and Javier stepped out. He closed the door behind him and the two of them were lit only by the pale light from inside.

I tried to take the goggles from Gus but he held on to him. "Camden, don't."

"Don't what?" I asked, even though I could see their black forms melding together, becoming one. Either he was standing in front of her talking to her or . . .

I ripped the goggles out of Gus's grasp. He turned around, slumping to the floor, not wanting to look at whatever it was that lay ahead for me.

I put the goggles to my eyes and looked through the viewfinder.

At first she looked like she was talking to Javier. Then his head disappeared. He went low, as if he were picking something up off the ground. That's what I thought he was doing, that he had dropped something, until I realized he wasn't coming back up. And then Ellie's back arched over the railing, her throat exposed, her hair hanging and her mouth open in passion.

I could hear it, traveling across the water to us. Her moans. I'd brought out those same moans myself, perhaps using similar methods. But I still couldn't quite grasp what was going on until I saw Javier appear in the night vision, like a green snake. His hands were all over her, his mouth at her neck, kissing down to her collarbones and chest. And Ellie, Ellie, my Ellie, my woman, she was succumbing to it. Even worse, she was enjoying it. After a while her hands went to his hair and she tugged on it, shoving him back downward.

That was about as much as I could take before it sunk in. Before I realized what I was seeing before my very own fucking eyes. Javier and Ellie. Together.

I hoped vomiting wouldn't make that much of a sound because that's the only thing I could think of doing to deal with all of this. I wanted to throw up, the bile filling my mouth, as if emptying my stomach would empty all the hurt and pain and hate that was filling up inside of me. I didn't know what else to do except wish for death and darkness and anything that would take this torture away. I felt like my heart was being ripped out of my chest and twisted around my throat, choking me.

I must have fallen to my side, because the next thing I knew my head was resting against damp crab trap netting and Gus was shoving two painkillers into my mouth and moving my jaw up and down, trying to get me to chew them.

That was the last thing I remembered before things got fuzzy and I stopped feeling.

CHAPTER TWENTY-ONE

Ellie

With the morning sun streaming through the bedroom window as it ascended over the sea, it was hard to imagine anything in life being that bad. For a split second, with Javier's arm wrapped around my waist, his chest rising and falling behind me, I could pretend that this was my life now: this room, he and I, the shimmering waves at our doorstep.

It was tempting, too, to ask for this to be my future. To forget about revenge, loss, and lies, and just forge through, making a new path. Why couldn't life be about us rolling in the sheets, enjoying each other's bodies, drinking beer and eating fresh fruit, running on the sand, eating at quaint little cafés, and buying fish every night from Pedro?

I knew the answer to that—it wouldn't be enough. Oh, it would be enough for me, to just live and not lie. But Javier would always want more. That was the tragedy of our relationship. Despite the years that passed, the passion that we shared, I would never be enough for him. He needed his revenge more than I needed mine. Perhaps when this was all over and his sisters were safe and Travis was dead, it could work. Maybe he'd give up all his power and live the simple life. Or maybe he'd keep it and convince me to join forces, to embrace the bad side. I didn't know and it was the kind of thing I could never ask for, because the two of us together were as much about deceit as we were about love. How could you ever have both of those and still call it even?

But, maybe, when you had nothing, you had to take what you could get, even if you knew it would hurt you in the end. A love that starts out under a lie is bound to kill you, and sometimes you lived to tell the tale.

A tear rolled down my cheek, cold against my warmed skin. I sniffed and felt Javier's arm around me, tightening. I wished I could say it made me feel safe. It didn't. Because I knew what I did last night and what I had to do today. I was going into the lion's den, under my own power, my own need for vengeance. I was going without protection. Without a safety net. Without a shield.

Alone.

"Are you crying?" I heard a groggy but concerned Javier mumble into my ear.

I swiped away the tear and rolled onto my back, willing the rest of the tears to stay inside, where they belonged. "I'm okay. Just emotional I guess."

"Angel," he said, holding me closer to him. "You did

so well last night. Travis saw you and you played it just right. You're going to do fine today."

"I know," I lied. I felt like I'd do anything but fine. Today there was a chance that I'd have to do more than see his face in a nightclub. I might have to talk to the monster, the very one I'd wanted to scar and burn all those years ago, the man whose death I used to dream about. How could I be fine?

Javier had his way of quieting my thoughts though. We had just enough time for a quick roll in the hay before we had to get up and get ready. As sure as I was that fucking him was fucking with my head, it was the only time I really got peace from what was going on around me. I liked to pretend that everything was going to be all right.

This was going to be the last time I'd see the fish shop for a while. Before the market, I was going to check into the hotel in Veracruz and spend the next few days alone, with only Enrico on the hotel staff to relay messages, though Javier did say he would try and meet up with me at some point if the coast was clear.

I had just finished packing my bag for my role as American tourist when I heard shouting from the kitchen, Javier laying into someone.

Curious, I came out and saw him spearing Raul with a most heated gaze—the kind you never wanted to see Javier give anyone. Raul was leaning on the counter as if he didn't give a shit, a line of coke on a colorful plate and rolled-up pesos beside him.

"What's wrong?" I asked, eyeing the drugs. Raul looked normal but wouldn't meet my eyes. It was then that I noticed Raul's "normal" was definitely always high; his beady, red eyes were a dead giveaway. I'm not sure why I never put two and two together—Raul was a coke addict.

Javier reached over and violently tipped up Raul's chin. "This motherfucker is doing shit right in the open now, where anyone can see it. No respect."

Raul ripped his face away from him and crossed his arms. "It's just us here, Javi. You never used to care."

"I always cared!" Javier roared. "You don't do this anymore, you got it?"

"Oh, not around her, is that what you're saying?"

"I'm saying you're done."

I frowned, wondering if there was some drug lord mantra like you could never get high on your own supply. I was pretty sure there wasn't, considering cartels didn't exactly have a code of ethics. Then again, Javier wasn't like everyone else. He had his own moral code, as warped and twisted as it was.

Raul bent over and quickly snorted up the rest of the cocaine. Then he threw the pesos in Javier's face and walked down the hall, bumping me out of the way with his shoulder. He disappeared down the stairs and I looked back to Javier, certain he was about to lose it.

He was close. Temples red, fists opening and closing, head back and staring at the ceiling. These moments with Javier were dangerous—you never knew which way he was going to go, and I couldn't blame him at all if he went apeshit on Raul.

I stood there watching him for a few moments then

thought better of it, thinking he needed privacy, and turned to head back to the room.

"Ellie," Javier called out, his voice hoarse. "Come here, please."

I'd be lying if I said that a few panicky butterflies didn't start fluttering in my stomach at that moment. I did as he asked, approaching him as you would a stray dog, unsure whether it would bite or lick you.

"Come closer," he said softly, eyes still on the ceiling.

I did, taking a very cautious step.

He raised his arms out to the side, pulling me into a hard embrace.

"We're going to have to get rid of him," Javier mumbled into the top of my head.

"Raul?"

"Yes. He's breaking the rules. He's disobeying orders. I know the signs when I see them. He's going to switch."

"Because of the coke? You run drugs into America, Javier."

"I don't use them, you know this. Drugs clutter the mind and the soul."

I bit my lip to prevent myself from pointing out his hypocrisy. Now wasn't the time. The truth was, I wanted Raul gone too. The drug use was just his way of sticking it to Javier. At least he was giving us a warning.

He kissed the top of my head. "Come on, let's get you checked in."

The butterflies reappeared. I was going to have to get used to them from then on in.

*   *   *

The hotel room was very nice, a bit overly "fiesta" for tourists really looking for that true Mexican feeling. The closets were shuttered teak, colorful striped rugs lined the terra-cotta tile floors, and the back patio was lined with glazed blue pots overflowing with bougain-villea and hibiscus. It was private and peaceful and, as Enrico closed the door behind him, leaving me sitting on the white-lace bedspread, very lonely. I wouldn't say I missed Javier, but it was the first time I'd been all by myself in a while.

The upside of that was that I was finally free. I could walk out the back door and disappear and maybe no one would find me again. I'd drift out there in the world, perhaps finding myself in the process.

Yet I didn't do any of that because of the very reason I turned myself over to Javier in the first place. Yes, I did it to save Camden. But it was my fate, my punish-ment for my past sins. And I had a feeling that if I ran again, they'd continue to catch up to me until I put a stop to them, once and for all.

I had to get to Travis.

Then the real freedom would come.

I sighed and looked over myself in the antique mirror. My hair was done up in ringlets again, my makeup still heavy-handed but appropriate for daytime. My razor blade necklace hung around my neck, a reminder of who I was and why I was doing this. My outfit wasn't risqué like last night's but still it was pretty. Floor-length black peasant skirt, black and hot pink Mexican print, off-the-shoulder top. I'd cut a flower from the patio and pinned it in my hair.

Before Javier dropped me off, we went over the plan one last time. I was to take a taxi to the market and spend a few hours acting like a tourist, stopping at every booth, smelling fruits, tasting samples, and haggling with vendors over leather belts. Travis would be making his rounds. Somehow I'd have to get myself noticed in the crowd. Now was the time to make the move, to flirt, or "whatever it was that you did to me," as Javier put it.

I had no idea what that was. I had been taken with Javier the moment I first laid eyes on him. It was hard not to be, as his magnetism came shining through. But Travis…I couldn't imagine flirting with him. I knew once I saw him, it would take all I had again to keep myself from hurting him. But I had to be strong. I had to be the con artist that I was meant to be: cool, collected, and in control. Or, in other words, I had to become like Javier.

I gave myself one last look in the mirror and swiped on bright pink blush to liven up my face before I headed out to the lobby. The day was sweltering, and vacationers were already lying by the azure pool, enjoying the sun's rays before it became too unbearable. Half of them looked like tomatoes already.

Enrico called me a cab from the front desk and wished me good luck, adding that he'd check on my room later tonight to see if I needed anything. I knew what that meant—he'd relay my messages to Javier. I didn't see why I couldn't just call him, why this had to be such a secretive operation. Perhaps the cartel had control over the phone lines too.

It certainly had control over the market. I had wondered what the point in all of this was, why I had to set everything up so delicately and convoluted when someone could just bring a sniper rifle to the market and blow Travis's head off. Once I got out of the cab, I understood how powerful the man was. He practically owned Veracruz, or at least its army and police force.

Everywhere you looked there were armed guards and army-fatigued police officers, automatic rifles at their sides. They were stationed at all corners of the market, as well as inside, patrolling the aisles, hands behind their backs. I did a quick sweep of the surrounding buildings as the cab driver counted the pesos I'd handed him. When you looked for them, you could find them everywhere—a face at a broken window, a couple of guards on the roofs. The entire market was being watched and patrolled from every single angle. Whoever was stupid enough to try to kill Travis here probably would not only fail but would die in the process.

All of this protection for one horrible man. A horrible man with far too much power and money.

A man I was supposed to stop.

It seemed laughable now.

The cabbie gave me back a few pesos—he short-changed me, but I didn't care. I shoved the money in my macramé purse, threw my shoulders back, and prepared to enter the chaos of Veracruz's Saturday open-air market.

Vibrant was definitely one way to describe it. I bet there was nothing you couldn't buy there. From hanging chickens and chilies to hand-tooled leather bags and expertly woven shawls, the market had everything you could want. A tiny part of me thrilled in this, pretending, just for a second, that I was a tourist looking for souvenirs from her trip to Mexico. I smiled politely at merchants, waved my hands dismissively at those who were shoving pig's ears in my face. I fumbled through my first lines of Spanish, drawing confused looks from a guy I was trying to buy silver earrings from, until I finally hit my stride and was able to communicate the basics. I walked away with the earrings, a white silk shawl, bags of miniature limes (they were cute and I figured in another life I could make margaritas out of them) and brightly colored chili peppers, a leather belt with a silver buckle that had BAD GIRL engraved on it, and a greasy paper bag full of churros.

I munched through one of the churros and made my way around the market for the second time, the sun beating down mercilessly. I stepped into the shade of an awning, part of a butcher shop where cow hocks were being hung on hooks and flies buzzed around greedily, and wiped the sweat off my forehead. I didn't want to look like I was searching for anything in particular, but I hadn't seen Travis yet. That seemed strange, considering he'd be easy to spot, no doubt flanked by a whole phalanx of bodyguards, as if all the stationary guards weren't enough. He really would want to be seen as the city's Don Vito Corleone.

I stayed in the shade until the sweat cooled and then set off again, this time walking down the middle aisles where the crowd was the thickest. A tiny little shopkeeper in a ruffled dress jumped out from behind her stall and started waving around sarongs, pointing to my skirt and yammering on about how I must buy one.

I did my shake of the head, hands waving no, combined with a polite and sympathetic smile, but the woman wasn't having any of it.

"You American, you buy," she said in broken English. She was pushy but her gap-toothed smile was so genuine that I felt bad for refusing her. She placed a sarong in my hands, getting me to pet the fabric, as if it were made out of precious gold instead of scratchy cotton.

I was still shaking my head, trying to be gentle about it, when my eyes went over her tiny head and focused on something in the crowd of shoppers.

A man, a white man about a foot taller than everyone else, had stopped down the aisle in front of one of the stalls. I couldn't see his face, just his profile from behind. Strong tanned neck, short black hair that glinted blue in the sunlight, and ears that stuck out slightly.

My heart hammered in my chest, demanding I acknowledge its presence.

It couldn't be.

Then he turned around and looked my way.

Looked right at me.

Blue, beautifully blue and soulful eyes behind Clark Kent glasses. Strong, wide jaw, full lips, straight nose. Model looks on a model body, dense muscular shoulders, biceps I couldn't fit my hands around. I knew because I'd tried. Tight black T-shirt that showed it all off, including a sling that went around one shoulder, propping up one heavily inked arm.

Camden McQueen.

I dropped the sarong, my bags, everything, caught up in his stare. It couldn't be him. Why was he here?

Had he really come for me after all?

An enormous wash of peace and heart and warmth came over me, giving me strength and resolve that seemed to resonate in my bones. I broke out into a smile so wide I thought my face would split in two. My chest was about to burst.

But he did not return the smile. He kept staring at me, over the heads of everyone bustling past him, the chaotic noise and movements. His eyes were hard, almost cold. Hurt. Something inside me was bleeding, just a trickle.

Then he turned around, started walking away. It wiped the smile clear off my face.

"Wait!" I yelled, trying to be heard above the noise of the market. I left my bags at my feet and started running down the aisle to get to him. I could see his head disappearing slowly, the farther he got away from me, the more the patrons, couples, families, tourists, got between us. "Camden!"

Why was he trying to get away from me? Did he not see me? Did he not recognize me?

I kept pushing my way through, knocking over people's bags, shoving them into each other, knocking over crates of fruit, yelling "*Lo siento*" the whole time. I squeezed past everything and everyone, ducking, dodging, trying my hardest to catch Camden.

And just when the aisle intersected with another aisle, just when I saw the space in front of me open up, someone stepped out in front of me. Not just someone.

Someone and his many bodyguards.

I nearly ran straight into Travis Raines.

My feet stopped in time and I wavered inches away from him.

He was staring down at me, a predatory smile on his face. I shot him a quick glance, forgetting all about the part I was supposed to be playing, and said, "I'm sorry."

I made a move to get around him—I had to get to Camden—but he reached out and grabbed my arm gently. His fingers met my skin, and revulsion engulfed me.

"Young lady, you look familiar to me," he said. His accent was strange, Southern, but he'd subconsciously picked up a Spanish cadence.

My brain was caught, bogged up, stuck. I had to act the part. I had to find Camden. I had to destroy Travis. I had to get out of there. I had to stop running from my past. I had to run after my future.

My future was getting away.

I swallowed hard, realizing that Travis was staring at me, waiting for an answer. If I didn't play my cards right, I wouldn't have a future to run away to.

"Uh, I don't think we've met before," I said, and smiled sweetly, amazed that my voice sounded steady. "I'm not from here."

"I can see that," he said, tone light and eyes . . . well, I tried not to look at his eyes, at their cold dark depths. I looked at his bodyguards instead, all four of them, big guys with faces made of stone. Each second I stood there was a second in which Camden got farther away. My Camden. Who had come for me, to rescue me, to make sure I was safe. My Camden, who looked at me with all the hurt in the world.

Oh God, what have I done?

My eyes drifted over to the stalls, hoping I'd spot him somewhere. Wishful thinking. Travis leaned in closer.

"Looking for someone?" he asked.

"I thought I saw someone I knew." Shit. I needed to hold myself together.

"Then you see how it can happen. I saw you last night. You were at my club."

"*Your* club?" I asked, taking in his bodyguards again because that's exactly what a young woman would do if this man was talking to her like this, surrounded by these thugs.

He grinned and clacked his teeth together, like he was taking bites out of something. It made my blood run cold. "Yes, my club. I own the Zoo. I take it you don't know who I am?"

You are the monster who ruined my life, I thought to myself, keeping my face as neutral as possible. *You are the reason I'm here and not running after the person who came after me.*

"No," I said. "An American, I'm guessing."

He cocked his head to the side, appraising me, something that Javier would sometimes do. The comparison made me feel sick.

How the fuck did my mother get involved with this man?

"Yes. You're an American too," he said. "California accent perhaps?"

I frowned, trying to remember what my fake ID had said. My fake name. My God, I'd forgotten everything already.

"You're good," I told him. "I grew up in California. Pismo Beach."

He clacked his teeth together again. Psycho.

"And what is your name, California girl?"

I swallowed hard. "Eleanor."

"That's a lovely name. Do people call you Ellie for short?"

My heart stopped for a moment. "No. Nora."

I had to get the fuck out of there before I really screwed things up. This was a bad idea. I wasn't going to pull it off. Javier had all kinds of wrong faith in me.

Travis touched my arm lightly. I forced a smile.

"Nora, would you like to have a drink with me?"

I opened my mouth to say no but something told me that no was out of the question with him. I don't think anyone said no to Travis Raines and lived to tell about it.

"Right now?" I asked.

He gave a slow nod. "Yes. Now."

"Sure," I said, forcing another motherfucking smile on my face. "I'm sure you're not a psycho ax murderer."

He let out a guffaw. "No, I'm not an ax murderer. I'm just an expat, a businessman, a capitalist. And I can show you a good time in Veracruz, Miss...?"

"Willis."

"Lovely. Miss Nora Willis. Come have a drink with me, Miss Nora Willis."

He held out his arm for me, as if any self-respecting

woman in her right mind would take it. I eyed it. "You never told me your name," I said.

"I didn't? It's Travis."

"Nice to meet you, Travis."

He led me around, back the way I came, where I picked up my bags, and I fought every single urge in my body to turn around and look for Camden. He'd come all this way for me, yet somehow I knew he was gone.

CHAPTER TWENTY-TWO

Camden

"I am going to fucking kill Javier Bernal."

The sentence hung in the car like a layer of fine dust. Gus put the bag of dried pork rinds that he was eating out of down and gave me a steady look.

"I believe it," he said, crumbs in his mustache. "But do you really expect to go into that shop with guns blazing and get out of it alive? No one just kills Javier Bernal." He resumed munching. "Besides, I don't think you really need to kill him. He's obviously not keeping Ellie there against her will."

My eyes seared into him, enough that his mouth jerked in surprise. "Sorry. I know this is tough for you."

"Tough" didn't even begin to describe it. Tough was easy. This was insurmountable. After we followed Ellie and Javier back to the fish shop, after I saw them... together...his hands and lips all over her, her head back, succumbing to him, I passed out from the pain.

Anyone else would say it was my shoulder, my gunshot wound sneaking up on me. It wasn't that. It was my heart being ripped in tiny, inconsequential pieces, bloody and cold. It was my pride falling down to its knees. It was everything I thought we'd shared turning out to be a lie and the woman I was chasing being nothing more than a ghost.

Gus let me pass out on the fishing boat until just before dawn, when the fishermen were coming to start their day. Then we went up the street, back to the stolen car, and hunkered down there for most of the morning, watching the fish shop, trying to decide what to do next.

I wanted to barge in there and shoot Javier right between the eyes. Part of me didn't even care if it was a suicide mission. But Gus was right. It wouldn't matter—it would feel good for a second, but the damage had already been done.

Gus cleared his throat. "To be fair, Camden, we don't know what's been going on here. Ellie might be playing a part."

"She's still in love with him."

"I don't think so. Ellie doesn't love easily. There's something else at work here, more than memories. We don't know what Javier is holding over her head or what he's promised her."

"You sound like you're taking her side," I grunted, glaring through the dirty windshield at the fish shop in the distance.

"I'm always going to take her side," Gus stated. I looked over at him and he gave me an apologetic smile.

"I'm sorry. I like you, Camden, but my allegiance is to Ellie."

"Why? Why are you doing all of this for her? What has she ever done for you?"

He blinked fast a few times, as if keeping back tears, and then turned his attention to his bag of pork rinds. "Love isn't just about keeping score, or what one does for another person and what another person has to do in return."

His words struck me. "You love her?"

He nodded. "I do. I'm not in love with her. It's not like that. I'm not like you. I care for her a great deal, more than she'll ever really know. It's...complicated."

I frowned, watching him for a few moments, trying to figure him out. "Everything that has to do with Ellie is complicated," I finally said, checking Gus's watch on my wrist. I was able to take another pill in about an hour. At this point it wasn't for the pain anymore—the pain in my heart had overtaken the wound in my shoulder, and no pill would make that go away. But it would give me a sense of oblivion that I so desperately sought.

I knew what Gus had been saying. I'd been a damn, damn fool. Always the fool, Camden McQueen.

"You'll work this out," Gus said. "You can get the chance I never had. Ellie has a good heart in her, hidden but it's there, and you bring that out. You're good for her and you're good for each other. Don't you forget that."

I wanted to. I wanted nothing more than to forget.

"Someone's leaving," Gus announced, and I sat up in the car, ducking down a bit. We were a block up the street, no one could really see us in the car. Still, it didn't hurt to be careful.

A man left the shop, walking down the street toward us. He was thinner than Javier and, as he came close, I recognized him. Raul.

Now I really had to duck. I put my head down as if I were looking for something in the glove compartment.

"He's gone," Gus said. "Didn't even look this way. Who was that?"

"Raul," I said, cautiously poking my head back up. "One of Javier's assholes."

"Everyone's got at least one."

We waited a few more moments, then Javier and Ellie stepped out of the fish shop and into the Range Rover. I wished we were in the GTO, not this piece-of-shit car. It would only have taken a few seconds for me to grab one of Gus's rifles from the back and blow his head off. I'm sure Ellie would have a bit of a shock if her Mexican lover's head exploded beside her, but I figured she deserved it.

I patted the dashboard anxiously. "Okay, there they go."

Gus brought the hatchback out onto the street, keeping far back from the Rover. We didn't have the cover of night anymore, and while Javier wouldn't be looking for me—at least I didn't think he would—he would be looking for anyone following them. He had very precious cargo with him: himself.

"Do you think he's taking her to the market to see Travis?" I asked, even though I already knew the answer. Something must have gone wrong last night when she was at the club and now they were trying again.

"It's possible, unless they're only going on an outing."

"How romantic," I spat out bitterly.

Gus gave me a look I didn't bother to acknowledge. I sat back in my seat, drumming my fingers on my knee, trying to keep whatever I had left in me together. I felt as if I were coming apart at the seams with each second that passed, the images of what I had seen in that sick, grainy, green light kept flashing in my head, settling over me like a gaseous cloud: toxic and deadly, a breeding ground for parasites. I was being eaten alive, consumed by broken love and betrayal and so much fucking hatred for myself, because I was the one who let this happen. I fell for the wrong girl over and over and over again.

"Take it easy," I heard Gus say. I looked down at my leg. I'd dug my fingernails into my knee, the skin beneath my shorts raised with drops of blood. It looked like the panther I'd tatted there had been bitten by a bigger cat. I stretched out my hand trying to relax.

We were in Veracruz when my watch went off and I popped another two pills, chewing them with bitter delight.

"Do you think they'll recognize the stolen car?" I asked woozily as we entered the city.

"People steal cars here all the time. No one's looking for it. Still, one of us should go back to the GTO and put it somewhere else. The neighborhood seemed fairly safe, but I wouldn't trust a soul in this city."

"By 'one of us,' I'm guessing you mean you." I tried

to raise my wounded arm to show him I couldn't drive but drooled on myself instead. These were the good moments, the ones where I was reduced to nothing more than a buzzing invalid.

"We don't have any guns on us. I've got a knife in my sock, that's it. We won't be able to do anything about Ellie until we're armed."

Even through my brief opiate haze, I had to admire Gus's dedication to this. I wanted to tell him that maybe there was no point in even going through with anything anymore—the Ellie we saw last night did not look like one who'd be willing to go with us. I'd remembered his Stockholm syndrome on steroids remark. This might be what we were dealing with. In fact, I hoped it was, because the alternative had already torn me apart.

We followed the Range Rover to a small hotel in the city, set amid lush rain forest, and watched as she Ellie got out with a bag. She waved good-bye to Javier like it was nothing, and the car sped off.

"Well, now fucking what?" I asked, the good part of the drug phase starting to wear off. "Do we follow Javier or her?"

Gus sucked on his lip. "I don't know. I wouldn't leave Ellie here alone."

I watched as Ellie entered the hotel, then I pushed my door open.

"I'm staying," I said.

"Camden, wait," Gus cried, trying to keep his voice down. He grabbed my bad arm for a second, long enough for pain to shoot through me. "Sorry, but just wait. Okay. Okay, you stay here. I'll go follow Javier and see where he goes, then I'll go back to the GTO and get our gear, okay? Stay with her and watch. Don't do anything until I get back."

I got out of the car and looked in through the open window. "How do I know where to find you?"

"Whether she's going to the market or not, meet me there at two PM."

"Where?"

"You'll find me." Then Gus hit the gas and the shitty little car took off down the road, trying to catch up with the Range Rover that was long gone.

I watched him disappear, standing on the side of the road a lot longer than I should have. Because I was afraid...afraid to walk into that hotel and see Ellie. I didn't know what I'd do now. I wasn't about to say anything, but even seeing her up close would be a sword in my gut.

I took in a deep breath through my nose, walked up the street to the entrance, and went inside. The lobby was cool, with high arched doorways that let the breeze in from the courtyard I could see in the back. A slim, eager-looking fellow was behind the front desk. My eyes darted across the tiled floor to see if Ellie was lounging in any of the wicker rockers or hidden by the plants. She wasn't—she must have gone to her room.

I went up to the front desk clerk with the nametag Enrico and asked about a room for the night.

"We have one," he said, flipping through the book. It had been a long time since I'd seen someone log details in an actual notebook, not a computer. "Shared bathroom, if that's okay."

I nodded. "Sure, that's fine. I'm curious, how much is your most expensive room here?"

"That would be the garden haciendas in the back. They run about three hundred U.S. dollars a night, but as you can see they are full."

He tapped the notebook, enough for me to glance down and catch the name Eleanor Willis. One of Ellie's fake names.

"Oh, well, maybe next time," I said. "How much for the shared bath?"

He told me it was sixty dollars a night, and I fished a wad of bills out of my wallet, using my Connor Malloy driver's license. For a while there I'd forgotten I was him. I was forgetting a lot of things about myself lately.

"Do you have any bags?" he asked.

Ah, right. I shook my head and shrugged. "First I mess up my arm mountain biking in the Baja, then Air Mexico loses all my bags."

The clerk gave me a sympathetic smile and handed me the key. I went up to my room, a tiny sliver of Mexico, sat on the narrow, squeaky bed for a minute, trying to gather up my thoughts and coming up empty. Then I decided to head back down to the lobby. I wanted to go into the courtyard, to the pool area where all the tourists were, but there was too much a chance for Ellie to see me, and I still didn't know what I'd do if she did.

I ended up going into the tiny gift shop and found a shirt to wear. The plaid one was starting to smell. I bought a black one that said Veracruz on the back in a nice script. The perfect tourist shirt, even though it was a bit tight. I decided to wear it out and was coming out of the changing room when I saw Ellie through the gift shop window, walking across the lobby.

I had to do something. I had to say something to her. Gus wanted to wait until we knew what the situation was, but I couldn't just let her walk by. Now that she was alone and we were in the same building, everything was different. I quickly paid for the shirt and rushed out of the store. But it was too late; she'd hopped in a cab and off they went.

I went back into the hotel and asked Enrico to call me a cab too. I was tempted to ask him a few questions about Ellie, but something told me to keep my mouth shut for now.

Of course, my goddamn cab took forever to arrive, and when it did I got the slowest fucking driver in the world who kept going on in Spanish, ignoring every attempt I made to tell him I didn't speak the language. By the time he dropped me off at the Veracruz market, it was packed with people and absolutely bustling. How the hell was I going to find Ellie there, let alone Gus?

I walked down the aisles, looking past the merchants, at every person who was squeezing through the crowd. I didn't notice anything unusual except for all the armed guards everywhere I turned. I didn't know if it was protected like this because that was the Veracruz way, or if it had something to do with Travis frequenting the market. Maybe it was one and the same.

I had finally stopped at a taco stand, needing something in my stomach, and was waiting in line with families carrying overflowing shopping bags when I felt the skin on the back of my neck prickle. It felt like lightning was kissing me.

I slowly turned around and, through the sea of people, I saw her face. Her beautiful, cruel face, looking right at me.

Only she didn't look cruel just then. She looked soft, her eyes dark pools, filled with things I wanted to read into, to dive into. She looked like an animal in a very large cage, an illusion of freedom around her but she could only run so far before she'd run back into herself.

Oh, Christ, this hurt more than anything in the world. How easily she had forgotten about me. How she must have tossed my memory to the wind, as she'd done before.

Then she smiled, recognizing me, like it really hit her, and I never thought she could look so much like an angel. She was glowing. And her radiance was breaking my heart.

I couldn't do this. I couldn't do this. I couldn't do this.

I turned around and walked away. I could hear her calling me, her voice thin above the chatter of the marketplace, but I kept walking. I'd come so far to find her and now I was running from the person I'd been looking for.

I pushed through the crowd, going as fast as I could without fucking up my arm, trying to keep my damaged heart still in my chest, trying to breathe through that inner pain, when I suddenly spotted a familiar beer gut in a Hawaiian shirt, speaking in Spanish to a pretty Mexican lady in front of a stand of socks and underwear.

"She's here," I said to Gus as I stopped in front of them.

Gus gave me a disappointed look. "Camden, this is Esmerelda."

I gave her a curt nod. Now wasn't the time for pleasantries. I looked back to Gus. "What do we do?"

"Okay, well then, let's go talk to her. This place is as good as any."

"Can you do it?" I asked him, feeling ashamed the moment I did so. I went on, "You're not as emotionally involved."

"Says you."

"I should keep my eyes open to see if Javier or Travis pops up."

Gus raised his eyebrow. "Javier wouldn't dare show his face here. Now how about you man the fuckup, put your big-girl panties on, and go get your fucking ex-girlfriend back?"

I felt like I'd been slapped in the face. It went red immediately and I hoped Esmerelda didn't understand a lick of English. But it worked. I shoved my pride aside for a moment and decided to do what we came here to do, what we had fought so hard for.

I only hoped it was all for a reason.

Gus shook Esmerelda's hand good-bye, and I led him back the way I came, hoping Ellie was still about somewhere.

"Oh, shit," Gus said under his breath. He'd stopped on the spot, causing a woman with a bag of fruit to collide into his back and let loose a string of Spanish obscenities. I followed his eyes. Beyond the crowd of people, where this aisle intersected with another, was a wall of men in black. Bodyguards protecting someone.

I knew who it was, even before Gus muttered, "Travis. We have to get out of here."

"Why? We're just tourists," I whispered back, ignoring the frustrated shoppers trying to go around us.

"What was that quote I said about casting doubt...?"

"Something about shadows," I filled in. "It wasn't very good."

He turned around, pulling on my good arm. "Come on, let's go down the next aisle and look over that way, see what's happening."

We went around and all the pain and heartache I was feeling over was replaced by a more familiar feeling: dread. With Travis in the picture, an actual living breathing real-life threat, someone more dangerous than Javier could ever be, the reality began to settle in. I started to feel like a real fucking chump, turning away from Ellie in the market like that. We stopped beside a shopkeeper selling poorly made pottery. No one else was there, and we were able to get a clear view into the next aisle over.

There was Travis Raines. Not at all what I expected. He was tall, reed thin with a shock of slicked-back gray hair. He was much older than I thought—well, at least in his sixties, as I assumed Gus was. However, Gus put out this air of being crotchety but harmless, and people probably underestimated him. There was no underestimating Travis. He oozed power, like it sustained him more than oxygen. Everyone, from the stoic bodyguards to the scared people walking past, giving him quick but furtive glances, were aware of this power, this energy, this...evil. That was dramatic but true.

Then there was Ellie Watt, or Eleanor Willis, as she now was. Standing in front of him, trying to look like any other girl. Of course I could see that she was more than any other girl. She was a heartbreaker. She was a temptress. She was lost. And now she was found, at least by me. I hoped Travis didn't pick up on any of those things. I hoped he saw her as a beautiful, average American tourist. I hoped she knew exactly what she was doing and that the confidence she was portraying was more than an act.

We watched them like a pair of creepers until Travis stuck his arm out for her and she accepted it, having him lead her away, the wall of bodyguards flanking her.

"The fuck. Where are they going?" I said. "What is she doing?"

The shopkeeper with the shitty pottery picked this time to get annoyed with us and shooed us away once he realized we weren't going to buy anything. I began to go after Ellie, but Gus reached out and grabbed me by the shirt.

"No," he said. "We don't follow him. We can't get away with that, not here."

I swallowed painfully. "How can we just let her go off with him?"

"We can. We have to. We don't know what her plan is. At any rate, we don't have an option. To follow her is to put her in danger and that's the last thing either of us wants, you got that? Look, we'll go back to your hotel room. I've got all the stuff now. Unpack and wait."

"Wait where? What if Javier or Travis follows her back?"

His mustache twitched. "We'll get you in her bedroom. You'll already be on the inside when she comes back."

If *she comes back*, I thought. Gus looked at me like he was thinking the same thing.

CHAPTER TWENTY-THREE

Ellie

I remembered being about eleven years old when my parents first started talking about leaving Mississippi. It was a hot spring day, hot like hell, and I was sitting on the front step of our trailer, watching the kids run down the street, laughing, having a good time. They were all wearing their bathing suits as kids tended to do when it got in the 80s with 100 percent humidity.

Not me. I sat there in the hot sun, in my own sweat, wearing jeans. They were baggy, really lightweight, and I had a hole in one knee, but it didn't make up for the fact that I could never be like one of those kids. I used to be, then in one night that all changed. After that, I fell asleep in tears because it hurt so bad, my teeth being ground into nothing because my mother refused to give me anything stronger than Children's Tylenol. During the day, when the pain was a bit better, I'd cry anyway because I could never be normal again. All I wanted to do was strip down to my bathing suit and join the kids in their search to find the nearest hose or sprinkler. But I couldn't. I didn't dare. Fear of being different, of being inferior, had consumed me at a young age.

So I sat there on the steps and watched the world go on without me. Behind me there was a screen door to let in the filthy breeze and behind that my parents sat at the table and started discussing my future. I don't know if they realized I was listening and could hear them or if they didn't care, but they talked about me as if I wasn't there.

My father was scared because Child Services had visited him at work, wanting to check in. I suppose they had come by when I was at school too. I hadn't really seen any of them, least not that I knew of. No one was asking me questions yet, but that's what they were afraid of. I wanted to tell my parents that I knew my lie so well I wouldn't do anything to get them in trouble. Funny thing is, I don't think they ever believed me. I bet they sat around in fear like I sat around in fear, thinking that one day I would turn on them.

Instead, they're the ones who turned on me. They're the ones who got up and left me one day, leaving me with my uncle.

Anyway, before that even happened, my parents were planning their escape. I remember it was my mom's idea for us to go to California. My dad was totally against it, and as I sat there on the porch and started thinking about how magical California sounded, how my uncle

Jim seemed like a real cool guy, I wondered why. My dad kept saying if we went to California, we were only going so we could see "him," but not her brother, someone else, and the last time my mother pulled a stunt like that, it had nearly gotten me killed.

At the time all I could fixate on was California and movie stars and the wild Pacific Ocean. Everything else went over my head.

Now all I could wonder about was how on earth my mother was able to have an affair with Travis. Not that she wasn't a gorgeous woman back in her day, that real Eastern European look, but why? How did it get started? What made my mother look at him and want him for herself? I didn't care how charming he was or how sweet he must have been to her—wouldn't she have looked at him and seen the monster underneath? Did she seriously think she could fix him? Redeem him? Was she ever in love with him, or had she just been a fool, foolish and reckless enough to use her own flesh and blood to get back at him?

The longer I sat across from Travis at a small, smoky bar that blotted out all the light and heat from outside, the more I couldn't understand her. How she could be with him and not be afraid for her life? Because I was her daughter through and through. And I was extremely afraid for my own life.

I eyed the bodyguards who flanked us on all sides. They never once looked my way. We had the whole bar to ourselves. Travis had gotten the owner to order everyone out. Not that there were that many people drinking in a jazz joint like that during the day, but still. He basically snapped his fingers and it happened. People did it as if their lives depended on—and I guess they did. The amount of power he had was sickening, to the point where people must have thought he'd have them executed on the spot if they didn't do what they were told. And there would be nothing that anyone could do about it. No police, no government, no army, no justice. Travis Raines and his new cartel owned them all.

At the moment, while I sat there in the booth across from him, he owned me. It went against every sniveling thread of pride I'd ever felt to admit that, but that was the truth and the truth was what it was. He had helped make me what I was, the con artist who never believed anyone was coming to save her, the girl who struggled to find the good deep inside. He had had his hand in it. And now he had my life in his hands. Because if Travis Raines found out that Ellie Watt was sitting across from him, the damaged daughter of Amelie Watt, I would be dead in a second. Even if he didn't figure it out, there was still a chance he would kill me for no reason. Just because he could.

"Would you like another drink?" he asked me. "Perhaps some water? You're looking a bit flushed."

I grimaced and put a hand to my forehead. Obviously the strain of the situation was showing on my face more than I thought. I needed to play it off. "Water would be great, thank you. I think I got too much sun today. I'm a bit dizzy."

He frowned subtly, just a darkening of the eyes. "That's a shame. I was hoping to take you out for dinner tonight. I own one of the best restaurants in town."

"You sure own a lot of things here."

He clacked his teeth together a few times and I resisted the urge to grip the edge of the table. "I own all of Veracruz. You will soon find this out. You speak the name Travis Raines and you'll see it in people's faces. The respect. The awe. For me."

Oh God, I wanted nothing more than to take my glass and figure out a million ways to break it on his head.

"Must be nice."

"You don't seem easily impressed."

I shrugged because that's what Eleanor Willis would have done.

"Maybe you'll get a chance to impress me tomorrow then."

I thought maybe I was pressing my luck, playing that hard-to-get kind of girl. Maybe he offed girls like that. But his eyes glinted hard with the challenge. The sick fuck *liked* it.

"Well, I shall rise to the occasion. Would you like a ride back to your hotel? Where are you staying?"

Now was the time to figure shit out. If I refused, would he follow me anyway? Would it better to be up front so he could follow me and I could see him do it?

"Yes, that would be great. I was going to take a cab, but if it would be no bother..."

"No bother at all." He smiled, face like an eel.

We left the bar and walked to the street where a massive SUV pulled up, seemingly out of nowhere, and he ushered me into the backseat. It was pretty similar to the one Javier had back in Ocean Springs, except the glass was exceptionally thick—bulletproof.

I was a mound of springy nerves the entire drive back to the hotel. I kept thinking how easy it would be for him to keep driving, take me away somewhere and shoot me. Rape me. Torture me.

To make matters worse, he picked up on this, shooting inquisitive glances over his shoulder as he sat in the passenger seat. "Are you all right?"

"Just the heatstroke. I should have mentioned I get carsick too," I said, hoping that would explain my sweaty palms that I unintentionally kept wiping on my skirt.

He shook his head as if I were just a giant mess. And I was. I was the biggest fucking mess, and I didn't realize how big until after he dropped me off at the hotel and told me that he'd come by for me tomorrow at 6 PM and to wear something stunning.

It was then, and only then, had I realized the gravity of the situation I was in. When I walked into the hotel and saw Enrico watching my every move, it made me realize how trapped I was, how alone. I had no one to hold my hand and tell me I was doing the right thing, that everything was going to be all right.

Camden.

I know I'd seen Camden, it hadn't been a dream. It couldn't have been. I saw him there in the market. He looked right at me. But the face I saw staring back at me wasn't the one I imagined ever seeing again. It was the face of a broken man, and guilt was starting to poke at me, telling me *I* was the one who broke him. This Camden who somehow found me in another country, only to turn and walk away.

I staggered past Enrico, telling him I had had too much sun and wanted to nap for a little bit. I hoped that would be enough to keep him away for the time being. I had something I needed to do, something I'd started but never got to finish.

I went through the courtyard bathed in twilight, walking faster as I went, until I got to the room. I wrestled with the old key for a few moments before the door opened and I went flying into the dark coolness. I locked the door behind me and flung myself on the bed. And I began to cry. Bawl. Sob. I cried because, at the base of it all, I was scared, mostly of myself. And if I couldn't trust myself, I had no one left at all.

I cried it all out of me and even when I was done, when it felt like I had nothing left inside, I rolled over onto my back and the feeling was still there. Disappointment in myself. For letting things go so far. If things went sour in the next twenty-four hours, I'd only have myself to blame.

I lay there for a few moments, praying for sleep to come and take me away, so I wouldn't have to face anything or do anything or be anyone anymore. I was drifting off when I heard it. The sound of metal, delicate; a hanger on a closet rail.

Someone was in my room.

To be more specific, someone was in my closet.

I sat up slowly, looking around for a weapon. I had been left there with nothing, not even my gun. What the hell had Javier been thinking? No, what had *I* been thinking?

"Who's there?" I asked, my voice breaking. "I know you're in the closet."

The hangers moved again. I held my breath and started calculating the distance from my bed to the front door. Could I make it out before the intruder caught me?

I had to chance it.

I scrambled to my feet and started running, my sandals sliding on the tiles almost bringing me to the ground. The closet door burst open at the same time and a large dark figure flew out of it, coming for me.

I was almost at the door, my hand reaching for the knob, when the person tackled me from behind with one arm going around my shoulder. Instead of pitching me forward onto the cold stone tiles, the person started to twist as we fell, his body taking the brunt of the impact. He landed on his back, and I landed on top of him.

The man let out a cry of pain, familiar and sharp, but my body was still on an adrenaline high and I tried to get off of him, to get away, to scream for help.

He was quick. Before I could move, his hand went over my mouth and he held me, the back of my head against his hard chest and grunted in my ear, "Ellie, it's me."

The sound of his voice immediately made me relax. I nodded against his hand and he let go. I flipped around and found myself face to face with Camden.

"You weren't a dream," I said, finding my breath again. I trailed my fingers down the side of his face, feeling the stubble, the strength of his features. "You actually came for me."

He flinched a little under my touch then his face

became all steel. He swallowed. "Of course I came for you. I told you I would."

I was lost in his eyes, the sincerity beneath the blue. How honest he was. I never considered that he would have kept his word. I never thought I was worth that.

Oh God, the guilt. Javier. He couldn't know about that, could he?

"How . . . how did you find me?" I asked.

He closed his eyes, resting his head back on the floor, wiggling his jaw back and forth. It was only then that I noticed the sling around his shoulder, his T-shirt soaked in one spot.

"Oh my God, Camden. What happened to you?" I got off him quickly and tried to help him up. He'd taken the fall for me so I wouldn't get hurt, though that couldn't have been good for his arm.

I hope he doesn't know. I hope he doesn't know.

"I got shot," he said, letting me get him to his feet. I'd forgotten how big he was.

I'd forgotten everything.

"You got shot?" I said when everything finally registered. "When? What?"

He grimaced and tried to move over to the bed. "I need to sit down. Do you have anything to drink? Something really stiff?"

"I don't know," I told him, running over to the mini-bar to check. It was stocked with small bottles of liquor. I grabbed four tequilas and two glasses and placed them on the bedside table, then made a move for my purse where I had put the bag of limes from earlier.

"I don't need lime," he said, trying to unscrew the

cap off the bottle with one hand, finishing the job with the teeth.

I had an unpleasant flashback to the tequila shot I'd taken with Javier the night before.

Did he know? Did he know?

He spat the cap out then emptied the contents of the bottle straight into his mouth. He did the same with another bottle.

I watched in silence, hovering nervously like a bird, wiping my hands up and down my sides, unsure what to do with myself or what I was to him now. He'd come so far, all this way, just to make sure I was okay. I didn't want to tell him what a mistake it was, that he'd wasted it all on a terrible, terrible girl.

He'd gotten shot. *For me.* And I was sleeping with the enemy, believing this man would never come save me.

Now Camden was watching me, his breath slowing. The look in his eyes was dark and calculating, reminding me a lot of the time he discovered me trying to rob him. Only he didn't have the gun to my head.

I wished he did.

"What happened?" I asked, before the guilt could eat me alive in silence. "How did you get shot?"

"Mexican police," he said, unscrewing the third bottle. His eyelids were drooping, his gaze lazy and, if I looked closer, full of something like contempt. "We were driving on the highway outside of Tampico. They took a shot. Lucky shot."

"We?"

He nodded slowly. "Me and Gus."

"Gus!" I exclaimed. "Where is he, is he okay?"

"He's not shot, if that's what you're worried about," he said rather coldly. "He's up in the hotel room."

"You're staying here?"

"Came all the way down to Veracruz to get you, Ellie."

I blinked, tried to say something intelligible, but nothing came out. I took a seat on the corner of the bed and put my hand on his knee. He eyed it until I took it away. Something had changed so terribly much and I was so afraid to find out what it was. He was looking at me with the eyes of a stranger.

I gave him a weak smile. "Well, thank you for coming to get me. I don't even know how you found me."

A shadow seemed to fall across his face. He looked like a shell-shocked soldier, older, wiser, harder.

He licked his lips. "It wasn't easy."

"How are Sophia and Ben?"

He let out a sharp, cold laugh. "Oh, Sophia and Ben? Oh, they're just fine. Especially since they got rid of their chump Camden."

His voice was twisting, slicing, going to a bad place. "What—"

He sat up straighter, sneering through the pain in his shoulder. "They're absolutely fucking fantastic. Maybe a bit mad that their little setup didn't work. Oh yeah, Sophia, her brothers, probably your little boyfriend Javier, they were all in on it."

My eyes widened at the term "boyfriend." I felt like my lungs dropped through to the floor. No...

He went on, louder, his eyes watering, blazing angrily into mine. "Nothing like finding yourself on the front cover of the *LA Times*, wanted for assault and homicide. Nothing like having to run for your fucking life while trying to track you down!"

I couldn't breathe at the memory of Javier reading the *LA Times*...

"Nothing like going to fucking Mississippi to find you and end up in your old fucking house that you shared with him and then learning what he had planned to do with you."

I shook my head, the tears springing to my eyes, unable to make sense of what he was saying, where this was going. Though he had been set up, he still went all the way to Ocean Springs to try to save me.

"What was the plan?" I whispered.

He leaned forward as if he were going to tell me a secret, eyes glinting. Darkness was falling fast outside of the window, but I was too frozen to turn on the lamp.

"Javier brought you there to kill your parents."

Ice. Pure ice.

"What, why?" It didn't make any sense.

Camden shrugged with his good shoulder. "'Cause he's fucking Javier and he's fucking insane, that's why. Just how brainwashed are you?"

"I'm not brainwashed."

He laughed again, this one more brutal. "Oh, that's a good one. So, tell me, what did he say or do to you to get you to come down here and kill Travis?"

"He told me he'd kill you," I cried out in indignation.

"And you believed him?" he asked.

"Of course I fucking believed him! I wouldn't have done it otherwise."

"If you believed him..." he said softly, rolling the bottles of tequila back and forth over the bedspread covers. He smiled once, to himself. "If you believed him, that he would do such a terrible thing to me, that he had that power"—his eyes flicked up to meet mine—"why would you go ahead and fuck him?"

The world was pulled out from under me. One fell swoop, and everything I had to stand on, everything I thought was solid was gone. I was falling, straight into my guilt. The tears rolled down my cheeks. I struggled to keep the sobs inside.

I couldn't look at him anymore. I couldn't look at myself ever again.

"I'm so sorry, Camden."

He waited a few moments, rolling the bottles back and forth, before saying "It doesn't matter."

"It *does* matter. I didn't do it to hurt you. I don't know why I did it."

"Because you're weak," he shot in. Another half shrug. "And you never really gave a shit about me."

"Camden, please!" I sniveled, reaching for his hand. He let me hold it, cold, no life in it for me. "Please, listen to me. I didn't think you'd ever come for me. I thought you would go on in your new life with Sophia and Ben. I thought I was alone and I'd stay alone as I've always been and..."

"Nice sob story, Ellie Watt."

"It's not a sob story! It's the truth."

"O ye of little faith."

"Well...I *don't* have faith in people. You know that."

"I know nothing!" he screamed. "I came all this

way for you because I thought you were in trouble and you aren't! You're in the kind of trouble you want to be in. I...know...nothing...about you." He seemed to have exhausted himself and lay back against the headboard, eyes rolling into the back of his head, which he gently shook back and forth. "I'm so fucking tired of being shit on."

"I know," I said quietly. I looked down at my hands like they were foreign objects. "You are the last person I'd ever want to hurt."

"But you did. Who else have you hurt today? Javier? Travis?"

"I don't know who I'm hurting anymore. Camden, please, you have to believe me. I didn't think I'd ever see you again. I slept with Javier because...because I loved him once. And he's made me believe that I belong with him, with this kind of life, that this is the best that I can get."

"He's right."

I looked up at him in shock. He was looking at me, our past written all over his face. I don't think I've ever had a knife stuck in me so deep. I don't know if I'd ever deserved it as much as I did then.

CHAPTER TWENTY-FOUR

Camden

I knew I hurt her.

Her face crumpled like a demolished building, pretty and strong in one moment, a ruin in the next. I knew she was hurting, feeling it, feeling everything. I knew she felt like absolutely nothing. Worthless. Rotten.

I knew she felt like I did. That's what I wanted.

She looked away from me, the tears frozen in her wide eyes, always threatening to spill over but never quite doing it. No release.

As angry as I still was, as bitter as the air tasted, there was a pang of sorrow somewhere in my chest. For fighting so dirty and hitting so low. No matter what Ellie deserved, how broken and utterly messed up she was, I still loved her. Deciding to not love her anymore wasn't going to be that simple.

Besides, I had to think about the big picture, about

Gus, about Ellie. My feelings for her, what we had shared, didn't even have to come into the equation. I came there to rescue her, to save her from all of this, and until the bitter end, that's just what I was going to do.

I only wished it hadn't hurt so much. I wished I had the strength inside me not to care.

"Ellie," I said quietly. I reached for the last tequila bottle and tossed it at her.

She caught it and stared at it numbly. She was in shock, dazed, lost in her thoughts and a million waves of remorse. I knew that look too.

I nodded at the bottle. "Drink up, baby."

She quickly screwed off the cap and drained the contents. She coughed a bit but got it down then chucked the bottle across the room where it landed on the tiles with a clatter.

My back twitched in response. That was going to fucking kill me in the morning. I couldn't tackle her in this place without hurting her. What was a little bit of extra pain for me in the long run? My shoulder was already killing me, my heart doubly so.

"Camden," she started, looking down, shoulders slumped as she sat on the edge of the bed. For the first time since I'd known her, she looked frail, easy to break. It didn't suit her. Another face of Ellie Watt, another person I'd have to get to know. "Were you… are you sure that Javier wants me to kill my parents?"

I nodded. "You believe me, don't you?"

She looked at me, all brown eyes. "Yes. I do. I'll never doubt you again."

I didn't particularly trust that. Ellie doubted everyone and everything that ever crossed her path. It was
hard for me to blame her when I saw it everywhere
she went. Even now she was discovering it with Javier,
though she surely should have seen that coming. Oh, I
couldn't wait to get my hands around that man's neck.

"I don't understand why he'd do that, why not just
tell me?"

"Gus and I have been trying to figure it out too. You
did say he had a twisted code of ethics and that he kept
his promises. Look what happened to Uncle Jim." *Yes,
look what happened to Uncle Jim,* I wanted to repeat it
for her benefit. He killed your uncle then you still slept
with him. You fucked a murderer.

The rage was dying to sweep in again. This was
going to eat me alive until the end of my life.

Only if I let it.

I took in a deep breath. "Ellie, I know that for whatever reason you must trust Javier or have some sort of
connection to him. I know you believe that what you're
doing is right. I understand the vengeance you want
with this man and I know what you'd do to get it. I only
want you to realize that you don't have to do any of this
if you don't want to. You can leave here with me and
Gus, tonight. We can put this behind us."

"Would killing him be so wrong?" she asked quietly. I had to fight the urge to wrap my arm around her
and bring her into me, to hold her close, tell her that I
loved her, that I wouldn't let another thing happen to
her. I'd take another bullet for her. I'd be there no matter what she chose, even if she wanted another lover,

another life. I would still be there when she fell. When she wanted to run. When she wanted to come home.

"Do you feel that killing him would change any-thing?" I asked. "Would it make a difference in your life, for the better?"

She mulled it over, her eyes searching aimlessly while the wheels in her beautiful brain turned. What-ever she'd say, I would understand. Because I knew what it was to have that anger so deep inside you, you think the only way you'll ever be rid of it is to be rid of the person who put it there. But only later do you real-ize what the truth is—that no one put that anger there. No one except you. And you have to live with yourself while someone else is dead or suffering or destroyed. Another body to add to the funeral pyre. Another weight on your already laden soul.

Finally she said, "I don't know. I've wanted this for so long, this retribution for myself. That if I kill him, I'll be free of everything that's held me down and told me where to fit in this world. Told me what I am. That if I kill him, the man who made me bad, I'll be good. Sometimes..." A tear rolled down her cheek, the dam breaking, the release. She sniffed. "Sometimes I'd do anything to be good."

Damn it. God damn it. My heart was breaking all over again, just when I thought I didn't have anything inside me to break.

"Come here," I said, leaning forward and bringing her down onto me. She lay with her head on my chest, sobbing quietly. "Hey, remember when we were kids and we'd lie like this on my trampoline?"

She sniffled. "I don't remember crying back then."

"No. No, we never cried in front of each other. We were too cool for that. It didn't mean we weren't crying inside. Or for each other." I cupped my good hand behind her head and held it there, took in a deep breath. "Ellie, I will help you with whatever you need to do. You won't have to go through this alone. If you want to kill Travis, for whatever reasons you have, I will be there for you. And when you're done, if you let me, I will take you back home. And if you want to back out of it now, if you want to disappear tonight and never look back, Gus and I will help you with that too. Whatever you've done or thought or planned or given up on, it doesn't change the fact that we came here for you. We came here to help you, Ellie, in whatever way you choose."

She stiffened on top of me, her limbs going rigid. "You can start by hiding back in the closet."

"What?"

She sprang up, eyes flying to the window. "Go now, to the closet, under the bed, hide. Somewhere! Go!"

There was no way I would fit under the bed quick enough, especially with my arm, so I quickly ducked back in the closet, sticking my good fingers through the slats and pulling it closed just as there was a knock at the door.

"Miss Eleanor Willis?" came a muffled voice.

I held my body as still as possible, my breath quiet, and tried to look through the slits without bumping into the hangers again.

From the angle of my view, I could see Ellie getting up and going over to the door and answering it.

"Hi, Enrico." She sounded drunk, a little too drunk. An act.

"Miss Willis," Enrico said. A large pause. I could tell he was looking at her oddly. "Can I come in?"

"Am I allowed to say no?"

Another pause. "No, miss. I'm sorry."

"Fine, come in." She walked away lazily and plopped down on the bed.

The door shut and he stopped in the middle of the room.

"What happened here?"

"Girls just want to have fun." She punctuated that with a giggle. She was going on a bit too strong and I had to wince, hoping Enrico bought it.

"Are you alone?" He started to walk to the patio entrance, the one I had come in through. He tried the door and I was glad I remembered to lock it.

"Of course I'm alone," she said. "Least I was until you showed up. Can't a girl have a few drinks in peace?"

He turned around and came back, stopping at the foot of the bed. Through the serrated slivers of my view, I could see his shoes and pants were both immaculately white. Enrico had seemed like a nice enough boy when I'd checked in, but he was obviously a friend of Javier's, which vetoed all innocent appearances.

"Miss Willis, your neighbors reported people yelling in here."

Pause. "So? Was I keeping them awake? It's not even nine o'clock."

"You were the one yelling?"

"Yes, so what? Free country, isn't Mexico?"

"*Who* were you yelling at?" he said, pleasant customer service patience being tested.

"Well, obviously myself. What, you never had a good yell, a good cry, a good fucking mental breakdown when you've been pawned and screwed over by various drug cartels?" Her voice was rising sharply near the end, and I could tell this wasn't an act at all. Despite always being shit on, I was starting to feel a bit sorry for her.

The truth was, I knew Ellie didn't do any of it to hurt me. Call me a fool, and I was, but I knew that deep down she'd do what she could to spare my pain. She cared enough about me for that. It still *hurt*, knowing that she believed I'd never come. I knew she never trusted anyone and I was just another lover to her who would one day break her heart and forget her name, but she should have known I wasn't like that. I wasn't like them. I wasn't like everyone else. She should have known what she was to me, that the only reason we were ever separated was because we didn't have a choice. I guess *she* did have a choice, though both of them were shitty ones. Her sacrifice didn't help us much in the end. It was all for nothing.

"Miss Willis, Javier wants you to know that you're completely safe here."

Javier. I almost put my fucking fist through the closet door but composed myself in time. That nasty, terrible blackness wanted company. I couldn't think about him, or her and him together, or how she could still do that to me, even if she never did it on purpose. I hated, hated, how easily he was able to win her back over, to make her doubt herself, to coerce her into doing such things. Sex was sex and I understood that. What I couldn't understand was his power over her. Or maybe I didn't want to. She was better than that. I believed it. I knew it.

"How am I safe?" she asked snidely, adjusting herself on the bed. "Because I just had drinks with Travis Raines and I didn't feel the slightest bit safe."

"You are safe here," he said, gesturing to the room. "He has people stationed all over now. There are two men just beyond the courtyard, on the other side of the river. If anyone comes in through there, they will find them. There are people at the front of the hotel too, and of course I am here. You can call me at all hours of the night. You are protected, wherever you are."

What Enrico, what Javier, was really trying to tell her was that she was stuck, held prisoner in her hotel. There was no way she could run off with me and Gus tonight or any other night. She was protected from one man and a captive to the next.

"Well, I guess that should make me feel safe," she said. "Until tomorrow night."

"Tomorrow?"

"Yes, Travis wants to take me out for dinner. Six PM."

"I see. I will let Javier know."

"You can tell Javier that I don't want to do it."

Pause. He walked over to the other side of the room. "I will tell him that. I do not know what his answer will be."

"His order, you mean."

"Yes, his order. I'm sorry if I come across a bit

unfriendly, but I have to follow his orders, and that may mean making you go out for the dinner tomorrow. Do you understand?"

The girl couldn't seem to go anywhere without someone threatening her.

"I understand," she said with a dejected sigh. "Listen, Enrico, can you do me a favor and get me another drink?"

He walked over to the minibar and opened the door. "Tequila is all gone."

"Then I'll take the bourbon."

"You Americans like to mix it up." He tossed the bottle to her and she caught it.

"I like to keep my liver on its toes."

"Well, good night, Miss Willis." Enrico walked over to the door. My breathing started to slow in relief. "I hope you can sleep well knowing how safe you are."

She cracked open the bottle of JD and drank it back before she said, "Good night."

The door closed. She waited a few tense moments before she went up and locked it. Then she went around to check the patio door again and closed the curtain there. She came back to the bed and lay down, her legs dangling off the edge. I could see the start of the cherry blossom tattoo snaking its way up her calf. It looked a bit rough, and for one crazy second I was concerned that she wasn't moisturizing it enough.

She went into the bathroom, almost forgetting that I was there. I wouldn't have put it past her. Then she came out, undressed, her top and skirt sliding to the floor and pooling around her ankles, reminding me of the obsidian shape of my dreams, then pulled on a T-shirt, turned off the main light, then the lamp and climbed into bed. Darkness.

I waited for ten more minutes, wondering if I should take a chance and say anything or if I should just hunker down in the closet and prepare for the night there. I wasn't going to chance leaving her room now, not when she was being guarded and heavily watched.

I pulled out Gus's cell from my pocket, checking it. He said he was going to see about getting a cell phone from a store in town, but so far I only had the line to his room. I'd have to call him in the morning and fill him in. I hoped he wasn't sitting up worrying about us too much.

Finally I decided to risk it and slowly pushed open the closet door. The room was dark except for the faded orange light of the illuminated walkway outside that came in through the flimsy curtains. I made my way over to the other side of the bed and got in, on top of the covers.

She rolled over to face me, her legs curled up in the fetal position, her hands clasped under chin. We looked at each other for a few seconds, and in that time I wondered how I was ever going to get past this. I wondered how I was even going to try. She could give me her excuses, but it wouldn't make much difference. It didn't take back what had been done and what had been done didn't take the love away. It only made me want to try and compartmentalize it, to tuck it away somewhere deep inside, a hint of hope shining among all the wicked and soulless things. That was the only way I was going to be able to get through this—locking it up and hoping it stayed in there.

Normally I would have kissed her, felt her body beneath my hands, do all those things to her that I had been dreaming of. I had wanted it, needed it, craved it. But I couldn't. I couldn't touch her now, not now. I don't even think she knew who her body belonged to at the moment. It certainly wasn't me. And the sooner I got over that bit, the better we would both be.

"I'll see you in the morning," I whispered softly. "They may be out there, but you'll be safe right here."

I could see in the gleam of her eyes that she needed me to come close, to put my arms around her and make everything all right. She was as vulnerable as I'd ever seen her. But I just turned over onto my back and let the tequila and heartbreak take me away.

CHAPTER TWENTY-FIVE

Ellie

I woke up right before sunrise, when the room was a purple gray haze, the air was decidedly heavy. It was a weird atmosphere, and it took me a few seconds to figure out where I was and who the man next to me was.

Camden. He was sleeping on his back, his glasses still on, lips parted. He was like a fragment from my dream, a faded portrait of masculinity, heart, and ink. My heart, that beating organ that had been so elusive to me of late, thumped loudly in my chest as I gazed at him, stirring me awake. How could I have been so careless with him?

In the end, he was here. Just like he said he'd be.

My mind fluttered over to Javier and the day ahead of me. I had believed that Javier would never put me in any danger that I couldn't get myself out of, but now I was starting to second guess things. How bad was his need for revenge this time around?

And he knew...he knew this whole time what had happened to Camden, that he was on the run, and he'd never told me. I guess he knew that if he had, I would've run away, I would've found some way to escape. With Camden on the run, Javier had no way of getting to him, of hurting him. I wouldn't have been coerced into this whole fucking mess.

He had wanted me to kill my parents. It was a ridiculous notion, and I could only figure that it was his way of trying to settle things with the people who hurt me. Maybe that's why he was doing it to Travis too. Though romantics would argue that was a sign of true love, it sat wrong inside of me, like food that wouldn't digest. Because as nearly noble as it seemed, why get *me* to do it?

I sighed and rubbed my hands on face. I didn't know what the fuck I was going to do. Last night, seeing Camden in my room, I'd been ready to run to him, leave with him and Gus, and try to make a break for it. I'm glad that we didn't. Javier's men would have shot them on sight. I don't know what his plans for me would have been. Perhaps, knowing Camden was really gone this time, I would have broken completely.

I was being yanked in different directions and it was tearing me up inside. I never fell back in love with Javier, my body spoke a different language than that, but he still tricked me. He still made me believe in the lies. How deep did his feelings for me go? I knew they never went all the way to the roots, I'd told myself that, but some tiny part of me hoped for his redemption, that I somehow held the key to his soul.

Perhaps that was exactly what my ego wanted to hear. Like it wanted to hear Camden tell me I was good. I didn't think I was going to get that either.

He was different too. His body shot, his heart blown out by what I had done. Last night I was so sure he was going to hold me close to him and make me feel the safety he was promising, I thought he was going to give me the protection I'd associated with him. Instead, he stared at me like I was a burden to him. A lost little girl he'd come after to bail out and now was stuck with the task. Camden was also a man of his word, and for better or worse, I knew he'd be there for me till the end—even if he didn't want to be. That's the thought that really stung, that dug deep, that he'd be there for me out of deep-seated devotion, a sense of obligation, not because he really wanted to be. I was afraid he'd start to resent me.

He slowly opened his eyes and tried to move. He stopped, groaning pitifully, face scrunched up in anguish.

"Do you want some Tylenol?" I asked.

He grunted and shook his head slightly. "No, I have some better shit than that. I just hate how happy it makes me feel."

I swallowed. "Maybe I should take some then."

He tilted his head, eyes on me. "Sometimes it's better to deal with the pain than mask it. It always comes back."

His lips were begging me to meet them with mine. Another spear of shame and regret rocked through me. I got up, went to the sink, and got him a glass of water.

When I came back, he was sitting up looking like he was in incredible pain.

"Is it your back?"

He nodded, took the glass of water from me. He fished two pills out of his pocket and finished the water. He wiped his mouth and exhaled. "Unfortunately, I won't be able to deal with this pain. Not today. Not when we have to figure out what to do."

I went over to the window and peeked through it. No wonder the air felt so heavy today. The sun was gone. Those dark clouds I had seen hovering over the sea for so long had finally rolled in and smothered us with a low, claustrophobic ceiling.

"What do you think I should do?" I asked, my eyes now searching the courtyard for anyone patrolling it. It was quiet, dead as anything, all the guests still asleep in their rooms or having their morning coffee and shaking their heads at the one day the weather decided to be a bitch. Well, it was still hurricane season. They should have known better. We all should have known better.

"I know I have to lie low here until you go," he said. He laughed and I turned to look at him. His eyes looked glazed, a lazy smile on his lips.

"Good shit?" I asked, taking a seat beside him on the bed.

He nodded, still smiling. Oh God, his dimples. I wanted him to keep taking these drugs, over and over again, so I could see them, so he could be happy and not hate me. I wanted him oblivious and loving me. I wanted my image in his eyes to be pure and good and untainted.

He sighed, leaning back against the headboard. "Ellie, I have something for you."

I waited while he went into his pocket and pulled out a small box that looked like a tin for tiny mints. He put it in my hand and told me to open it, his words slurring slowly.

"Shouldn't we do this when you're not high?" I asked.

"It's pretty self-explanatory." He waved at it.

I shrugged and opened the tin. It was a tiny red dot of plastic, no bigger than the end of a pencil.

"What is this? Wireless mike?"

He shook his head. "One more guess."

"A tracking device?"

He smiled again and my heart jumped. "Bingo. Put that on the underside of your necklace."

I looked down at the razor blade and lifted it up.

"I'll help you in a few," he said.

"I've got it," I said, taking the dot out of the tin, sticking it to the back of the necklace. From Javier's mike the other day, to the tracking device, I'd turned into a walking instrument. I guess it was better than being a walking weapon.

Camden fished his cell from his pocket and waved it at me. "I'm not really sure how but as soon as I bring it to him, Gus has you in the system so we can start tracking your every move."

"What was the original plan?"

He shrugged his one shoulder, head rolling to the side. "We didn't know. We weren't sure if you'd come with us, if you'd want to leave. If you'd even come back from Travis. We could only hope."

"And what do you hope?"

He straightened his head and gave me a steady gaze. "I hope we can all be here together."

I looked at my hands, wringing them together. "I have to go with Travis tonight."

He swallowed hard. "So you'll go with Travis. And then you'll escape."

I raised my brow. "How?"

"Well, you said you'll be going out for dinner. We'll be tracking you. We'll know where you are. You go to the bathroom window or through the kitchen or however you can figure it and we'll be there waiting for you. We'll find you. And we'll all leave together."

I shook my head roughly. "No. He's got people everywhere."

"I know. We saw them. But he's got his people looking out for him. They won't be watching you. Once you're there with him, they won't have a reason to. You're just an American tourist to him, one hot piece of ass. He's going to work on impressing you and you're going to be impressed, then he'll have no reason to worry why you're taking so long in the bathroom."

The way he was telling me what I had to do was familiar. But this time it was comforting because I knew he had my best interests in mind. I knew I could trust him 100 percent, because I'd left him in the dust in Palm Valley and he was here with me now. This could work. I could get out of all of this.

"I just..." he began and trailed off.

"What?"

"I just hope that once we leave, that you can leave it for good."

I gulped. "You think I'd return to this place?"

"Not this place. Not this city. The place inside you. The place where killing Travis still sounds like a good idea. I know you want him dead, Ellie, and there's nothing wrong with that. But once we leave, we have to let it go. Everything and everyone."

I know he meant Javier by that. I nodded. "I will do that. I will leave."

"You will, but does that mean you *can*?"

Outside thunder rumbled ominously.

He exhaled loudly. "Looks like a storm is coming. You better get ready for your day. You never know when Enrico will stop by with a new message."

"You better get back in the closet then," I said.

"If only my father could hear that," he said, attempting a joke. His brow furrowed in pain and I had to wonder how he was dealing with everything. Not only me or his gunshot wound but Sophia turning on him and being wanted by the police. His father had to know too, the man Camden could never be good enough for. My poor, poor Camden. He'd taken enough.

He got up and used the washroom quickly, had a banana, and went back in the closet. I got ready and waited, waited long enough so that when there finally was a knock at my door, I was ready for it.

It was Enrico. I opened the door and a gust of electric air came in.

"Just checking in on you," Enrico said. "Any problems last night?"

"No, I went to bed. Looks like a storm is coming."

"There's a Category One hurricane off the coast. Nothing to worry about, just no suntanning today."

I smiled politely and stared at him until he cleared his throat.

"The other reason I am here is that Javier has a message for you."

My gut twisted. "What is it?"

"He wants to meet here at this café at eleven AM today." He handed me a business card.

"Is this a good idea?"

"That is not for me to say. Have a good day, Miss Willis. I will have the cab waiting for you out front a half hour prior."

Enrico turned and walked away. I knew Camden was in the closet, catching all of that. At least he could finally come out after I left, assuming that Javier's men would be trailing after me. Then he could activate the tracking device and I would have his protection.

I got ready for the day, feeling slightly self-conscious with Camden there, hiding out of sight. I put on a simple strapless maxi dress and fluffed out my hair with my fingers, doing a quick sweep of makeup.

At twenty after ten, I grabbed my purse and left the room, whispering "See you later" to Camden, hoping he had heard me. Hoping that I would see him later. I had no idea what Javier had planned for me now. Everything was turned on its head.

The café wasn't a long a cab ride from the market, and I got there early. I didn't see Javier anywhere. I sat down at one of the tables inside, the threatening clouds producing wind that whipped scattered loose napkins around on the streets like white tumbleweeds.

I waited there for an hour at my table, finally indulging in a crepe and some fruit, when the waiter slipped me a note. It said *"mujeres baño andale"* in unknown cursive handwriting, perhaps the waiter's.

I looked up at the waiter but he was already walking past and delivering food to someone else. I got up and made my way through the café to the woman's bathroom, trying to stay cool. Suddenly I was very afraid.

I opened the door and stepped in. There were only two stalls. Both looked empty but their doors were closed.

"Javier?" I whispered tentatively.

A pair of shiny shoes stepped down from one of the seats. I held my breath as the stall door opened and Javier stepped out. Everything felt so fucking different now. I had to keep it cool.

He nodded at the door behind me. "Lock it."

"Okay," I said, and turned around to do so.

When I turned toward him, he was right there behind me, grabbing my head and kissing me hard. His tongue snaked around in my mouth, his hands going down my sides, cupping underneath my ass until he pressed me up against the door.

It was different now. It had been wrong before and I knew that, but now it was another shade of wrong that was about more than just me. It was about Camden. I couldn't do this to him knowing what I knew now, what I should have always, always known. Even if Camden didn't want anything to do with me after this was all over, it couldn't even be an option. This had to stop.

"Ellie," Javier whispered as he pulled his lips away and started biting down my neck. I felt powerless, frightened and cold. "Ellie, I need you. I missed you."

Lies, lies. Too many lies. His fingers went down to my thighs, gathering up the length of my dress. His other hand went to his pants, started undoing his fly.

"Javier," I said, trying to keep my voice steady. "This isn't the time."

"There's always time for this," he said, nipping at my collarbone, near the edge of the razor blade. I held my breath, dying inside.

"No," I said. I ducked under his arm and went to the opposite side of the bathroom, hands at the wall.

He had his cock in his hand, stroking it, the look on his face one of lust and madness.

His smile was lopsided, wickedly amused. "No? You don't get to say no, Ellie."

I narrowed my eyes at him, pulled down my dress. "I'm saying no now. Don't you want to know how my fucking date with Travis went last night? Don't you want to know if he touched me, threatened me, hurt me?"

He looked taken aback, enough so that he put his dick away and zipped up his fly. He walked over to me, smoothing back his hair. "Okay. If it's so important for you to tell me, but I already heard it from Enrico."

I swallowed down the anger that was building up. That he could send me off to be with such a monster, the monster who did those things to Javier's own family, and not even care to hear about it.

"It doesn't matter," I spat out. "I guess you know about the plans for tonight?"

He smiled. "Yes, I do. And it's perfect, Ellie, just perfect. This couldn't work out better. Dinner. Food. Tonight is when you'll do it."

A wave of horror flashed through me like the lightning strikes outside. "When I do what?"

"When you kill Travis."

My mouth dropped open and my hand automatically went to my necklace. "I am not doing it. I'm not killing him. I'm leading you to him. I'm working as a mole. I am not your assassin. I am not your weapon."

"You've always been a weapon," he said, coming closer and pulling something out of his pocket. "That's what makes you and me so good. This time you're the weapon and I'm the one holding the trigger."

He brought out a necklace with silver angel wings as the pendant. He flicked the edge of it and the angel wings opened up, a locket. Inside was a tiny, tiny vial of powder.

"What is that?" I said, barely breathing.

"It's poison," he said matter-of-factly. "Tonight you'll put it in his food. He will die."

"I . . . I can't . . . I won't. They'll know I did it!"

"They won't. I'll be waiting for you outside, Ellie. I'll be there."

"No." I shook my head. I wouldn't do it. And though I could have pretended for the sake of pretending, to make things go easier, to get him out of there, I wanted to let him know that I wouldn't. That he couldn't make me do everything he asked. That I was stronger than he thought I was.

"This whole time," I said sadly, "this was your plan, wasn't it?"

He furrowed his brow. "It's better this way, Ellie. You have to be the one to do it. It's the only way you'll get your revenge."

"You need your revenge too."

"Yours is more important."

"Or maybe my life is more expendable than yours," I said bitterly.

His face contorted as if I had slapped him in the face. "How could you say that?"

I chewed my lip and held out my hand. "Just give me the damn necklace."

"No, I'd rather put it on you," he said, reaching for the one around my neck.

"No!" I yelled, ripping out of his grasp. But it was too late. His hand closed around it and he ripped it off. He stared at the razor blade in his hand. The tracking device staring up at him.

Fear took a hard, sharp hold of every part of me.

His eyes burned, blazed, unable to accept what he was seeing.

"What is this?" he seethed, his face reddening.

I could have come up with a lie, if I really tried. But there were no lies left in me.

"What is this?" he screamed. He grabbed my face in his hands, squeezing my chin and my lips, the pressure burning against my bones. "Who gave you this? Tell me!"

"Or what?" I tried to say. "You'll kill me?"

His eyes widened, all whites around the yellow gold, his pupils black as night and mean as sin. His grip on my face became tighter and I started to squirm from the pain.

Finally he screamed, "Fuck!" and turned around, kicking in the bathroom stall door. He spun around. "Where is he? Huh? Where is that tattooed mother-fucker?"

I rubbed at my jaw, cowering away from him. "I don't know."

"You don't fucking know!" He marched over to me and placed his hands at my throat, pressed me up against the wall. "How can you not know?"

I took my hand and dug my nails into his palms, driving them down, making him bleed, staring right back at him, trying to fight through the air I was losing again. I would not lose again.

His eyes twitched as they searched my face, searching for the truth. When he realized he was already getting it, he released my neck and let me breathe again.

I took a moment to recover, swallowing painfully, and then said, "I don't know where he is. And that's the truth."

He walked away, shaking out his shoulders, going in a circle around the room. The bathroom door jingled and he lifted his head and yelled, "Fuck right off!" He then turned to face me and, instead of anger, his face was slack with something else...bitterness. Heartache, if he had a heart that could ache.

"Did you sleep with him?" he asked, voice barely above a whisper.

"What the hell is it with you men and sex?" I said. "Like who gets to fuck who really means anything. No, I didn't sleep with him. Are you happy?"

He laughed caustically. "Am I happy? Oh, angel, my

dirty, rotten, lying angel! No, I am not happy. I won't be happy until you do as I've told you."

He came over to me and quickly put his hands around my neck. I thought he was going to try to strangle me again, but he just put the angel locket around me then delicately straightened the pendant so it was resting on my collarbone.

"You have no idea," he said, soft and hard all at once, eyes focused on the angel wings, "how badly I want you to hurt right now. Because I didn't think you could ever hurt me again, not like you once did. But you have." He lifted his eyes up to mine. "You betrayed me when all I've done is give you my heart and promise you a new life."

I couldn't say anything to that bout of crazy. He pressed the pendant into me and walked away, shaking his head, holding my razor blade necklace in one hand.

"Your Camden will be tracking me now instead of you—he's going to get quite the surprise. And you're going to do as I've told you. You're going to go for dinner with Travis. You're going to kill him." He put his hand on the lock, then turned his head to the side, eyeing me. "Or I'll kill your Camden, for real this time. I'll deliver his head to your doorstep."

He unlocked the door and stepped out into the café, leaving me alone in the bathroom, wondering how the hell I was going to get us all out of this alive.

CHAPTER TWENTY-SIX

Camden

After Ellie had gotten ready for her meeting with Javier and I'd spent a few minutes grappling with the urge to scream, I got out of the closet and, very slowly, very carefully made my way back into the main part of the hotel.

Gus was in the room looking like utter shit. For once I got to tell him that. He hadn't slept at all, waiting up all night for me. I think he thought for a moment that perhaps Ellie and I were making up for lost time, but he figured out pretty quickly from my expression that that wasn't the case. I had to say, he looked a bit disappointed, as if the crotchety old man had been rooting for us as a couple that whole time. I guess I had been rooting for us too.

I couldn't dwell on that, I couldn't think about it. I just had to keep going and stick to the new plan. We activated the tracking device on Gus's phone and were able to see where she was on Google Maps. It was actually pretty relieving to follow that flashing blue dot as it made its way through the streets of Veracruz to the café.

"So she's just meeting Javier?" he asked, after the blue dot had been immobile for quite a while.

I nodded. "As far as I know. She should be coming back here after to get ready for her dinner with Travis. I guess we should get going just before six. That way we can be out and ready to follow her."

"I agree," he said, his eyes on the flashing light. He frowned. "Hmmm."

"What?" I leaned over and he showed me the screen. The blue dot was moving away from the café, in the opposite direction of the way Ellie had gotten there. She was heading north and fairly fast, in a car, not on foot.

"What do you think that means?" I asked. "Do you think Javier is taking her somewhere?"

"Maybe. Or maybe it wasn't Javier that asked her to meet him."

I looked at him sharply. "Who, like Travis?"

Gus shrugged quickly. "I have no idea. I don't think we can afford to sit here and speculate."

He was right about that. We ran out of the hotel and into the car. Gus had taken back the GTO. No one had touched the thing, and I couldn't blame them—with her scratched sides and smashed side mirrors, she looked like she was destined for the trash heap. But I knew better—I knew what she was capable of and I knew that today we'd need her speed and handling more than anything.

"You think the cops are still looking for this?" I asked as we cruised along the streets, trying to get the car and the blue dot to match up. I wished I was the one behind the wheel, but Gus had proven himself with the car so far.

"I doubt it," he said. "Mexico is a big country and we could be anywhere. People disappear easily in a few days. We'll still be careful, though."

We followed the blue dot as it went north along the Fidel Velázquez Highway, getting farther away from the city. I started to get a bad feeling about all of this, as the buildings became more and more industrial.

My shoulder started to ache; I was all tensed up. "I don't know, Gus."

He nodded. "I know. This isn't right. Something's wrong."

"I think she's in danger."

He gave me a grim look. "That kid is always in danger."

The blue dot finally came to a stop at the end of a long road that ended into what looked like nothing. Ten minutes later, we were approaching the blue light. Gus took the GTO down a street with a few empty warehouses flanking the sides. At the end of the road was an office building with broken windows and a handful of cars parked outside. That was where she had to be. Unfortunately, the software didn't allow us to triangulate her position any closer.

"Either Javier has her," I said, watching the area carefully as Gus pulled to the side of the road, a few yards away, "or shit has hit the fan with Travis. How many guns do we need?"

Gus exhaled. "Whatever it is, I hope it's enough." He turned in his seat and started pulling them out of the bag in the backseat.

"This might hurt for a second," he said, and jammed my gun into the sling. Pain shot up my arm like rockets. "But it's a good place for it."

I winced, tears in my eyes, and looked down. He had placed it underneath my arm. No one could see it. "Fine. Give me two more as decoys."

He handed me two small revolvers. I stuck one in my waistband and held the other one in my hand. That morning I'd put a knife in my sock.

Thunder rumbled in the distance as I eyed the Coffee-mate. "Think it'll work a second time?"

"Don't even think about," Gus told me. He shoved a gun in his waistband and took another one to his lips, kissing it. "Maybe this baby will get to see some action." He smiled and then the light went out of his eyes. I knew how he felt. There would be blood. I couldn't let myself hesitate even once when it came to pulling the trigger, not when it came to saving Ellie.

"All right," I said, giving him a heavy nod. "Let's go see what trouble we can get ourselves into."

We got out of the car and started hurrying down the sidewalk, guns to our sides, trying to be fast and inconspicuous all at once. It wasn't easy, though there was no one on this dead-end street. Heavy drops of rain began to fall. I was grateful for something to distract me from my nerves that were buzzing through me.

We were almost at the building, heading toward the side to see if we could see in the windows, when

I heard a gun being cocked. I knew that sound wasn't necessary—it was there to make a point. To let us know we'd been caught.

Gus and I froze at the sound, making split-second decisions in our heads. We had no choice but to turn around and see.

We did.

Javier was a few feet behind us, on the road, gun pointed at my head. Beside him was Raul, his gun aimed at Gus.

"*Buenos días, gringos,*" Javier said with a smile. "Kindly drop your fucking guns and put your hands up or I'll blow your heads right the fuck off."

Gus and I exchanged a look. Defeat.

We did as we were told.

Javier waved his gun at us. "And kick them over, you know how this goes."

I kicked mine angrily, as did Gus, guns clattering across the cracked pavement.

"Now," Javier said, walking toward me, moving like a snake. I half expected his tongue to come shooting out, forked at the end. "I am going to frisk you for the rest of your weapons." He stopped right in front of me, lips pressed together in a tight smile. "Try not to enjoy it too much."

I closed my eyes, breathing in deeply through my nose, trying to dispel the anger that was punching me in the gut, in my lungs, in my chest. That rage would come in handy right about now, but rage acted without thought, and I needed to play this next part so damn well or Ellie would be lost to me forever.

I almost controlled it but when Javier's hands got to my family jewels and he groped around them and said, "I can see why Ellie chose me. My balls are bigger," I let that rage out for just one second.

I spat right in his face. Well, since I was a lot taller, it kind of went on his forehead and trickled down into his eyes. I grinned at him, enjoying the look of revulsion and fury that flashed through him.

"Fucking pansy," he sniped, and then took his gun and jabbed the butt of it right into the bullet hole on my shoulder.

Everything went fuzzy and black and I could barely keep my lunch down. I collapsed to my knees and spat out bile, the pain overtaking me, ruling me.

Then Javier kicked me in the shoulder, same spot, and I rolled over onto my back, swells of unconsciousness overcoming the waves of pain. Then I remembered Gus standing beside me, and Ellie, and I knew I had to do what I could to stay awake and stay alive, pain or no pain.

I remained on my back breathing hard until Javier reached down and ripped me back up until I was on my feet, swaying unsteadily.

"Hey now," he said, lightly slapping my face until my eyes were open. "Hey, Camden, hey, Camden, you better stay awake. I am just getting started here with you both."

Javier glared at Gus while Raul started scooping up the guns they found on us. They hadn't found the one in my sling. I wanted to look at Gus to see if he had noticed, but I wasn't about to give anything away.

"I didn't think I'd see you ever again," Javier said to him, frowning and seeming a bit uneasy. "You're one of the few good ones left in her life."

I raised my brows and swallowed away the residue of pain. "You two know each other?" I tried to hide the surprise in my voice but I couldn't hide much of anything, except my gun.

Gus was watching Javier, not me. The old man never looked so angry.

"No," Javier said slowly, carefully. "I'd only heard about him. You're a famous man in the Watt circle."

"And so are you," Gus grunted.

Javier tapped his gun against his leg, seeming to think. "I suppose it's better they think something of me than nothing at all. They are here, you know. Her *parents*."

That was news to me, but it wasn't the news I wanted. "Where is Ellie?"

Just then another man came around the corner, someone I didn't recognize, holding a gun to his side.

Javier glanced at him out of the corner of his eye. "What is it, Peter?" he asked testily.

Peter glanced at Gus and me then said to Javier, "Travis Raines is having a dinner party tonight."

Javier's brow scrunched up. "What?"

"At his house," Peter added for effect. "Ellie isn't going out for dinner, she's going there. To his house. To the compound."

Whatever this meant to Javier, this was bad news. And if it was bad news for Javier, it was probably bad news for Ellie too. I looked at Gus, who had an enlightened yet miserable expression on his face.

"Oh shit," Gus grumbled.

Javier's eyes were wild, thoughts spinning, and he nodded ever so slightly at Gus, as if he understood what Gus was realizing.

"What the fuck is going on?" I said, wanting an explanation.

Javier shot me a look and swallowed hard, worry furrowing his face. A look I'd never seen on him. The look was gone quickly.

"Ellie," he said slowly, looking back to Gus, "will be at Travis's tonight. Unfortunately, we won't be able to get in there without a fight. The place will have heightened security staff who, I'm sure, will find the cyanide vial on her necklace."

Her necklace. Of course. Javier had given her one and taken the razor blade with the tracking device. Cyanide. He was getting her to kill Travis Raines tonight.

"Her parents are there. They work for Travis now." Javier looked up at the sky and rubbed the side of his face. "They'll see Ellie. And her cover will be blown." He brought his head back down to face me. "She's as good as dead."

And you put her in her grave was all I could think. *You set her up to fail from the beginning.*

"So what the fuck are you going to do now?" I asked, spitting out the words. "You're just going to leave her there?"

Javier narrowed his eyes into reptilian slits. "I don't know what choice I have. We can hope for the best."

"And to think, you thought you were good enough

for her," Gus said, shaking his head with disappointment at Javier.

Javier whipped his head around and shoved his gun in Gus's face, right up under his chin. "You don't know anything, old man," he sneered. "You don't get a chance to interfere in her life, you gave that up. I don't want to kill you because I know what you are and how much you mean to her, so don't you fucking piss me off!"

My eyes were drawn to Javier and Gus, wondering what the fuck Javier was talking about, so I barely had time to realize what was going on. Raul now had his gun raised at Javier's head and Peter was reaching for his own gun, perhaps to protect him. But the movement from Peter was enough to bring Raul's gun toward him. Raul pulled the trigger, blasting Peter in the head. The sound brought out Javier's well-honed reflexes. He spun around, his arm suddenly around Gus, using him as a shield, his gun drawn.

Raul fired and ended up shooting Gus right in the gut.

I was screaming. Running for them. Javier pulled the trigger and shot Raul before he could fire again, and a bloody Gus slipped through Javier's arms.

Javier pulled the gun around to me but I was too fast. I was already there. I was already the black beast.

I tackled Javier, my bad shoulder down, not caring about the pain. I dove right into his chest, throwing him back into the concrete wall of the building, his head smashing against it, leaving a bloody smear that was diluted by the rain.

Even with one arm in a sling, I was able to beat the

fuck out of him. I punched him over and over again, relishing the feeling of my bleeding knuckles, the blood from his face, the feeling of breaking cartilage.

He tried, several times, to get up, to fight back. He put up a good, dirty fight, my shoulder being his number one target. But I was beyond the pain now. I was something else. I was rage and I was wrath and I was twenty-six years of hell.

I brought out my gun from the sling and held it right against Javier's temple, spitting in his face one more time, watching the spit mix with blood and rain. "You can't give me a single fucking reason why I shouldn't pull the trigger."

He looked up at me, eyes golden against the mask of blood on his face. He licked his broken and bleeding lips, slowly, sickly, and said, "No. I can't. So kill me. And let this all be over with."

I pressed the gun harder into his head, the anger shaking me from my bones. "No. This won't be over because Ellie is still out there. She's going to Travis's and there's a chance she's not coming back. You better fucking hope that she poisons him and does it well because that's the only way she'll get out of there."

"Camden." I heard Gus groan from behind me. I kept the gun at Javier's head and looked at him. He was lying back and holding onto his stomach, blood running from his mouth.

"Stay cool, Gus, I'll get an ambulance," I told him.

"You go get Ellie," he said, barely getting out the words. "I'll be fine."

I turned and looked at Javier, hoping I could burn

him alive with my eyes. "I'm going to go after Ellie. I'm only letting you live so you can get Gus to the hospital. If he dies, it's on you. And I'm going to be sure that Ellie knows about it."

Javier swallowed hard, and for a second I worried that he might die before Gus. A strange thing to worry about. I decided to call the ambulance on my way to Travis's, just to be sure. I couldn't trust this man for anything, not even to stay alive when I needed him to.

I got to my feet. "Do you understand?"

He nodded, breathing hard, his nostrils flaring.

"On second thought." I pointed the gun at him and for once he looked as if he thought I might pull the trigger. He was actually afraid of me. "I could just kill you now and be done with you and call an ambulance myself."

I held it there for a few moments, pointed at him with all the fire inside me, before I lowered the gun and walked over to Gus, kneeling down beside him. His face was white, his eyes dull, but he was alert and looking at me. I patted him on the arm and gave it a good squeeze.

"You're going to be fine, Gus." I pulled the cell phone out of his pocket and eyed Javier, who was still lying there, propped up against the wall like a rag doll. I nodded at him. "Tell me where Travis lives, Javier."

He seemed to consider my request, as if he weren't going to answer me, and for a second I thought maybe he really would let Ellie go on this suicide mission. But he motioned for me to bring the cell over.

I handed it to him and with a bloody hand he began

to enter an address into the GPS. He handed it back to me as the new coordinates began triangulating. A flashing red dot.

"You go in there like this, you're going to get yourself killed before you even step foot on the property," he sneered. "You can't do this alone."

"You let me worry about me," I said, getting up and looming over him. "And if I ever see your face again, I will kill you. You won't know when it will happen, but it will happen."

We stared at each other for a few tense seconds, his yellow, poisonous eyes hating every inch of me. I was sure my look was no different.

I tore my eyes away and glanced over at Gus. I swallowed hard, praying this wasn't the last time I'd see him.

"I'll see you in a bit, Gus," I told him. Then I turned on my heel and started running for the GTO. Running for Ellie.

CHAPTER TWENTY-SEVEN

Ellie

Once I went back to the hotel and saw that Enrico wasn't at the desk, I went upstairs and started going down the hallway, calling out for Gus and Camden, hoping they were in one of the hotel rooms. I needed to warn them, to get to them before Javier did. But they weren't anywhere, and when I went back downstairs and asked the front desk lady if she could call them for me, there was no answer on their end.

They would have seen the device going off with Javier and thought it was me, deviating from the plan. Now there was a whole new plan, one that Gus and Camden were walking straight into. I hoped to God that Javier would keep his word and kill Camden only if I didn't go through with the assassination. I should have made him promise it.

That was the only thing that kept me going, kept me putting one foot in front of the other, the fact that if

I did everything I was told, they could be saved. And Gus, dear sweet old Gus, he wasn't an idiot—he was a trained cop and a hell of a lot of other things. He was the wild card, someone Javier wouldn't be expecting when Camden turned up.

I got out of the shower, trying to calm my breath and keep my limbs from shaking, trying to go ahead and do the things I needed to do to survive and get out of this. I picked out a dress from the closet, the place where Camden had hidden, watching out for me, never obvious but always there. The dress was long, green and glittery like mermaid scales, which would have made me feel absolutely beautiful if I had been wearing it any other time, but now it was just a cloak for my murder, a means to an end.

I pinned my hair up and made my makeup look sweet and sexy. I'd definitely act the part tonight. I was no longer afraid. I was determined to carry this out. I would get rid of Travis Raines and then figure out a way to get myself out of there and back to Camden and Gus somehow. Through hell and high water, they found me. I could find them. I'd been through worse.

I eyed the necklace, hoping it would hold together and keep my secrets hidden. Those dirty angel wings. So Javier thought I was rotten too. I guess I shouldn't have been surprised; he'd been telling me how bad I was all this time.

At five thirty I went out to the lobby, where Enrico was still nowhere to be found. Funny how he disappeared all of a sudden. I wondered if that was because Travis was coming here or perhaps Javier had called in all of his troops to deal with Camden and Gus.

I swallowed hard and started sliding the pendant up and down its chain. No fear. I could do this. This would be done.

A white limousine pulled up outside and the driver came into the lobby, elegantly dressed with a jaunty cap and dark glasses. He called out, "Eleanor Willis."

I paused, waiting a moment, letting the fake name sink in, before I stood up and gathered my black shawl around me. "That's me."

The driver showed the way to the limo. It had been raining on and off all day and it was just starting to sputter again, the wind driving it into my face. I had put on waterproof mascara, insurance against the weather and against any tears I'd be shedding for whatever reason. I wouldn't get through this day without tears or blood.

The driver pointed to the heavy, dark sky and said, "It will be sunny tomorrow."

I gave him a sad smile. I didn't doubt tomorrow would be anything but sunny. I got in the back of the spacious limo, somewhat surprised that Travis wasn't there.

"Are we meeting Mr. Raines at the restaurant?" I asked.

He shook his head. "Mr. Raines is having dinner at his house. He is there already tending to his guests. He is having a dinner party."

I sat back, stunned. A dinner party? How the fuck was I going to escape from a dinner party? How was Javier going to get me, let alone anyone else?

And just like that, I'd let the fear back in. Maybe this

really was a suicide mission. Maybe it always had been planned this way. Ellie Watt, the sacrifice that everyone loved to make.

My heart cried out for Camden, the only one who never saw me that way. I held my head back, staring at the lights on the roof of the limo, trying to keep the tears back. I stayed like that the entire drive until the limo pulled off the main streets of Veracruz and started to head inland toward a group of low hills, lush with greenery and heavily gated mansions sprinkled throughout like hard candy.

Travis's place was at the end of a very long and narrow cobblestone street lined with flowers that seemed too bright for nature and palm trees that stretched as tall as the eyes could see. It was like entering a tunnel, but there was no light at the end of it.

The limo paused at the extremely large gates where the driver waved something at the man at the booth. The man came out and the rear window went down. He looked in the back, at me, and then nodded. He returned to the booth and the gates opened for us.

Travis's house took my breath away. I didn't want it to, but it did. It was so much more impressive than the one I had to sneak into as a child. It was beyond sprawling, with many wings and beautiful balconies, shinning white and gold under the lights. Dark clouds billowed above it. I wouldn't have been surprised if the skies opened above it and Satan came fluttering down on black wings.

The limo climbed up the long, sweeping driveway and stopped in front of the door, where carpeted steps led up into a hall inside made of granite and marble. It was like a Hollywood movie premiere, with beautifully dressed people everywhere. The driver held the car door open for me.

I smiled in thanks and got out, saying "This is pretty big for a dinner party."

"Oh, this is only the cocktail preparty. The dinner party is for very special guests. It comes later. You should feel privileged that Mr. Raines has invited you, Miss Willis."

I studied the man, someone's father or grandfather, who seemed to have no problem working for one the vilest men in the country. Maybe that's what you had to do here to survive. Maybe these people were no different from me. Trying to turn a blind eye to what they knew was wrong, shielding their hearts, trying to live another day.

I walked up to the door, getting curious but pleasant glances from Veracruz's elite. The men admired my breasts, the women envied my dress. A bodyguard, the man I recognized as the bouncer from the Zoo, had a list and was checking names.

"Your name?" he asked.

"Eleanor Willis," I said. "I didn't bring my passport."

"That's okay, I am just checking."

I smiled at him. "Oh, good. My friend Connor Malloy might be coming here later."

"Is he on the list?"

I peered over at the list. "He should be."

The man scanned it. "Doesn't have his name here."

"Well, I'll speak to Travis about it. He'll be an

American, tall, black hair, tattoos, glasses. Like a hot muscley nerd."

The man nodded absently, not really caring. "Check with Mr. Raines, please."

Then he looked at the next person coming up the stairs. I moved past him, chewing on my lip. I had no idea if Camden would show up here, how he'd get away from Javier, how he'd even figure out where I was. But if it did happen, I hoped I had given him just a little bit of help, maybe a few seconds bought.

Suddenly a woman all in black appeared in front of me, waving a metal detector. "Miss, we need to check you."

I nodded, my thoughts racing to my necklace. My nipple ring beeped first, prompting another somewhat embarrassing explanation, considering this woman was in her late fifties and seemed disgusted by the whole idea. Then the necklace beeped. The woman ran the detector over it again and then lifted it off my collar-bone, feeling underneath.

I held my breath, trying to seem normal, trying to act like everything wasn't resting in her hands. It didn't say poison on the vial, but I still had a feeling it would get bad for me. At the very least she'd confiscate it, thinking it some sort of drug, and then what did I have? My only hope was that drugs weren't taboo at a party in a drug lord's house.

But the woman pressed the necklace back into my neck and smiled at it. "*Precioso,*" she said, and let me go.

I moved far enough away from her before I exhaled loudly, letting it all out. That was close. I was in and

I was okay, but I didn't know for how much longer. I needed to hold it together.

Too late for that.

The crowd parted and Travis Raines appeared in front of me in a tuxedo, bodyguards on all sides of him.

He smiled at me and raised his arms to showcase the house. "You came, Miss Eleanor Willis. What do you think of my house? Isn't it the loveliest house you've ever seen?"

I pasted a smile on my lips, and the next thing I said wasn't a lie, "Yes, it's the nicest house I've ever seen."

"Good, good," he said, and clapped his hands together. "Since you are new here, let me show you around and introduce you to the guests."

It was the most terrifying and boring hour of my life. He introduced me to literally everyone, saying my name "Miss Eleanor Willis" to every single person there. And there were a lot of people. I estimated at least eighty, milling about and looking pretty.

The whole time I kept thinking about the necklace, I kept thinking about how I was going to do it and when. How would I get his food, what if I slipped up and he caught me? How long did the poison take to work? Would I have time to give it to him and then excuse myself to the bathroom? Would anyone suspect me? Did I have to sit there and watch him eat it and die? Because for all the terrible things he'd done, for the devil that he was, I didn't know if I could do that. My heart would take no pleasure in murdering him, in seeing him die before my eyes. I always thought I might, that I would swim in it, but now that I was here and it was a reality, poison at my neck, I knew the act would haunt me. Just because someone deserved to die didn't mean I was the person to do it.

But for tonight, for here, I had to. I was the angel of death, walking arm in arm with Lucifer.

We paused by the open doors to the veranda where many people were sitting about on brightly colored deck chairs, watching the thunder and lightning storm off in the distance. From there you could look down the large grassy sweep of finely cut lawn and illuminated garden. In flashes of lightning I could see the lawn went beyond the lights and disappeared into jungle. It looked like it continued for acres and acres, and it was all Travis Raines's.

Travis was beside me, talking to someone whom he introduced as the senator of something. I wasn't listening to a word they were saying. My eyes were caught on someone across the room, a striking man in an ill-fitting suit and an arm in a sling.

Camden. He was here, somehow. Just standing by the wall, his eyes on me, sending me signals. Trying to say something. But what? He was here, he was alive. He was *alive*. I looked around, trying not to be too obvious about it, to see if Javier was too, if it was a trap. Or maybe a dream, maybe a nightmare. But I didn't see him, not Gus, not anyone. Only Camden. He jerked his head toward the hallway, motioning for me to go out that way, to meet him there.

I told him I would with my eyes and was about to tell Travis I needed to use the bathroom when a woman stepped in front of me with a tray of champagne.

"Would you like some champagne?" she asked, and I nearly burst into tears at the sound of her voice. *This* woman. She was looking at the men, a phony smile pasted on her lips, one that lingered on Travis a little too long. Then she looked at me and for one second I could have been another pretty girl on the arm of the man she had once loved.

Then there was a flash of recognition, recognition that messed with her features, making her look less like a thin, middle-aged woman with highlighted brown hair and tall Estonian cheekbones and more like a woman having the fright of her life. Because this, this was absolutely as frightening as it was fucked up.

She dropped the tray, it falling in slow motion, the champagne flutes tipping and the fizzing liquid spilling everywhere.

"Ellie!" she exclaimed. And that's when I knew it wasn't a daydream of mine. It wasn't something I'd imagined over and over again because what I'd imagined didn't have my mother working for Travis Raines.

My mother.

This was my mother.

Mom.

She was there, standing in front of me. After all these years, she was here with me.

And in that moment, that cry that escaped from her red lips, she and I both knew what was happening. That Travis was looking between the two of us and putting two and two and eleven and twenty-six together.

I had, maybe, a few seconds. In one second my eyes flitted over my mother's shoulder to Camden. He was already running toward me, a plastic bottle in his hand. He knew; he'd seen this was coming.

In the next second, I spun around and ran like hell. I ran as fast as I could, grateful, for once, that I was never able to wear high heels, and shoved people out the way, leaping onto the veranda. I don't know what happened behind me, I could only focus on the lawn in front, the lights, the darkness behind it all. Suddenly there was a small explosion, a burst of something going off, though there was no heat and no light, but there was screaming and coughing and gunfire and suddenly Camden was at my side, running alongside me.

There was no time, no space in my lungs to talk, no way to figure out what had just happened and how that could have been my mother, my mom, who had left me in California all those years ago. The one who made me a freak, who left me as one. How could she be here? How could she be with that man, the one who ruined me before everyone else did? How could she do this to me?

My vision was getting blurry and the rainclouds burst open again, in time to hide my tears. I kept running, Camden at my side, limbs pumping up and down, bullets whizzing past us. I had no idea how we were going to get out of this alive.

I should have killed Travis the first chance I got. Now the necklace was still around my neck, and it was useless.

A machine gun went off in the distance, the rattle of bullets. We were heading for the jungle, for the darkness and depth that promised shelter and shade. We moved just inside the first trees, where a wide but overgrown path had cut through, when we were suddenly illuminated. A row of lights went on a few yards in front of us, lights that belonged to a Jeep or a utility vehicle. Someone appeared at the top of the vehicle, standing on the seat, gun propped up over the windshield and aimed right at us.

Camden made a move to go in front of me, to block me from the gun. The gun went off, the single shot ringing throughout the forest. I screamed and gripped Camden as he became a shield, feeling for where the bullet would have gone into him. I felt like my heart had been shot too.

Camden gripped my arm right back and said, "I'm okay," as the man with the gun fell from the Jeep and landed on the hood. What the fuck?

The bushes rustled to the left of the Jeep, and another man stepped out into the lights. I couldn't see his face, only his silhouette, but I'd always recognize him.

"If I were you two, I'd get the fuck in this car, or this will have been a big waste of my time," Javier said.

I exchanged a glance with Camden, not understanding any of this. He didn't look at ease, but he glanced behind us at the Jeeps that were rolling over the lawn and coming for us, the gunfire in the distance that wouldn't stop until we were hunted down. It was either go with Javier or die there. It wasn't an easy choice, but I'd gotten pretty good at making hard decisions.

"Come on," Camden said, squeezing my arm and pulling me over to the Jeep. Javier had already hopped into the driver's seat, and I climbed in right beside him. Camden had scarcely climbed in before the Jeep started speeding backward along the rough path, our bodies knocking against each other from the bumps and dips. When the clearing opened a bit, Javier brought the Jeep around in a quick spin and we went off following the path through, the way lit by the headlights.

I had so many questions, but why Javier was there wasn't one. I didn't want to dwell on that, not now, not when we had to focus on our escape.

"What's your plan?" I asked him.

He glared at me and I realized how fucked up his face was. From the cutting look that he briefly shot Camden, I could tell he was the source of all the blood and bruises.

"Before I kill your Clark Kent over there, my plan is to get us the fuck out of here."

"How?"

"Let me show you how Mexicans drive."

Once bullets started flying at the Jeep and we were lit up from behind, Travis's men entering the path, Javier turned off the headlights and turned to the right. Against the flashes of lightning, we could see the bushes and trees lighting up in front of us. Another flash of lightning and we were seconds from colliding with a tree. Javier yanked the wheel just in time, and we went bounding out of the jungle and back to the smoothness of Travis's groomed lawn. The house glowed in the distance, people running in all directions, guns going off, but who knew where or at what because at the moment they weren't after us.

That moment lasted about a minute, until people could hear the roar of the Jeep and we drove onto the area that was lit. Then guns were going off at us. People were taking aim from all directions. There wasn't enough time to shoot, we were swerving wildly and bouncing down around to the front yard where people were fleeing the mansion in a convoy of fancy cars and limos. The gates were open, trying to let them out.

"Hold on," Javier yelled, and he sounded like he was smiling when he said it, like this was all a fucking game. A gunshot came from the side and hit the door of the Jeep as Javier aimed the vehicle at a red sports car that was trying to leave through the gates. I held onto Camden for dear life, he held onto the roll bar, and Javier held onto the wheel as we all braced for impact when we rear-ended the red car, sending it flying, crashing into the guard's booth. We were stalled for just a second, enough time for the guard to get out his gun and aim it at us, but Javier was faster and shot him in the head first. Then he thrust the car into gear and slammed his foot on the gas. We rocketed forward and raced down the street. There seemed like a light at the end of this tunnel when you were facing the other way.

We sped through the streets, not slowing, not stopping, weaving in and out of the Sunday evening drivers until Javier thought we were far enough away. Then he pulled the Jeep down a lonely road and parked it with a lurch.

A heavy minute passed as the rain started falling again. With no roof above our heads, all three of us were soaked quickly. We sat there breathing hard, me between the men, trying to find some sense in this ever-growing mess.

"What happened?" I asked. "My mother...why was my mother there?"

I looked at Camden who was looking at Javier. I turned to look at Javier.

"Why was she there? You wanted me to kill my parents? I don't understand."

He stared right back at me, and I realized how many secrets the man had been keeping from me. "Your parents were never any good," he stated.

I felt the sting even though I knew the truth. "I still don't understand."

"Your parents used to work for Javier. And then they switched and went to Travis," Camden filled in over my head.

"Fuck you, you pansy." Javier sneered. "What the fuck do you know about anything?"

"I know this pansy beat your fucking ass, American style," Camden shot back.

Shit, there was going to be more bloodshed if I didn't stop this.

"You guys!" I yelled. "Where is Gus?"

"I left him with Javier," Camden said, his face falling. "He was shot. He was alive when I left him."

"You did *what*?" I screeched, looking at Camden wildly. "Why the fuck did you leave him, he was shot!"

"I had to come get you," Camden said angrily. "We didn't know that you were going to be having dinner at his house. If we'd known that, I would have never let you leave today."

"So where the fuck is Gus, Javier?" I asked, my eyes slicing into him.

He rubbed nervously at the dried blood smeared all over his forehead. "He's gone."

"Dead?"

He smoothed his hair behind his ears. "No. They have him."

"Who the fuck is 'they'?"

He looked at me like I was an idiot. "Who do you think? Los Zetas."

"How the hell did they get him?" I looked between the both of them and slammed my hands down on the dashboard. "The fuck!" I screamed.

Javier sighed and looked away. I was so close to clocking him upside the head and reopening a few wounds, I didn't give a shit if he had come and gotten me and Camden out of there. I knew he hadn't rescued us because he'd had a change of heart. He licked his lips and gave me an apologetic glance. "After Camden left, I waited until I could hear the ambulance. I left Gus there and went into the building. I knew the cops would show up soon after, Zetas cops, once the medics discovered Peter and Raul's bodies and that I'd be as good as dead. I went upstairs to hide. I watched the ambulance come. He was alive. They put an oxygen mask on him. They took him away. They got to the end of the street. Then a black car came out of nowhere, stopped the ambulance. Shot the driver. Opened up the back. Took Gus out, shot everyone else. They put Gus in the car. And then they drove off."

My mouth was open. It took effort to close it. "And that was Travis? He was at the party..."

"I guess Raul orchestrated this. We won't know because I shot him. And he, by the way, is the one who shot Gus, not me." Javier cast a furtive glance over at Camden and continued, "I'm guessing they mean to take you, Ellie."

Camden cleared his throat. "They would have taken Ellie at the party. I was watching Travis's face, he was truly shocked when he found out about Ellie and her mother."

"He was probably planning on taking Ellie later, for vengeance, without knowing who she really was. Now, he probably has Gus. And this whole fucking thing is far from over. Now Travis knows everything." Javier scratched at his chin thoughtfully, "Your parents won't be around for much longer either."

That was enough. I took my elbow and smashed Javier right in his already broken nose. Then I crawled over Camden and jumped from the Jeep, running down the road until I tripped over a pothole and went flying.

Camden was soon at my side, helping me back up. I waved him away, wanting just to lie there, let the rain wash me away.

"Ellie, come on," he said softly, bringing me up to me feet. My dress was all dirty from the mud, as dirty as I felt.

I blinked back the tears and stared up at him, the side of his face illuminated by the headlights. "What do we do now?"

He cocked his head at me and smiled, just a bit. "We do what we've always done. The right thing. We go get him back."

I shook my head. I was so damn afraid. "I can't do this again. Javier's right, Travis knows me now. Everything has been blown wide open...my parents...it's what that asshole wanted." I glared at the Jeep but was only blinded.

"That asshole isn't going to get what he wants much longer, Ellie. We don't need him. You and I, we will get Gus back."

"You wouldn't last a day." Javier was suddenly behind us. My God, he could be sneaky.

"Oh, fuck off," Camden said. "You should be grateful your brains aren't spilled all over the wall."

"You didn't have the guts," he retorted, stepping right up to Camden. As much as this spelled disaster, as sticky as this all was, Javier kind of had a point. We wouldn't get that far. Camden had gotten to me with the help of Gus and his contacts. Together, Camden and I had nothing.

"You still want your sisters safe, don't you?" I asked Javier.

He nodded, and I saw the first flash of pain come across his brow. "I have to get to Mexico City," Javier said. "That's where Violetta is. She's the closest to him now, the easiest one for him to go after. I have people here who can help me, who *will* help me. I just don't know if it's enough. Now that Travis knows I am here…"

He didn't have to finish the sentence. We all knew far too well what he would do.

"Okay," I said, looking between the men. "Javier, we'll help protect your sister if you help us get Gus back. And my parents, if we can."

"How the fuck can you protect my sister?" he asked angrily.

"Javier," I said. "Who else do you have right now?

Who else is here with you? Peter? Raul? You can't do this alone just as we can't."

"I have my people."

"Those same *people* turned on you. What makes you think they'll stay loyal now?"

"Raul I knew..."

"And yet look what happened. Who knows who else Travis has won over? At least you know where you stand with us."

I don't know why I was pressing so hard for Javier's help, especially when earlier he'd threatened to deliver Camden's head at my doorstep, but there it was.

He shook his head back and forth but walked back to the Jeep. "I don't like this."

"None of us like this!" I yelled at him. I looked up at Camden, pleading a bit with my eyes. "I don't think we have much of a choice."

Camden's eyes cut into Javier as he got back into the Jeep. "You always have a choice, Ellie. Always. This will have to be ours." We turned and headed back toward the Jeep. Camden leaned into me and whispered, "At the first legitimate excuse, Javier is gone. I'll kill him if I have to."

I would have chalked that up to Camden being overprotective. But I recognized the dark gleam in his eyes, the absence of guilt, and I realized he was stating the truth.

Camden had changed. We *all* had changed. The past was behind us. And I had no idea what our future was.

THE END

ACKNOWLEDGMENTS

I knew once I'd finished *Sins & Needles* that following it up with an equally good sequel wasn't going to be an easy task. Expectations were high, deadlines were looming, and I had three volatile characters who were dying to take me on a wild and emotional journey. But, powered by energy drinks and the Bourne Trilogy soundtracks, I completed *Shooting Scars*. I couldn't have done it without the following people: my wonderfully supportive parents, my hardworking and honest team of beta readers (Megan Simpson, Megan Ward O'Connell, Emily Franke, Claribel Contreras, Barbie Bohrman, Nina Decker, Brenna Weidner, Stephanie Brown, Taryn Celluci, Jamie Hall, Kayla Veres, Rebecca Espinoza, Shawna Vitale, Amanda Polito, Lucia Valovčíková, Natasha Tomic), *everyone* at Halle's Harlots, the badass fight clubbers Madeline Sheehan, E. L. Montes, Gail McHugh, Cindy Brown, Trevlyn Tuitt, and S. L. Jennings for their tireless patience with me, the talented Najla Qamber, Maryse

Black, Kara Malinczak, my cool, calm, collected agent Scott Waxman, Samantha Howard, Farley Chase, my editor Latoya Smith for her passion and clarity, the whole team at Grand Central Publishing for taking a chance on me, Kelly St-Laurent for her encouragement, and, last but not least, Scott MacKenzie for being there for me every single step of the way.

When a sadistic criminal kidnaps her friend and her mother, con artist Ellie Watt has only one chance in hell of getting them out alive – using two dangerous men who love her to death ...

Please see the next page for an excerpt from

PROLOGUE

THE GIRL WOKE up screaming.

The pain that had engulfed her the night before hadn't subsided while she lay unconscious, lulled to sleep by the drugs the doctors had given her. The pain wrapped around her legs, defying the morphine that seeped through her young veins.

She tried to sit up in her hospital bed and look around the dark room. There was no one there, not even her parents. She started to shake and cry, not understanding what had happened to her, not able to deal with the agony that had taken over.

She was alone and forever damaged.

Finally one of the night-shift nurses appeared at the door and came running over to her.

"What is it, Ellie?" the nurse asked, but the girl couldn't speak. Her sobs were too powerful. She could only shake her head and moan pitifully, tears streaming down her face.

The nurse knew. She quickly administered more

drugs through the IV drip that went into the girl's arm. The girl had been horribly burned on her leg, one of the worst instances the nurse had ever seen. The doctors had done what they could, but without insurance, her parents were unable to pay for any reconstructive surgery. A skin graft could have saved the girl from having horrible scars in the future.

Her parents weren't even around. They had been sitting in the waiting room for most of the day, but at night they'd gone elsewhere, leaving the girl alone in the hospital. The nurse was extremely suspicious of them—everything from the furtive way they kept leaving the building to the way they explained what had happened to the girl.

Though it was believable that the girl came from the type of low-income family that would allow her to search for car parts on a nearby trash heap, the whole story about accidentally spilling battery acid on her leg didn't ring true. The nurse thought it sounded like her parents were probably running a meth lab instead. Even worse, they could have been neglecting or abusing the girl. There was definitely something wrong with the story, but the girl had been in so much pain that neither the doctors nor the nurses could find out what her version of events were.

Except now. The girl's sobs were subsiding as the morphine began to take effect, working quickly in her eleven-year-old system. The nurse watched her carefully, debating whether or not she should try and ask her. This was a job for Child Services, not for her, but there was something about the girl she wanted to protect. It was like she could see the child was already damaged before the burns on her leg happened.

"Ellie," she said gently, smoothing back the girl's fine blond hair. She was going to grow up to be a stunning woman, already showing promise in the usually awkward preteen phase. That made the nurse feel even more sickened for her, knowing her beauty would be marred by the scars that would come.

The girl opened her wide brown eyes and looked up at the nurse. Her face was wet from tears and she looked scared despite the subsiding pain.

"Ellie," the nurse went on, "are you able to tell me what happened to you?"

The girl blinked, unsure of what to do or say. She could barely remember what happened herself but knew that what had happened was wrong. And even though her parents hadn't told her yet to keep quiet about Travis Raines, the bad man whose house her mother made her break into, she knew all too well to keep her mouth shut. She was the daughter of con artists, after all, and truth was never an option.

Still, there was a part of her that wanted to tell the nurse what happened. She wanted to get the Travis man in trouble. She wanted him to be put away for what he did to her.

"I...I don't remember," the girl said, so terribly afraid she'd tell the truth.

The nurse studied her. "Do you remember looking for car parts?"

Car parts? The girl had no idea what her parents had

told the doctors. The confusion came across her face, just long enough for the nurse to pick up on it.

"Ellie, what was the last thing you remember?" the nurse asked quickly. "How did you burn your leg, did your parents do this to you?"

The girl's face fell as she tried to figure out what to do.

"What the hell do you think you're doing?" Amelie Watt yelled, appearing at the doorway.

The girl cringed at the sound of her mother's voice. In her increasingly delirious state, she was worried that she may have done something to anger her.

Amelie marched into the hospital room, her eyes blazing at the nurse.

"Why are you questioning my daughter?" she yelled, furious, her arms waving. "That isn't your right."

The nurse stepped back from the girl but refused to apologize. "I'm concerned about her."

"Your only concern is to make my daughter better." Amelie crossed her arms, head held high. She was a striking woman with exotic Eastern European features: high cheekbones, a strong jaw, and dark, sloe eyes. She gave off the impression that she wasn't afraid, but she couldn't hide the tremor in her voice. "Why are you waking her up in the middle of the night anyway? Let my poor baby sleep."

The nurse raised her brows. "Your baby was crying in the middle of the night, screaming from the pain. I was the only one around." She let those last words sink in like daggers.

Amelie sucked in her breath and shook her head.

"Don't you dare question my parenting skills. We had to leave to get some sleep at home. It's the only way we can be there for her."

The nurse stared back at Amelie, wondering if she should push it further. She glanced at the girl who was staring at her mother with a mix of admiration and fear. Perhaps there was no use digging around here. If the girl really was being abused or neglected, Child Services would find out about it. They'd already been notified anyway. The Watts could deal with them in the morning.

Finally the nurse sighed and said, "You've got five minutes before I'll need you to leave the room. She'll need to sleep and the drugs will keep the pain at bay."

Amelie narrowed her eyes and then looked to her daughter. The nurse left the room, closing the door behind her.

Amelie relaxed visibly once she heard the door shut. She came closer to her daughter and placed a hand on Ellie's thin, tanned arm, wincing at the sight of the IV going into it.

"Baby," she whispered. "What did you tell them?"

By now the girl was slowly losing consciousness, eased into a comfortable state by the morphine. She licked her lips and said what she knew her mother wanted her to hear. "I didn't tell them anything, Mama."

Amelie gave her a pained smile. "That's my baby girl. When you're feeling better, we'll let you know what to say. For now, tell them that you were looking for car parts at the dump and that was the last thing you remember. You got it? The last thing you remember."

"But..." the girl started, "But the man. Travis." Amelie shuddered at the sound of his name. "He needs to be punished. He needs to go to jail."

"He will be punished one day, baby," her mother said. "One day, he will pay. But that's not your job. We'll take care of it. I promise."

Her mother stayed with her, holding her hand.

I'll make him pay, the girl thought. Then she fell asleep.

CHAPTER ONE

THE STORM RAGED on and inside I was screaming.

I was sitting in a stolen Jeep with no roof, parked on the side of a dirt road beneath a wavering canopy that occasionally let a spattering of rain pelt me in the face. Despite the warmth of the tropical night, I was cold and soaked to the bone in my muddy evening gown. On one side of me was Camden McQueen, on the other was Javier Bernal. One more light than dark, one more dark than light. Both men had come for me. Both men had loved me. And both of them I had seriously underestimated.

There really wasn't much time to sit around and try to get my head on straight. But after everything that happened—after Javier had manipulated me into coming with him to Mexico; after trying to convince me to kill Travis, his cartel rival; after that went horribly wrong and we had to go on the run in an explosion of gunfire—I knew a panic attack was just waiting to devour me, to incapacitate me, to take me out of the game. I could feel the fear buzzing through my veins, threatening to tear me up from the inside out. The fear of losing everything—Gus, my mother, my revenge, my purpose. I feared Javier and what he might do to Camden. I feared Camden and the way he'd changed toward me. I feared myself and the things I might do to try and make sense of it all.

We had only been in the Jeep for about ten minutes, heading back to Veracruz, when I'd told Javier to park the car so I could have a moment. He reluctantly complied, finding an area beneath some massive trees that shook from the howling winds. Both men were staring at me, and I could only look down at my hands as I rubbed them up and down against the mud on my dress, the coldness seeping into my palms. They both knew me, knew my attacks, and that alone had me screaming internally, wanting to run. I couldn't even look at them. I couldn't even accept the situation. Javier and Camden. The three of us having to work together, let alone sit in a Jeep together without them killing each other. And I was in the middle.

My mind raced back to our escape. *My mother. Dear God, my mother.* I really never thought I'd see her again, let alone at a drug lord's party, but there she was, serving motherfucking champagne. She was working for Travis of all people, the man who poured acid down my leg when I was just eleven years old, the same man who my mother wanted to rob that night in Mississippi. What the hell had happened to her? After everything we had gone through as a family, after all the pain I suffered, the inquests from authorities, the move to Palm Valley to stay with Uncle Jim and her eventual abandonment of me, why was she here with him now? And where was my father?

I swallowed, my throat feeling thick, and debated about asking Javier. He had known this all along, knew where they were. He'd even wanted me to kill them for some sick, divine purpose based on that damaged moral code of his. This whole time he knew and he was using me.

I couldn't even be angry at him over that, though. I should have known better, I should have expected this. I was so damn angry at myself for falling for his old tricks, for slipping into a past that would have been better left buried. I listened to his sweet, sweet lies, and I believed them, like the naive girl I used to be. I hated myself for losing my faith in Camden and putting it in Javier instead, and hated myself even more for the damage I caused. That was another reason I couldn't look at him. Every time I looked at Camden, I saw the ways he'd changed. He was stronger, tougher, and more ruthless. He was also hurt, scarred deep inside by what I'd done. He now had the kind of scars that even his skilled hands couldn't transform.

"Are you okay?" Camden asked, his voice low. My knee was touching his knee. My other knee was touching Javier's. I could feel them on either side of me, hear their breathing, both their bodies tense and rigid as we sat there in the darkness. This was so awkward. So fucking awkward.

And from the looks of it, with Gus and my parents in the clutches of Travis Raines, my cover being blown, the three of us having to make our way through Mexico together, awkward was the least of my problems.

I nodded, still looking at my hands, even though I wasn't okay. None of us were.

Javier sighed loudly. Something about his manner made me look over. Somehow it was easier to look at him, maybe because I didn't feel guilt when I did.

"What?" I asked. I pressed my fingers into my thigh to keep my nerves from misfiring.

He tilted his head toward me, and though the only light came from the glow of the Jeep's dashboard and the far-off flashes of lightning in the sky, I could see the gleam in his eyes. Unreadable, as always.

"I'm just wondering how long we're going to sit here in a fucking tropical storm," he said simply, a false smile spread across his face. "That's all."

Camden sat up straighter. "At least the rain should wash all that blood off your face."

Javier's eyes flicked over to him. "Are you sure you want me to help you get your fat Gus back? Because I think I'm the one doing you both a favor. Aside from saving your behinds, of course. I don't recall either of you thanking me yet."

I exhaled through my nose. "Just give me a few minutes. I need to figure out the plan."

Javier let out a dry laugh, rain running off the tip of his nose, and eyed me incredulously. "The plan? You're not in charge of the plan, angel. If you want my help, then you're doing it my way."

"Fuck that," Camden spat out.

I finally had to look at him. His eyes were raging beneath his glasses that reflected the dull glow from the car, and he was gripping the door handle like he was about to break it in two. Oh God, I didn't need this. But then again, it was partly my fault. Maybe I did need this. I deserved it.

"Camden," I said, trying to placate him with my eyes, "please, let's just ... let's just stay calm and think."

"I am calm," Javier answered as Camden opened his mouth. "I need to go find my sister, Violetta. That's my goal first and foremost. Then I'll help you get to Travis and Gus."

"And my mother?" I filled in, daring him to be honest.

He gave me a short nod, though he was looking off onto the dark road. "Yes ... and your mother."

Now was the time to ask him. Better now than never.

I took in a deep breath. "Where's my father? I didn't see him at the party."

He raised a brow and looked over my head at Camden. Why, I had no fucking idea. I turned to look at Camden, but he was staring back at Javier like he didn't even know who he was.

"Javier," I repeated. "Where is my father?"

He frowned at Camden and looked back at me. His face went stony. "The man you call your father is dead."

Every limb on me froze. My lungs sucked in warm air and raindrops.

"Dead?" I asked, feeling like I was choking.

Dead.

My father was dead?

No.

Javier's eyes softened momentarily, but only for a moment. "I didn't know until I got here."

I let it soak into my bones. My father was dead.

The good parent.

The weak one.

Dead.

With my mother working for Travis, I truly was an orphan now.

"Oh God," I said, finally finding enough air. I leaned forward, trying to ward off another panic attack, and Camden's warm hand met the small of my back, just enough to let me know he was there. His touch somehow strengthened me. "Oh God."

"I'm sorry," Javier said.

It took a few moments before I realized what he said.

I immediately whipped my head toward him. "No you're not," I seethed. "You wanted me to kill them. You sick fucking bastard, you wanted me to kill my own parents. You brought me here for that. You are not fucking sorry!"

Javier stared at me impassively, his features forever reptilian, smooth and calculating. No emotion. No anything. How could I have ever thought there was something warm inside him?

"You're right," he said, turning his attention back to the empty road. "I'm not sorry. I'm glad he's dead. He deserves it for what he did to you. But I am sorry you feel this way, right now."

"Like I wouldn't have felt worse if *I* killed them?"

He shrugged. "Obviously now I know how that would have played out. Apparently you don't hold the same grudges that I do."

I felt like elbowing him in the nose again, seeing it

break over and over. But Javier was one of those men who could take the pain and make it work for him. He had too much of an advantage over us at the moment, and he *liked* it when I hated him. Maybe more than when I loved him.

"How did he die?" I asked, grinding my teeth.

"I don't know," he said. "All I know is that there is one less person to hurt you."

"You are so fucked up," Camden muttered, his hand tightening on my back.

Javier merely grinned at that, his teeth white in the darkness, taking no offense at all. "Whatever I am, you need me more than I need you. And because of that, you'll do as I say."

"Sounds like a deal with the devil," I told him.

"My, my, angel, how quickly you've changed your tune now that this tattooed ape is back in your life." He eyed Camden. "You know, just because you're here now doesn't mean you've won anything."

"I only came to get Ellie back," he said, his voice quiet but full of animosity. I knew that Camden was keeping himself on a very tight leash. I also knew that when he didn't, well, I didn't have to look long at Javier's bruised and bloodied face to know what happens.

"Oh, of course," Javier said with deliberation. "But is she really back?"

"Javier, shut the fuck up," I said. "If you've got a plan then tell us what the plan is, because the longer we sit here arguing, the farther Gus gets away from us."

He slowly looked back to me. "That has been my point all along. Are you able to think now? Is your little attack over? Because I know what worked last time you—"

"Get on with it," I cut in. Neither Camden nor I needed him to finish his sentence. The last time I had a panic attack around Javier, we ended up having sex in an orange grove. I was vulnerable, driven by lust, desperate for closure and lured back into my own past. I had a million excuses for why I fucked him, but what bothered me the most was that at the heart of them all, I did it because I wanted to. I needed to. Now, looking at him, knowing how much he had and hadn't changed, I hated myself for being so weak, hated my body for betraying me so easily.

He held my gaze and I knew in the dimness he could make out the raw anger in my eyes. He was thinking, wondering how much more he could toy with me. He now had the ability to get a rise out of both Camden and me anytime he wanted. He was a man with too much ammo, but perhaps he'd always been that way. He stockpiled it like a squirrel preparing for winter.

He shifted the Jeep with a lurch, causing me to fall into Camden, and pulled the vehicle back onto the dirt road, the rain whipping us as it continued to fall in heavy drops. We sped in the direction of Veracruz, where the city lights were casting a dull orange glow on the bottoms of the storm clouds.

"The first step is to get rid of this car," Javier said, his mouth set in a grim line. "They'll be looking for it."

"There's always Jose," Camden said.

I looked at him incredulously. "You have Jose?"

He gave me a small smile. "The car's a bit battered,

but yeah I have Jose. It brought me and Gus down here. All your stuff is still in the trunk."

Thank God, because all my other stuff was in the hotel room that I wouldn't be returning to. The only thing I had on me was what fit into my clutch purse: Eleanor Willis's passport (which was pretty much useless now since Travis knew it was a fake), some makeup, a few pesos, and that was it.

"Right," Javier scoffed. "I'm sure the car isn't wanted by a few people either."

"You mean other than you?" I asked.

He grunted. "The past is the past. We're better off getting something more inconspicuous, don't you agree?"

"We're getting my stuff out of the car, at least," I told Javier. "You can add that to your plan."

He made another disagreeable sound but didn't argue. "Fine. Get your stuff. Get a new car. Head to Mexico City to check on Violetta."

I frowned at the mention of his sister. "Check on?"

He nodded. "I'll tell her to get out of town, go to Marguerite or Alana's in Jalisco."

"And she'll listen to you?"

He bit his lip for a second. "She knows what happened to Beatriz. She'll listen."

"Who is Beatriz?" Camden asked.

Javier shot him a look as he brought the Jeep onto the main highway. "None of your fucking business."

"It's one of his sisters," I quickly told Camden. "Travis murdered her."

"Of course he did," Camden said with a sigh, leaning

back into the seat. I finally had the strength to watch him for a few moments. The wind was ruffling up his dark hair, his glasses reflecting the lights of the few cars on the highway that were braving the storm. His jaw was strong, lips full but held together tightly. I knew he was tormented but I didn't know by whom. Was it Javier?

Or was it me?

He took his glasses off and wiped the rain off of them with the sleeve of the tuxedo he had gotten for Travis's party. It took effort, his brilliant blue eyes wincing with pain. His shoulder was still messed up from being shot.

"Do you have any more of your painkillers?" I asked him.

He closed his eyes and nodded while he slipped his glasses back on. "Now's not the time. I'll deal."

"Well you certainly dealt with Javier's face," I said. It slipped out before I had a chance to take it back. I wasn't about to start provoking the monster, but it was easier said than done.

And provoke him I did.

Javier's grip on the wheel tightened and he slammed on the brakes so we went skidding across the highway. I screamed, the tires squealing beneath us, as we came to a shuddering stop on the shoulder and he shifted it into park.

"Jesus!" Camden yelled. "Are you trying to kill us?"

Javier immediately whipped out his gun so it was in front of my face and pointed at Camden.

"No. Now I'm trying to kill you," Javier sneered, staring down the barrel of the gun.

"Then fucking do it," Camden said, his eyes blazing, meeting the challenge.

"You shouldn't tempt me," Javier countered.

My eyes darted between the two of them and the gun. It wavered slightly, betraying Javier's smooth exterior. He was damn angry, angry enough to do something stupid. He didn't need Camden egging him on.

I raised my hands slowly, careful not to touch the gun that was inches away. I spoke carefully, trying to keep my voice from shaking. "Please, please, Javier, Camden, let's just…let's just calm down."

"Shut up," Javier said, his eyes flitting to me and back to Camden. "This is all your fault."

"How is this my fault?" I exclaimed and then realized it was. I needed to keep my mouth shut. We all did. I looked between the two of them and said, "Okay, I'm sorry. It is my fault. Obviously we're not getting anywhere if we can't get along."

Javier's grip tightened on the gun. "This isn't a matter of getting *along*, angel." He licked his lips and nodded at Camden. "Tell me, Camden, how did you manage to escape from your ex-wife and the mighty Vincent Madano?"

Camden frowned at him, his jaw tensing. "How do you know about that?"

Javier grinned. "I read it in the newspaper like everyone else."

"Bullshit."

"I have to say, I'm impressed," Javier went on. "Vincent Madano is not a man you can just mess up and walk away."

"How well do you really know them?" I asked Javier, remembering that Camden had said something about it all being a setup, that Sophia and her brothers and possibly Javier were all in on it. The exchange, the kidnapping—it was all for show. All to get me away from Camden and maybe to put Camden in danger.

It must have been driving Javier crazy to have Camden here with us. Camden could not be caught that easily.

"I know them well enough," Javier said. He loosed his grip on the gun, shook the rain off of it, and put it back in his waistband. I exhaled in relief. "But I suppose that's neither here nor there at this point."

I was sure that Camden wouldn't let it go that easily. Just how deeply was Javier tied to his ex-wife and her brothers and why? But Camden only gave Javier a final glare before turning his attention back to the darkened farmland we had stopped beside.

"Let's just get Gus back," he said and pressed his lips together as if to prevent himself from saying something else.

Javier watched him for a few moments before putting the Jeep back into drive and returning us to the highway.

We sat in unbearable silence as we made our way into Veracruz, yet it was safer than saying anything. I felt like we were a word away from incinerating each other. Camden only spoke up to give directions to where he had ditched Jose.

Unfortunately it was a bit too close to Travis's compound for comfort. We pulled down a quiet residential street only a few blocks away, the leafy trees blowing wildly in the wind, the rain having thankfully dropped off. The sound of helicopters buzzed in the distance.

Javier eyed the sky and I asked, "Are those his or news choppers?"

He nodded slightly. "They're his. The news wouldn't dare cover this."

"Turn right down here," Camden told him, and we came down another street, this one more narrow, with the trees blocking out the streetlights that were few and far between. This was still a well-to-do area, though the houses were smaller and spaced farther apart, all behind tall gates and walls. I did note that it was a dead-end road, which meant there was only one way out if something were to happen to us. We couldn't be too careful, not with the choppers circling in the distance, their spotlights occasionally lighting up the sky.

"There she is," Camden said, pointing to the end of the street where jungle seemed to have taken over and there were no streetlights. I could barely make out the shape of the car in the darkness.

"She?" Javier asked, eyebrow cocked. "Its name is Jose."

Camden shrugged. "Guess she's a cross-dresser."

Javier sighed, shaking his head in disgust, and pulled the Jeep up to it. "Let's make this fast."

We hopped out and it was only now that we were closer that I saw what Camden meant by "battered."

"Holy shit, Camden!" I cried out at the sight of the poor vehicle.

"What the hell did you do to my car?" Javier yelled, his hands thrown up in the air.

The GTO had the paint scraped off all along one side, the windows on the driver's side were all shot out, the driver's side mirror was missing, and the front was totally crunched up with only the right headlight intact.

"*Your* car?" I asked Javier once I managed to look away from poor Jose. "What happened to the past being the past?"

"Now's not the time to argue semantics," Camden interrupted us. "She's broken but she's a survivor." He fished the keys out of his suit jacket and tossed them at me. "Just like you."

I caught them and he held my eyes for a moment before walking past me back to the Jeep.

Javier scoffed, though I didn't know if it was for the state of the car or Camden's comment, and made his way to the trunk. He bumped it with his fist. "Come on, let's get her open."

I was about to hurry over to him when Camden suddenly said, "Fuck."

I spun around and looked at him. He was frozen in the act of taking off his jacket, his good arm free, his head cocked upward, eyes searching the sky. The sound of the choppers had gotten louder, and over the tips of the waving trees I could see the spotlight in the sky, the blades whirring.

"Yeah, no kidding fuck," I said. I turned to Javier and quickly ran over to him, trying to get my keys into the trunk of the car. I kept fumbling, missing the lock just as the wind blew my hair back and we were lit up by the spotlight, the helicopter coming closer. We were in their sights, no doubt about that. We had been spotted.

"Hurry up!" Javier yelled at me before ripping the keys out of my hands.

Camden hit the side of the Jeep with his fist. "There's no time!" he yelled. "We have to go!"

"No!" I yelled back as Javier got the trunk open. "Not without my stuff!"

Suddenly the ground in front of Camden started exploding with bullets as a steady stream of them came off the approaching chopper. We all cried out, dirt flying everywhere.

Javier quickly slammed the trunk shut. "Then we're taking Jose. Get the fuck in!"

He went for the driver's seat as Camden came running over, taking my hand and pulling me to the passenger's side. He shoved me into the backseat, telling me to lie down, and barely got in the car himself before Javier was gunning the engine and driving the car backward. I could feel the wheels spinning for grip beneath my head and tried to sit up just as the sound of more bullets filled the air. I was tossed back down as Javier put the pedal to the floor and turned the wheel, the sheer power of the rear wheels grinding until we did a 180 and were facing the right way. The chopper was now directly above us, and I could feel the wind its blades created flowing through the smashed windows, the spotlight blinding me.

"Hang on," Javier said, "this is going to get ugly before it gets better."

He pressed down on the gas again and the car roared loudly before it lurched forward and we were all pinned back to our seats from the force. This is exactly why I loved this car. I just hoped it was stronger than it looked at the moment.

We raced down the street, the chopper in hot pursuit, the whir of blades and bullets gaining on us. I leaned forward between the seats, reaching for the glove compartment, waving my hand at it when I couldn't reach. "My gun, give me my gun!"

Camden gave me an odd look but opened the compartment and handed me the gun that was thankfully still in there. It wasn't my Colt .45—that was in the trunk still—but it would do.

"What are you doing?" Camden yelled as I quickly checked the clip and slammed it back in.

"She's being a good girl," Javier said just as the trunk was bombarded with bullets, sounding like metal fireworks being set off. "Fuck!" he yelled and swerved, trying to lose them, as I attempted to lean out of his window. I wedged myself up against the back of his seat and faced behind us. The wind whipped my hair around, the spotlight blinding me, but I managed to keep the gun aimed upward at the helicopter. I had no idea if this would work like it did in the movies, but I figured it was better than just sitting in the backseat and doing nothing.

Only problem was, Javier kept swerving and throwing me off balance and the chopper kept moving out of my sights. You'd think that would mean that their bullets weren't any closer to hitting us, but that wasn't quite the case. One hit the trunk again, a dangerously close call, just as Javier brought the car spinning around the corner and onto another road.

"Where do I shoot?" I screamed above the noise. "The fuel tank?"

"Shoot the fucking person who's shooting at us!"

"Right," I muttered. All I could see against the light was the outline of the chopper, not anyone inside. Still, there was a faint red glow whenever the gun went off, so I just aimed there, firing off a few rounds and hoping they went somewhere.

Suddenly the windshield in the back of the car was hit and I screamed as it exploded into a million shards of glass. Obviously I hadn't hit the gunman yet.

"Keep shooting!" Javier yelled as he brought the car around onto another street. We were leaving the hidden, residential hills of the wealthy and coming into the more open and busier suburbs of Veracruz. It was well lit and now there was traffic we had to contend with.

The chopper ducked down lower and sped up as we slowed to navigate around the cars on the road. The sound of horns, irate yells from drivers, and screeching tires filled the air. I took aim once more and fired again and again, hoping it would hit at least the windshield. But the helicopter came closer, the wind from the rotors shaking my arm like jelly, its landing skids almost coming down on top of us until Javier swerved the car to the left and the chopper had to rise quickly to get above a tall semi-truck in its path. I took the time to grab my arm with my other hand, trying to steady myself, to ignore the cramp in my lower back, the pressure of the door frame against my shoulder.

Come on, Ellie, I told myself as the helicopter came back again, much faster now and much lower, as if it didn't give a fuck anymore.

"Drive faster!" I yelled but wasn't sure Javier could hear me over the noise. I took in a deep breath, trying to see past the hair flying in front of my face, and started firing.

I fired and fired but it just came closer and closer.

And then there was a dull click.

There were no more bullets left in my gun.

And my other clip was in the glove compartment.

We were fucking screwed.

Don't miss Book One in
The Artists Trilogy

Read on for an electrifying extract ...

PROLOGUE

This will be the last time.

I've said that before. I've said it a lot. I've said it while talking to myself in a mirror like some Tarantino cliché. But I've never said it while having a pool cue pressed against my throat by a crazed Ukrainian man who was hell bent on making me his wife.

It's nice to know there's still a first time for everything.

Luckily, as the edges of my vision turned a sick shade of grey and my feet dangled from the floor, I had enough fight left in me to get out of this alive. Though it meant a few seconds of agony as the cue pressed into my windpipe, I pried my hands off of it and reached out. Sergei, my future fake husband, wasn't short, but I had long arms and as I pushed aside his gut, I found his balls.

With one swift movement, I made a tight, nails-first fist around them and tugged.

Hard.

Sergei screamed, dropping me and the pool cue to the sticky floor. I hopped up to my feet, grabbed the stick, and swung it against the side of his head as he was doubled over. When I was a child, I was never in a town long enough to get enrolled in the softball team, which was a shame because as the cue cracked against the side of his bald head, I realized it could have been a second career.

Hell, it could even be a first career. I was quitting the grifting game anyway.

Sergei made some grumbling, moaning noise like a disgruntled cow giving birth, and though I had done some damage, I only bought myself a few seconds. I grabbed the eight ball from the pool table and chucked it at his head where it bounced off his forehead with a thwack that made my toes curl.

For all the games I played, I'd always been a bit squeamish with violence. That said, I'd never been busted by one of the men I'd conned with my virgin bride scam. I chalked this up to "kill or be killed." Self defense. Hopefully it would be the last time for that, too.

Not that I was doing any killing here. After the pool ball made contact with his head and caused him to drop to his knees with a screech, I turned on my heels and booked it into the ladies' washroom. I knew there were two angry-looking men stationed outside of the door to the pool room, and they definitely wouldn't let me pass while their friend was on the floor hoping his testicles were still attached.

The ladies' room smelled rank, like mold and cold pipes, and I wondered how long it had been since it was cleaned. The Frontier wasn't the sort of bar that women hung out at, and that should have been my first tip that something was awry. The second was that no one even looked my way when I walked in the place. It's like they were expecting me, and when a dodgy bar in Cincinnati is expecting you, you know you're on someone else's turf. Third thing that should have tipped me off was the pool room was in a basement and there were an awful lot of locks on that door.

But, as I balanced my boots on the rust-stained sink, I found there were no locks on the rectangular window. I slammed it open and stuck my arms out into the warm August air, finding soggy dirt under my hands as the rain came down in heavy sheets. Just perfect. I was going to become Mud Woman in a few seconds.

Mud Woman was still preferable to Dead Woman, however, and I pulled myself through the narrow window and onto the muddy ground, the cold, wet dirt seeping into my shirt and down the front of my jeans. I heard Sergei yelling his head off and pounding on the bathroom door.

This had been a close one. Way too close.

I scrambled to my feet and quickly looked around to see if anyone had noticed. So far the bar looked quiet, the red lights from inside spilling through the falling rain. The street was equally quiet and lined with Audis and Mercedes that stuck out like gaudy jewelry among the decrepit meat-packing buildings. My own car, which I reluctantly called Jóse, was parked two blocks away. I may have underestimated the situation but I was glad I still had my wits about me. When an old friend emails you out of the blue and asks you to meet him at a sketchy bar late at night, you do take some precautions. It's too bad I hadn't clued in that it wasn't an old lover of mine but Sergei, out for revenge.

I took advantage of not being seen and ran as fast as I could down the street, my footsteps echoing coldly. By the time I rounded the corner and saw the dark green 1970 GTO sitting on the empty street, the rain had washed the mud clean off of me.

I wiped my wet hair from my eyes and stared at the glistening Ohio license plate. It was time for that to come off, and I mentally flipped through the spare plates I had inside. I knew I'd never set foot in Cincinnati again after this, and now that I knew this had been a set-up, I couldn't be sure they hadn't noticed my car. I had a wad of Sergei's money—which I'd been keeping strapped to the bottom of the driver's seat—and apparently he was the type who'd follow up on that kind of thing. He was the type that would hunt me down. I should have figured that from our email exchanges. This wouldn't even be about the money anymore, but the fact that I pulled a fast one on him. But what do you expect when you're trolling for virgin brides on OKCupid?

Men and their stupid pride.

I supposed he could try and hunt me down. He could try and follow me from state to state. But I knew as soon as I got in Jóse, he wouldn't be able to find me. I'd been hunted before and for a lot more than money.

And they still hadn't found me.

Yet.

Hearing distant but irate voices filling the air, I quickly opened the door and hopped in. My instincts told me to just drive and never look back, and unfortunately I knew I had to listen. I had to leave my pretty apartment, my safe coffee shop job, and my yoga-infused roommate Carlee behind. It was a shame, too. After living with Carlee for six months, the flexible little thing had actually grown on me.

I'll mail her something nice, I told myself and gunned the engine. Jóse purred to life and we shot down the street, away from the bar and from Sergei and his buddies who were now probably scouring the streets looking for me.

It didn't matter. I was used to running and always kept a spare life in the trunk. Spare clothes, spare driver's licenses, spare Social Security Numbers, and a spare tire. As soon as I felt like I was a comfortable distance away, I'd pull into a motel under a new name. I'd change the plates on my car. Yes, Jóse wasn't the most inconspicuous of vehicles, but I was sentimental about the car. After all, it wasn't even mine.

Then tomorrow, I'd figure out my budget. Figure out how long I could go before I'd need a legitimate job. Figure out that moment when I'd have to stay true to my word and make sure that this truly *was* the last time.

I careened around a corner then slowed as the car disappeared into traffic heading across the Ohio River. With my free hand I opened my wallet and went through my spare IDs. Now that I was going to go legit, I didn't have much of a choice.

I took out the California license that said Ellie Watt. I'd need to change the expiration date and photo since the last time I set foot in the state was seven years ago, just after I turned nineteen. But it would do. I was Ellie Watt again.

I was finally me.

Oh joy.

Find out where Ellie and Javier's dark, breathtakingly sexy
and dangerously toxic love story began. . .

On Every
Street

The Artists Trilogy – Prequel to Book One

A beautiful, damaged con artist after the drug lord
who was her ruin.

A dangerous and seductive henchman for the enemy,
who she can't help but fall for.

With body and heart battling with the deepest desire for
revenge, no one will walk away from this con a winner.

'At that moment, this man saw me.
The real me underneath the bombshell mask.
I felt like he must have seen everything.'

Utterly explosive and shockingly sexy, join
Ellie and Camden on their addictive journey. . .

Sins
& Needles

The Artists Trilogy – Book One

A con artist escaping to her hometown to leave her
grifting life behind.

A figure from her past who's bigger, badder and sexier than
before, and with a thriving tattoo business.

The two come head to head and enter a dangerous bargain.
The wild ride has only just begun. . .

'He filled me with light. With effervescence. With hope . . .
"I love you," he whispered.
"From now until the end, under any name you choose."'

The Artists Trilogy comes to a spectacularly wild,
raw and breathless conclusion. . .

Bold Tricks

The Artists Trilogy – Book Three

A beautiful, scarred con artist on the hunt for revenge.

Her only hope in hell is to turn to two men who both
love her to death.

An unlikely, uneasy trio must play the deadliest game of all.
In the vicious battle of past and present, lover and enemy,
life and death, what will it take to survive?

*'Both men had a stake in my heart at some point
in the game. This ever-changing game.'*

headline
ETERNAL

FIND YOUR HEART'S DESIRE...